# SIEGE OF COMEDIANS

# SIEGE

## — OF —

## COMEDIANS

### A NOVEL BY

## SUSAN DAITCH

DZANC
BOOKS

**DZANC BOOKS**

2580 Craig Rd.
Ann Arbor, MI 48103
www.dzancbooks.org

Library of Congress Catalog-in-Publication Data available upon request

The story of Fair Brow is quoted from Italo Calvino's *Italian Folktales*, Pantheon Books.

*The All-Purpose Mourning Stadium* appears courtesy of artist, Patricia Smith.

Text on page 257 is from https://www.weltmuseumwien.at/schausammlung/#kulturkampf.


ISBN: 978-1950539338
First US edition: September 2021
Interior design by Angelica Gillespie
Cover by Matthew Revert

Printed in the United States of America

10  9  8  7  6  5  4  3  2  1

# SIEGE OF COMEDIANS

# CLAY HEADS TALKING

# CHAPTER ONE

THE MOBILE PHONE COMPANY'S logo was a rotating aqua and orange Mercator map that folded into a globe as it turned. Over and over again the lobes of the momentarily flat map turned three dimensional and curved into a ball then unfolded back to the flat map. The animation appeared on a screen in the front window of the store, a branch of the Global Pathways Wireless. Located on Martin Luther King Blvd, sandwiched between a Mickey D's and a Starbucks, this branch was busy for mid-day, midweek. A woman and her son were considering an upgrade. A group of teenage girls were looking at new phone cases and deciding which ones had decent bling potential. A man holding a Wildlife Conservation Fund backpack by a strap had only wanted to replace a lost charger. The two people who worked in the branch were happy to have so many customers, because most people solved their problems in front of a computer screen or other device, so walking talking humans who strolled into the store had become less and less common. Their jobs depended on good service, so they were eager to provide it, though they kept half an eye on the teenage girls who looked, to the manager, like a gang of shoplifters. Both manager and employee wore aqua and orange striped polo shirts. Once in a while an older customer who had lived on the east coast would tell them these were Howard Johnson colors, but they had no idea who Howard Johnson might have been or why he would be known by the colors that symbolized Global Pathways Wireless.

When the bomb went off, windows shattered outward onto the pavement and a fist of black smoke burst through the screen that had, until a second ago, been filled with the endless loop of the spinning globe. Almost immediately the air smelled of toxic melting metal, plastic, burning USB cords, and paper. Greedy yellow flames reached for the McDonald's and the Starbucks, but they had working sprinkler systems. Global Pathways did not.

By the time the fire department arrived and put out the blaze, only a few of the retrieved bodies could be identified. The five that were burned beyond recognition were sent to a lab in New York to have their faces reconstructed. The lab in New York was really only one or two people who specialized in reconstructing heads and thereby finding identities. This is a very specific skill.

# CHAPTER TWO

THEY ARRIVED AT MY studio via FedEx. The blackened knobs that had once been heads were not a pretty sight, I can tell you. Sometimes I hope I'll find something surprising in the minute chambers and alleyways of human remains: diamonds or emeralds tucked in jaws, lodged behind molars, but all I lifted from the crates and boxes were bones in need of major facial reconstruction. In the case of the Global Pathways victims, there was enough skull to flesh out the faces and heads in clay. When nearly finished, they looked decently lifelike. Five people: a middle-aged man and woman, a young man in his late teens, early twenties, and two very young girls, maybe twelve or thirteen. The younger man had wide-set eyes, a short thick nose, and a broad face. His teeth were mostly intact and in no need of orthodontia. Perhaps he'd had braces when young which meant he came from a family who could afford expensive dental work. That was all I knew. Any or none of them could have been the human time bomb. The horror of their last minutes on earth—those expressions are unknown. My job is to measure the space between eye sockets, to mold calm and straightforward appearances in clay over bare bone because identification needs to reside in neutrality, not terror. Terror is not useful for ID-ing and only causes trauma to surviving friends and family who have to view the clay reproductions. It's hard enough as it is. To look at and understand the fear and pain in their loved ones' last moments on earth—what would be the point of that? I've never sculpted a screaming face.

Holloway, the detective who called from Missing Persons, couldn't resist telling me heads would roll if I didn't turn this one around quickly. His sense of humor tended to link obvious phrases or truisms with the gruesome nature of our work, so when on a job with Holloway, it was no surprise he didn't ever react to the horrific ways life could end. He never gagged or had to look away no matter what had been done to body parts. At the same time, he had a penchant for looking at a crime scene as a fulcrum for unseen forces and would speak in a tone of wonderment, as if he were the first to note phenomena: the influence of high tides, rhythms of underground vibrations created by subway cars, mice and rats' fear of open spaces or, as he called it, rodents' agoraphobia. He was obsessed with Fermi's Paradox, and would, in the middle of an investigation, talk about the possibility of humans being absolutely alone in the universe, that there is no planet out there somewhere with another Holloway and another Iridia Kepler sifting through the same evidence and coming to a conclusion way more quickly. It wasn't my job to go to crime scenes, for the most part, but he would talk to me about them. Why was the weapon distinctly left facing east? Why were candles positioned on the windowsill? Sometimes I wanted to say to him, Don't get your eye stems in a tangle, it's just random and haphazard, but then he'd figure things out in unexpected ways. While he was speaking to me over the phone I imagined him in the morgue instructing the coroner's assistant to box up the skull and have it messengered immediately, all in a day's work.

My studio is a fourth floor walk-up in Sunset Park, a former warehouse, a warren of other studios and small businesses. I also live there which is illegal, but this is what I can afford, and the management company who works for the absentee landlord doesn't seem to snoop around as long as nobody burns the place down.

The first thing I have to do when the heads arrive is boil them to remove any excess bits and pieces of lingering decay or charred flesh. The pots on my stove aren't the stuff of television cooking shows. I warn the rare guy who comes home with me not to look at anything on the stove, but few can resist the temptation. Once a professional climber who led teams up the Rockies and into Death Valley, someone you'd think would be pretty tough, peeked under a lid and left screaming, saying, *No really, I'm fine* from the stairs, *I'll be in touch*. I knew he wouldn't call again, but I was okay with that.

The heads from the Global Pathways fire weren't much to look at, but I've seen worse. I lifted each one out of the cooled pot, held the skull, or what was left of it, up to the light. After boiling, the skull gets placed on a stand, and clay built up to resemble the muscle, fat, and skin that used to be there. I do this based on the information the bones give you, and really, they can tell you a lot. The plane from the cheekbones to the mouth, the space between the eyebrow and the crease in the eyelid. One of my anatomy teachers said there is a word in French for that space, but in English we're so squeamish about body parts we don't name anatomy so readily, or we use metaphors: the crook of the elbow, ball of the foot, white of the eye. I worked on the explosion heads almost twenty-four seven.

Were the five acquainted? Can't say. Such personal knowledge is never within my purview. When they were finished, I placed them facing one another as if having a conversation. Does physiognomy betray psychology? Does a face tell you who a person is inside? To what extent do people's faces reveal who they really are? Some days I believed personality was completely exposed by the codes that features gave away, but other days I was sure faces were just an arrangement of sensory and communicative organs.

This I can say: death came instantly. The five probably never knew what hit them or why they died as they did. The clues in the bones and the remains of the store—scorch mark patterns, chemical residue trails, the molecular giveaways—are part of a breadcrumb trail that revealed Global Pathways was a shell company. Details came to light, and weeks later, these made the news. Global Pathways was compared to Truman Used Auto Parts of Kansas City, Missouri, a concern that funneled money to clandestine arms dealers or Divine Nail Salons of Jersey City, a cash-cleaning vector for Serbian gangs. Global Pathways stores were cleaning for human traffickers who hid their cargo in container ships, suburban homes, boarded up shops in malls. The violence visited upon the Oakland franchise was a warning, a way of severing an arm while exposing the bone at the same time. The snaking pattern of connections was not my puzzle. That was for the police. My job was to give faces to those who lost theirs, so they could be identified. Was one of them an unwitting carrier of the device? The clay wouldn't tell me. I leave that for others.

# CHAPTER THREE

My mother and father were arrested when I was eighteen. They didn't show up at my high school graduation, but that wasn't unusual, for them. If school was a city institution, it was, as far as they were concerned, a necessary evil. They would have home schooled me if they had the time, but growing pot is a full-time job. As growers and sometimes in the distribution business as well, my anarchist parents might as well have been corporate lawyers for all I saw of them, but corporate they emphatically were not. They named me Iridia after Iridium, an element found on meteorites and only present on earth when an asteroid hits, then the earth is peppered with the silvery white metal. The last major shower was 66 million years ago, and as a result of that pummeling, it was curtains for the dinosaurs, one theory goes. For me it meant having a name that rhymed with a sexually transmitted disease. I grew up watering rows of plants under a ceiling of grow lights in the basement of our ramshackle house in Red Hook with a view of Governors Island, knowing from an early age, not to talk about what my parents did exactly. I made things up as I went along. They worked from home, so I might say they fixed computers or wrote catalog copy, or blogged about sinking old subway cars to form new coral reefs. The idea you could grow oysters in Buttermilk Channel sounded reasonable. Mollusks filter pollution. Just don't eat them.

After graduation, the house and the basement farm were gone. My parents were in jail; the IRS took what was left. I was on my own. I packed my bag, enrolled in night school studying drawing and anatomy, working days in an orthodontist's office, living with an aunt who called my family the Crackpot Keplers. At the office I had names and teeth to imagine lives for. Mickey X had an overbite, Dexter Z had very few chompers left of his own, Ellie Y needed no work whatsoever that I could tell, but the orthodontist was in love with her, and therefore made a mold of her teeth—cost covered by insurance. Everybody has their stories, their reasons.

When a man and woman, passengers on a plane that crashed in Long Island Sound, could only be identified via dental records, it fell to me to pull their records and compare X-rays to make a positive match. Besides X-rays, the orthodontist kept a cabinet of molds of teeth, of before and after, so you could see how much better you would look if you signed on to the recommended treatment, adjustments, braces. If you couldn't pay, there was only *before*. No *after*. Only one of the two mystery passengers had been a patient of his. The teeth told stories. The woman had both a before and an after set. She had a name and contact information. As far as I know, the man remained unidentified.

The crash victims got me thinking about working with bones and clay. I took more anatomy classes. One of my teachers was flown to Buenos Aires to put faces on skulls when, decades after people disappeared, remains began to be found. When he returned he showed us an animated image of a real skull damaged by blunt force, revolving in space, constellations of white points appearing around the bone only to melt into lines that became a representation of skin, eyes, brows, lips, hair, and then a name with a history, a date of birth, and a date of death. Next picture: a photograph of the people who had looked for her. Other examples followed. Lost children, newborns taken from their parents could now, as adults, be reunited with grandparents, and look at reconstructed faces to see echoes of their own. I became a certified forensic sculptor. Working in law enforcement was the last thing my parents would have wanted for their daughter. Maybe that's what propelled me toward restoring the faces of the anonymous.

# CHAPTER FOUR

DETECTIVE HOLLOWAY'S OFFICE OVERLOOKED Jamaica Bay, close enough to the airport so planes were frequent, even dense in the sky. I like these edges of the city when you're so far on the brink, there's barely any evidence you're in a metropolis, because you aren't. You're in a transit zone, a launching pad, a high diving board, and everything you know is at your back. The Global Pathways case was under national investigation, so I was called to the city branch, local division of the Federal Missing Persons Bureau. Missing Persons is my bread and butter. Who else has need of my services? No one.

I waited in his office, taking in window cactuses, an electric Turkish coffee maker, a picture of him with the State Poet snapped at Brooklyn College, another of him with José Calderon. I wouldn't have minded fixing myself a cup of coffee, but making myself at home probably would be considered unprofessional. There was a bag of grounds beckoning from a shelf, but I'd have to leave the room to find water, no water fountains on this floor, only vending machines. I lifted the coffee pot by its gooseneck spout, a place you shouldn't put your fingers, just as Holloway walked in. He took the silver object out of my hands and put in back on the window sill, next to a dwarf cactus, as I said oh hello a little too loudly and emphatically, as if poking through his things, sticking my fingers where they didn't belong was just part of waiting after all, and anyone would know that. That was something I remembered from my mother during the dope farm days. Anything weird, just act like you own the place. She did, and that attitude worked, until it didn't anymore, i.e., she was arrested. I don't know how you claim ownership when you're in jail. I'd rather not know how that's working out for her now.

Holloway was younger than his voice would have led anyone to guess. He had what might have been permanent bed head, and wore a narrow tie that gave him an eighties punk business look, like he just stepped out of a Robert Longo *Men in the Cities* drawing, but he smoked an e-cigarette flavored to give off clove and cedar-smelling vapor. If this had been invented when my parents were still producing, they would have been avid consumers. I inhaled, inducing nostalgia for something that never was. An eggshell-size cup of Turkish coffee would have been a hospitable offer, but this was a gesture that didn't seem to occur to him.

"Iridia, what I have to tell you won't come as a surprise. We had a complaint about you. I wanted to give you the news in person, because it is not pleasant or fair, but can't be helped." Holloway poured liquid from a bottle labeled Suicide Bunny into his e-cig.

"I wanted to give you the news in person, because it's serious."

"Leo Sancton?"

Holloway nodded. I knew. I was half expecting it, but I still felt that stomach drop when the roller coaster has reached the top of its steepest incline, is about to hurtle down to who knows where, and you only hope it stays on the rails, and the safety bar isn't more rusted than it looks.

Sancton, the other forensic sculptor, competed with me for jobs. There wasn't enough work for two of us, and a program called Electronic Facial Identification Technique, or E-Fit, was making both of us obsolete anyway. Leo lived by an old school dirty pool credo. He had seniority over me and could not afford to retire. Sancton had no computer, no cell phone, no electronics of any kind. He worked out of his cluttered house in Whitestone, where as far as he was concerned, Ronald Reagan was still meeting Gorbachev on Governors

Island, and clay deliveries arrived at his door after he made a call on his cracked, held together with duct tape dial phone. I knew all this about him because there are so few of us, anymore, though I'd never met the man or seen pictures of him. Neither had Holloway, but Leo was known by reputation. From time to time he would use that phone to remind whoever I was working for that Iridia Kepler's mother and father were convicted felons serving time in Federal penitentiaries, and therefore she should absolutely in no way be assigned or trusted with cases that involved National Security, drugs, mail fraud, or anything else he could come up with. I felt sorry for Sancton, but I needed to eat, too. If I don't work for Missing Persons, I don't work. Most people haven't got extra skulls laying around the house that need identifying. We just found this guy in the basement and wondered who he might be? I've never gotten that request.

❖

I didn't want to go back to taking molds of misaligned incisors but didn't want to lose the roof over my head either. The pot farm, rows of plants swaying slightly from a ceiling fan in the summer, just before harvest, these plants cast a very long shadow.

"So, listen, Iridia, I'm going to overnight a couple of Henry 8s to you. As a favor. The heads were several years old when we found them, and we found them some time ago, but see what you can do at this point. I'm sorry, but I have to give the current cases to Leo. He's less competent, but Leo's clean. You aren't. I'm sorry, Iridia, really, I am, but my hands are tied. I have no choice. I'll need to verify your address."

Henry 8 is slang for Henry the XIII which means the corpse and the head were found separately. I stared at Holloway.

"You don't have the rest of the bodies? Not for any of them?"

"There were no bodies," Holloway explained. "All we found were the heads, and there wasn't much left of them as you'll see. The individuals were found in a swamp near the terminal. Facial tissue was fairly decomposed, as to be expected by the time they were found."

"Anything found near the heads?"

It helps if there are any bits and pieces, clothing, movie tickets, receipts near the body, but all Missing Persons had found beside one of the heads was a gold earring, a horseshoe, diamond chips representing nail heads; it was positioned where an ear might have been. It was possible this belonged to one of the victims, or not. The inspector told me the gold horseshoe would be in the box, and I should attach the earring when that particular head was complete.

"At first we thought they were brought in on the tide, coming in from Jamaica Bay." Holloway jerked his own cranium in the direction of the water. "When was the last time there was a severed head lying within spitting distance of a runway? But around the same time other heads turned up in Chicago, San Francisco, and L.A., slightly more intact than what we've recovered, but also near airports. One turned up on a luggage carousel in O'Hare. At first it was thought to be a baggage handler involved in a prescription drug smuggling operation, but that was a dead end."

He was throwing me a hopeless, dried out old bone, literally, before I was cashiered. In the awkward silence I looked around Holloway's office. There were no family photos on his desk. Among papers pinned to a corkboard was a note with FaceIt.com scribbled across in Sharpie and a cartoon of a fellow describing, according to the speech balloon, a blond man with a narrow face, while the artist drew a woman with a round face and dark curly hair.

"Look at it this way, Iridia, the camera pans around a room, say, someone's home office. There are thousands of objects in that room: books, papers, lamps, chairs, photographs in frames, cat toys, but only one or two of those things contain a clue as to who your man really is. According to the information everyone knows, according to what's public, he might be a real estate agent, a professor of genetic engineering, owner of race horses or a basketball team, lieutenant governor of a swing state, a pharmaceutical giant, oil baron, whatever, you name it, but he or she is also something else that is not public. That other activity or identity represents a danger, an illegality, so the person will go to great lengths to keep it hidden, but needs the tools of his trade, needs access. The person could be involved in money laundering on a grand scale, insider trading, a Wall Street Ponzi scheme, illegal arms deals, a hacking mastermind. If only you could spread every object out across a football field and examine each one, but you can't. Also, you don't have infinite amounts of time. The thing you're looking for will not be the obvious object to reveal this meaning, this code, but rather they are the elements that are ordinary and easily overlooked, tossed by the wayside. You have to find those one or two things which expose events heretofore concealed. You're looking for the crowbar to put under the manhole cover. You need to see what's underneath, and the clock is ticking. The problem is, the crowbar doesn't look like a crowbar. If it did, it would be easy to find. The original owner of one or all of those heads may have known that other identity or activity and the nature of the key to it."

"If these heads are so important, why don't you give them to Sancton?"

"Did I say they were important? I don't know. Maybe they are. Haven't a clue. In any case, Sancton is a blunt instrument."

"How long have they been sitting in the evidence room?"

"Since you were labeling and cataloguing the city's gnashers in an orthodontist's office."

"A case so cold, I'll get frostbite."

I imagined a scenario in which a pair of clowns stumble on something valuable, high risk, secret, but they don't know what it is: plutonium, anthrax, yellow cake, an ampoule of a viral agent so dangerous, whole cities could be turned into ghost towns, wiped out in a matter of hours. Or maybe the clowns found a recording of a despot engaged in an activity so grotesque and repulsive or so dangerous, the exposing of this activity will bring down his government. So their lives are in danger, but they're clowns, so they don't know what they have. Not a clue. They become aware that someone is following them, but they're clowns, so no one believes them. They're eliminated in such a way so that they can never be identified, even if found, and their fate quickly descends into the land of obscurity, cold cases. In identifying them, I run the risk of becoming Clown #3. Ordinarily, I don't feel like the woman who knew too much. No one sends me letter bombs. I'm too far from the investigation, whatever it might be. I go about my beeswax, but if anyone did want to tamper with evidence, the pots boiling on my stove would be a good place to begin.

"Iridia, if you don't want the job, just say so."

"If you're paying me, I can't say no."

"All right, then. Expect a package. And you're only working on one head at present, right?"

I nodded, figuring which bills I could put off in what order.

"A messenger will pick up whatever you're working on to take to Sancton."

When I got home, I could toss the thing into a clear plastic bag to hand to the messenger, but then why make him suffer, people staring, pointing, creeped out by a real skull dangling from his bicycle handlebars as he makes his way to Whitestone.

Holloway called a car to take me home, throwing the empty bottle of Suicide Bunny into the garbage as he spoke. The glass hitting metal made a surprisingly loud clanging sound upon impact.

# CHAPTER FIVE

THE MESSENGER FROM THE Port Authority Police was prompt. On my way down in the freight elevator, I ran into a woman who had the studio next door to mine. Nora Schwan most emphatically did not live in her studio, so I didn't see her all that often, but wasn't crazy about running into her. With asymmetrically cut hair, large black-framed glasses and tight psychedelic pink jeans, she was hard to avoid. If she only knew what was in those boxes I was picking up. The last time Nora looked in through my door, she saw all the clay heads, and dismissed me as the kind of artist who got caught in the nineteenth century, not worth bothering with. The truth is, I'm not an artist. Not only am I my family's worst nightmare, but for the artists who have studios here, I'm so far beneath them, I'm in China.

She said excuse me as if I was the maid, moving across the lobby like she owned the place. The rows of small mailboxes reminded me of the orthodontist's cabinet of molds. A notice for a photographer who did headshots launched me back to the classroom where my teacher showed a photograph of a skull whose surface looked like a lunar landscape but with a neat hole at the back. Nora gave the impression that nothing dogged at her heels. If she knocked into the messenger, if the boxes had fallen, I'd like to say it would have been her head I'd be delivering to Port Authority, but probably not, probably I wouldn't have said anything.

The messenger held an electronic clipboard for me to sign and cautioned me about the *This Side Up – Human Remains* label. Nora stared at us for a moment, then proceeded to clear a space on the bulletin board that hung in the lobby. It was always layered with notices for everything from sublets wanted to dog walking offers. She pulled down and crumpled other signs before throwing them in a bin, then tacked up an announcement for a group show, her name featured prominently. The theme of the show was Coney Island, though the gallery was in another waterfront neighborhood. Task completed, she turned for a moment and looked at my clay-splattered T-shirt. I even had clay in my hair.

There was a brief flicker of curiosity about who buys what she referred to as *my heads*, but I evaded the question. They are in no way my heads. I am paid, but no one really owns them.

"After I bring these upstairs, I'm going to the corner diner for coffee, can I get you a cup?" I offered in case I'd misread our brief interaction. She shook her head. No doubt Nora wouldn't swallow diner coffee even if it were the only drinkable beverage between here and East Patagonia. The invitation to the opening clearly wasn't extended to people like me, but it was in my old neighborhood. I decided to go.

# CHAPTER SIX

BONES CAN TALK. The jaw and eye sockets reveal the most. The nose keeps information to itself. I plot out tissue thicknesses, try to be aware of asymmetries in the set of the eyes, the mouth, the sides of the nose, put small pegs in a shallow layer of clay and build up from there. There are twenty-one points of the skull that determine facial tissue, density, curvature, and I look for them like an acupuncturist looking for critical meridians. This is what matters in my job. Getting these numbers right. We all have these mostly invisible and unnecessary to know measurements until we're just a skull, then these depths have to be reimagined to get the face right. Hair is, in some ways, the easiest, because you're fairly free to imagine whatever seems legitimate. Facial features you cannot imagine into existence. You have to work with what's there.

It took a few days, but I worked fast, only slept a few hours, and almost finished the three heads. The first two were women, the third so thin on remains I couldn't be sure. While the clay was still wet, I put the horseshoe earring in the left ear of one, then took it out again. When the soft clay heads were finished, I'd make synthetic molds of them, then cast in a harder clay, one that will cure in two days, though it can take longer. When the final cast is finished, I remove the soft clay, so the bones can be returned. They are evidence, and the only remains the family might have.

There was one head remaining, but for this one, there was so little bone left, I didn't have much to work with. I built up a face based on what was there, but something wasn't right. Did I make a mistake with the nose? The mouth? In the geometry of the face, had I thrown something so far off, it couldn't be corrected? What if the person hadn't wanted to be found? They had set up a false trail, so they could disappear. What I knew: somewhere there was an identity no longer inhabited by any living person.

There was a possibility the head belonged to a stand-in, a body double, working for a despot, dictator, potentate.

I drew a face on a wooden ice cream spoon, flat line for the mouth, L for the nose, winking eyes.

A knock on my door. A person appears who says, that's my head, that's me. Mystery solved. That's not going to happen.

But someone did knock on my door in the middle of the night. I assumed it was one of the artists from down the hall, and therefore walked slowly, in no hurry to ask who's there? I pictured an unknown neighbor wanting to borrow a serrated knife, a jar of turpentine, looking down her nose at what she considered my anachronistic sculptures. "Like, why?" I could hear her snicker.

But it wasn't anyone from my hall or even from my building. It was a man who introduced himself as Leo Sancton, smelling of canned fish and toothpaste, salty clay under his fingernails. Unshaved because no one had visited him since the second Clinton administration, so why bother? Wasting no time, he walked right over to the troublesome head.

"You're having difficulties with that one. I can see." He jabbed a thumb in the direction of the pile of curved bones that were supposed to be reassembled to form someone's skull. He picked one up as if it was a pottery shard found on an archeological site, key to understanding a vanished hamlet, a kind of relic, the remains certainly were not.

"So here's the deal," Sancton got right to the point, "I want you to do my head in clay and say the skull is mine. No one knows where

I am, no one has seen me in years. I'm unlocatable in this century, and I want to disappear."

"I can't do that. You're here now. Can I offer you a cup of coffee?"

"No thanks, not at this hour, but I wouldn't say no to something stronger."

I did have something stronger, a shot of vodka in a souvenir glass from the Everglades, which he accepted gladly, downed, then asked for a refill.

"Fill it up to the gator this time, please and thank you. Well, my dear, you don't have a lot of good choices, do you? You can't send back a heap of nothing. Your job is precarious as it is. Make the head that of yours truly. No one will be the wiser. How do you know the bones are even human?"

"DNA, Leo, it's been invented. Holloway knows you're alive and on the east coast. It will never work."

"Holloway doesn't know squat. He has no idea where I am, and he has no idea who you are. He knows about your parents, but he doesn't know what you did. How about this, sweetheart? I let him know that you were part of your mother and father's business. That's the icing on the cake. You were no innocent bystander, and once the cat is out of the bag, you're done. No way will you ever be assigned or trusted with cases that involve National Security, drugs, mail fraud, or any number of other actions." He held up a piece of paper. I could see handwritten lines and the impressions of typing. "I can send this anonymously. It can be on the desk of Missing Persons in a matter of days."

I didn't let him in on the not a secret to anyone but him that there were far faster ways to send the document.

"I was a minor."

"So you were even more useful." He shrugged like it was no concern of his what age I was. "Running with corner boys, making deliveries."

How did he know this? It only happened a few times. It could have been a calculated guess on his part.

Then Leo arranged his face into a pleading expression. It wasn't entirely convincing, but I was a captive audience. He held up his glass, turning it with his fingers: panther, spoonbill, manatee, but if he was signaling a refill, I didn't move. Okay, he shrugged as if dealing with a very slow person, and explained that in ancient Rome, if in a play, a character was supposed to die, for that scene, the actor would be replaced at the last minute by a condemned prisoner who would actually be killed on stage. As far as he was concerned, he was that actor, and someone had been killed in his place. He could now go off stage and carry on in whatever way he pleased. I told Leo his life was not a play, and I had no interest in sabotaging this case, cold though it may have been.

He picked up a piece of jawbone and held it up to his face, "See, this curvature here, it's not so different, not so farfetched. Like I said, no one will ever know you're doing me this little favor. The crime is still the crime. What does it matter who you slot in as a random bystander? What I've learned from this business: the dead are the dead. You could tell them to go fuck themselves, but they can't. That's the point."

When deterioration is so advanced, it's hard to identify remains, and no identity will take up residence, will adhere, so bingo, the late Leo S. can move in. It's not as if he planned for someone to die in his place, I hope, but only that it was someone's bad luck he wanted to take advantage of, so he could reinvent himself in another location.

I shook my head.

"Believe me, Holloway gets this letter, you never work again."

"Why do you need to disappear? What the fuck, Leo?"

No one was after him, he'd committed no crime, turned no state's evidence, squealed on no one, he knew no one to squeal on. He didn't owe money to sharks, but felt as if he did, and if he remained Leo S., these sharks who were not after funds, but after him in some other way, they would bury him. Leo wanted his own private Witness Protection Program. He had it all set up, all he needed now was to get rid of Leo S., and become this new person. Rubbing his hands together, as if it was a done deal, Leo was making me uncomfortable, but what danger did the old guy really present? I had no answer, just that he creeped me out, and I wanted him to leave. I could do nothing for him.

"Look, maybe you're okay with applying droppers full of Quink Ink to dried out typewriter ribbons in order to restore them to working life, but I know when the boat has sailed, and I wasn't on it, and if I could be someone else, even if only for a few years, that would be a relief, free from ghosts of clay past. Is it too much to ask? You know I'm the kind of person who waits for the mail, who waits for the phone to ring because it hardly ever does. It's time for me to go, but I'd like to go in another format."

I assured him, I didn't feel obsolete, and there were no typewriters laying around in my studio. He wanted to outrun his own position on some massive dial, the needle pointing to archaic, that's it, pal. He was lonely and saw no other way out.

"Stop the clock, Iridia, you can do this for me."

"Who are you going to become?"

"One of those people who sits in glass booths and sells movie tickets. I'll read in between shows. No one will notice me."

"Hardly anyone goes to the movies anymore, and when they do, movie tickets come out of machines."

Perhaps he had no definite plan, but he was serious about his need to disappear, to kevork but still be alive.

"I don't want to expire alone, found months, years later, or maybe not until the whole block, surrounding blocks, the whole shooting match is underwater, then a diver finds what's left. Who was that guy? Kill me now and get it over with." He fiddled with a shell-like piece of cranium.

"What's in it for me?"

"Look at it this way, you're eliminating your competition."

"Okay, Leo," I said. "Take a seat."

He pulled up a chair and tilted his head slightly back so he looked like a Roman emperor as he posed. There was no way his scheme would work, but he wouldn't budge, so I began to work on his head. The bones were a Rubik's Cube without color, but then, the head really did begin to look like him, and as I hollowed out cheekbones and nostrils, Leo's jaw relaxed, he appeared visibly relieved, as if he was watching his own reincarnation. I told him to hold still.

When the head was finished, he smiled, and pushed himself up from the chair, but as he prepared to leave, he handed me a photocopy of the letter he could still put in the mail should I back out of our agreement.

"For your perusal and for your records, just to remind you, no funny business, Iridia."

As soon as he was gone, I sliced off his face, and got back to work.

There is something in the business of making things known as inherent vice, which means the seeds of deterioration lay in the unstable chemistry of some materials used. Maybe any object's destiny is to self-destruct, it's just a question of how fast. Hungry bacteria, mold, external agents all do their job from without, but from within, molecular arrangements expand and contract at different rates causing miniature earthquakes, shifting of micro-tectonic plates that do considerable damage. The destruction of inherent vice is down the road, but for the moment, my heads are very durable; they can and do outlast the originals.

Light from my dusty windows fell across their noses, cheeks, chins. I didn't know what words came out of their mouths, what food went in, whom or how those mouths had kissed, or what other body parts might have entered them. Not for them or for any of the heads I ever worked on. When I'd finessed the last curve of an ear, the crease under an eye, and the clay was dry, I'd jacket them in plastic bubble wrap, pad their boxes with Styrofoam peanuts, seal them up to send back to Missing Persons. Job finished, but what work would follow, I had no idea.

# CHAPTER SEVEN

ON THE ROOF OF our old building, as a child, I painted faces on clothespins and made up stories about the people I invented, as my mother clipped them to the clothesline where my characters held our sheets in order to let the wind do its work. When I was a little older the roof was a good place to listen to music and be alone, if I needed to be, though my parents mostly did leave me alone. Once, I fell asleep and woke in the middle of the night, one arm numb from pins and needles. I'm not sure they even noticed I wasn't in my room. The door to the upper floor of the house was jammed, so I was stuck up there. I sat down on the cool tiles, looked at a speck of blue nail polish on my little toe. The fleck was impossible to peel off, but I thought if I could focus on one small thing, I wouldn't panic or feel trapped. There was no way to climb down. The fire escape was out of reach, and its railings were rusted through anyway. People in the house next door were having a loud fight. I looked up at the sky. Somewhere up there was an asteroid with my name on it, my mother used to remind me, and she did finally rescue me that night, frightened and angry, where were you, etc. I miss that house, but I'll never live in anything like it again. It's still boarded up, but Basque seafood restaurants, ramen noodle joints, cafés full of people on devices now surround it. I don't think it's all bad, but there's no place for me anymore.

The gallery showing Nora's work was only a few blocks from the defunct pot farm. Some of the houses and apartment buildings that marked my walk from home to the school bus were still the kind that had aluminum awnings over the front doors, some had been demolished and rebuilt with a lot of glass in front. The site of the gallery had formerly housed a bodega that did business with my parents. What had been a storefront almost entirely papered over with signage for brands of cigarettes and lotto tickets was now a floor to ceiling glass window. All this transparency is deceptive. You think you can see in, but you really have no idea what's going on. I stood outside for a few minutes reviewing my ghosts before going in. The corner boys watching and selling, hands in pockets, confident and dark-eyed. My parents who smelled of cedar oil used to mask pot smells. Little Gene, sometimes known as P'ti Jean, the giant lookout who had a clear view all the way to the end of the warehouses. They all rolled up their wares and flew into the sky. What was I left with? Time to come in out of the cold. I didn't know anyone in the gallery crowd but would have been surprised if I had.

There were black and white photographs of Coney in winter, stark and deserted, huge blown-up pictures of the Mermaid Parade, self-portraits as the Cyclone went into rapid descent. There were a series of paintings of Incendaria, a young woman covered in a maze pattern tattoo like a New Guinea tribesman. Her face is full of piercings, and she eats fire at the sideshow. I'd once seen her on the F train, men and tourists staring at her and making wisecracks. It was nasty, and I felt badly for her. Coney Island is the last stop on the F train. She was probably just trying to get to work.

Being in a group of people I don't know makes me feel like I'm treading water in the middle of the Atlantic. I don't know how to talk to strangers in crowds. The life of a group, like molecules that bond and cleave in patterns that are impenetrable, drives me to look for the exit sign. I swallowed the last of my bitter white wine, but as I tossed the cup in the trash, I realized there was one more room to look at.

It was a large sculpture made to look like a shooting gallery, complete with repetitive ice cream truck-like music coming from a speaker attached to the counter. The heads were on a sliding track, like a conveyor belt. Some of the clay heads were labeled in case an alien landed from Mars and needed identities: Donald T., Donald R., Kim K., Kanye W., but others were just ordinary and nameless. The celebrity heads had been glazed and fired, but the commoners were just dried clay. I was mesmerized and stood in line waiting to try out one of the guns. When my turn came I picked up a carnival weapon, aimed, and shot. A sound like firing went off, but no pellets were discharged. I guess you weren't supposed to be able to actually destroy the heads and perhaps the point of the sculpture was about the powerlessness of the average citizen. I handed my rifle to the next person in line and stepped back. Then, as the conveyor belt continued to move heads, there was one I recognized. It was one of the heads I'd been working on, the one that had been found with the horseshoe earring. This one was more precise, more life-like as if it had been created from a living model who posed for the artist, a person clearly more skilled than I was. He captured a sense of who the person was, whereas my finished products are just a set of identifiable features.

A label on the wall told me that an artist named C. Finzi had made *American Carnival*. If Finzi was here, I wanted to talk to him.

Nora stood near her photographs engaged in conversation with two men. It looked like she was wearing a floor length black and silver dress, but when she stepped so her feet were apart, it became apparent that she was wearing something like tights, the inseams connected by a large triangle of parachute silk. When she moved her arms, silk connected her sleeves to the sides of her dress, all the way to her ankles. The material contained spines of rubberized ribs to keep its shape, especially when airborne. Nora was wearing a wingsuit. She looked like a giant talking bat or flying squirrel who used words like aerodynamic and canyon precipice. In theory, while wearing this suit, she could jump off a nearby building and glide through the air. There were fluorescent stripes along the edges of the wingsuit, so she would look like a floating star if she jumped at night. Nora had wanted to experiment with LED lights in a performance piece with other gliders, but no, she was not going to jump tonight. Look, she twirled around, no parachute backpack, always used for serious long distance jumping. As she twirled, she accidentally knocked into my arm, and I spilled wine on her sleeve. She assumed it was one of the men and so said to them, no big deal, no one will see the stains three thousand feet up. I took this opportunity to ask if she could point out or introduce me to the artist who made *American Carnival*.

"Why?" Wingsuit fluttered in agitation.

"Because I'd like to meet him."

"He's over there." She pointed to a man in a black knit hat, black shirt unbuttoned to reveal the edges of tattoos of what looked like a map of the Outer Hebrides. "He's talking to the gallery owner, so you shouldn't interrupt him." Then in a flash of silk, Nora turned her back to me.

Thanks, Nora. Jump from one of these warehouses at night, and it'll be your face I'll be putting back together.

C. Finzi was talking to a man who scanned the room while appearing to listen. I waited, pretending to stare at the paintings of Incendaria until his conversation was finished.

"I've updated the shooting gallery," he explained to the dealer. "In 1942 Coney Island was closed so American soldiers could train on site using the shooting galleries to practice marksmanship. Their targets were iron replicas of Hitler, bullets pinging off. Casings could still be found years later."

"This is what you want me to tell buyers?"

"You shoot and aim, feel like you're firing, there's a sound, but nothing comes out, so the heads go on rotating. There's no prize. There is never any prize. That's part of the point." He explained this to a gallerist who, while appearing to listen, deftly separated himself to talk to someone else.

"Finzi?"

He turned in my direction, not smiling, as if my presence triggered the departure of someone more important. I had the sensation the jagged edge of his Hebrides tattoo was moving up his neck, or maybe my eyes were just drawn to it.

"Call me Ziv."

I wasn't a buyer, a collector, or dealer, and on the scale of engagement value in the gallery, I was at the bottom, also known as a waste of time. In the future, there will be some way to assess individuals so you can know origins, professions, aspirations, the kind of information you don't have time to stop and look up, but the information will hover over people's heads in screen format. Call it a rudeness eliminator or rudeness accelerator, depending on how used. I didn't pretend to be anyone who had any business at the opening, but came straight out, told him who I was, and what I did.

"That head, that one." I pointed to the clay head just as it appeared on the conveyor belt.

"Donald Rumsfeld?"

"No, the one with the horseshoe earring. Did you know her?"

"Not at all. I found the clay head in the garbage. I find all my material in the garbage. That's the point of my assemblages. Everything can be found somewhere. In the trash, in a junkyard."

"Still, it looks like her, the face I just finished."

"How do you know?"

"Well, I don't, but my version is workmanlike in comparison, even though I had the actual skull. Your version, or whoever did this, captured the spirit of the person, as if she could spring back to life and talk to us. She has a soul."

"I don't believe in souls." Ziv looked distracted. I was losing currency with the word soul, which I had my doubts about anyway. "It's just dried-out mud. Oceans rise, or it gets rained on, and she's mud again. That's all."

I sensed Ziv was about to pull the eject lever on me, and down I would drop into the basement, but he went on to explain to me that he used to work as a waiter in a place where a lot of food was thrown out. Even when the owner was asked if he would join other restaurants in donating food, he refused, so Ziv posted to a network of dumpster divers, giving them the address. He hoped that to this day behind the restaurant they were dining on oysters and the accumulated dregs of many champagne bottles.

"Nothing had to be made from the ground up. There's plenty of stuff already kicking around that can be repurposed, why add to rising levels of uselessness?"

"Do you remember the address where you found her?" I didn't want him to float away and needed to know if there was anything more he could tell me about the head revolving on *American Carnival.*

"Near the canal, not far from here. I'll take you there when the gallery closes."

I was surprised he wasn't hanging out with friends afterward. I thought that was what you did after openings, occasions to celebrate, to go from gallery to bar, but Ziv seemed to want to get out of there as soon as it was over, as if he needed to punch out of a time clock. Maybe he wanted to blow someone off, maybe that someone was Nora Schwan, who glanced in my direction every once in a while, like she wanted to float over on an air current, tap me on the arm and ask me what I was still doing here.

The gallery would close in thirty minutes. I got another glass of wine, wandered outside, and sat on a stoop. A cruise ship, so long I couldn't see the prow or stern, distorted the horizon and made it look like the coast of New Jersey had moved closer.

Ernesto, that was the name of the bodega owner. His counter had run directly in front of where black and white photographs of Coney in winter now hung. He'd kept a gun under the cash register. A real gun, not an imitation pop-pop. I wondered where Ernesto was now. In my memory he was a ghost, just like the Coney Island ghosts who used to play on the beach, because there's no place else to go, and eat fifty-cent hot dogs, all part of a lost city.

# CHAPTER EIGHT

"It was here."

The house was a block from the canal. Fortunately, it wasn't an apartment building, but a single-family house with trash discreetly placed out front, so we didn't have the impossible task of guessing who'd tossed out a head or possibly a bunch of heads based on real murdered people. The name above the buzzer was Ice. It was a semi-dilapidated building of yellow brick, basic four walls, a garage on the ground floor, one floor above that where the occupant lived, and a billboard for a tile company cantilevered from the roof.

"I'm going to ring the bell. You don't have to hang around," I said.

"No, I will, if you don't mind. I'm curious." It was late, not too late to be ringing a stranger's bell, but still, I was glad to have Ziv for company.

The garage door went up, and a woman with hair in shades of yellow that ranged from platinum to marigold greeted us. Her garage was full of stuff: props, furniture, and pieces of sets, but also bits and pieces of drawings. Once again, I was struck by this person's artistry. The front of the workshop was populated by figures of Depression-era characters: hobos, burlesque performers, industrialists in top hats, one angled as about to dive off a ledge. They looked like they just stepped out of a Reginald Marsh painting, George Gershwin playing in the background. What play this was for, she didn't say, and I wasn't sure what all the figures were made of. My heads got the job done. The goal was to learn who you were looking at. Her work revealed personality, as if the figures were about to break into speech. I could see that instantly, and I think Ziv was impressed, too. I was curious about how she invented out of thin air. How do you decide how features assemble themselves? I had to work with proof, with evidence. This woman was free to imagine faces, except when she used models, and even then, she was an artist while I occupied a zone of just the facts. Ms. Ice lifted a full suit of armor out of her way as if it were made of cardboard which it was. I also noticed a cage with a small alligator in a corner in the back.

"Lemon Ice." She held out her hand. "You must be the Morrises. You're here for Frankie," then pointed to the alligator. "I'm so glad you were able to come tonight. She really needs to be reintroduced to the wild as soon as possible. Poor thing probably spent her whole short life in a dark closet."

I explained that we were not a couple named Morris and were not taking Frankie anywhere, but she had already lifted the gator from her cage and was petting and talking to the animal in human baby talk.

"Oh, hello, sweetie pie. How's my little Frankie? Ready to go back to the swamp?"

Lemon kissed the alligator at the tip of her snout. Frankie was not exactly a baby. She was about three feet long, far from fully grown, but still had teeth, and a jaw that could no doubt do some damage.

"What's your real name?" Ziv was nothing if not direct.

"Didn't I just introduce myself? Lemon Ice." She pointed to a poster for a band called the Y-Spirals.

"I used to be in a group. Y-spiral is a skating spin. Here, hold Frankie." She handed the alligator to me, then demonstrated (though without the spin) by pulling her foot up above her head. Ziv looked particularly interested in her flexibility. "We all took names relating to skating, but I liked the idea of a new identity, so had it changed legally. The band had a short run. Now I make props, paint scenery, have a sideline rescuing animals, mostly reptiles."

"I used to have a girlfriend who worked at the Bronx Zoo. Once a retired veterinarian tried to let all the elephants out." Ziv was like a spellbound cartoon character who walks off a cliff, legs still making the motions of walking, head looking the wrong way as he drops.

"I remember that was on the news. I sort of wish he'd been able to let them out, but on the other hand, what would they do in the Bronx?" She turned to me. "Is Iridia your real name?"

I nodded, Yses, that's my real name, Iridia Kepler. Frankie was blackish green, rows of ridges down her back, and she pulsed in my arms as if I needed reminding that she was alive. Hoping the alligator had been fed recently, I pet her the best I could, given the ridges. Do you even pet a reptile? What's their skin nerve receptor situation? Does it even matter to them? Frankie shut her eyes, so whatever I was doing must have lulled her into a kind of sleep.

"When I was in the Y-Spirals, I did business with your parents. They were known as Moon Dust, but when they were arrested their real names were in the papers."

My name had been in the papers, too. It wasn't supposed to be, but it was. Lemon wasn't telling me anything I didn't already know. My parents were incarcerated in Michigan and California respectively. I live paycheck to paycheck and hadn't seen them in years. Ziv had that oh-this-is-new-information look in his eye, but the story of the Moon Dust Keplers was not a conversation I wanted to have with a guy I just met who made art out of trash, or reminisce with a woman who kissed alligators. Images of my father and mother in showers, carrying trays of prison food to bolted-down tables, looking for visitors who never appeared, all of this was something I put in a box and tried very hard not to look into. So Lemon Ice had been one of their customers. So had a lot of people.

"Frankie belonged to a fence. When he was busted the police called me to take the animal. She'd escaped the closet and was hiding in between a stack of Play Stations and a huge flatscreen TV in an abandoned garage the fence used to store surplus merchandise. The police know me. You might say I run a kind of hotel for snakes, and what have you. They stay here temporarily until I can find people who will put them back in the wild. Female alligators like Frankie are particularly endangered and are going to become increasingly rare."

"Why?" Ziv asked like he was dying to know and maybe he really was. Lemon Ice replied as if she assumed everyone was as fascinated by the subject as she was.

We learned that alligators make their nests in decomposing plants on a bank, in a swamp, wherever. If the temperature in the riparian zone is above 93 degrees, all the hatchlings in the clutch will be male, if it's cooler, they will all be female. Gender is determined by temperature. Until a certain point in their egg development, sex can go either way. It's completely decided by degrees above or below 93. Global warming means more males, then males only, then no more alligators whatsoever. Then she asked us, if you aren't the Morrises, why are you here?

When I told her why we rang her bell, I only said that Ziv had found the head in her garbage, and wondered what her connection to it might have been.

"You went through my garbage?" Lemon looked shocked. "I did that portrait years ago but kept it around for a while."

"The head was just sitting there on a pile of Styrofoam burger boxes, crushed cans, and a bundle of undistributed menus. If there had been other heads or theater props, they were gone by the time I arrived." Ziv explained what he did, making art out of stuff people throw away. To Ziv every object was worth something and should be recycled. He felt it just as odd that she'd put so much work into the portraits and then got rid of them. Lemon explained they were for a play that got cancelled, so she was stuck with them, and why keep pieces of dry clay? They were unusable. It had been some years ago, and they sat around in her studio until she figured out what to do with them. To Lemon, nothing material was precious. They were just things. I tried to imagine all these heads in a cluster on the curb waiting for sanitation trucks.

"I included heads of a few friends at the time, thrown in just for fun. The one with the horseshoe earring, her name was Ada."

"What was her last name?"

"I don't know."

The figure of the suicidal industrialist was on rollers, so he could be moved back and forth. Ziv pushed the guy right and left until Lemon gestured that he should stop.

"He's kind of fragile, you know?"

Ziv retreated toward a closet-size construction made of old keyboards assembled to look like part of a spaceship control panel.

"But she was a friend? You didn't know her last name?"

"I hadn't known her that long. She was a runaway from somewhere, quite a few places, I think. She never told me all of it. I didn't want to pry. She helped me in the studio briefly, and I paid her in cash, as she requested. Ada had no green card, no visa, no working papers, no driver's license, nothing."

In other words she was here illegally. I didn't want to tell Lemon that her disappeared friend had been found, or part of her had been. There was no body. Let her think disappeared could mean still alive somewhere.

"How did you meet her?" Ziv asked from the space capsule.

"I was cutting through a department store, and I get sensory overload in those places, so I try not to really look at all the little alcove environments, like if you buy this shirt, this chair, your life will be optimistic and prosperous, you know? It's a maze, and I just keep my head down and aim for the Fulton Street exit. That's what I was doing, but out of the corner of my eye I saw this person who was talking softly but urgently, very skinny, patchy do-it-yourself hair dyed like peacock feathers, so I noticed that, plus Cleopatra black wings around her eyes, green jeans, vinyl jacket with fake fur trim. She was leaning over a jewelry counter surrounded by an array of black and white velvet boxes. The salesgirl was also very young and genuinely eager to show her potential customer as many choices as she required in order to ultimately make a sale. Cleopatra wings, who I would later learn was Ada, tried on this one and that, held her hand out in that universal gesture of elegance as she looked at each one in turn, and each ring fell short to be replaced by another. I stopped my dash, mesmerized, as if watching a play in which something isn't right, and you're about to find out what that something is. From a few yards distance, in order not to be obvious, I spun a stand of gold chains. A second woman appeared out of nowhere, Ada's accomplice, and asked the salesperson a question, something like, where's the shoe department? Is it toward Jay Street or on the sixth floor? In the seconds that the salesgirl looked away, Ada slipped one of the gold rings into a fur-trimmed pocket and replaced it with a ring of plastic, I could tell from a short distance. By the time the salesperson turned her head back to her customer, Ada was already halfway to the revolving doors that led to the street. I was right behind her.

"There was a lot of foot traffic, office workers and court employees on lunch break, people milling around, selling stuff from tables: hats, gloves, knockoff bags, cell phone cases. Once she was a few blocks from the department store, Ada positioned herself between a woman selling Christian-themed romances and children's books and a man singing along with a boombox. She held up the ring and shouted, gold ring for sale! 14 karats! It was hard to hear her, and her accent sounded Russian, but not exactly. A kid brushed past me as he ran up to her and snatched the ring out of her hand. He disappeared into the crowd. She tried to run after him, yelling that he was a thief, but he had vanished, and she was left standing in the middle of the sidewalk, looking stunned as people streamed around her, some staring, most oblivious. Then out of an electronics outlet her accomplice materialized and demanded her half of the money. If she didn't have the ring, she must have sold it and kept all the money for herself.

Accomplice did not believe a boy, any boy, had stolen the ring, and she pulled out a small knife.

"The accomplice was shorter than Ada, bug-eyed, stoned or something. She came at Ada. The first rule of theft is that you don't draw attention to yourself. Even if there's a problem, you exit and continue on quickly and as invisibly as possible. Her accomplice had no sense, was like a screechy helicopter drone. She slashed and dove, but only scratched Ada's arms before she was pulled off.

"A few people in the crowd, guys alert to fights, separated them. The police were called, and Ada grew agitated. I was closest to her, and in the chaos, she grabbed my arm, whispering, sweating, barely coherent. If the police were called, she was afraid they would send her to someone named Oygen or Oyster or Oxygen or what? Or they would arrest him, but she would have to pay. It made no sense to me. This man had a house on an island that didn't look like an island. Staten Island? Long Island? Maybe. A burly guy, the security guard for the electronics outlet, was more focused on the other woman, the one with the knife. She became hysterical, also talking about a house, arching back and forth rapidly, as if she were having a seizure, but she was no match for the security guard.

"Ada made gagging sounds like she was about to throw up. I'm not sure if she really was going to be sick or looking for a way out. People back off if they think they're going to get sprayed, so I said, 'Let me get her to a bathroom. There's one in the McDonald's around the corner.' I tried to let go of her arm, but she clung to me as we walked around the corner, past the McDonald's, and into the subway. Within minutes, we were underground, speeding to a very different part of the city. She stayed in my garage for a few days and helped me out."

"Doing what?"

"At that time I had a big job, a modern version of *Orlando Furioso*," Lemon explained.

"Is that something to do with Florida?" I asked.

"It's a play based on an epic poem by Ariosto. There are three hundred characters, some human, some phantoms. There weren't three hundred actors, but the stage needed to appear to be occupied by armies, by monsters, by townspeople."

She explained *Orlando Furioso*, written in the sixteenth century, was about the war between Charlemagne's Christian paladins and the Saracens, but for hundreds of years the play was adapted as a marionette show mostly in Italy and Sicily.

"One of the things I was hired to make were life-size puppets the actors could get into and walk around in. I used the clay heads for some of these characters. Ada loved the story and was excited to have her face included."

"Which character had Ada's face?"

"There are a number of forbidden romances in the story. Orlando is in love with Angelica, a pagan princess. Infidel, Ruggiero, is in love with woman warrior, Bradamante. Ada was the basis for Angelica, and one of her friends, who turned up later, was the model for Bradamante. The Saracens had black hair, black armor, turbans, curved swords.

"The play presented an interesting mechanical challenge. Some of the figures had to be constructed in such a way so that when their heads were cut off, they could easily be reattached for future performances."

Lemon brought out the last of the Saracens and showed how his head could be removed and replaced.

"We all got into cutting off heads. Ada would speak in what she imagined was Angelica's voice, and her friend would take another part, sometimes in English, sometimes in their own language."

"*Furioso* was the biggest job I've ever taken on. In fact, it seemed endless. The stage was meant to represent all of earth, and not only that, but there was a trip to the moon which I planned to paint to resemble Georges Méliès' moon, you know the one that gets the rocket in its eye. When Angelica marries someone else, Orlando goes mad with grief, and his friend Duke Astolfo rides a hippogriff to the lunar surface to retrieve his brains. It made me wonder if Ada would become mad with grief when Angelica and the rest would be shipped off to the theater, but we never got that far."

The Ada/Angelica head had ended up in the garbage. She spoke of her regrets, actually glad Ziv had rescued it, she would go to the gallery to see *American Carnival*, then she returned to the subject of the *Orlando Furioso* production.

"I needed to make armor, velvet capes, plumed helmets, shields, swords. It was a ton of work, one of the biggest jobs I ever had, before it got beached. Sometimes my boyfriend helped out, and while it lasted I was happy to hire extra hands. Ada was very deft with small moving parts as if she'd worked as a clockmaker, though I'm sure she hadn't, because who does anymore?"

I shifted Frankie from the crook of one arm to the other. It felt like she was getting heavier, like a dead weight that was only increasing its center of gravity as we talked. I had an image of snapping jaws and there goes my right arm from the elbow down. I also worried about the animal shitting all over me. Lemon must have read the look on my face, but she didn't offer to take Frankie back.

"Alligators have slow metabolisms. She's still digesting her last meal and shouldn't be hungry."

I didn't find *shouldn't* to be reassuring.

"Did Ada talk about herself at all? Anything about the house she ran away from?" If I could bring something outstandingly useful back to Missing Persons, a punched Long Island Railroad ticket, a talking Saracen, Ada's notes hidden in the homburg of the self-destructive industrialist, there was a chance I could get my job back. I needed that one object, that hinge between the garage and my own personal mayhem.

"I got to know her a bit during the days we worked together. I had a few lizards at that time, and I was rambling on about how unfair it is to lizards that when talking about humans, if they are compared to a lizard, that means they are sly and devious, not to be trusted. There is no scientific evidence that lizards have this character or any other character for that matter. They just are who they are. This was a new expression for her. The correlation doesn't exist in her language, but she said she preferred them to the human variety. That got her talking about her life before the shoplifting incident."

Lemon walked toward the part of her workshop where Ziv was holding up a hacksaw, and I saw this as an opportunity to put the alligator down, but Lemon shook her head.

"If she wakes up and scampers off, I'll never find her."

"Alligators can scamper?"

"On land, yes. They can even walk on two legs, but not for any distance."

"Good to know. Did Ada say where she was from?"

"She was from Zagreb, Sarajevo, Belgrade, the story changed, or maybe I wasn't paying the strictest attention while I was trying to figure out how a puppet could lose its head but then easily reattach it within minutes. The original Sicilian marionettes were operated by a series of iron rods with hooks at their ends, themselves a lethal weapon. Ada was very skilled at painting faces. She had studied art in high school, in another life.

"Did I mention the giant sea monsters called orcs? There was an orc, a fantastic many-headed monster, she called Oygen. I learned this was also the name of the man who kept her and others in a house in Long Island. Maybe near an airport. She said they heard planes all the time, and there were motels nearby. He trained the girls, the less attractive ones, to steal. At first, they practiced breaking into houses and spotting marks at train stations on what I figured out was Long Island. If they made mistakes, came back empty-handed, they were beaten. Success meant, in theory, your debt would be reduced, but it only seemed to increase with incalculable interest, and at least one girl was so seriously beaten that she died, but a few of them did become more skilled and were graduated into being brought into the city. One of Oygen's gang brought them in, and here they were charged with stealing mostly jewelry and cell phones, things which are small and easily lifted. The cell phones had to be sold like greased lightning before owners turned them off. Whoever bought them would be left with an inert piece of plastic, but by then Ada would be long gone and unfindable. The city offered crowds, more shops, and the promise of anonymity, but you had to be quick. If the gang of thieves didn't make their quota, the punishment was dire and collective. Everyone was beaten, everyone suffered, and it was all the slower person's fault. That person would feel the wrath, not only of Oygen, but of everyone in the cell, and in this way, no one had friends or alliances. Everyone suspected and hated everyone else."

She finally took Frankie from my arms and put her back in her cage. Until that moment, Lemon had been talking in a very speedy way, but when she described the beatings, she slowed down. Now she spoke in whispers.

"It wasn't just beatings, but also they were forced to have sex either with Oygen or with men who paid him.

"There was a definite hierarchy in Oygen's operation. Some of the girls were sex slaves. Ada and the darker ones were considered less desirable, but they'd all had their turns in windowless sheetrock rooms painted pink and smelling of dollar store disinfectant spray. Once in a while they were taken to a motel somewhere. Nobody, or few at any rate, would pay for these lesser girls, so mostly Oygen used them for other rackets, but sex with them in place of cash payment could happen at any time."

"Once they were in the city, why didn't they just escape? Go to the police?"

"They would be deported. Affiliated gangs back home would finish them off. Oygen told them he knew who their families were in whatever town or village or city they came from. If they ran away, he would have their families killed. If Oygen were arrested, the revenge would be terrible."

"And they believed him?" Ziv asked.

"They had no reason not to. They had seen what he'd done. He showed them pictures on his phone of horribly mutilated bodies. He spoke to them in their language, and if he didn't, he had people working for him who did."

"But Ada did run away." I said.

"As soon as she turned the corner with me, as soon as we walked past the McDonald's, she couldn't go back to the house on Long Island. She didn't even know my name, but I was someone, an American living in this city. If she went back, it would have been the third day in a row she'd returned empty-handed, which meant another beating and forced sex with an associate of Oygen's. What did I know of this world? I knew nothing. I understood garage band business, mating habits of reptiles, and making props for theater productions whose tickets cost a small fortune. That was all."

I did know something about people who traded their bodies for what my parents called injections of good times, tabs of imagination, never calling those substances by their names. It wasn't what they traded in. Injections or tabs of imagination gone wild; this they avoided and claimed it was not a territory that shared a border with them, and maybe they were right, but it was there nonetheless.

"Oygen paid for their airfare, insisted they were going to learn how to be nurses in America. They would make a ton of money, but when they arrived, before that was even remotely possible, they discovered they owed him tens of thousands of dollars for their seat on a plane, for a falling-apart house and food scraped from other people's plates. When she told me the amount of the debt, I couldn't believe it. It was a debt that could never be repaid."

"How long did she stay with you?"

"A few weeks, maybe longer. I don't remember exactly. Toward the end of her time working for me, though I didn't know it would be the end, two other women showed up."

"Do you know where they were from?"

Lemon shook her head.

"I used their heads as models, too, but then *Orlando Furioso* was cancelled. I got my fee, and so of course I paid Ada and the two other runaways. I'm not sure how they found her, why she contacted or trusted them. They couldn't believe you could earn cash in this country for doing something that would end up nowhere."

"So that's why you threw out the heads?"

"I had all this stuff in my workshop, and as you can see, it's not that big. I didn't need the heads anymore, so put them in the trash."

"There was only one in your garbage." Ziv said.

"Someone beat you to it." Lemon shrugged. "The last time I saw Ada, we were going into the city to buy plastic jewels from the bead stores on Thirty-Sixth Street. There was a fire in the subway. We were standing on the platform. It was actually pretty scary. The tunnel was full of black smoke, so thick it was like a solid thing like a giant fist speeding toward us. Someone said it was a bomb. There's always a catastrophist in the crowd. It would turn out to be a massive track fire, maybe fueled by oil or electricity—something that wasn't supposed to be where it was, but not a bomb.

"You couldn't see anything, but we felt our way to the street, a maneuver that was only possible because we had been standing near a flight of stairs. Others down the platform were in total darkness, coughing, liable to fall over the edge of the platform onto the tracks. There was a big crowd gathered on the street, spectators and those who had gotten to the surface. The police and firefighters hadn't arrived yet. They'd be there in seconds, but at that moment, when no one was being cordoned back, and it was pretty chaotic, Ada recognized a man, or he recognized her. He was wearing the red jacket of the Bayern Munich soccer team, not something you see every day, so I remembered it, but she ran as soon as they made eye contact across the crowd. I knew better than to call out her name, to draw attention to her, but she disappeared into the mob. I never saw her again. Later I learned many people suffered from smoke inhalation. Two people who didn't make it out in time died on the platform.

"I thought Ada would find her way back, but she never did. She never answered her phone or the texts I sent. I reported her missing, but the police had no leads, no information, no last sightings. Ada and her friends were invisible; they didn't exist. I kept hoping she was alive somewhere, although I was running out of stories to tell myself that would explain her silence."

We were all quiet for a few minutes. Lemon gave Frankie more water, poked her fingers in the cage, whispered soothing sounds in what might pass as alligator talk, then she let us know it was time for us to depart. She worked at night, and she wanted to be alone. It wasn't a hostile request. I had asked questions without saying exactly what I did for a living, but she must have caught hints of bad news, news that was worse than she could have imagined, and her answers were worse than I could have imagined.

Ziv expressed his apologies, shaking hands with one of the remaining *Furioso* knights when he stumbled into it on his way out. We walked out into the night as if we, and everyone we knew, still had all the time in the world.

# CHAPTER NINE

"SO, YOUR PARENTS WERE dealers?" This really interested Ziv. I was used to interest of this kind, and sometimes I ignored it, sometimes the curiosity was a little too gleeful, the speaker imagining because he knew my parents were old school pot dealers, then he could infer all kinds of other things. It was a night full of strangers, as far as Ziv was concerned, a story he would tell friends about two women he'd never seen before or since, who made clay heads of the living and the dead and who does that?

I didn't want to talk about them, so I told him the only thing my mother was afraid of were snakes. When she was little, her mother told her about a python named Franz who escaped from the Vienna Zoo which was not far from where my grandmother lived until she was about ten. Franz not only got out of his cage, but managed to board a tram, traveling quite far on the Ringstrasse, getting off, and disappearing into the city. You could never be sure where Franz would reappear, hungry and trying to adjust to a different climate from the one he was used to. As an adult, my mother no longer believed this was or had ever been a true story, but she would tell it to me in my grandmother's accent. I never met Ottilie. She overdosed before I was born. Ziv had no interest in Franz, I could tell. He wanted to know about the dealers. I had my standard story.

"My parents weren't murderers, but who's to say they didn't provide an entrance ramp to big troubles for some people? I don't know. Maybe. Maybe not. The story went that they taught music in schools, but programs were cut, and I believe this was true. They played trumpet and electric keyboard on the street and on subway platforms. Acoustics were passable, and the money was decent. Despite a small itinerant following, they got arrested or harassed by police, because you're not supposed to perform without special permits or something. As pot growers they started with just a few plants for personal use, then started growing for other people, and then more people. After a few years, the business was all they had." My grandmother, I was told, was not squeamish about naming body parts, and my parents, in their business dealings had learned from her, making liberal use of schmucks and putzes, each word having connotations far beyond the simple definitions.

We were drinking tallboys in his huge studio in an abandoned warehouse, not far from Lemon Ice's garage. The warehouse, one big shell of brick and pirated electricity, was different from the converted one I worked in that had been turned into floors and rooms. Ziv's squat probably wouldn't stay abandoned much longer, developers had been seen walking around the perimeters, and surveyors had set up their equipment, peering through things that looked like telescopes, taking measurements. You might think no one would want to build so close to a part of the canal where garbage barges dock, where the ground under your feet is known to be so toxic, it will take a superfund to clean up, but no one seemed to care, including Ziv.

He knew Nora Schwan from a road trip. She hadn't been on the trip, but she was a friend of a friend who had been. I was half listening, there was so much to look at in his cavernous space. Walls full of photographs, bits of written texts, found objects from odd pieces of hardware like hack saw blades, fan belts, old toys' innards. He assembled these things together to construct his sculptures, but I didn't know what to say to him about his work, what it all meant. The effect of all the objects that used to be one utilitarian thing with a job to do, say a hack saw, turned into something else entirely, like a bunch of other hacksaws welded end to end to form a picture frame that from a distance looked like something baroque and fussy – it was overwhelming, so I just stood there in silence. There were bins of discarded plastic bits and pieces organized according to color: red, blue, green, clear. Plastic is cheap, in some cases it's worthless, but his assemblages of those faceted suitcase-shaped boxes that once contained strawberries or tomatoes, for example, when fit together as a freestanding wall, in the dim lighting, the pieces of throwaway plastic looked like a screen of fist-sized super diamonds, ghostly but dazzling. Nearby an array of Blue Rhino propane gas tanks framed a smaller grid of old televisions. Ziv put his hand on my arm and showed me around as if I needed steering, which I probably did.

There was an army tank made of aluminum roasting pans entitled *The Unknown Knowns*, a stained glass window made out of soda and beer bottles from something called the *Dresden Series*, a cloudburst made of tin cans and kitchen utensils. What the finished objects looked like had nothing to do with the use or meaning of their components.

When Ziv talked about how he began to use what he scavenged because he couldn't afford to buy things that cost money, I understood. When I came home to an empty house after my parents were arrested, I had nothing. It was an animal that was familiar to me, always at my heels, so I felt Ziv and I had something in common somehow, though I also felt this was a late-night illusion. When he pulled out a stale, bent joint and offered it to me, this was the last thing I wanted. The last. I don't want to remember the house with the clothesline on the roof. In a registry of loss this is a department of slippery slopes I need to turn my back on, or at least try to.

"How do you sleep with all those skulls just a few feet away?" he asked.

"Like a baby." There are things that keep me up at night, but these relics of people I never knew do not make the list.

Ziv put his hand in my hair, sort of roughly, and I felt his lips, then his teeth on the back of my neck, like he was trying on a role he wasn't all that sure of either.

Another time, I said, I have to get home. Did I? Not really and yes absolutely.

# CHAPTER TEN

WHEN I GOT TO the street I texted Holloway's number to Lemon Ice. The head had a name and an identity, and Missing Persons would want to speak to her. Lemon didn't respond, so I swung by her house on my way to the subway. It was not an hour to expect an answer, but Lemon had said she worked at night. The canal in the early morning hours is about as close to a natural environment as you can get to in this part of the city, and I know that isn't much, but there are gulls and life in it somewhere, even if it's only the white biofilm on the bottom of the canal. The exact composition of the film is unknown, but it's thought to have some curative potential for degenerating human cells targeted by one disease or another. The lesson: what appears to be a dead zone might have medicinal elements buried in it. Like small pockets of ice discovered on a planet that had previously been considered little more than a rotating piece of cold rock, you look closely and learn perhaps life is possible in the worst places. Hurray, we're not alone! But it's a mistake to be too optimistic about the canal. Once, a wounded baby whale wandered into the channel by mistake, and though its waters really are more toxic than healing, the sight of the animal a few yards from the junk barges was a reminder that we're only destructive guests here, guests who spill and break, who tear up the house and don't leave until they're dead. The whale was looked after by a marine vet then towed back out to sea where it was known to have died a short while later. These were my distractions as I stood on the Ninth Street Bridge before making my way back to Lemon's building.

The garage door was halfway up, and the lights were still on. I ducked under and called out to Lemon. The Depression-era figures were still in place. Her workshop tools lay scattered on a table in the back near Frankie's cage. The wire door was wide open, and the cage was empty. I remembered Lemon putting the alligator back, but couldn't remember, or hadn't noticed whether or not she latched the door. If she hadn't, I imagined the animal slithering out of its cage and heading to the canal, adapting and surviving in the chemical-laced liquid only to mutate into a mammoth beast with rows of teeth Mack the Knife sharp, a transformation that was, however unrealistic, difficult to entirely dispel. I hoped the Morrises had arrived in the middle of the night to transport Frankie to the Everglades, but I watched my step as I looked around.

Amid the box cutters and hot glue guns on her workbench were a bunch of photographs, mostly pictures from plays, followed by pictures of Lemon Ice with her defunct band, the Y-Spirals. At the bottom of the stack were images of lab monkeys and rats being tortured by equipment I couldn't even begin to figure out the purpose of. A monkey in something that looked like an electric chair. Animals clearly awake and conscious during surgeries. The next and last picture was of Lemon throwing blood, or a substance that looked like blood, at a pair of women wearing fur coats. The women wore big sunglasses, but their mouths were screaming. I imagined Lemon in battle gear with her golden hair sticking out, bottle of red fluid ready to be thrown, scoping out the fur coats, approaching them, getting ready to spring. The animal pictures were disturbing, but it wasn't unusual for someone involved with animal rights to have them.

Out the back of the garage was a weedy lot, empty except for a small child's plastic swimming pool. This was probably where Lemon gave the animals a walk if they had legs, or a crawl if they didn't. I stepped up to the pool, remembering that alligators can move quickly, scampering on two legs if they feel like it. The water was murky, not dumped and refilled in quite a while. Otherwise, there was nothing in the yard that I could see except withered Queen Anne's lace and skunk cabbage. What I couldn't see, I didn't want to get too close to. If she had snakes or lizards at her reptile hotel, I would prefer to give them a wide berth. I looked for a gate, but there was no way out of the yard without going back through the garage.

As I made my way through the props, wending my way back to the half-open garage door, I followed a different path through her stuff from the one I took to enter, first stumbling into the spaceship made of old keyboards. A sign over what might have been its dashboard control panel stated it was a Sartrian vessel, as opposed to a Martian ship. I hadn't really looked at it earlier, a comic assemblage of old technology used to make something futuristic, but as I circuited a pile of mannequin parts, there was something sticky under my feet. A puddle of blood spread out from a heap of arms and legs.

Lemon's body was sprawled just behind them. There was a series of bloody hyphenated marks along her neck and shoulders. The teeth marks were close together, but her neck was also bruised. Her eyes were shut, but she was still breathing, and I stayed with her until the ambulance came, and then she wasn't breathing anymore.

# CHAPTER ELEVEN

"WE'VE CONFIRMED YOU WERE with Mr. Finzi, but you were with Ms. Ice just before she was murdered and again right afterward."

Holloway sounded noncommittal. He was just reporting where the facts, as far as he was concerned, lay. "If her death wasn't an accident, and she knew her killer or killers, there may have been elements that were already in place, paving the way, though neither you nor Mr. Finzi were yet aware of any of them. Iridia, do you know what a tropism is?" He filled his e-cig from a bottle labeled Sucker Punch, and exhaled over the empty animal cages.

"The way plants lean toward sunlight."

"The turning of all or part of an organism in a particular direction in response to an external stimulus." Holloway was neatly dressed, even in the middle of the night. I wondered what he watched or read when he was by himself: documentaries about whether or not we're alone in the universe, because Holloway seemed very much alone in his own universe. With all the infinite number of galaxies and the possibility of millions of planets capable of sustaining life, somewhere there's another Holloway making similar, but not quite identical decisions, who finds the Ada/Angelica character, a woman who couldn't be forced to convert to Christianity, and this other interplanetary theoretical detective intuits a series of steps that lead to the man who wielded the knife while earthling Holloway is mortal, hampered, loads more Sucker Punch into his e-cig, and maybe just watches porn when he's alone.

I was distraught, but he didn't seem to see that. Remembered from my training: cases in which the guilty called 911 in order to construct a picture of innocence, the simulation of alternative facts on a nonexistent planet. Is that what Holloway was thinking?

He looked around the workshop, taking me aside as we stepped around the empty cages and bags of food for various kinds of animals in the back. The array of tools, any of them easily weaponized, the clusters of props and figures in various states of being ready for the stage were mute, but Holloway felt that, even in their speechlessness, they had some capability for relaying information. Please, Holloway, don't talk to me about crowbars and football fields.

"Something was about to happen right after your first visit, even though you didn't know it. I believe there are elements, energy, what have you, something that if read correctly can be interpreted. I don't think Lemon Ice's murder came out of nowhere. Tropisms were already indicating action, you just didn't yet know what that action was going to be. When something is premeditated, and the parties know one another to one degree or another, there is a kind of environmental preparation or signs that if found and read correctly can foreshadow and point to the killer. The victim uncharacteristically cleaned the place, hid power tools, locked up dogs that should have been let out."

I'd been following Ada's story, holding an alligator, what was out of place or unusual in a garage I'd never been in before? Holloway was asking me to think like a baggage screener who missed the knife in the suitcase. He wanted me to go back and try to remember what I might have overlooked in the X-ray. It sounded logical, but did Holloway's theory have some basis in experience or did he list toward the hocus-pocus? I wasn't sure. There are often elements, out-of-the-blue phone calls, texts, leaving the door open, things, gestures, that don't register at the time. Holloway could discuss method of death as coolly as a veteran coroner, as if he were discussing an electrical system rather than a deceased human being, yet he had an earnest and dreamy look about him when he talked about energy.

"Think back to your last minutes with Ms. Ice. Any signs hidden in the grass but marking the road for what was to come? Anything that if you knew then what you know now, it would all make sense."

"There was an alligator in her workshop, but she wasn't fully grown. A couple by the name of Morris may have arrived between the time I left and the time I returned. They were supposed to take Frankie."

"Do you know anything about these Morrises?"

"Only their name. Lemon may have a record of them somewhere." Apart from the photographs I hadn't looked through her personal stuff.

"Who wants to own what will become a man-eating alligator? That can't be a large number. They could be drug dealers."

Was this a personal jab? Yes, I knew of a few who kept exotic pets. It was a thing with dealers. They came to our house with Burmese pythons around their necks, assuring us the snake or snakes were passive and sleepy. My father would take them from our guest and drape them around his neck in long cool loops as a gesture of curiosity or trust, I suppose. My mother did not.

"It was Lemon's understanding that the Morrises were going to release Frankie back into her natural habitat, probably in Florida."

"The senior reptile man is coming down from the Bronx Zoo. I don't expect we're looking at the Creature from the Black Lagoon, gills, lungs, webbed feet, and all." Holloway was just letting me know.

The Creature from the Black Lagoon would have been sympathetic to Lemon. He kills the characters who have their eyes on destroying the rainforest.

Holloway was no longer listening to me. An officer took my fingerprints, and I could see they were daunted by the task ahead. There were so many surfaces to dust, in theory, I suppose it could take years to finish, and even then, there would be so much floating, moorless, identity-less data in whatever prints, both human and animal were recovered. How could it all be sorted through? Holloway was spellbound by the opportunities of the workshop, so he was done with me for the time being.

"The heads are almost complete, but not quite. Will you be wanting Leo Sancton to finish them?"

"If you're almost finished, okay, but if the case shifts to high priority in the next day or so, then yes, I'm afraid a messenger will take the heads to Leo."

"As long as I get paid for what I've done."

"Of course, and if you think of anything else that might be of interest, anything you might have forgotten, be sure to let me know immediately."

# CHAPTER TWELVE

Ziv was downstairs, and I buzzed him up. I'd been up all night, or what remained of it, which wasn't much at all. It was now late afternoon. The police had been to see him, but he'd been able to go back to sleep following his questioning. Nora, who knew nothing, was in the hall, and as she peeked through my open door, I turned a skull to face her, and with one of my hands on its head, I smiled from my own private Yorick-land. I had a great time at the opening, Nora, thanks for the invite.

There was only a second in which I could think this way, to talk to my neighbor with masked sarcasm. Otherwise, I was drowning. It's one thing to work with bones, it's another to watch someone die.

Ziv walked in, animated, all caffeinated manic action, tying pieces of information together as if the woman we'd met only for an hour or so was a collection of data points. He knew I'd just gotten up, and he sat at a table, scrolling through headlines from years earlier, the time the three heads were discovered near Kennedy. There were photographs of the swampy area near the airport. People talked about being afraid to fly, although there was no evidence the heads had anything to do with airplanes. Conjecture ran toward people forced to walk into propellers, dropped from helicopters, satanic ritual. The captions under the pictures referenced *Head On a Platter, Head Over Heels, Head Buried in the Sand*, and *Heads Up!* The investigation went nowhere and the deaths were forgotten. This, I already knew.

The heads were almost done, then I would make a mold, and cast. They were perched in a troika on one of my worktables. Ziv looked at the forensic charts I'd tacked up that help the sculptor determine ethnicity based on skull measurements and told me it looked like fascism, and yes, German Nazis had catalogued all kinds of faces, and connected numerical values to race, but that wasn't what I was doing here.

My phone rang. It was Holloway who informed me the Morrises had been picked up, but they'd had a flat tire while driving through Maryland and never had gotten further north than Baltimore. The couple were professional gator wrestlers turned animal rescuers, especially known for wrangling reptiles from the Tampa Zoo after a hurricane tore through, freeing the large-jawed creatures who needed to be corralled before they could snack on flamingos and manatees. They were devastated, they said, to learn about Lemon Ice, and also sorry Frankie was at large. The Morrises offered their tracking services, but the Bronx Zoo reptile guy was on the job, so the former wrestlers were sent back to Florida.

Missing Persons found no Oygen in New York state, even narrowed down to Long Island. Which town? No idea. Once they had faces for the three heads, they could do more effective identity tracking, even if the three women were illegal aliens.

The Global Pathways heads, that fire, had been tied to a human trafficking organization, I reminded him, but Holloway knew that. Global Pathways was a West Coast operation that limited its scope to moving people from Southeast Asia.

I coated the heads with polyurethane resin to make the molds, and while they were drying, I asked Ziv if we could go to Howard Beach. Ada had been kept prisoner somewhere near an airport, near airport motels, where prostitutes could come and go and no one noticed anything about them, not their accents or the makeup that might have been worn too thick because of what it covered. Ziv had a green 1998 Toyota Tacoma. The backseat was full of junk he collected. We drove on the Belt Parkway, circumnavigating the western edge of the island till we arrived at Spring Creek Park and the neighborhood near Kennedy Airport.

We drove around looking for a small motel, the kind that people would book if they had to stay overnight somewhere between connecting flights. There was a Belleville Motel on the Cross Bay Boulevard, on a commercial strip between an automotive repair franchise and a Gold's Gym. If you had to stay there, it would be easy to make your flight, but also easy to drive into Long Island. Within minutes, you'd be there.

Sitting in the Belleville parking lot, I saw a woman get out of a black Mercury Sable, followed by a large man. They went into the office, presumably to pay, obtain a key, and get to business. The man had a paddle-shaped head, sharp nose, brown and gray hair tied into a ponytail. The woman was wearing a vinyl jacket trimmed with fake fur. Both wore reflective sunglasses. They came out of the office a few minutes later, opened the car doors to let two little boys out, and removed a suitcase from the trunk.

We sat for an hour, but there was nothing to be learned from those who came and went from the Belleville Motel.

Ziv pulled out of the parking lot and drove a few blocks to Bay View Clamhouse, telling me this would be a quick stop, then I could get back to work. There was a neon sign out front with a dancing drunk clam perched on top. The clam was meant to be soused. It was holding a martini glass, and its face made of neon tubing blinked between two different expressions: what passed as clam normal and lurching blotto. The menu posted by the door sported a quote from Walt Whitman.

*"Yes: there was a clam-bake—and, of all the places in the world, a clam-bake at Coney-Island! Could moral ambition go higher, or mortal wishes go deeper?"*

The Bay View had a nautical theme: nets on the walls, pieces of driftwood, pictures of Coast Guard cutters and men holding very large fish. At this hour, not too late, but not exactly right after work either, the bar and restaurant had an air of collective relief, a work day was over, and you could pretend for a moment the early morning train ride back into the city was light years away. A woman at the bar was drinking alone, pinkish cotton candy beehive, Amy Winehouse black wings coming from the corners of her eyes. She wore a tight silver satin dress with star-shaped rhinestone buttons, necklace made of knobs of crystal, a worn imitation leopard skin coat draped over the back of her chair. She looked tired but optimistic, and while other people were looking into screens, she was reading. When she tilted it up against the bar I could make out the title, *Kant und das Problem der Metaphysik*. When she ordered, she spoke with a Spanish accent. I imagined she was waiting for a stranger met online, she's hopeful, maybe this time will be different. She had her eyes on the door when we walked in, and smiled at Ziv, but he didn't notice. I felt his hand on my shoulder as the hostess seated us in a booth.

"It'll be fast. I promise."

He ordered calamari for two. It was not fast.

"The only witness to Lemon's death was Frankie, and Frankie has disappeared." It went without saying that Frankie was incapable of speech, but according to Holloway's theory of tropisms, there might be some evidence in the condition of the alligator, something in the way she was handled and released, but I had no idea what that something could be. Holloway must have had an inkling of how Frankie could "talk," or he wouldn't have called in the reptile man from the Bronx, who, should they find the animal, could read the nicks and markings of a hide like Braille. Could alligator skin be fingerprinted? Poor Frankie slithering out of Lemon's garage, looking for what pleasures could be found on the bankless polluted canal.

Ziv looked up escaped alligator and found a few animals had recently escaped from a circus camped near the airport. A saltwater crocodile, the kind native to Australia, swam across the channel and turned up in a playground in Mill Basin. A baboon was cornered foraging in a Pretzel Tyme in Kings Plaza Shopping Center. The exact numbers and kinds of animals kept by the circus were not known. There are others that could be still out there, managing to survive in the Salt Marsh or swimming further out to Long Island. It could be a longed-for escape, depending on the creature, but eventually winter will come, and unless the animal at large is a bear, there is no happy we're-all-finally-free sigh of relief for the wildlife of the circus. Animal rights groups were angry, and circus people were angry at the animal rights groups. Lemon freed animals when she could. She probably annoyed a lot of people, like that vet who released the elephants.

When the calamari arrived, I couldn't eat it. Ziv reached over and speared a couple from my plate.

"You don't like it?"

"The suctions look like they were cut from the back of a very small bath mat."

"I picked up some bath mats a few weeks ago from a dumpster. They were still in their packaging but someone threw them out. I rolled them into tubes and stacked them like logs."

"A life raft. A Kon-Tiki made of bath mat logs instead of balsa wood."

Ziv suggested we work together, but I have no affinity for invention. I have to work with what's there. He commented that I worked for the city who locked up my parents, as if I didn't know, as if I needed to be reminded.

"Yes, they felt the same way, the Crackpot Keplers. My parents' identities needed to remain hidden—I understand that—but some dead scream out for their names and faces to be known. Fairness, of not getting away with murder, is an idea, that's all. It's generally elusive and maybe not ever completely attainable. I'm a solo act, not an artist. As long as there are bones and clay, I can keep working, but I'm thinking I should find another city, or maybe not a city at all."

A tall balding man in a Key West T-shirt walked in the door, swinging car keys on his index finger, and the face of the woman in the silver dress lit up.

"Where would you go?"

"Someplace north where the ground freezes, remains are preserved, and the work is easy. No cartels. No money laundering. Death by polar bear."

"It's a mistake. Don't go." Ziv speared a couple more rings of calamari but didn't eat them.

"Imagine this is the Earth," I picked up a ketchup dispenser in the shape of a tomato, "and this," I tapped the top, "is the absolute edge of what you think of when you think about Europe, Russia, Canada, the place where Frankenstein hunted his demon monster, the geography seems empty, but in fact contains, so I'm told, a thrill or terror beyond consciousness."

"It's not empty. You'll find the descendants of animals that greeted the Ice Age rather than flee south: wooly mammoths, saber-tooth tigers, dogs like wolves, the kind who hunt in packs. They've had time to evolve. Glaciers move slowly. You can't be sure they were actually creeping forward at all. Actually, now they're mostly retreating. You'll find deadly viruses, thawed out and back on the job."

"There are no elephants or tigers in the Arctic."

"Seriously, don't go. There's no garbage there. I'd have nothing to recycle."

"Okay, Ziv," I said, pushing nearly empty plates to the center of the table. "Let's get out of here."

He wanted me to come home with him, but Missing Persons needed those heads. I had a deadline that couldn't wait, even if it was my last job.

# CHAPTER THIRTEEN

IT WAS NIGHT WHEN I returned to my apartment, but it seemed like the middle of the day, as if I'd slept on a long-distance flight, waking up at an airport in a country that was sort of familiar, but that I didn't wholly recognize.

I put my key in my door, and it moved at that very slight touch. It was already open. Had I forgotten to lock it? This was possible. You had to go through a locked door at the entrance to the building, walk through a courtyard, then through another locked door which required a different key to get to the back part of the complex where I lived. The few clandestine residents, like myself, and people who only worked in the building, were always milling around, in the halls, or working with their doors open. The former warehouse always seemed very secure, so what did it matter if the lock itself was flimsy. Anyone who broke into my studio would think they'd stumbled into a Halloween fun house without all that much fun involved.

The biggest threat I could imagine was the management company, making a midnight visit to let me know it was illegal to live here, informing me and everyone who did so that we had twenty-four hours to get out. This was always a risk, that we'd be thrown out, but management didn't come round so far into the night and just make themselves at home till you got back. I pushed the grain of the wood paneling with my index finger, and it swung open effortlessly.

Strains of Glenn Gould playing and breathing as he played came from someone's device. Glenn Gould, as far as I knew, had no access to my apartment, or to any other in the vicinity. The light switches weren't working. I'd paid my bills, but they were dead. The answer was that the light bulbs had been taken out.

A small pool of illumination clicked on from a desk lamp that had been moved to my worktable where the three heads were positioned. The cone pierced nearly total darkness. A shirtless man had his back to me, performing on an air piano along with the recording, breathing audibly along with Glenn Gould. From his wrist, up his arm, over his shoulder, across his back, then down his other arm was a tattoo of, I would guess, eighty-eight keys, though I didn't count them. He was sweating slightly as he played, and his skin glistened, black and white rectangles rippling as he played a space a few inches above the table. Then the waltzing of his long white fingers stopped, he took out a piano wire and sliced the faces off the three heads. Brown clay noses, cheeks, lips crumpled to the floor, where he stepped on them. Resin coating was a crunched and folded mass.

I froze, listening to the sound of wet clay squashing underfoot, a perceptible noise despite the Glenn Gould. What I thought in that second: if I shout, my real face could be sliced off next. The pianist rolled the silver wire into a coil and turned to face me, said my name, and asked me if this, he swung the wire toward the mess, had been my work? His face was hidden by what must have been a customized rubber mask of Leonard Bernstein. What lay underneath? A Manson-like psychopath, wild-eyed and slack-jawed? I nodded. The mask muffled his voice, but it increased in pitch.

"Your phone, please." He extended a hand, and I walked across the apartment to drop it in his palm. Examining it, as if the thing would tell him something, when finished, the mask looked back at me.

"You're going to have to do these faces over, I'm afraid. We can't have these people identified."

"How?"

"Eyes, nose, mouth, Iridia, you've been doing this for years. You will make up mugs that look like no living, walking around human. Invent whatever you like, but do it now." He gestured toward the three stumps sitting on my worktable.

"I don't make up faces. I'm not an artist."

"You will tonight, or you'll find yourself laid out next to your friend who made Saracens drop their noggins."

Bernstein handed me a small wooden spatula, not a knife which is what I would have used at that point, and tilted his head toward the stumps in a gesture that could only be interpreted as get to work. I didn't move. The rubber mask told me nothing. If he was losing patience underneath it, I had no way of interpreting his expression, but he kept talking, slowly, as if to a child.

"The human face is linked to identity. Neanderthal faces are no longer walking among us Homo sapiens except in some small, barely detectable percentage. Faces on milk cartons, on Most Wanted lists still on paper in your post offices, barely register to anyone. By and large no one gives a shit, but just in case, insofar as these are destined to go to Missing Persons, they can't be accurate."

Lemon had described Ada's accent as sort of Russian, but not exactly. Bernstein's was like that. *No one* sounded like one word, his mouth a lingering o, hard landing on the protracted n. He grabbed my arm and pushed me to the table.

"What do faces tell you? What is the language of the face? For these three, that language must become obsolete."

Bernstein played the air piano for a few minutes, then began to speak again, talking as if he'd been quiet for a long time, lost the habit of speech, and now couldn't stop. He was speedy; he was on something. In his impulsiveness, it was possible I would end up like Lemon Ice, like Ada. There was no reason to assume otherwise.

"My employer lives in a house behind shrubs cut like boxes, but this makes his home look like that of his neighbors. He rarely speaks to them because he has zero interest in their lives, but also because he doesn't want them up in his business, and unlike yours truly, he's a man of few words, you know?"

I didn't know, but I nodded. He didn't name the man Ada referred to as Oygen, the kidnapper she was afraid of, the gangster in whose house there were basement prisons while aboveground everything looked ordinary, so I don't know if that same Oygen was the Leonard Bernstein's boss, or if there was someone else and Oygen was only a middleman. Bernstein talked too much, but he was not going to name names.

"People come. People go. Everywhere in that house, a Babel of languages." He paused for a minute as if thinking about a house I hope never to see. How would someone like the pianist be found and hired? Perhaps he was a cousin or a brother, known for talent, ruthlessness, family loyalty? The flood of nervous talking began again. If there were one hundred secrets about this boss, it went without saying Bernstein wasn't supposed to divulge any of them, but he risked revealing a couple of them. I guess it made life interesting.

"There are languages that are extinct, or nearly so; languages that once had hundreds of thousands, maybe millions of speakers: Seminole, Livonian, Bantu, Judeo-Persian. Now zilch or pretty close to it. There are no zoos or nature preserves for languages threatened with extinction. Having a written form helps, but if you look at, say, Yiddish or Latin, that's no guarantee the life raft of writing will get you to a shore where you can flourish again. How does a language, a set of codes is all, plummet down to bupkis? One century it's the omnipresent language of diplomacy, the market, the bedroom, the military, the next minute it's squashed like a bug. War, annihilation of native speakers, vast migrations, slaveries. Of this, there is no mystery. What if termination should be the fate of your beloved English, the Anglo-Saxon devil that absorbs, expands, makes his own? It could happen. It's not so farfetched. All these documents, papers, books, websites, blogs, twitterfeeds, rendered inscrutable gibberish.

All down the gurgle hole, thousands of years from now maybe, but still inevitable. Meaning that what was once a route to clarity is now ocean bottom, opaque frigid mud, mostly lifeless except for those fish that have evolved to have no eyes because there's no light down there, so why bother? So, too, sweetheart, go these faces you've worked so hard on. They need to be unreadable. They must go the way of the dead English of the future and become unrecognizable. Faces of no one in particular."

"Missing Persons is waiting for these three."

"Of course it is, and you're going to accommodate Missing Persons with all the skills you possess. Here's what I suggest, and I make this suggestion very strongly. Refashion," he pointed to the anonymous lumps, "these to be other faces."

Then he stepped back and with a sweep of one tattooed arm, worthy of a television game show host revealing a prize, he moved the desk lamp to the other end of the table. On a square of frayed canvas lay a pile of cash. In another sweep of his arm, he collected the four corners of the canvas so it became a pouch. He held the bag in one hand, silver wire in the other.

"Your choice."

There was no alternative. I pointed to the bag.

"Wise move. Take it now while you're still able to speak fluently and can enjoy the cash. So, this is what will happen. You're going to give these domes new faces. I'm going to sit here and watch you. When you're done, you'll call Missing Persons to have a messenger come pick them up. As soon as the new heads leave, this," he pointed to the bag, "is yours. But I'm not going to ask you again. You don't mind if I practice while you work?"

I shook my head. It was a ridiculous question. He replaced the light bulbs so I could see what I was doing.

I stood inches away from the face that had been Ada's and slowly scraped the spatula into what had been her cheek, pushing clay into some idea of a cheekbone. What choice did I have?

"That's good, Iridia. I think you're getting the point I'm trying to make here."

But then I stopped engraving eye sockets and stood very still.

"Whatever I dream up won't correspond to the bone structure."

"Bones go back to the dusty old evidence room. No one sees them. You can do whatever you want."

The rubber Bernstein nose was very close to mine as he bent over, so we could, as much as it was possible, be eye to eye. He was no longer playing an invisible piano. The silver piano wire taut between his hands wrapped around my neck in an instant, tightening, slicing into my skin. I started to choke, couldn't breathe. The wire felt like a hot slow knife. Tears streaming, I coughed out I'd get back to work. Leonard Bernstein allowed no room for debate about the subtleties of the art.

Adding noses, brows, and chins where they'd been sliced off, I re-sculpted the three faces in record time. Instead of working on one, finishing it, then moving on to the next, I worked as if on an assembly line: three mouths, three sets of ears, three hairlines, nostrils, holes poked in the lined up noses, boom, boom, boom. The pianist practiced his invisible instrument, recordings of Glenn Gould repeated over and over. Since my internal clock was on a day for night setting, I wasn't tired, and I didn't want to nod out only to wake up with a wire tightening around my neck. Bernstein was playing and talking and playing and talking, only stopping to make coffee from my stovetop espresso maker. The man seemed to know where everything was, as if he'd been in my apartment before, and perhaps he had been. He poured himself a small cup that he was able to fit under his mask when he lifted the edge, turning away from me so none of his face was visible. I wanted to see what lay underneath, but, on the other hand, it probably wasn't in my best interest to be able to identify his features, or for him to suspect that I could.

Next, I coated the clay with polyurethane resin, but when I tried to open the windows to diffuse the fumes, he stopped me, tapping his bare wrist in the universal gesture of running out of time. His invisible watch was speeding up. Finish fast or you poison yourself. Perhaps he thought his rubber mask filtered out the toxic vapors. It wouldn't, and I wasn't masked, so to speed up curing the resin I waved a blow dryer aggressively around the heads like a mad barber, switching from left to right as my arms got tired. Meanwhile Bernstein continued to practice.

The molds were cast, clay poured into them, and those left to dry. I was starving, having not eaten since I pushed the calamari back to Ziv at the Bay View Clamhouse, and I asked Bernstein if I could make some food. I decided to make a sauce that would have the most forceful smell I could think of: onions, mushrooms, fistfuls of garlic, basil, rosemary, oregano, thyme. The kind of smell that would have Nora Schwan knocking on my door to complain. The air pianist didn't notice that I was using knives, or he was so preoccupied with playing he didn't consider that I needed access to them. I turned my sharpest knife over and over before I smashed the garlic, but I couldn't bring myself to plunge it into the line on his spine that separated middle C from D flat. I thought about it, lifted the knife, but put it down again. Bernstein kept playing. Despite the powerful smell, he shook his head; he would eat nothing.

I put the horseshoe earring in one of the three heads, chosen at random. Once the molds were cast, I had to remove the clay from the skulls, and they, too, would be sent back to Missing Persons. If someone skilled enough held them up to the new faces, they would realize that the bone structure and features didn't match. Anyone who had seen the faces I'd originally made would know these were very different, but those unlucky pairs of eyes belonged only to Nora Schwan, who had looked in for a minute, and to Ziv.

When the heads were dry, Bernstein handed back my phone, just long enough for me to call Missing Persons as instructed. It was early in the morning. Holloway had just gotten in and was no doubt enjoying a quiet moment with Suicide Bunny. Believing I was talking about the original heads, Holloway said nothing about being surprised I worked so fast, and assured me a messenger would be at my door within an hour. The department's check to me would appear in the mail as per usual. There was nothing left to say.

Bernstein admired the curvatures of cheekbones, the slope of the noses, the style of the invented haircuts. He compared them to three-dimensional maps, and that is exactly what they are, except these three were maps of Atlantis, Camelot, Middle Earth, places that don't exist. Isopleths of non-people, my new specialty. I packed up the clay heads along with the original three skulls, loaded them on a hand truck, and waited for the messenger. Once again, the Bernstein watched but never offered to do any heavy lifting. He talked while I wrapped and packed.

"The clay effigies are silent, deaf and mute." He tipped his head toward the boxes. "Clay is inorganic, right? You got your minerals, your earth, but earth always contains some living things. The odd bacteria, DNA from your hands, like the pottery shards that contained blood and virus proteins from an Iron Age German who collapsed from Crimean-Congo hemorrhagic fever virus. Deadly virus! Don't touch! It's back! So in a way, the clay can speak whether we like it or not. These heads, because you touched them, contain evidence of your hands." He rubbed a shoulder blade, right under white keys.

"So you're saying that whatever happens from here on out, I take the fall for falsification. Is that it?"

"Of course. That goes without saying. Let me pose another question. How do those who are born deaf acquire language? Are we hard-wired for language? You know the theory, that every child is born with innate coding for universal grammar, its categories, mechanisms, and constraints. UG treats the cerebral cortex like its own private soccer pitch. How is finding a much-sought-after word like scoring a goal? As humans we want to know causes and to be able to identify who did what to whom. It's good for evolution to know these things, but it can be dangerous for you, Iridia, so as we part, you have your cash, but keep this in mind: if you want to stay among the walking around upright humans, keep your trap shut."

What the fuck else was I supposed to do, Mr. Enlightenment.

"I'm not an idiot."

"Glad to hear it."

When the messenger rang, Bernstein told me to buzz the man in and instruct him to come upstairs, to pick up the boxes in the apartment. The pianist needed to watch the transaction but not be seen. He stood behind a screen that separated my bed from the rest of the studio, so the messenger never saw the half-naked man in a rubber mask observing my every move, listening to every word I said.

Task completed, elevator doors closed, Bernstein handed back my phone, and without another word left the cash on the table, put on a jacket, and disappeared down the stairs. I assumed he would take the Bernstein mask off before he got to the courtyard, so I ran to the hall window, but all I could see was his back and long hair that he reached up to tie into a top bun. Then he was gone.

Returning to my studio, I opened windows to let the polyurethane fumes disperse. I wanted to do more than change the air, I wanted to get rid of every object Bernstein had seen or touched, to hoover everything away, like some kind of bedlam Claymation: buildings, people, the city itself melted to prelapsarian moss and lichens whose clumps of leaves and filaments resembled faces. I couldn't reduce everything around me to plants, so I ran out of the warehouse and under the shadow of the Expressway, then turned west toward the bay, almost to the Narrows, finally collapsing in a park. When I woke, it was evening. I made my way back slowly, as if measuring every block. It was a way not to think.

My studio was dark, and the building was quiet. I looked at the modeling tools left in the sink, clay hardening along a serrated knife edge. The money would help for a while, for years, if I was lucky, but it wouldn't last forever. There was no one to stop me from continuing in my profession. Would a nose have this arch or that dip? In the orthodontist's office, cheery anodyne music in the background, while I looked for the teeth of a crash victim, I stopped mid-search, clay mold in hand, and worked out a way to make a leap to a trade, a profession recreating faces from bones. If I couldn't do that kind of work anymore, I needed another means to jump to something else, but I was stuck on a ledge with no parkour abilities whatsoever.

The heads do their job. In time they become friable lumps: there goes the nose, now the head resembles a sphinx, the ears—both go Van Gogh style. All that's left is the mouth, and as Leo might say, the mouth doesn't tell you squat. They look precise but can be entirely wrong. Given the opportunity to try on someone else. Why not?

Human DNA has been found on Da Vinci's drawings. This was a surprise? The hand touches paper and sheds pieces of itself, invisible to the naked eye. Bacteria, too, they live, multiply, travel from exhibit to exhibit, globetrotting, oblivious, tracing their lineage on that single piece of paper going back thousands of what passes for virus or bacterial generations, all the way back to Leonardo or an assistant, touching a mushroom, an apple after it's been bitten, a thimble of espresso, that drink newly arrived from Constantinople, then touching the paper again, transferring the little devils to paper made from linen rags. So that drawing, admired for its red chalk lines that describe bags under the eyes, the deep groove under the nose (no front teeth), that image stared at, and stared at, and studied for five hundred years turns out be full of unseen guests, a bio archive of one-celled wiggle pusses and stationary why-bother-I'm-content-heres. Amid the hair, beard, fox marks, etc. microbiologists have found the pneumonia virus and microorganisms ordinarily at home in the intestine, leading one to believe folks didn't wash their hands all that regularly, and now look who's here five hundred years later, and still going strong. The portrait is thought to be of the artist himself, but not everyone agrees this is so, there is still some dispute over the identity of the sitter. If that's Da Vinci's DNA, then problem solved, though not so fast, just proves he likely drew the portrait, not necessarily that he was the sitter. No one is exactly sure where in the church of Saint Florentin his remains might be, so a DNA match may not even be possible. Hundreds of years later, the identity of the microbes is more of a sure thing than Leonardo himself.

I moved tubs of clay and jars of resin to the hall. Any artist who wanted my supplies could have them gratis. Then I turned on my laptop, clicked on a news channel. Quarter past the top of the hour, the news turned local. A man fell or was pushed in front of a subway, suspending service on three converging train lines, Port Authority commission formed to study the disappearing coastline, and there was a fire in an abandoned warehouse near the canal. Sparks, the reporter said, had leapt from the burning building to the water, igniting the surface of the heavily polluted canal, turning it into waves of fire. The image of the block on my screen was a familiar one, and despite the smoke in the background, I knew exactly where the fire had been. One fatality, male.

I ran out the door, asked a guy in the courtyard if I could borrow his bicycle, okay, great, thanks, jumped on, lock still wrapped around the handlebars. At the first intersection I nearly collided with another cyclist who yelled gofahyoself. Though I was twenty or thirty minutes away, the smell of smoke began when I was a few blocks from Ziv's address, then it grew stronger, more acrid. The other buildings on the block were still standing, and the flames were out. What was left of the building was cordoned off. Yellow tape circled the lot, but the place was deserted. I ducked under.

Roof gone, windows blown out, wood struts and beams rippled carbonized black. Some brick walls still stood, though barely, in a shattered formation. They were the idea of walls, rather than walls themselves. If you knew what Ziv's possessions, his furniture, his kitchen, his work, if you knew what all that looked like, you could identify a few things, lumps of melted saw blades, monkey wrenches, a blue shell of a propane tank, that if it wasn't empty would have been one hell of an explosive.

# CHAPTER FOURTEEN

*Dearest Iridia,*

*As you know, I've been working in the laundry for about a year, and in general, it's neither good nor bad, just a jailhouse job. There are far more disgusting things to handle than a bunch of old sheets, but lately I've been finding notes mixed in with the bundles, notes that seem to be directed to me, like fortunes in fortune cookies, and who's to say if they're on the mark or random? Who is sticking the notes in there, and how that person knows that I, and none of the inmates who work at the laundry will find them, I have no idea. I've asked the dozen or so others who work this shift, and no one else has discovered any notes. Just me. Someone who has access, is positioned, and has perfect timing, knows my schedule and habits, how I do my job.*

*The woman in the cell to the right of mine was found hanged by a sheet, which makes no sense to anyone. Her death was determined to have been a suicide, but she was due to be released in six months. Why do yourself in, when you're about to get out?*

*The resident of the cell opposite mine has been hoping for new DNA evidence to exonerate her from a murder conviction. A child in her care died, but she swears it had nothing to do with her. Last week, news reached her that a fire in a Cincinnati lab, destroyed equipment, storage, and evidence went up in smoke along with it, and there go her chances down the drain. She'll be here forever.*

*Two women sitting on either side of me in the cafeteria fell instantly and violently ill, as if a fast-acting poison had been sprinkled on their Jello.*

*Odd, huh? I mean, stuff goes on all the time, but this feels like a tightening noose. In the realm of prison calamities, why does it look like I have immunity, but may not always. Disaster creeps closer to my cell. I have nightmares and daymares of fire, of flooding. I'm locked in and can't possibly get out. And what's with the notes?*

*I know how things work here, and my fear is not that I'm in a sandwich of bad shit; I'm in a vice that's closing.*

*The notes are handwritten in block letters on regular typing paper cut into strips, but not so small that I wouldn't notice them. The fact they're handwritten is more ominous, in the way the human voice over the phone with its cadence, pitch, tone, inflections, is scarier than a text, or the way a robot that really looks like a human is much more terrifying than a collection of tin cans and LED lights.*

*I hope you're well and are working, though as you know, I wish you were doing something useful with your talents instead of carrying water for a branch of the police department. I know, I know, the remains of loved ones deserve to be identified, and common murderers should be behind bars, absolutely. Cold-blooded killers are no strangers to the population here, and I've made the acquaintance of more than a few. But Iridia, darling, the source of your paycheck still sticks in my craw, and I'm sorry, it always will. I know your father, wherever he is, in whatever hole, feels the same way. It is one of the great tragedies of my life that I, or rather we, couldn't support you so you could become the artist you deserved to be. You certainly had the ability. I still have one of your drawings up in my cell. It was drawn on the roof: a jagged skyline with a sun and rainbow.*

*I would love nothing more than to have a visit from you but understand flights, hotels, car rentals, are all expensive. In place of an actual visit, please write more often, and it wouldn't hurt you to call once in a while, would it?*

*Love you always,*
*Mom*

Slips of paper, the notes, had been included in the letter. I shook them out.

*Dead languages can be the key to freedom.*
*Save face, say nothing.*
*Face your fear, and it will disappear.*
*Tongue-lashing is a prelude to a nocturne.*

The postmark on the envelope indicated the letter was mailed the day before my visit from the pianist. I'd done what they'd asked, there was no need to threaten my mother, no need to communicate *if you don't comply, we can get to your mother and father, too, don't forget.* What Oygen, Bernstein, or whoever, were trying to tell me was clear: you took the money, we're done, you and us, but you get to live with this fear.

In the hallway, Nora was screaming. I dropped the letter from yesterday's mail on what remained of my worktable, and opened my door. Someone from another floor was trying to reassure her while she was shouting, barely incoherent. The storefront gallery had been broken into and vandalized. The work in the show had been slashed, shattered, paint thrown on walls and every conceivable surface. I have to admit I didn't think this was the biggest tragedy to occur in the world, but listened closely as she went on about lost images of Coney Island and irreplaceable drawings.

"What happened to *American Carnival*?" I asked.

"What do you think?" It was almost an accusation. "The whole thing was flipped over which would have to take more than one person, then it looked like someone took a jackhammer to every part. A pile of garbage was all that's left."

I put the cash in a backpack and threw some stuff in a suitcase. On my way out of the building, I stopped to look in my mailbox. There was new mail in it: credit card offers, menus from restaurants offering discounts, and a letter from my father's prison. I didn't touch it. The letter would be returned to sender. If my mother and father didn't know where I was, the precariousness of their relative safety couldn't be used to threaten me into creating counterfeit heads or keeping my mouth shut.

# CHAPTER FIFTEEN

HARRY LIME FAKES HIS death in *The Third Man* and disappears into the sewers of Vienna. Underground tunnels were not a place I wanted to visit in any city, but I knew a little German, and I liked the idea of becoming someone else, if it was at all possible. My grandmother was born in the Leopoldstadt district, formerly known as Mazzesinsel or Matzoh Island, and once I heard that concept, I drew images of a bedrock of matzoh: here's the Cenozoic Era, Mesozoic, Paleozoic matzoh layer, but as the water levels rise, no flour-based component can maintain its structural integrity. A soggy mass crumbles, and then it's all washed away. Though she died before I was born, I knew a few facts about her. Ottilie escaped the city on a train in 1939. She ended up in New York, but in the beat poets of Washington Square, the displaced cafeteria intellectuals of the Upper West Side, Borscht Belt comedians, in the general elbowing raucousness, there was no foothold for her in the following decades. If you asked her how she was, just as a general greeting, she might answer an expression which translated literally as, at night it's dark. Ottilie bounced around, only to succumb to a fatal combination of Benedryl and slivovitz. My mother, who was on her way to becoming a pot distributor, was, at that time, playing music somewhere in the West 4th Street subway platform.

If Leopoldstadt had been made Brooklyn's twin borough in 2007, then Coney Island's Viennese partner was the Prater, and if the two amusement park districts were mirror images of one another, than the Wiener Riesenrad Ferris Wheel, where Harry Lime told his friend Holly Martins that people were just dots, was the Wonder Wheel where from the top, you looked out over tens of thousands of animated dots plus the Atlantic Ocean.

During the day the Prater, despite sites like GunFun Shooting Club, Hotel Psycho, Extasy, and Volare, looked like a refined Coney, though the extra fussy design filigrees that Coney did without, didn't necessarily make the amusement park any less whack. Harry Lime wasn't the only one to make deals here. At night the Höllenblitz with its Méliès-like demons and waterfalls was lit up, cars on rails disappearing inside, screams making their amplified way out. While the corpse puppets and mummy creatures of Hotel Psycho never slept, the place might only appear deserted. As I walked around, music would blast from the odd mostly empty bar, and then the pathways were dark, quiet, and empty. Mechanisms designed to make people scream lay around every corner, and I was reminded of my midnight travels through Gowanus, the night of Lemon Ice's murder, though in actuality, I encountered no horror show, no set of three creatures who appeared out of the noxious fog and gray gusts of concrete powder, no helpful Uber driver on a cigarette break, no bicycle messenger, no talking alligator emerged from the canal rasping advice in an amphibious pidgin.

I had enough money to do whatever I wanted to and thought about trying my hand at making heads, faces, drawings based on random observations or entirely speculative, but with no crime to solve dogging at my heels, insisting on verifiable likeness. With whatever leaky pen or stub of a pencil I had on hand, I drew faces obsessively so I wouldn't have to think of what I'd left behind, then following the advice of what must have been a somewhat dated guidebook, I found the address of an art supply store famous for its history going back to before the First World War. In the book there was a photograph of jars of brilliant rare pigment: Scheele's green, Tyrian purple, white lead. At the storefront of what I thought was its location, shades were drawn over the display windows, and when I opened the door, a woman framed by wooden carvings glared at me. Mangers, martyred saints, clowns on skis, cuckoo clocks of various sizes and mechanical complexity loomed. They seemed to inflate, crowd one another, lean toward me. I coughed out in broken American-accented German that I had the wrong address. It was not an art supply shop and perhaps never had been. There was some mistake, or I misread the guide. For a moment I froze as the woman glowered at me, and I felt like an animal in Lemon Ice's garage filled with knights and Saracens, impossible to interpret the cardboard people on all sides, but knowing you don't belong there. I never tried to find the correct address for the shop.

There was news of refugees approaching from Hungary, those who had been stopped and prevented from traveling further north, images of children watching Tom and Jerry cartoons outside the Keleti train station in Budapest where the police had barricaded them in. On a bus, the street, in the elevator of my small apartment building, you heard bits of conversations about not letting them into Austria, and it was Germany's fault. Germany, they said, had laid the table, now the hoards were rushing in from the east. A kebab cart on my corner was overturned, chunks of lamb, onions, spilling to the pavement, tins clattering, pools of oil. I heard the screaming, threats yelled, and footsteps running away from the ruined cart. The air smelled of cumin and garlic, the shadows the Turkish vendor left behind, still, hours after his disabled cart was towed away.

The opposite of the two-euro thrills of the Prater were the halberd thumping baroque museums like the Belvedere Palace. Most exciting thing: at the top of a vast marble staircase, a cleaner polishing the huge naked statue of an Apollo. He started with the head, then systematically moved lower and lower down the god's body, and I wondered, what is dirty for the cleaners who work here? What level of dust, corrosion, layer of biofilm is a cause for concern? When is it the deciding moment to have a good time, put on a show, and clean the naked stone people? Because then the Volksprater concept of dirty creeps in: touching the body parts that on humans would be considered private and hidden by clothes. You could tell the cleaner, back to the spectators, but occasionally turning around, was enjoying this.

More often than not, I walked through room after room of gilded fillips and curlicues. The portraits of Franz this and sword of Emperor that hung like fogged windows into eras when the sun revolved around the earth and a mosquito bite could kill you. If you were a seventeenth century person, all these canvases and objects were like the internet. They told you alliances, status updates, divine affiliations.

The images made as much sense to me as Lenny Bruce explaining Jewish versus goyish did to my grandmother. She didn't understand why Eddie Cantor, the "Apostle of Pep" was, to Bruce, bland and pandering, while Ray Charles was Jewish. She was baffled as to why Viceroy was Jewish while Camel with its alpine ads was firmly in the goyish column. Why was the Navy goyish but the Airforce Jewish? These demarcations made zero sense to her. This, I knew from my mother, and she died of laughter trying to explain, while Ottilie, in her own way, would say, darling, how have I landed in this dreckfest? So I felt staring at paintings of unknown but inbred royals with droopy lips and unfocused stares. I wasn't sure where I'd landed, and yet if the gallery where I saw *American Carnival* hadn't been vandalized, but magically preserved, how would those objects and photographs be read decades or hundreds of years later? A future anthropologist might conclude everyone living in the twenty-first century belonged to a society of gawkers and mawkers, constantly on display. In a thousand years, relics of Coney Island will look closer to images of forgotten royalty who died from treatable illnesses, who no one ever told, ya' too damn inbred, then we will to the jetpack-live-forever travelers of the future.

Until I found the Grosz painting. It stopped me in my tracks. Men with bandoliers of ammunition, guns, fires consuming overturned cars or trucks, large city buildings tilted at chaotic angles, about to be consumed by fire. George Grosz painted *Street Fight in Vienna* in 1934 when he was already in New York. Ottilie may have seen the actual fighting that year, while Grosz had his eye on the door and left years before. Fascism was a kind of knocking he recognized, and he packed his bags. Ottilie's family waited until it was too late.

What kind of knocking had Ziv recognized? Going through drecknests of dumpsters for material to make his installations, were there signs he was capable of reading, signs in the garbage a city throws away? The hills of lithium batteries, the circuitry in a phone that looks like an aerial map of a small city, all the things that in their sheer quantity are the breadcrumb path that leads to prematurely melting glaciers, he said. So, he hurried back to his warehouse, sack of precious plastic and Styrofoam bits and pieces, as if they were golden, and in a way, they were.

Ziv liked the idea of Grosz, impoverished, selling a painting to cover a few hundred dollars in car repairs, living on Long Island, and decades later, there's Mr. Oygen in residence down the street, hoarding people. His business card, if it existed, would advertise his ability to turn slaves into goldmines.

# CHAPTER SIXTEEN

I STARTED RUNNING IN the morning because it was something to do. There was no work for me here, and it was odd not to have an assignment, the urgency of deadlines and identities waiting to be known. Somewhere back in Missing Persons were three heads that bore no resemblance to any real person who ever walked the planet, and Holloway and his team were scouring every database, every blind alley to find these women who were phantoms in more ways than he would ever realize. A woman with a horseshoe earring got on the A train bound for Howard Beach with no memory of Trinidad-born Michael Griffith chased by a white gang into traffic where he was killed by a car in 1986. She doesn't remember because she's not real. I invented her, but she knocks on Detective Holloway's door and introduces herself. She tells him, there's something you need to know.

A body believed to be Leo S. washed up just under the express-way at the point where the highway becomes a bridge and vaults over the river. Marine life had made a meal of the carcass, so there wasn't a great deal left. Missing Persons had never met the man in person, so his demise was noted, but no notice posted, no flowers sent, because there was no one to send flowers to as far as anyone knew.

When talking birds, parrots and cockatoos, are released back into the wild, native birds with the same abilities mimic them in turn, so you could be walking in a jungle or Telegraph Hill in San Francisco or Greenwood Cemetery in Brooklyn (places where parrot flocks are known to roost) and you would be surprised to hear someone (before you realized the source of the scream was avian) screech, for example, dickhead, dickwad, dickhappy, dicktator, dickhawker, dickhunter, dickplodockus, and so on. Dirty-mouthed birds are funny. They aren't supposed to know what they're repeating, it's just sound to them, though there are ornithologists who think they do know. There was the case of the parrot who witnessed a murder and repeated the victim's last words, identifying the shooter. Somewhere in the fake heads I built are talking parrots. Will I feel relieved when Missing Persons figures it out? And do I really want them to? Being unmasked or hiding safely in a city that, if history had gone a different way, could have been mine, and I'd be speaking German in this low crime city, so low, so nonexistent I'd be working as a tour guide, a teacher, a cataloguer of Habsburg armaments. Who knows? Come on, Holloway, find me, extradite my ass, guilty of tampering with evidence.

Sometimes those dots Harry Lime described stopped in place and keeled over, as he knew they would, and he absolutely did not care, as long as he was making money. Bodies, motionless dots, turned up in the park. In other words, faceless people followed me everywhere. One morning, three turned up.

The police had cordoned off the area around the Riesenrad. It was so early in the morning, the wheel was still lit up, music growing fainter and fainter, the operator was having trouble bringing the entire mechanism to a halt, but finally the sound trailed off. The cars of the Riesenrad aren't like the buckets of the Coney Island Wonder Wheel. They're more like miniature train compartments, and people, couples, can book a car, have dinner in it, and admire the view of the city as they circle. People don't start queuing up until later in the morning, usually, but a few tourists who wanted to beat the crowds had stood in line. Eventually the operator opened the door to a carriage that already had occupants: three headless bodies, deposited there during the night.

Two of the bodies were women, and it was guessed, based on their clothing, that they were strays whose origins lay in the crowds arriving through the Balkans or from war zones to the east. Rumors began with a statement made anonymously to a man holding up a phone, spreading outward from the police cordons to the edges of the crowd, but the bodies belonged to a population that, if they went missing, no one reported it. If family or friends were in the city, these were people who remained silent. It was possible they didn't speak German, didn't want the police or courts to know their identities at risk of being shipped back or flown to a desert island in the Pacific that once belonged to Australia, a no man's land. No one wanted to end up in such a place, so they tucked their photographs, the only concrete evidence that the vanished ever existed, into back pockets. Someone near me in the crowd whispered the murders were no doubt the work of gangs who hung out at the Praterstern Station. Everyone had their stories, their explanations that provided answers of some kind, whether true or not.

Unable to run further, I walked to a café on the edge of the Prater. Workers were coming in off the night shift: security guards, ambulance drivers, orderlies, they drank as if it was midnight, because for them, it was. They mixed with office workers, one group shedding their on-the-job selves, the other about to launch themselves into another day. I didn't know Oygen or the Bernstein's real names or faces, but did a search on my phone for news of the city I'd left behind, along with the words *traffickers, smugglers*, within a small window of dates. There was a picture of a man who could have been the pianist. I now thought of him as the Pianist, like Metamorpho, Atom Smasher, or Sandman, or any number of superheroes and supervillains. The tattoos, though distinctive in real life, were hard to make out in the photograph. The man had been arrested and deported, so he and Oygen could be here, could be anywhere. Like the Watchers in *Justice League*, there is always someone behind who you think is in control. At the pot farm I'd read my father's *X-Men* comics, so I knew, even superpowers can't defeat every possible brush with death. Sooner or later, even the most intrepid can be fooled despite the ability to fly, climb, predict the future. But they can also be reborn, rise from the smashed atom ashes, and there they are again, getting off a plane at the Flughafen Wien.

# CHAPTER SEVENTEEN

I NEVER CHECKED MY old email address. The icon sat in an upper right-hand corner of the screen like an indecipherable relic from a Bronze Age language. I was afraid if I clicked on it, an alarm would sound in a distant basement or maybe in a submarine, and a man who looked like Roy Cohn circa 1965 would put on his headphones; my exact location would appear on his radar screen, followed by the buzzing sound of a drone overhead. I'd catch a nanosecond-long glimpse of the aerial wingsuited bug before my vaporization. So I didn't click on that icon ever, until I read about the Riesenrad bodies. The heads once attached to those bodies had been found in Hotel Psycho, Prater horror house, a dark ride full of pop-up skeletons and screaming faces, so no one noticed these were real. Until I learned about the night shift cleaner who found the genuine once-living-and-breathing heads, I hadn't even been tempted to look at my old mail, but then the memory of working, and the possibility of doing so again, of building identity and a face from minimal information, all that tapped me on the shoulder. If I got the call, the message, Iridia, we only want you, I wouldn't answer, but despite the risks, it would be nice to have a momentary flash of feeling needed. So I opened the mail I used to have. Just a peek, it would only take a second.

The screen was instantly striated with bar after bar of deletable nothing, until I saw zivf@gmail.com. Dated only two weeks earlier. There was no subject heading. I opened it.

*Hi Iridia –*

*Yes, it's me, Ziv, feet on the ground, not writing from afterlife limbo. My corporeal self wasn't transported anywhere you wouldn't recognize. You and everyone else were misinformed: I wasn't incinerated in the warehouse fire. Who was it, then, whose charred bits and pieces were piled by the door? Who else was in the building? I have no answer for that question, but there were crews of runaways, dumpster divers, gang members on the outs with their gangs, graffiti painters, all of whom camped out in the building from time to time. Sometimes there was no one there but me. That night, there was someone else in the building. Exactly who it was, will most likely never be known.*

*Missing Persons' mistake was to send the remains found near the barred door (and, yes, the door was barred from the outside) to Leo Sancton, half blind, trembling hands, no internet access. You would have known immediately that Yorick wasn't me, but Leo, magnifying glass in hand, saw my picture in the print newspaper that landed on his doorstep, read I was missing, presumed dead in the blaze, so he reproduced what the photograph, not the bones, told him. He wanted to retire and collect his pension. Can you blame him? Dead is dead. Identity, the driving force behind his career, no longer matters so much. In a few years, no one remembers the person, and a few years is a blink in cosmic time. An old man like Leo is more than aware of this. In the end, we're all just molecules of calcium, phosphate, and salt. I was Leo's last job, I hear.*

*The skull sent to his home in Whitestone belonged to someone, but not to me. I'm still here. My work is entirely destroyed, as is much of my face. I'm living, hiding out, sequestered in Lemon Ice's unlocked garage. I don't know how long it will be before the landlord hauls everything out and evicts me. It's been quite a while, and I'm beginning to think the place has been abandoned, even by long-lost reptiles. Until then, I try on masks and make myself at home.*

*As soon as I was able, at night, hoodie pulled over my head, I made my way to your studio; it was empty. What people didn't take had been thrown away. Your phone was turned off. I don't know if you'll get this email, but if you do, please let me know you're okay. I need major surgery to have my face reconstructed, but there is no hope of my ever having the kind of money to begin the process. I would love to see you again, but don't want you, or anyone, to see me.*

I wrote back to Ziv immediately. How could I send him money for surgery, I wanted to know. He asked where I was, and this I wouldn't tell him, not yet, and I couldn't send him money via a bank account which would betray my location, so I sent him half of what I had using bitcoin, and he was very pleased to use that kind of transaction. Facial reconstruction costs the earth. Did he have insurance? Of course not. Ziv could now make an appointment with a plastic surgeon, but a month passed before I heard from him again. The surgery was still out of reach. The doctor was optimistic that there was enough tissue to, if not totally restore his original face, make him look human, to look like everyone else. No one would stare at him, and he'd be safe from those who set the fire. He would have a new face that would be unrecognizable to anyone looking for the old Ziv. The doctor's waiting room was full of before and after pictures, some hard to look at, but the afters were dramatic in their naturalness, and in some cases, real beauty. Remembering Ziv's face, his expressions of skepticism, anticipation, of relief when doubt was resolved, I sent him everything I had. I just clicked and did it.

Weeks passed, and I couldn't stop myself from checking the forbidden mailbox constantly. I wrote to him, had he had the surgery? How did it go? Could he send me pictures of his new face? I would tell him where I was living, and he could fly here. Then I stopped and didn't send that one. There was no answer. I never heard from him again. Perhaps he died in surgery—it happened, people did—or maybe there was no Ziv. I mean, maybe Ziv did die in the fire, and the person writing to me was someone else. Bernstein, even, getting his money back and laughing all the way to the bank. I would never know.

I looked at faces in the street, wondering if one of them was Ziv, but no one looked back at me with any kind of recognition, only annoyance. In any case, the money was gone. I had to go back to work.

# CHAPTER EIGHTEEN

THE LAB WAS LOCATED off Saint Ulrichsplatz near the Museum of Natural History. The Weissberger Lab wasn't a forensic lab and rarely worked on humans. There was so little crime in the city, we would have almost nothing to do. The lab was associated with the museum, and mostly what we worked on were remains not even local to the city, but sent from elsewhere, remains of creatures that occupied not the fork in the road between man and apes, but on the tines very close to the point of separation. I called it the Weissmuller Lab, but no one I worked with got the joke. The Weissberger was a clean, white, well-lit lab that smelled of acetone, latex, and burnt coffee. Though a lowly technician, I had my own work table and enjoyed conversations over lunch, a fly on the wall, for the most part.

Once skeletons were put together and studied, models were constructed for exhibitions. Bones were fleshed out: muscle, skin, hair. Sometimes there were very few bones to go on, maybe ninety percent of the face was missing and had to be imagined anew. Low foreheads allowed for greater bite power and diminutive brainpan size, at least that was one theory. Creatures like Lucy arrived, and the square ape mandible gets smaller; the intermediary skulls line up on the cladogram branch that eventually leads to us.

The eye sockets of the skulls that list toward the ape end of the spectrum were huge, and a paleontologist I worked with stuck his forefinger in one, twirling the skull around in hula-hoop fashion.

Speaking in English, he would say things like, Don't forget, the apes for all their talents sit on one side of the divide, whomanns on the other.

We were also sent bones that weren't heads, like the Lebombo Bone, found near the South African border. These were notched tally sticks, 43,000 years old, made from baboon fibula. Each notch was meant to mark phases of the moon, that was the assumption, no one knew for certain, but these tools were another signpost in the road where we waved adios to the apes. The exact location of that signpost was the lab's unspoken charter, and it kept moving. Name one thing that could be definitively established once and for all as the true separation point between humans and apes, the question was often posed. Use of fire to cook food. The ability of creatures to imagine the future or have a concept of it that would go beyond, say, storing food. I imagined Bugs Bunny moving a sign repetitively from place to place, back and forth, with determination and tolerance until finally collapsing in frustration. Not here, over there, but can you be sure? I can't.

There was anxiety about the possibility of big overarching mistakes, the moment when the underpinning of everything the lab was founded on would suddenly be proven false. An example cited: dinosaurs were considered lizards until evidence tilted them closer to birds. What errors could the lab be making of similar guffaw-inducing magnitude? Their uncertainty was a new workplace quality for me. Missing Persons assignments had appeared to navigate more solid ground, at least that was the impression: this is what you have, this is what you do, here are the provable results. In the realm of uncertainty and conjecture, the skull spinner asked questions like can consciousness be created or enhanced, the basic electrons and atoms be tinkered with, CRISPR style, so apes could be more like whomanns? If so, then could consciousness become like an ingredient you can add as if making a cake? Meanwhile, it was someone's job to order more of the synthetic fur that got adhered to models whether truly simian or one of the intermediary wayfarers that was almost, but not quite, a tool-making, food-cooking, language-with-tenses whomann.

# CHAPTER NINETEEN

A WOMAN AT A table nearby spilled coffee on her jacket, but she laughed it off. She told her friend she was planning on quitting her job that afternoon. The spill was what an invisible costume designer would have painted for the film about her life, about what the next few hours held in store. No one at my office, she said, knows what I'm talking about. It's as if I'm speaking a dead language. They get some of it, but not much, and I've had it. Her face was frozen, as she'd had a fair amount of Botox, but she also seemed happy; she was about to solve one big problem, though another was just down the road in the form of *what next?*

The Pianist had talked about dying languages, as if that loss was equal to the degradation of faces, of those craniofacial markers we need to match face to ethnic group, race, clan, family, then bingo, name and social security number if they have one, followed by medical records, education, search history, shopping habits. Coded in the clay, beside my own bacteria with its DNA stamp, were the lies I constructed and sent to Missing Persons. My DNA could also be found in the clay models of the lab, but it's unlikely anyone would care. There was no criminal intent when I made those faces. Holloway might still be looking for tropisms, for the one object out of a thousand, and he might figure it out, how I'd sent him features that bore no connection to the bones at hand. He had the resources to find me, feet up, revolving on the Riesenrad with my own personal invisible Harry Lime.

As I left the café, I saw a group of people in costumes headed toward the center of the city. They were dressed as clowns, princesses, wizards, someone's idea of a Turk in a turban, curved sword at his side, perhaps meant to be a jinni. A cluster toward the back of the crowd wore rubber masks: Angela Merkel, Vladimir Putin, David Bowie, Jay-Z, and among the group was a Leonard Bernstein. He turned and stared at me. Was it the same Leonard Bernstein? Impossible to know. The woman who was planning to quit her job joined me as we watched. The American president was visiting, and the local Clown Army had promised mayhem, she explained.

I followed them, but lost sight of the Bernstein. Other clowns joined in as we walked, and soon I was surrounded, unable to move or leave the crowd. Traffic stopped, cars let us pass, some cyclists joined in.

Vladimir Putin, standing near me, pulled all kinds of things from one of his voluminous patch pockets: a whistle, wind-up false teeth, a plucked rubber chicken, whoopee cushions, elastic euros, stretchy until they snapped, and finally a second rubber mask. A lizard? I asked. No, a chameleon. He put it on my head, explaining the plan was to deliberately put all kinds of junk in their pockets, making it more difficult and time-consuming for the police to search them.

We reached the palace on the Ringstrasse where the president was meeting the prime minister. Was it the Belvedere, the Urania Observatory? The Parliament building? I didn't know. Even the grand buildings I'd seen, I'd never viewed all of the exteriors. There were always other sides, other angles, baroque, encrusted with figures and decoration, fountains and symmetrical and asymmetrical gardens. You could never see everything. So what were those buildings? The clowns were staring straight ahead, focused on the soldiers who ringed the palace. Tanks were stationed on corners. Pepper spray, teargas, bullets, the Grosz painting come to life in another century with another set of actors. The palace was impossibly distant and defended. What was the point? We surged forward anyway, toward the line of police in riot gear, helmets, shields, faces covered by visors. We got so close we could see their faces under the bulletproof plastic. A few of the soldiers and police were laughing so hard they broke rank and let the clowns pass.

A man in a Rosa Luxemburg mask was slowly emptying his backpack for a trio of soldiers. He pulled out a bright orange water gun, held it up in the air and appeared to be saying something, the way the mask moved. One of the soldiers grabbed his arm and twisted it behind his back, while the other dumped the remaining contents on the ground. It was just a piece of plastic filled with water. People laughed as the crowd pushed forward. The soldiers were losing patience. What if there had been acid in the gun? What if someone did have an explosive? Windows and sentries blown out, soldiers, police, marchers' body parts all mixed and scattered from the palace to the street.

Who would reconstruct my face? Who would claim me or even know I was missing? No more memories of my parents' pot farm, no one to say her name sounds like an element found on an asteroid, the charts of facial anatomy: muscles, bones, characteristics of races and ethnic groups that bear an unfortunate similarity to the racial investigations of the Third Reich.

Someone botches the job of my reconstruction, intentionally or because there just aren't enough skull bones left to figure out what I looked like. In the afterlife, I'm not myself at all. I become the Queen of Sheba, Molly Picon, Judy Holliday.

The inside of my rubber mask was damp with the sweat of the last chameleon-wearer. It smelled like sour yogurt. I gagged, but I have to admit that for a few minutes I felt happy, part of the mob. Though already I knew before long the helmets and masks would come off, and then, maybe, you see people as they actually are.

# THE PROPAGANDA ARTIST

WHEN CARLOS THE JACKAL kidnapped delegates at the OPEC conference in Vienna, Martin Shusterman asked his parents to change the channel. He was more interested in the progress of the Viking 1 destined to land on Mars, followed by Viking 2 which would land on the scalloped topography of Utopia Planitia. Because of solar ultraviolet radiation, extreme aridity, and oxidation of soil chemistry, Mars was considered self-sterilizing, and therefore not even microbes would find the planet in any way hospitable, but Martin hoped the spacecrafts would locate some form of life thriving in that climate of deprivation. The image of creatures climbing over rocks, tapping on the arachnid legs of the Viking's landing gear was too seductive to dismiss out of hand. The images of a nondescript boxy office building located on Karl-Lueger-Ring, even if there were gunmen inside, held no interest for Martin. It was too far away, too foreign but still terrestrial, and had nothing to do with his imaginary life.

They had a neighbor who did not have a television, so he would come over and contribute his opinions on Carlos the Jackal. ("Poor security. Anyone could just walk in. What do you expect of a city that names a street after Karl Lueger, the mayor whose theories about race were like the rings of Saturn: some groups needed to be kept so far on the perimeter that they could no longer be said to have feet on the planet. To this end, he closed the country's borders and sneered at neighboring Hungary, calling its capital Judapest. What do you expect of such people?") Myers had no off switch. He would go on and on about the news of the day: the Weather Underground bombing of the State Department, assassination attempts against President Ford, the Red Army Faction bombing of the Axel Springer Verlag offices in Hamburg, demanding amnesty for the Baader Meinhof gang.

When the Apollo-Soyuz docking mission occurred in orbit, Myers smelled a rat. Nothing Soviet was a harmless photo op, he said, adding, *launched from Baikonur Cosmodrome in Kazakhstan* in a fake Russian accent, as he helped himself to a beer Shusterman's father put on the table. On the Shustermans' black-and-white television, the Apollo capsule backed away, blocking the sun from the Soyuz, causing a man-made eclipse. In this way, the cosmonauts Myers was so suspicious of were able to photograph the sun's corona.

As he cringed at Myers' Boris and Natasha accent and his pronouncements of authority, Martin reminded himself that if there had been a zoom out to a camera on an airplane wing, the city would look like a scattering of Pez, bevel-edged pastel bricks. Continuing to zoom out, camera, now on a satellite would record the image of his parents' living room as less than the size of an atom, soon a relic of nothing. Like the raptors in Mongolia who didn't see the mudslide that buried them in a nanosecond, in a blink they, too, would be gone. At least for the raptors, millions of years later, their fossils were found and now sat fourteen miles away in the Museum of Natural History. Humans at that moment, sitting in their grid of Pez, as seen from the air, would be lucky if they were ever as preserved as those random raptor bones. He hoped if he thought about it long and hard enough, Myers would go home.

FBI Special Agent Myers wore a derby, an *alte kahker* who would tell a young waitress a joke, holding her hand, calling her dear, until he got to the punch line, a man who resembled Jack Benny, but who looked in the mirror and saw Cary Grant. Shusterman was just out of high school, but Myers annoyed him no end, and he found it hard to believe the man ever worked for the FBI, though his parents insisted it was true. The life of Mr. Myers was not a mystery he wanted to explore.

At his parents' insistence Shusterman had played the cello, and he was decent, but not nearly good enough to play professionally, though all his teachers commented that he did have an uncanny ear. He could hear music and repeat note for note, just not particularly well.

Shusterman took the subway into Manhattan, getting off at West 4th Street for no reason, just a random stop. He passed a couple playing music in a station, tossed some change into a Dutch Masters Cigar box, then stared down the tunnel for a south bound E train.

Later, in a tenement apartment perched near the Holland Tunnel, he bought pot from a guy who talked about Nixon, wiretaps, and the FBI not only going through John Lennon's garbage, but trash cans near the BQE. Shusterman knew one thing; if he didn't leave the neighborhood he grew up in soon, he would be stuck in the Pez grid forever.

Shusterman played the cello in cafés, imitating *Nuevo cancions,* if a singer was hanging around, or variations on tangos that no one could really dance to. He traveled from Lima to Santiago to Tierra del Fuego to Buenos Aires where he stayed for several years. In Buenos Aires he had a girlfriend, Abril, who was a student at the university. They met while he was playing in his bumbling way, sliding from one song to the next, and no one was paying much attention to him, but she did. During a break, she asked him where he was from, and he talked too much and in a nervous torrent of disconnected references: his neighbor in New York was a spook; his cello teacher was a tiny man, who escaped Berlin by hiding in a bass case that was loaded on a train. When he emerged, he was in Zurich. Hitler had referred to Switzerland as the little hedgehog he would soon squeeze, and he occasionally found himself using the word, hedgehog, to describe situations that seemed safe and well defended, but were actually vulnerable and not nearly as safe as the hedgehog, smugly and in great delusion, thought. That's us, that could be us, thinking we're safe, when who knows what could happen?

Shusterman felt like Groucho Marx talking while eating crackers in bed, but couldn't stop himself. Abril didn't seem to mind, or perhaps she wasn't really listening. He regretted his words as soon as they left his mouth, but she wanted to see him again, and he was amazed that someone wouldn't mind the crumbs in his tangled, not-washed-very-often sheets. Embarrassment didn't hold him back even though, as soon as she left a room, Shusterman felt he was an idiot, and yet, even if he was, when she said see you later, she meant it.

After a few months, he asked Abril if she would like to move into his apartment, and she agreed. Shusterman couldn't believe his good fortune. The kid who strained his eyes at the television screen, hoping to find some twitch of life on Mars, was a person he no longer recognized, at least that's what he told himself. She had a lot of friends who filled their apartment from time to time, other students who came from all over the continent, and though his own Spanish wasn't quite fluent, he could tell, just by listening, not only whether the speaker was from Chile or Venezuela, but what part of the country, or even the city, a person was from. They found this extremely entertaining in a complete gringo.

There was an old man, Karl Sauer, who lived across the courtyard whose accent intrigued Shusterman. At first, he thought he was German, and though he did claim to have lived in Berlin, his accent, with its longer vowels, betrayed his origins in Vienna. Once, when the door to Sauer's apartment was open a crack, Shusterman glimpsed dark wooden carvings, lots of them, of Tyrolean peasants, gnomes on skis, the Last Supper. In the dark Tyrolean carvings in their density and clutter, Shusterman saw a nightmare of folk art and the roots of the idea that certain kinds of foreigners should be thrown down a well as a matter of course. Then, in calmer moments, he thought he misread and jumped to conclusions. Sauer was just an old man who collected things.

Shusterman stopped repeating the hedgehog story. He was happy in the city where Italianate buildings, the balconies that nearly touched overhead on narrow streets, were so different from the grid of his childhood. He worked on his accent to erase any trace of who he'd been. Playing soccer in the park, a decent player in a defensive position, he felt part of a team, part of something. If he didn't smoke a pack of Nobleza Piccardos a day, he would have been even better.

Shusterman and Abril planned to get married, but then, one by one, their friends began to disappear. Shusterman knew people, students, were picked up in the middle of the night, taken to the stadium, to secret prisons, dropped from helicopters into the Rio de la Plata never to be seen again. He stopped repeating the hedgehog story or even using the word at all.

One night he and Abril were caught out in the city close to midnight. Even women who sold mangos, guavas, blackened corn and tamarind soda on the street were gone, but the streets weren't completely empty. Some liked to play chicken with the gangs and the police. They heard footsteps, shadows moved. Abril saw two girls, about thirteen and fourteen, sprint away from them. Hands moving along a dark wall as if for balance, they followed the pair down a narrow street, watched them pause at a doorway; one put a hand over the other's mouth, stifling a scream or a hysterical laugh, then they disappeared. Beneath their feet a trickle of blood ran across the sidewalk, over the edge of the curb and pooled into the street. They followed the trail to a door which Shusterman pushed open. Behind the door lay a cobbled passageway that led to a courtyard and other apartment buildings. Music, laughter, and the sound of raised voices could be heard in the distance. A girl lay unconscious, curled into a ball. A wound to her head was bleeding. One arm hung limply. She was very small, perhaps not much older than the two girls who fled. Her jeans were torn and her tube top was pushed down to her waist. Abril covered the girl with her jacket, and Shusterman lifted her in his arms and carried her back to their apartment.

They washed and bandaged the girl, who whispered a babel of sounds before she regained consciousness. She refused to give her name, and they left her to sleep, a mango drink by her side. When they awoke in late morning, she was gone, along with Abril's jewelry and a radio. A desk had been ransacked. Abril pulled drawers out and tipped them over, looked under every piece of paper and every book on the desk. Her identity papers were missing. At the time they returned to the apartment, she had taken them out of her jacket and put them on the desk. It was perilous to leave your house without identity papers in your possession, even if only for a five-minute run around the corner. If the police stopped you, it was the first thing they asked for. Abril shrugged; there was nothing to be done, she would apply for new ones the next day.

A few days later Abril failed to return home from her late afternoon class. Shusterman waited in the café down the street. He played the cello for an hour, then stopped, unable to continue. The owner served him an espresso with a shot of whiskey in it. The café was quiet, grew busy, then less so as people went home. It grew dark, street lights came on, then as shops closed, the street turned darker. Shusterman was the only person left in the café.

Her family tried to find her, but no one knew anything. If you made too many inquiries, you disappeared too, and this could go on until there was no one remaining to make inquiries. What few friends they had left were afraid to speak to him. All he could find out was that she had left the university around five, had been seen walking down Avenida Córdoba, but disappeared shortly afterward, and was never seen alive again.

Karl, he noticed, tried to avoid him when it looked like they were about to cross paths in the building. The man would abruptly turn, take the stairs if he was waiting for the elevator or steer to a far side of the courtyard and avoid eye contact with Shusterman.

One night when he couldn't sleep, Shusterman decided to retrace Abril's footsteps, what he imagined her footsteps would have been. It was after midnight and dangerous to go out, but his imagination kept cycling with the idea that if he looked closely enough, he would find something: a lost shoe, a gold earring made from dangling concentric circles, a trap door behind which, for some reason, no one had looked before, and there he would find her, thirsty, tired, grimy, just waiting for him to unlatch the entrance. He got dressed and slipped out of the building. At first all was quiet. Around a corner he could hear a *nasone* carved long ago by a nostalgic Neapolitan stonecutter. The stone water fountain was in the shape of a Minotaur and seemed to drip water according to its own unpredictable lunar system. As he walked further toward the center of the city, he heard an argument from a shuttered storefront, a woman's singing wavering in and out of earshot, but when he approached the Balvanera district, the sound of traffic picked up. Who were these late-night travelers? If they drove unmarked Fords or Fiats, it was better not to know.

On Avenida Corrientes he stopped for a moment by a boarded-up kiosk. A bundle of clothes under the newsstand's awning began to move as if awakened by his footsteps, and an elderly woman in a large black hat, wrapped in a red blanket, lifted her head to look at him.

"Mister, mister," she pulled at his pant leg, then hoisted herself up. "I'm looking for Zelaya Street. Do you know it? Can you take me there?"

She was a member of the Aymara tribe who occasionally came into the city from the Andes, traveling across the pampas, to sell brightly colored striped blankets, and he started to give her directions, then realized she couldn't read street signs. Zelaya was a short street, only two blocks long, and not far, so he walked her to it.

"My daughter works for a household, a rich family. Very nice."

They found the address, but the woman became nervous, she wanted him to leave, so he nodded goodbye and wished her well. It was possible the story about the daughter was not true, and she had other business or perhaps no business whatsoever inside the house. As Shusterman turned to go, the woman reached into her bag, and held out an arrow to him, a gift for showing her the way. He tried to decline, but she insisted he take it.

"Don't touch the tip," she warned, tilting her hat forward, so it was difficult to see her eyes. She pretended to touch the end of the arrow, her finger stopping a hair from the point, then made the universal expression of a corpse. He took the arrow, left the woman in the doorway, and headed back to his route for Avenida Córdoba.

Abril had told him a story about a class trip to the Andes during which a boy had hiked off alone and gone missing. Search crews looked for him from the air and on the ground, in the foothills, and up into the mountains, but no trace could be found. All who knew him believed he was lost forever. There was no way he could survive without water and food, directionless, far from any village. Then, a year later, he turned up on an ostrich farm. From a blow to the head he had suffered amnesia, had no idea who he was, and so became adopted as a worker on the farm, herding ostriches, collecting eggs and feathers, assisting with the slaughter. This was actually dangerous work if a bird was pissed off or felt threatened. In comedies, a second blow to the head might right the situation, but no such blow by an ostrich returned him to his former identity. On the farm he was discovered happy and well, if disoriented. His family drove him back to Buenos Aires, but it took years for him to readjust to being the person his family and friends continued to expect him to be. The same thing could have happened to Abril, Shusterman thought. She could be working in a basement sweatshop, sewing T-shirts for export, unconsciously waiting for the second blow to the head to return her to the person she was. Shusterman stared at cracks in the sidewalk, at panes of glass beveled into leaded windows, anything that would provide some kind of hand or footprint, the trail of an amnesiac just waiting to be recovered.

As he turned onto Boulogne Sur Mer he startled a boy, maybe fifteen or sixteen years old, who was spraying graffiti on the side of a building. The loopy letters mimicked those he'd seen on subway cars and on the sides of buildings, mostly in the Bronx and Brooklyn.

"I'm looking for a plaza. I have things to sell," the boy mumbled. Shusterman, with his long hair and torn jeans, probably didn't look like someone who would turn him in, but he clearly wasn't taking any chances. In a flash, the spray can vanished. The boy reached into his backpack and laid some objects on the ground: lumps of fool's gold, a set of wooden pipes, some packs of cigarettes, and a couple of Zippo lighters. Perhaps he thought of Shusterman as an easy mark, a strange man out in the middle of the night who spoke with an American accent.

"Here." He handed him the arrow and mimed touching the tip, then turning into a standing corpse. "Out at night you should have something." Shusterman tried to imagine he was like Apollo giving Paris the arrow that would slay Achilles, though he actually felt a little ridiculous, like a character in a comic who doesn't know what he's doing and is about to be flattened in the next panel. The boy seemed very pleased to have the gift, and in return he gave Shusterman one of the Zippo lighters. It was blue and had a crown embossed on it. "Stay clear of Avenida Córdoba," he warned.

"But that's where I need to go," Shusterman explained.

"Then be careful. They are picking people up tonight."

The boy put the arrow in his bag and was gone, leaving an orange spray paint can rolling in the gutter. Shusterman kept his eyes down, but also scoured doorways, windows, alleys, so his progress was slow. Soon it would be daylight. He found nothing. Picking up a cigarette butt stained red, he sniffed it, then put the thing in his pocket. At the intersection of Córdoba and Talcahuano, right at the plaza, a soldier stepped out of the dark. He was very young, and tottered when he walked, a little drunk or high or both.

"Papers," he slurred. "Where are you going?"

"I'm looking for my girlfriend. Maybe you've seen her?"

"Maybe I have," the man said as if genuinely thinking, for a moment, that he could be of service. "What does she look like?"

"This tall." Shusterman put his hand up to his shoulder. "Long dark brown hair."

"Same as yours?" The soldier leaned into his hip and gave a half smile.

"No. Hers is longer. Brown eyes. She was wearing a red shirt."

"Ay, yes, a red shirt. And she had a crescent-shaped scar under one eye, no?"

"Yes, she has such a scar." Shusterman took a step toward the soldier, stopping short of grabbing him by the shoulders. "Do you know where she was taken?"

"Your girlfriend has a butt shaped like an avocado." He made a big ass shape with his hands.

"No." Abril was very thin. He was describing someone else. The soldier was drunk and knew nothing.

"She had blond streaks in her hair, was wearing a lot of gold jewelry, and this you can't miss: a line of falling dominoes tattooed around her neck, and silk underwear that was peacock blue."

The soldier was laughing at him, making it up as he went along. He might have been in the squad that picked up Abril if this was his crew's turf. Picking up so many, night after night, week after week, each frightened face melted into the next, quickly forgotten. He probably didn't even look at them.

They were done. Shusterman held out his hand for his papers.

The soldier pointed his gun at Shusterman, but it jammed. He shoved Shusterman hard against the wall. In a matter of minutes, the rest of his squad would appear. He didn't need to shoot the American—let someone else do it. Shusterman tried to push the guy off, but it was like pushing a bear, not exactly an angry or hungry bear, but one who was acting more on instinct: this is what I do. They both smelled like sweat and cigarettes. Shusterman tried to say something, but as a fist pushed into his mouth, all that came out was a garbled blast of syllables. Shusterman swung, not really knowing what he was doing. The sound of knuckle hitting jaw made a noise like a piece of wood snapping. The soldier scrambled to his feet, but the pavement was wet and slippery, and staggering, the man fell backward, landing hard on his spine, head cracking on the pavement. Shusterman picked up the gun and swung the butt at the soldier's face, hard enough to knock him out. A tooth fell to the pavement.

He sat on the ground near the body and quickly looked through the soldier's pockets. Others would arrive soon. His name, a driver's license, his few pesos didn't matter. There was nothing on him of any use or value. He stuffed everything back into the man's shirt and pants. Shusterman considered pocketing the wallet to make it look like a robbery, but there was no point. No one in his or her right mind would rob a soldier. Standing, he kicked the gun aside. He didn't want the weapon but didn't want to leave it either. His route lay too far from the river for a detour to carry it to the banks to toss it in, and to be found with it would be an instant death sentence.

Voices were getting closer. He tried to smash the gun on the ground, but it didn't break. Picking it up, he ran around the corner where he'd seen a dumpster in front of a clothing shop that had gone out of business, and threw it in. Amidst the bundles of flattened boxes, tangles of string, shredded bags and naked mannequins, whole and in parts, you could see, if you looked closely, a Browning Hi-Power nestled between an extended hand with elegantly posed fingers and the stump of a plaster leg.

SHUSTERMAN UNLOCKED HIS DOOR and stood still, listening. Someone, a man, was in the back of his apartment singing Cole Porter's *Let's Do It, Let's Fall in Love*. He picked up a heavy glass bookend, an object from Abril's childhood—it was in the shape of a horse, the figure riding it had long ago been snapped off leaving a lethally sharp half-man—and made his way quietly down the hall.

The singer was seated at his kitchen table drinking a Cerveza Quilmes, smiling like an aged Puck in a Derby hat.

"Well," Myers said when he saw him. "Look what the cat just dragged in."

"I live here, that's what the cat dragged in. What are you doing here, Mr. Myers?"

"Time to come home, Shusterman," said Myers, all smiles as if sitting on the Shustermans' backyard terrace for a Labor Day barbeque.

"My home is here."

"Your girlfriend isn't coming back. You know that. It's only because your mother is more on the ball than you think that you're still alive. She reads the papers. She knows what's going on down here, and she talks to me."

It occurred to Shusterman that his mother had seen Myers's Glock, years ago, but his father never mentioned its existence. His mother might have seen other possessions and articles of Myers' clothing or person that few ever saw. This was not something he wanted to dwell on. He wondered how much snooping, as Myers had made himself at home, he had done. A quick glance through the apartment didn't indicate drawers or papers rifled through. There was no point in asking how he got in.

"Don't be a pain in the ass. You're next on the list, Marty."

"How would you know?"

"It's my job to know, trust me. You're going to be picked up next, my boy. Pack your things. I've booked a flight out, and you're going to be on it."

Myers suggested Shusterman think about time, not as linear, but a loop, like a doughnut. He'd come back someday, but right now, he needed to leave. It sounded like he knew what he was talking about, but it was Myers's job to sound like he knew what he was talking about.

"A fucking doughnut," Shusterman said. He left with Myers and regretted it for the rest of his life.

❊

Shusterman enrolled in a linguistics program at Brooklyn College, and supported himself repairing instruments in a midtown music shop. The last of its kind, even then, and professional musicians of all sorts dropped off immensely valuable violins, cellos, electric guitars, gamelans, tablas, almost anything that made sequential patterns of sound. The shop owner seemed to know each and every one of them on a first-name basis, and their conversations about everything from tuning to touring were a window into professional lives glimpsed from a distance. Shusterman worked in a backroom, and he could have happily stayed or started his own repair business until one of his professors told the story of the Yorkshire Ripper case. For Shusterman, the story was about pure sound and concentrated listening. It began with the man known as the Yorkshire Ripper, responsible for the murders of thirteen women. He sent the police a tape, or so the constabulary believed.

*I'm Jack. I see you are still having no luck catching me. I have the greatest respect for you, George, but Lord! You are no nearer to catching me now than four years ago when I started. I reckon your boys are letting you down, George. They can't be much good, can they?*

His teacher did a surprisingly good imitation of the accent. Forensic voice analysts narrowed down the particularities of the Wearside pronunciation, syllable by syllable, to the Castletown area of Sunderland, and focused their search for the Yorkshire Ripper to that area. Billboards were set up, hot lines, the tape was played on the radio. Unfortunately, the recording later turned out to be a hoax and delayed the capture of Peter Sutcliff, the real murderer, who was from Bradford, some ninety-five miles away. Citizens from Bradford spoke with an identifiably different accent.

Returning to a version of his own voice, the professor continued, we are the only animals with complex speech organs, our ability to assign language to the passage of time and projection into the future is one of the markers on the road that separates us from apes. He walked from one end of the blackboard to the other, rolling chalk down the palm of his hand, curling his fingers up just before it could fall to the floor. Though killer whales, some birds, and monkeys communicate via a collection of sounds that can be read as heading toward language, we alone are a species that can say, *let me then tow to pieces, while still chasing thee, though tied to thee, thou damned whale! Thus, I give up the spear!* He held up the chalk as if it were a harpoon.

Shusterman became intrigued with the clues in speech, those embedded identity tags that couldn't be altered or erased. Interested in how humans were said to be hardwired for language and the involuntary aspects of speech, he studied language acquisition, how children marshal sounds into meaning. A guest lecturer talked about forensic linguistics. Listening to voices, the man said, is like looking around a room, trying to determine which object, among thousands, appears ordinary but is really the hinge between ordinariness and malfeasance on a grand scale. You hear some small variation in the cadence, a currently used accent masking accent of origin, and a layer of identity and criminal intention are revealed. Shusterman enjoyed searching through sound as if he were hearing voices, which in a way, he was. After graduation, he moved to Washington DC to begin training in forensic speech identification.

In DC it was suggested Shusterman specialize in Arabic. He could hear some differences, between Beirut and Cairo, that was easy, between Cairo and Alexandria required a little closer listening. He reasoned wars came and went. Someone who had specialized in the subtle differences between various Laotian or Vietnamese dialects during the 1960s and '70s would now be listening to wiretaps on Southeast Asian gangs in St. Paul, Chicago, New Orleans. With globalization there were fewer distinct groups of enemies. A cell or a gang could include people from all over the world, could be at your doorstep or a few feet from it, not in another hemisphere. Someone could take the E train in Queens, for example, traveling through distinct neighborhoods whose residents span the globe, picking up recruits along the way. He stuck to American speech. It was what he knew.

There were forms he had to fill out that asked if he had any prior convictions, and the honest answer was no, he did not, not in the United States, but in another city he had, though never arrested, committed a crime, maybe it would be called resisting arrest and assaulting an officer, maybe something worse. It was luck, not necessarily skill, that sent the soldier into the fall that cracked his skull. If he'd been wearing a helmet, he would have been able to scramble to his feet, but he hadn't. The man could be dead, expiring minutes after Shusterman ran off, or could be brain damaged, sitting in a wheelchair. Shusterman told no one about that night. Shusterman didn't talk about Abril either, and sometimes he imagined she was still alive, suffering from amnesia like the boy who ended up on the ostrich farm. She was a strong swimmer. What if when dropped from the plane, it was flying low, the pilot thought he was high enough, but he miscalculated, and instead of landing flat, which would be lethal, Abril had twisted like a high diver, and then swam to the surface, and made it to shore?

❇

His first case back in New York involved the voiceprint of a man reporting a murder to 911. The caller turned out to be the murderer. This was not uncommon for some kinds of psychotics, or so he'd been warned, but the subtle differences in voice between real panic and good acting were treacherous to pin down with absolute certainty. The tapes began with screaming.

*No blood, no wounds, maybe she had a heart attack. Come quickly. No, I don't know how to do CPR. I just walked in, and she was lying on the floor, face down. She's not breathing. Come as fast as you can.*

In some weird Norman Bates sort of way, the murderer felt sympathy for his victim. It would never have occurred to Shusterman to make a phony emergency call, to say, hey, I found this body on Avenida Corrientes. For a man sitting in an apartment in Babylon, New York, looking out at a revolving Midas Muffler sign adjacent to a strip mall, maybe calling 911 seemed like a viable option. There was almost a singsong quality to his real or projected panic. 911 calls were often of poor quality with a lot of background noise, but once cleaned up, they offered all kinds of information. Shusterman testified in court, played back voice tapes, compared samples of actual graphed voiceprints projected on a screen so the jury could see the differences. The 911 call, Shusterman was sure, had been a way to taunt the police. There had been other evidence as well: the man had been an abusive boyfriend with previous arrests, and he had terrorized the victim's family. The jury was out for less than an hour. The man was convicted.

He got more cases involving unknown identities. Even though there was no name or affiliation, Shusterman could give an idea of where the caller might be from, and if geography could be narrowed down, likely place of origin, possible associates, milieu traveled in, class, education, sometimes occupation, that could be more important information than a single name and identity. Especially when considering a cell or a militia, as opposed to an individual, however dangerous that person may be, you want to know what pond the guy is swimming in, Shusterman would say. Each voice has unique acoustic properties. But even as he considered the pathway taken between the source of sound in the larynx and the chambers where resonances and other characteristics created distinctive patterns, he sometimes felt less than one hundred percent sure. For legitimacy, voice analysis needs more than just a reliable ear. Even with scientific backup, his line of work still wasn't as widely accepted as fingerprints.

Being an expert witness in court made him nervous, even if he was sure his assessment was accurate. He would explain spectrographs to the jury and point out that while the tones they heard in Exhibits A and B might sound different, the core voice was the same in two recordings. Speech disorders, accent, and dialect variations left their marks, and his analysis confirmed what he had heard on the tape. You see the same peaks and valleys. Listen again. Hear how both speakers say *irth* in birthday cake.

A difficult case of armed robbery and hostage-taking came up, which had a jumble of recordings of untraceable cell phone calls made by three different people, or were the calls made by only one person? He ran tests for the usual identifiers, testing duration, frequency of certain words and sounds. The samples were limited both in quantity and quality, but he analyzed the onset time of each voice, the spacing between enunciations, and the nasalization of vowels, a highly individualized marker. Patterns of certain sound waves canceled or attenuated each other. Some people, actors in particular, can be skilled at disguising their voices, so to even a highly trained ear, to someone who may have perfect pitch, they would believe the voice issued from very different speakers. The computer, however, could not be fooled. Shusterman disagreed with the computer. The evidence remained in identity limbo.

Speech analysis wasn't a perfect science, and Shusterman was occasionally beleaguered by doubts. Had he helped to send the wrong person to jail? Had his ear been slightly off or had those vocal trimmings that decorate the core soundtrack tripped him up? Certain cases in particular haunted him. Others he was dead certain about. He played soccer in the park, but he never told his teammates exactly what he did or who he worked for.

As Shusterman became more skilled, cases involving lone psychopaths gave way to bigger cases. He examined voiceprints for the Department of Alcohol, Tobacco, and Firearms, for the IRS, listened to mafia surveillance tapes for the FBI, recordings of possible terrorists tapped by Interpol. Sometimes he was assigned a bodyguard. On occasion he knew he was followed.

He began to prefer working alone in an office, analyzing patterns of sound waves, resonance and antiresonance characteristics, plosive spikes, and slopes, phonemes. Atoms of speech flooded the screen, waiting to be interpreted. Looking at the topology of a voiceprint was like looking at a cross section of the Earth's crust, he imagined telling Abril as if she were sitting with him. Here's the Jurassic layer, the Mississippian layer, but these outcroppings, what you see, that's the most recent, so that's what the eye or ear registers first, but there's a lot of history underneath. Shusterman was adept at finding that hidden piece that the suspect didn't want known, that trace of years spent in Shaker Heights or East Los Angeles, but not too far east, or Jersey City, despite the suspect's attempt to portray himself or herself as someone else. He was like a seismograph, registering that vocal tremor or slight change in pitch that indicated anxiety and perhaps the airing of a stretched truth. You just never knew what he would find. Shusterman became known for hearing things you never thought possible.

❊

He saw Special Agent Myers for the last time when he visited his parents. Shusterman hadn't seen Myers in several years, but he heard about him when his mother would drop his name into conversations, and he knew the man would appear from time to time in their house. For the most part, he made himself scarce when Shusterman visited, but that night, there he was, smiling and telling jokes, standing too close to Shusterman's mother, as if there had never been a trip to pull Shusterman out of his apartment, put him on a flight, and send him back. Shusterman's mother returned with a tray of beer and chips, and Myers asked her about a family down the street who made a bundle when they sold their house. He had a drink, a fistful of chips that crackled loudly as he chewed, and left shortly afterward. Shusterman never saw him again.

❊

## ADVERSARIA: ACCORDING TO SPECIAL AGENT MYERS

*In Hôtel Terminus: The Life and Times of Klaus Barbie, Marcel Ophuls talks about "controlled ignorance" when discussing lists of war criminals. Who would be arrested and who would be let go? Sauer benefitted from controlled ignorance in Vienna after the war, until a pair of disgruntled black marketeers tried to throw him over a balcony (as was the case with Barbie). He told his handler, a German-speaking American from Chicago, that communists were on to him. He needed to get out of the country.*

*Ophuls interviews Eugene Kolb, former major in the United States Army Counter Intelligence Corps. Kolb is sitting in front of a Christmas tree, describing how collecting intelligence is more successful in a friendly situation, like taking someone out for a meal, as opposed to interrogation in a threatening or formal setting, an office or prison, for example. "Is that where interrogation would be most effective?" Ophuls asks. "Over bratwurst?"'*

*When Sauer was interrogated, he must have given a very convincing performance. Did his American protector believe of the Austrians, as Kolb did of the French, that their secret services were riddled with communists? The Americans didn't read French papers, didn't know Barbie was a mass murderer, or so some of them claimed. If Klaus Barbie could slip through, for someone like Sauer, getting out of Austria would have been akin to a piece of cake.*

*Sauer would also have escaped via the Vatican's Ratline, financed by the United States. His identity was a sleeping giant, unrecognized, left alone. No one remembered who he was or had been. He lived under his own name in Buenos Aires. No one cared.*

Shusterman complained to Abril that human ears, even highly trained ones, were becoming expendable, and sometimes his results were no longer admissible as evidence. There was software that could do what he did, and the software sent no invoices. Machines with microchips for ears were more accurate to sensitivities of voice and accent identification, even recognizing the most elusive group: people with brain trauma who sometimes found themselves speaking in accents from places they'd never lived. He wasn't sure he should tell her this, but she was fading out, then gone, so he continued. For reasons unknown, these victims were capable of doing an almost perfect job of affecting the adopted accent. He apologized and asked her to come back, but she had vanished.

His last project was a map of American regional accents. It was meant to visualize how migration, as reflected by accents, mirrored the spread of certain diseases. The indeterminate boundaries were marked by saturated colors that faded to indicate the lessening of intensity: blue Okie accent spreading to California, Acadian green migrating from Canada to Cajun territory. When the map was finished, he found himself balancing when to pay which bill first and how long he could put off others. What Shusterman had entered into as a reliable vocation became obsolete. Myers, who'd once thought this profession was such a good idea, was now a resident of a facility called Hillsdale Memory Center, an institution for people with dementia, and didn't know what software was.

One of the soccer players wanted to learn how to lose his accent for an audition as an American lawyer for a television pilot. They practiced in the park after the game, then as the day for the audition grew closer, the man came to Shusterman's apartment and listened to tapes of interrogatory performances from *Perry Mason* to *Law and Order* to *Suits*. Shusterman guessed a theatrical performance wasn't the same as what happened in an actual courtroom. Studying different styles of American judicial speech, they came up with a kind of middle ground accentless English. The amateur soccer player got the part and sent other actors to Shusterman. That was the beginning of his second career.

"Say the a with an ah sound. Hahrt. Hell's hahrt, I stab thee... Let's listen to the tape again."

He was training an actor starring in a film about the life of Herman Melville, and it was a headache. Intercut with scenes of Melville's childhood, growing up with a mentally ill father, the director was inserting scenes of Ahab chasing the giant albino sperm whale. The actor who was to play both the adult Melville and Captain Ahab needed to speak in two distinctly different accents. Shusterman guessed Melville's accent was merchant class Anglo-American. The Melvilles weren't recent immigrants, but there might have been a hint of Liverpool, because of their associations. Shusterman was familiar with an 1889 recording of Walt Whitman in which the poet pronounced world as *woild*, so there was probably a hint of o pronounced oy and dropped r's. Reading Whitman always helped with nineteenth-century East Coast urban accents. Though the director was shooting scenes of the madness of Melville's father, and the entire family living eight in a room, Shusterman insisted the writer probably spoke in the patrician tones of Henry James or Edith Wharton with a touch of Whitman's Brooklyn. The director argued no, he wanted an accent with dropped r's, almost American, but still close to England. Ahab, the director imagined, spoke with a mid-Atlantic Cary Grant sort of accent. The actor would be saying his lines on a moving platform meant to represent *The Pequod*, while water machines sprayed him soaking wet.

The director said *Mobay, Mobay, Mobay,* like Cary Grant saying *Juday, Juday, Juday* in *Only Angels Have Wings.*

Shusterman went to the New York Public Library and read through old New York City newspapers and magazines to get some sense of the rhythm of early nineteenth-century speech. He owned a large archive of voices speaking in accents, mainly, but not exclusively, English speakers from all over the world, but there were gaps in his collection. He played the Whitman recordings over and over, listening to the pauses between words, the plosives, the fricatives, the places where his voice goes up. His office, a specially converted room in his apartment, had the sweetish smell of old audiotapes, and every available foot of wall space was occupied by his collections of recordings in a variety of formats. A dozen tape recorders all in working order were displayed on floor-to-ceiling shelves. There was little wall space left to display Shusterman's diplomas or certificates. In place of these he had hung a still from *Singin' in the Rain* in which Gene Kelly and Donald O'Connor sing "Moses Supposes His Toeses Are Roses" during a session with a speech coach.

Ahab stood and addressed the photograph of Gene Kelly and Donald O'Connor jumping in the air in front of a series of diagrams of the parts of the human mouth.

*Towards thee I roll, thou all-destroying but unconquering whale; to the last I grapple with thee; from hell's heart I stab at thee; for hate's sake I spit my last breath at thee. Sink all coffins and all hearses to one common pool! and since neither can be mine, let me then tow to pieces, while still chasing thee, though tied to thee, thou damned whale! Thus, I give up the spear!*

He was a talented young man whose face was handsome in a nineteenth-century kind of way. It was a look he wasn't entirely hap-py with, and so he tended to counter his Lincoln-era good looks by shaving his head into a furry bleached Mohawk and being a goofball when the opportunity presented itself, humming the theme from *Jaws* when an actress stormed off the set or pranking a shot by throwing an inflatable sex doll overboard during a storm.

"Emphasis on *thee*. No pauses in the middle of a clause."

Captain Ahab repeated *from hell's heart I stab thee* perfectly.

Their session ended, and the man left, his lines echoing in Shusterman's head.

Who came from Hell's heart? An image of a magma-encased core gave way to a *Metropolis*-like underground. Or Hell's heart could have been city streets, empty and apocalyptic, shot in black and white, a site ruled by someone he used to know. It was an apartment not far from the Rio de La Plata, home of a man who dreamed of a city of snow, ruled by princes and archdukes—but Hell's heart also had a chamber down the hall, the one Shusterman left in a hurry, the one he'd thought he would live in forever.

Shusterman sat at his laptop and typed "Karl Sauer" into the empty space under the Google logo. When he'd lived in Buenos Aires, a computer in one's house wasn't even an imaginary thing, and in all the years in between, the fate of his neighbor wasn't a question he'd asked himself or anyone else. When Buttinsky Myers told him how Sauer came to be his neighbor, the internet still hadn't yet been invented, and even if it had, Shusterman wouldn't have wanted to know.

He clicked on *Images*. First up: a black-and-white picture of Karl Sauer having beers with men on the easily identifiable Avenida Rivadavia, dated during the years Shusterman had lived in the city.

The names of the men were listed in the caption. He looked them up. A director of a mining company, a rancher, a man who worked at an address that Shusterman recognized as a bureau, a sort of registry that may have had links to the death squads or those who commanded them or not, no one really knew for certain. He thought about the relationship between those two words: *death* and *squads*. How does *squad* prod, contradict, or encompass death?

Remembering his search in the middle of the night during what were his last twenty-four hours in that city, Shusterman had gone on a journey to find a lost person, lost to a squadron who did the bidding of unseen and unknowable phantoms. On his way, he encountered three souls who he helped or who helped him, who gave him something or a piece of advice or warning that, in the course of the night, he would find useful in his search. Even the soldier's story gave Shusterman a few minutes of hope, even though it was false. In fairy tales, the successful use of gifts results in survival, wisdom, acquiring a fortune, marrying a prince or princess. What did Shusterman get? He never married, he had no fortune to speak of, and those anonymous souls who had taken from him lived happily ever after, he was certain, like Sauer in his apartment surrounded by reminders of exile, but still, he was alive and well-off. Shusterman dreamed of tube tops, ostrich eggs, Zippo lighters, spray paint cans, an arrow coated with tree frog venom, one of the most toxic substances in the world.

Alma Mercado, his neighbor in Buenos Aires, had dyed blonde hair, chewed wintergreen gum, and carried around a copy of *Tiempo y ser*, the Spanish translation of *Being and Time*. She had dropped out of the university, didn't have regular work, but seemed to support herself with a patchwork of jobs proofreading for law firms, painting apartments with a couple of friends, odd bits of translation, and walking dogs that lived in adjacent buildings. Because of all these forms of employment, she knew things. It was from Alma that Shusterman heard Sauer could have whispered Abril's name in the right ear. Perhaps Sauer was several degrees removed from direct contact, but it wasn't difficult to inform, a lot of people did, and you didn't need to know the people Sauer seemed to have known from the photograph.

Alma was easy to find. She had a website for translation services for legal documents, Spanish to English and English to Spanish. There was a picture of Alma dressed as a matador alongside a picture of herself dressed as a tourist wearing shorts printed with stars and stripes. She looked much the same as she had when he used to run into her on the stairs. Her contact information was posted, so he wrote her an email, though it felt like trying to grasp a toy in one of those machines where you have to use a mechanical arm. The thing or word he wanted often slipped out of grasp, grammar uncertain.

It was 1 a.m. in Argentina, but within an hour, he received a reply. The first paragraph was a chatty entrance ramp: How nice to hear from you after all these years! You became an accent coach! I remember how you could tell if someone was from Lima or La Paz! She suggested they Skype and within minutes Shusterman was back in his old apartment.

"Look familiar? Your old place was bigger than mine, so when it became vacant, I moved in!"

Alma had never been an awkward talker. His neighbor was as smooth as a slide in a water park. That made their reunion, after so many years, less awkward, and for that, Shusterman was relieved. Alma walked out onto the balcony and turned the laptop so the screen faced the street, tipped it down to the cars parked below, then back up the stone façade of the building opposite. It was the middle of the night, so Shusterman couldn't actually see very much, but it was enough. Alma's face froze until she went back indoors where there was a stronger connection. Her head and shoulders blocked the view, and Shusterman was glad of it. He hadn't expected to see his old apartment, and it was a jolt. She poured herself a glass of wine, asked if he could do the same, and he did.

"The day after the last day I saw you, though I didn't know it would be your last day in the city, I saw a man who said he was your uncle fumbling at the door to your apartment, humming *the hip bone's connected to the thigh bone*. He spoke Spanish badly, with a funny American accent, and he told me you had forgotten to pick him up at the airport, but he had keys. *Shusterman is a busy fellow*, he said to excuse your forgetting, and he smiled at me, the kind of smile that's like a wink. The guy must've had keys because he got into the building, so I believed him, because he was so clearly an American and because he spoke with such confidence."

"He's not my uncle. He did not have keys."

"So he was picking the lock? I couldn't really see."

"Yes."

He asked Alma about their former neighbor, a man who, in Shusterman's memory, was like Dr. Caligari himself, traveling with portable collapsible coffins for easy repeated use.

"Karl Sauer. Karl Sauer. A nose so thin and sharp, like a goldfish fin you could probably see through if you looked hard enough, cilia waving with every exhale. I cleaned his apartment every other week. He saw me reading Heidegger and thought he could trust me, but it turned out he was more interested in Dassin than Dasein. Cleaning is a license to snoop, but when I worked for Sauer, I wanted to get in and out as quickly as possible, but sometimes I did look around.

"One of the creepier things lying around among his carved wooden knick knacks: a troll couple. How cute! Well, not exactly. They were porn trolls with moveable parts, sort of like a Bavarian version of erotic netsuke but larger. The broad base of the fucking trolls contained a drawer which, of course, I opened. Inside the drawer I found old yellowed propaganda scripts written by Sauer in Vienna in 1941."

"Did you find anything else?"

"All kinds of things. A list of aliases. Notes in the fucking trolls drawer also revealed he had been consumed with two men."

"Who?"

"Ernst Deutsch and Karl Freund."

"Sauer didn't work. Where did his money came from, do you think?"

"That I couldn't tell you. I found no evidence of a source, and believe me, I looked."

"So he died in the apartment with his trolls."

"No. Nowhere near it. About a year after the Berlin Wall fell, Karl returned to Vienna. By 1990 he had long outlived his usefulness to anyone. No one here had the slightest interest in the old man. It was dangerous for him to go back, but he did. He left me an address to forward his mail, and of course, I had his keys. He meant to visit only for a few weeks, but he never returned."

"So you had time to really search his apartment."

It was rented out to a new tenant almost immediately. I kept a few things: photographs, some papers and books. If he turned out to be a famous most-wanted Nazi, I figured I could sell the stuff. Most people here think Barbie is a doll. So far, no one is interested in Sauer's bits and pieces. The only person interested briefly was Juan Carlos Zenaida, a man who worked for a television station. I met him when he was shooting the exterior of our building, many years ago. He was making a documentary, but he died before it could be completed, and I was never able to sell him anything. Zenaida told me that Sauer shot a film of the Disappeared in an idyllic setting outside the city, a film that was meant to convince the world that those who had been murdered were alive and prospering, though at the time of shooting, their hours were numbered.

"Like the footage of the beautified concentration camp, Theresienstadt, shown to the Red Cross."

"Of course. That was where he got the idea. Sauer was a propaganda artist. That was his calling, to convert skeptics and critics into true believers."

"Do you have any idea where the film is now? Did you find it in his apartment?"

"No. I think he took the film with him to Vienna. The negative was destroyed, and according to Zenaida, there was only one copy. As with the Theresienstadt propaganda film, all but twenty minutes were destroyed."

That was all Alma knew about Karl Sauer. She was tired and needed to get to sleep, but before they signed off, she raised a glass to Shusterman, and asked that they not let so many years pass before they spoke again.

"It bothered me a bit all these years because you didn't stop in to say goodbye to me, and I thought you would have done that much, but Abril had disappeared, you were distraught, and to drop out of sight was rarely a temporary condition in those days. Everyone was suspicious of any gesture, any word, that didn't seem completely normal and routine. I have to say, I missed you, Shusterman. There were times when my fingers hovered over the keyboard, as soon as keyboards were invented and tied to the Web. It would have been so easy to type in your name, and I thought to try to find you, but I didn't, and I'm sorry."

❈

## ADVERSARIA

*Ernst Deutsch was an Austrian Jewish actor who escaped to Buenos Aires. Deutsch played Rabbi Loew's assistant in* Der Golem. *He was the object of Sauer's particular animus, but Ernst and his family slipped out of his grasp. He never found any of them. Deutsch later appeared in* The Third Man, *playing "Baron" Kurtz, friend of Harry Lime. That the actor was able to return to Vienna while Sauer was viewed as a criminal, an outcast, infuriated him beyond words. Later he had some misconception that the family of Karl Freund, a Jewish cinematographer who shot* Metropolis *and* Dracula, *was in Buenos Aires. Freund had managed to escape, but he never lived in Argentina. Sauer was wrong. Freund immigrated to Los Angeles, where he would go on to shoot* I Love Lucy.

※

Karl Sauer had little Web presence, but Zenaida did. YouTube provided pieces of his unedited, never-released documentary about Argentina's Dirty War. There was a shot of Shusterman's old building and the addresses of other informers. Some lived in gated estates in suburbs; some, like Sauer, lived in apartment buildings and were not so well off. The voiceover said he had few known associates and mostly kept to himself. There was a close-up of Sauer and a shot of a list of informants. Sauer's name was on the list, highlighted when the voice said: *Karl Sauer.* There was also a document with names Sauer had submitted to the death squads. Shusterman paused and zoomed in. Abril's name was on the list.

Shusterman wanted to revive the fragmented documentary he saw on YouTube so it would get thousands, millions of views. He wanted everyone to see what he saw. If he were to go to Vienna to look for Sauer's film of the Disappeared, he needed money to make the trip, to take a leave from his work. He was almost able to retire, but in order to do so, and to travel, he needed one last big job he could overcharge for.

Then a blockbuster project found him. The call came from the production team for *Siege of Planet of the Apes.* The director wanted him to invent an accent, tiers of accents dependent on class and station in life, for a cast of intelligent apes, that is to say actors in monkey suits. They wanted someone who would be familiar with a certain transgressive frame of mind, accents that hid other accents. Shusterman with his various professional experiences, the producers believed, was their man.

The movie was to be shot mostly at Silvercup Studios in Queens, so the actors would be trained in the city. The act of speaking through the extensive masks, prosthetic facial apparatus intended to make humans look simian, made the actors sound as if they had blocks in their mouths and that, too, had to be remedied. Shusterman was intrigued and delighted.

He studied the speech patterns of dolphins, killer whales, crows, parrots, and apes, especially chimpanzees, in terms of language capabilities. Given an ape's anatomy, what kinds of sounds could they produce beyond the calls, hoots, and screeches they were known to emit? Speech depended on the evolution of the larynx deep in the throat and the position of the tongue. The first kinds of speech may have originated in instincts generated in the subcortex. *Ouch! Watch it!* You live in a hierarchical group, not just with family, but organized according to clans as well. You figure out how to make tools, weapons, a warning system alerting others to the presence of predators, but also to food possibilities out there in the jungle or desert or plains, and you need to talk about all of this. *Ouch* and *watch it* evolve to *WTF*.

He studied what apes could do. Facial expressions and hand gestures (opposable thumbs!) edge toward verbal language. Grinning, for chimps, signifies fear and anxiety, not humor or pleasure. Trust is communicated by putting a companion's fingers in your mouth. More than one researcher's digits were severed when they let monkeys take their hands and put their fingers in between their chompers. It was someone's job to put the sliced digits in a bag and drive to the hospital for reattachment, if possible.

Chimps could be taught to smoke cigarettes, ride bicycles, unicycles, and eat with utensils, but not even Nim Chimpsky could marshal sounds into sentences of more than three words. Chimps could exercise deception, Machiavellian-style, organize the ouster of their leaders, the alpha males, by the primate equivalent of backroom dealings. Shusterman read about the legendary Herman, raised by humans, then given to the Tampa Zoo. Herman had been observed retrieving lettuce stolen from him by a mischievous female, but then he turned around and gave the greens to the thief in an act of generosity and forgiveness. Countless humans were incapable of that kind of gesture.

Wittgenstein said, if a lion could speak, we could not understand him. But Shusterman believed this was wrong. Chimp Nim could ask for a banana. There was that. Unless Wittgenstein meant nobody truly understands anyone anyway; all language is fatally flawed whether humans are hardwired for it or not. Those circuits are just a bunch of amino acids, glial cells, axons that list toward ultimate entropy, kaputzsky.

The producers of *Siege of Planet of the Apes* said, wait a minute. In the first *Planet of the Apes*, the animals spoke English, some with British accents, even. Subsequent movies worked backward through the stories that lead up to the final scene of the first 1968 movie where the Statue of Liberty is buried in sand. Look at *Rise of, Dawn of, Escape from,* etc., the producers insisted. In all these, intelligence-enhanced apes figured things out. Just go with it, they said. Don't worry about the position of the larynx. Shusterman's instincts went the way of *Nim will never understand the past tense or a split infinitive.* The gap was unbridgeable, but he was being paid to just go with it, so in the end, he did.

He researched the accents of people who had been in comas or had brain damage and emerged with foreign accents, though the patients in question were only ever monolingual native English speakers. He studied the class accents of London, Johannesburg, and New York, and the overlays of accents brought by immigrant groups to those cities: Russian, Jamaican, Brazilian, Bengali. It was still a dream job, and he charged through the roof. No one complained.

On the set, the few times he needed to be there, he watched as actors were zipped into ape suits, some much larger than the actors themselves, so air had to be pumped in. As he rounded a corner between sets, he saw a male ape bent over a female ape. They looked up and said they were rehearsing. Shusterman had no idea who they were, nor did it matter to him. There was no need for the actors to say anything to him. He had read the script several times and knew they weren't rehearsing. No scene of ape sex existed in the movie. It was possible the actors didn't even know one another since, once they were in costume and had been to makeup, no human faces were visible. Shusterman marveled at hidden hooks, eyes, and seams that concealed rows of zipper teeth. The costume department was ingenious. On impulse, he took a picture of the apes with his phone, but Shusterman had no intention of posting it anywhere. The couple in ape costumes didn't seem concerned that he snapped them. They were unidentifiable, and others, before he ambled along, had taken their pictures, too. What did they care?

To the young actors, Shusterman was invisible, but mostly the apes were played by older actors, and it was possible the fucking apes were his age. In his worn Levi's and raincoat with wide lapels, his unchanged outgrown haircut, the 1970s were still present for Shusterman. The clock wasn't really moving forward. The minute hand clicked back and forth between 7:25 and 7:26, not able to overcome gravity, and the unseen mechanical hiccup that kept it from ever reaching 8.

A sea of monkey extras swept past him in waves of sienna brown, black, and tawny-tinted fur that, up close, resembled fine shag carpeting.

<hr />

## ADVERSARIA: MOVIE PLOT

Siege of Planet of the Apes *opened with an opulent desert city populated by humans. It was never clear exactly where this city was meant to be—the Sahara, Mongolian steppes, somewhere in arid central Australia, or a hybrid combination of all of them. What mattered was that the city was geographically isolated. It rose from a digitally enhanced landscape. Sandstone towers turned coral in the sunset. At the street level, people rushed past cafés and takeout stands, neon-lit and raucous. The ape-controlled territories were elsewhere, and the populations had no contact with the other. There were rumors, but little concrete evidence, so each cast the other as a combination of marvelous and brutish, and in this there was a great deal of accuracy.*

*Ape-opolis, which the director called Ape-istan in private, had become religious, autocratic, and strictly hierarchical. Each class needed to have a different accent. Royalty lived in palaces that looked like Versailles with an arboreal tone in design and decoration. There were soldiers, merchants, teachers, circus performers, and, most importantly, a watcher class employed by ministers and generals. Their motto was: No secrets here! We live in openness and harmony!*

*All, or almost all, worshipped a harsh and vengeful god represented on altars and shrines that combined fragments of King Kong toys and pieces of divine simian anatomy pillaged from empty Hanuman temples and other zoomorphic structures in parts of the world they had no names for. The artisans who constructed the shrines were part of a brotherhood of atheists whose position in the Ape-opolis pecking order was like that of the long-gone Jews who sold Christian souvenirs at the steps of the Vatican; they were seen as secretive outcasts doing a job forbidden to true believers. Each ape who worked on the shrines was assigned his or her own personal watcher. They knew this, but shrugged the watchers off for the most part. Often, in hopes of throwing off the confidence of those doing the surveillance, the ape artists smiled and waved at their observers when they were identified watching them. This cavalier attitude would, in at least one case, prove to be a mistake with fatal consequences. Watchers had a fair amount of power, and their reports could lead to imprisonment or worse.*

*Though the ape society was sharply divided along class lines, they had no slaves. The desert humans, on the other hand, most certainly did. The script didn't go into exactly where the slaves came from, but their origins, it was taken for granted, lay in conquered territory. The ruling elite were expansionist and militaristic, but master and slave all spoke with the same accent. Since they all sounded the same, this uniformity gave the impression that human society tended to be classless, a dangerous misconception, exploited by both slave and master.*

*The rhythm of the desert city was disrupted when scouts arrived from the east, reporting on the riches of the apes and highlighting the divisiveness and discontent within their distant cities, which made the apelands seem ripe for a takeover. The scouts described ape watchers thrown off cliffs. New, more numerous, watchers took their place to no avail. Arboreally-themed palaces became infested with termites, woodpeckers nested in the gilt spandrels and lunette vaults. Ape-opolis was a mess. The desert humans knew animals, even these apparently intelligent animals, were below themselves on the food chain. The generals were sure they could march out, conquer, and return in a matter of weeks. Quarters were built in anticipation of new slaves being brought in, slaves who could understand English, but who were not quite human. A ministry of potential employment was set up which determined the apes could be used for construction on heights, mining, and possibly food service.*

*War was declared based on trumped-up charges, the kidnapping of a caravan of schoolchildren on a field trip, and within days a long stream of troops filed out of the capital city in a march bristling with tanks, big guns, fighter planes overhead, and hundreds of slaves. The humans were in no doubt all the spoils and riches the apes possessed would soon be theirs.*

*The apes were taken by surprise. By the time sentries in their towers spotted the marauders, it was too late. Hordes of hairless invaders quickly encircled their city. From turrets and ramparts, even perched on gargoyles, humans were viewed with fear and revulsion. The ape army fought viciously, but many were killed on the parapets. The humans had far superior firepower. Within the city, food became scarce. Animals not normally eaten were consumed. The sculptors working on shrines laid down their chisels, hot glue guns, and soldering irons. Even they, the more or less non-aggressive untouchables, were drafted into defense. Fearing they would be cannon fodder, many trudged to the city walls and peeked over the parapets at their adversaries, whose shaved heads and bare arms filled them with horror and awe. The humans looked up at hairy faces in much the same way.*

*The siege went on for months. In their excitement and lack of good data, human generals hadn't accounted for the possibility of their own food running out, or the probability that other ape armies from other parts of what passed as the Earth would plunge into their encampment like, as the director described it, bloodthirsty renegade samurai descending in the middle of the night to avenge a usurped throne. Long story short: despite odds in their favor, the humans lost.*

*Routed into retreat, the slaves were left behind, and this was where the movie really picked up steam. The apes adopted the human slaves for studies and experimentation. Why were they ape-like, but not quite? Underground laboratories were punishing in their tortures and filth. Set design had plenty of images of actual locations where animals were used in experiments.*

*Shooting was well underway, but unresolved questions about the ending remained. The director and producers discussed interspecies love and seduction, but this was considered too disgusting, really, and a distraction. The point was the slaves were still slaves. The apes adopted human behavior. In the end, some slaves escaped with the outcast apes, the ones who questioned the blind faith of their brethren's religious devotion. As they galloped across the plains into a new future, there were no guarantees as to how an experimental social venture would turn out. Inherent violence lurks in everyone's DNA, the scriptwriter said.*

*Last scene, a slave shoots a wild dog at random. The dog was minding its own business, not harming anyone. Cruelty is present, always, no matter what. Violence is inevitable. The thing lurking within, like the creature bursting out of John Hurt in* Alien.

Shusterman enjoyed visiting the set, seeing the construction of palaces and laboratory gizmos, but for the most part, the actors and makeup people had to travel to his apartment/coaching studio for the training sessions. Reciting lines while wearing an ape head complete with prosthetic muzzle presented a particular challenge to speech that had to be worked through. The makeup people set up their tables and mirrors in his bathroom, which was small, and their equipment spilled into his bedroom. Pieces of fur and boxes of powder were scattered on the floor because there was no room for everything.

A man and a woman who had been cast as skeptic artists, apists working on the shrines, had long, important speaking parts. The actress's makeup was exceptionally complicated. She wanted to come across as sexy as possible, like Kim Hunter in the original movie, and among the additional details, required extensive false eyelashes, for example, to be visible below the patches of fur that constituted her brow. There was only space in Shusterman's small apartment office for the makeup people to work on one of them at a time, and the actor was done first. Though time-consuming, his needs were simpler in comparison. Time gobbling was fine with Shusterman. He waited on his balcony overlooking a quiet street and mentally added up the contributions to his Vienna fund. These were all billable hours.

When the actor was finished with makeup, he joined Shusterman on the balcony to smoke. Shusterman kept a large bottle of water nearby, initially meant to irrigate a few plants he'd stuck out there, but in fact, he wanted to be prepared to douse the guy in the event his head, encased in fake fur, caught on fire from the cigarette. It grew smaller with each inhale, and the glowing shreds of tobacco were within a couple of millimeters from what the man called his ape-stache before he stubbed it out. People on the street below looked up at the smoking man with an ape head, but no one, as far as Shusterman could tell, raised their phone to take any pictures.

There was a scene in which the apists, working on a grotto-like apse framed by minarets, finally confronted two of their watchers lurking behind rocks, and this scene became critical for establishing their speech patterns. Their lines were sarcastic in substance, and Shusterman experimented with a combination of Scottish and the outer borough accent he grew up with. Both were known for deadpan deliveries when a deeply cynical comment was called for. He had the actors listen to a Scottish football sportscaster yell when Lionel Messi scored a difficult goal, one which shouldn't have been possible, a chance created out of very little opportunity. *Wot a play! Positively magisterial!* Shusterman played the recording over and over. He put his hands on their lips and jaws, then placed their hands on his face to demonstrate how lips and jaws should move or be held to reproduce that accent. He opened his mouth to demonstrate where the tongue should tap around against teeth or palate. The actress was professional. The makeup people giggled. Then he had them listen to Judy Holliday in *Born Yesterday.*

*Are you one of these talkers, or would you be interested in a little action?*

Shusterman pronounced *talker* the way Holliday did: *tawker.* This was an example of what was known as the "coil-curl merger" when *heard* became *hoid.* Another feature of the accent was the hard landings on final consonants, *t* and *d.* It was spoken mainly, but not exclusively, by people born in New York before World War II. Agent Myers had this accent, but he had tried to modify it with varying degrees of success, depending on who he was speaking to. It usually made itself known. *Bear with me, Shusterman, my boy. You need to leave, now. Now* drawn out into two syllables like he was some kind of Kennedy. Shusterman had replayed that moment over and over, apologizing to Abril for not staying, for not continuing to look for her.

"*Tawker. Tawker. Tawker.*" He looked straight at the ape actress as he spoke. "Repeat after me. *Or are you interested in a little action?* Note how pitch goes up, then down, high, low, high, low."

The skin visible around her eyes turned bright pink, then reddish. At first, she had trouble moving her jaw with the ape-shaped mandible adhered. It was lightweight plastic, specially cast for the film, but even with air conditioning, she complained her face was coated with sweat that was beginning to drip down and soak her neck. Rivulets ran from the base of the fur ending at her collarbone down to the fabric of her cut-off *Dancing with the Stars* T-shirt. Before devoting herself to acting, she explained to Shusterman, she had been a competitive ballroom dancer. It made sense, casting her; though she didn't have to dance for her role as ape artist atheist, there was a gymnastic element to the part that required scampering up rock faces, turning somersaults, and a fair amount of running. Shusterman was sympathetic to someone who hadn't been able to earn a living doing what she'd been trained to do. When standing close to her, he could detect wafts of tiger balm, menthol, and clove oil that had been rubbed into strained muscles.

The actors were very good, and learned quickly, but something wasn't right. He scrapped the accents they'd practiced and switched to a tone that seemed to imply trust and pragmatism, the opposite of sarcastic, more implication of what you see is what you get, or at least that was his interpretation: northern American Midwest. The actor listened to new recordings (*For a premium ice fishing experience, you need a portable TV satellite dish*) but rubbed his simian jaw, visibly pissed off. He felt Shusterman was wasting their time, trying one speech pattern after another. He didn't like the nasally flat a's, and thought they sounded thick and dumbass, but the director liked the contradiction between the received ideas connected with the flat accent and the acerbic content of the lines. Shusterman was sincere in his search, but at the same time, he was consciously, if not conscientiously, on the clock. Despite undercurrents of rancor, the two artist apes learned the upper Midwest accent with proficiency, declaring their two-fisted atheism with lines like:

*Evolution will not be televised.*

*Divinity is a cultural construct.*

*Prove it!*

Followed by:

*Pass the hot glue gun. His tail got unhinged.*

And to the watchers:

*Suck this, Eyeballs!*

The last scene Shusterman was needed for involved scientist apes performing medical experiments on the captured humans. A different pair of actors arrived at his apartment. The scientist-torturer apists were quiet and brooding. They stared at Shusterman's still from *Singin' in the Rain* as if the gleeful faces of Gene Kelly and Donald O'Connor contained clues to a pending apocalypse. Shusterman explained prosody, pauses, intonation, rhythm, timbre, and stresses. The apes tended to speak in anacoluthons, fragments, as if full sentences were just out of linguistic reach, but the audience would get the idea. The pair of actors took notes and practiced their lines like opera singers.

Initially the accent he chose for these characters was Germanic, Berliners, say, who had been in the United States for a number of years, so their accents would be modified, not broadly identifiable, but still even an untrained ear would detect Teutonic origins. There were many possible models. On his way to the subway, an animal rights activist handed him a flyer featuring animal acts that they felt demonstrated unnecessary captivity and cruelty. Among the examples were Siegfried and Roy, German-born entertainers, who performed with white lions and ivory-furred Siberian tigers. He watched interviews with them at their estate, "Little Bavaria," outside Las Vegas, where, he noted, Leni Riefenstahl had been one of their visitors. He listened to her accent, too. *I knew nothing. I knew nothing. I knew not a thing about any of it.*

The German-inflicted accent was easy to imitate, but something wasn't right about it. In expressions as common as *good evening, Doctor,* Shusterman saw Karl Sauer scurrying down a hall, calling over his shoulder *buenos noches* with the accents of time spent on Alexanderplatz. Also, the apes sounded hilarious with this accent, *das electrodes ist comink unglood.* Their roles were not meant to be comic.

He watched clips of Ronald Reagan. The showmanship behind which shivs were drilled into anonymous backs, the rouged cheeks, the tilt of the head with its slope of shiny dyed hair, the reassuring tone, as if to say we can all agree on the right thing to do here. Sell arms to Iran despite the embargo, use funds to arm the Contras. Invade Grenada. Threat to American freedom. That hazard was described by his critics as thirty-two guys in sneakers, but Reagan wasted no time sending in US Special Forces, Navy Seals, Team Four. A blankety fog of intonation that masked meaning, that's what Shusterman wanted. *There, there, you're going to be fine, better than ever, while I add a drop or two of strychnine to your IV.*

Then Shusterman listened to Margaret Thatcher. The speech of the former prime minister reminded him of blocks of granite. With her stresses and emphasis on certain adjectives and gerunds, it was hard to listen to, even so many years later. She had had a tutor from the National Theater who trained her to deepen her voice, speak slowly, so she had an authoritative, all-knowing affect. Mrs. Thatcher had been great pals with Reagan. The two had very different vocalizations, but Shusterman devised an accent that was a hybrid of the two.

"What are the anatomical features of their brains?" asked one of the actors after donning his ape head. He said his line in the measured, repetitive melody reminiscent of the Iron Lady's cadences: anatomical.

Among the questions the scientist apes had: what was the relationship between left and right hemispheres of the brain? If you severed the connections between the two halves, how would people communicate? Apes had a great deal of medical technology, but had not developed X-rays, so the only way to find out what was inside the body was surgery. They were interested in how the brain was organized, how memory and visualization worked. What were the language centers? The apes spoke as if, rather than cells and neurons, they would find, once they opened up human brains, maps and instructional manuals. The humans were justifiably terrified. Thatcher/

Reagan apes said the word *neocortical* with tongues that glided over syllables, sounding benign, but hiding menace and pain.

Apists wondered what traits, if any, might tie them to humans. Do humans experience empathy? If humans owned slaves, making a case for empathy was a tall order. Using a more Reaganified accent, an actor savored the emptiness of the central word of that sentence, empathy, and gave it a deceptive "look at me" stress. The humans recognized themselves in mirrors, but what, exactly, were the components and limitations of human consciousness? How are emotions and cognition interconnected?

❊

## ADVERSARIA: END OF THE MOVIE

*The apes surmised humans lived in large social groups, but their affinity for and use of slaves caused the apes to question how humans were socialized.*

*Electrodes were taped onto the humans' heads. The apes had other humans beaten in front of those whose brains were hooked up to machines, as they went berserk with horror, terror, and agony.*

*The apes, who alternated between walking upright and on all fours, observed that because of the evolution (they used that word) of the big toe, humans walked with one foot after the other. The constant upright posture meant lungs were positioned differently, breathing varied, and because of these alignments, humans could do something apes didn't fully understand: laugh. The expulsion of guffaws, which the apes linked to non-language sounds and the humans' particular method of breathing when standing, could not be reproduced in the captured slaves. There were no knuckle-draggers among the captives; even when they were put in low-ceilinged cages, they tended to hop in a squatting position, but then once captured, none of the humans laughed, especially after viewing the torture of their confrères. Laughter had been distinctly observed when looking down on*

*the human troops in their days of confidence, before they were defeated
and scattered. The apes had a vocalization that resembled laughter, but
it was more of a general screech, not the particularized sounds of human
mirth. The apes didn't have jokes or comic routines of any kind, but it has
to be said, they didn't really know what they were missing.*

*When humans were autopsied they were found to have something in
their hypothalamus that the apes did not: nucleus accumbens. This, the
surgeon apes conjectured, was the part of the brain that understood jokes
and generated a respiratory audile response. Could it be transplanted if
there were ape volunteers? One of the atheist apists took the gamble.*

*"Crocodiles look like they're smiling, but they most definitely are
not," said one of the skeptical scientists in a voice that sounded as if he'd
just arrived from the Australian outback.*

*His colleagues proposed looking into reptile brains, too, but while
they were debating the finer points of neurosurgery, two of the slaves escaped, and the movie plot proceeded quickly to its final chase scene.*

❈

Shusterman's work was done. His bags were packed.

# ADVERSARIA

*Sauer was last seen alive talking to the animals as he made his way around the Schönbrunn Palace grounds, which is the Vienna Zoo. Back in a city he hadn't seen in decades, he became increasingly disoriented. He banged on glass barriers and screamed at the orangutans until he was removed, tried to herd the free-ranging peacocks by using a trash can lid as a shield like some lost knight, scolded a zookeeper about what he saw as the mangy conditions of the sea lions. Then the zoo lost sight of him, and it was assumed he'd calmed down or left the park. Hours passed. No one reported him anywhere, then somehow, he accessed the rhinoceros enclosure located in a far isolated corner of the park, and once in the enclosure, Karl made himself at home. He shouted that the white rhino was a reincarnation of Leni Riefenstahl, though she was still alive. Whispering terms of endearment, he encircled the rhino's neck with his arms.*

*A child, impatient and skipping ahead of his straggling family, saw him in the rhino environment, and the boy sprinted back, shouting that a man was riding the rhino's nose. The father ran to get help. Before the invention of the cell phone, there were few ways to find someone other than to put one foot in front of the other as quickly as possible. Meanwhile, the rhino shook Karl off and responded to his attempts at interspecies affection by charging him, her horn piercing a lung, severing an aorta.*

*Whether he had help or climbed in on his own, a man who thinks a white rhino is Leni Riefenstahl is in trouble. Looking for Göring, got a goring.*

One Viennese rhino in particular had a neck that looked as if it were constructed of accordion folds, his head a mechanism for locating and consuming food at the end of the appendage. Was this a descendent of the beast who skewered Sauer? No way to know. Shusterman stood on the viewing platform of the rhinoceros enclosure at the Tiergarten Schönbrunn. The corral was also home to nilgai, blackbuck antelopes, and chital, a kind of deer native to India. None of the animals would have shared a habitat in the wild, but they roamed around their pen ignoring one another, at least while Shusterman watched them. It would have been easy for an adult to hop over the fence, climb down the boulders, and have a chinwag with the animals there. He could have been over the fence before anyone could grab his arm to try to talk him out of the leap, but he just stared at the animals, imagined the old man he remembered as Karl Sauer hugging a white rhino and whispering, *Leni, darling*, in its ear.

When he lived in Vienna during the war, Sauer had probably visited the Schönbrunn. The state of the zoo, in some ways, reflected the city's fortunes, and this might not have been lost on the propagandist. In 1944, some citizens limped along in a fog of *why bother?* Those who had waved flags from the sidewalk with passion and efficiency now felt *why go to the trouble of sweeping the stairs?* The whole building could be pulverized in the evening's attack. The zookeepers charged with hoisting Zoo Director Otto Antonius' beloved swastika flags all over the cages and pathways of the zoo, may have, by then, abandoned their posts. If you loved animals, it was unbearable to watch them starve in captivity. Yet, if you didn't go into work, it's possible hungry citizens could break in to kill hippos for schnitzel or flamingos to roast with white wine and herbs, if any white wine and herbs could be found. This happened in Stalingrad, in Paris, in Budapest. Imagine, however, once the barred cages are reduced to rubble, any animal still alive is now free. In the park there's grass! Herbivores can eat for the first time in days, weeks, longer, who knows? They gorge themselves. They mosey over to the amusement area, the Wurstelprater. Its rides are in ruins, but what do they care? More food to forage: sausage heels, cones of spun sugar, cast off cookies in the form of misshapen Alpine trolls. Then, the foraging animals find each other, and for the carnivores this is good news, otherwise there were only squirrels and sparrows, tough unsatisfying little devils to be ground up via back molars. Surviving animals wander into the city, past Freud's house, past palaces and churches, knocking over statues, and scaring unarmed citizens to death. Armed citizens shoot them. It will be winter soon, anyway. None of them could survive snow and ice. The zoo was heavily bombed during World War II. Died in the bombardment: elephant and hippo, followed in death, as the Allied advanced, by the double suicide of Otto Antonius and his wife.

The zoo was rebuilt after the war, and at some point, cages gave way to approximations of native environments. In 2009, two artists, Christoph Steinbrener and Rainer Dempf, constructed installations around the zoo: an oil crane in the penguin zone, a drum labeled *Toxic Waste* in a fish tank, a Mercedes Benz submerged in the rhino pool. The drum didn't really contain lethal chemicals, and the crane wasn't real, but their point was to demonstrate what environmental degradation looks like. By the time Shusterman arrived, the Mercedes Benz had been removed, but he read of how the rhinos were fascinated by it, and he wondered about the connection between a rhinoceros reincarnation of Leni Riefenstahl and a Mercedes. Perhaps it was true, and the rhino, a descendent of the one who gored Sauer, became the reincarnation of a woman who missed her car.

A woman asked Shusterman if he knew how to get to the *Haus des Meeres*, House of the Sea, she was looking for alligators. She had an American accent, so he answered her in English, that he didn't know, he was a visitor, just like she was. In her answer, that she wasn't a visitor, but had moved to the city, he guessed she, too, was from New York. She said that she was, and got that shocked, how-did-you-know expression on her face, an expression he hadn't seen in a long time, and it gave him some satisfaction, but she looked uncomfortable that he'd guessed correctly, here in the middle of a very different city.

"Look here," he said trying to be helpful, he had a map of the zoo, explaining he was old, he needed paper. "Are you sure you want the *Haus des Meeres?* It looks like there are alligators over there." He pointed to the lower righthand corner of the map. "We're here." He pointed to the lower left corner."

She thanked him, explaining she'd mixed up east and west. Schusterman tried to prolong the conversation. He liked hearing the familiar accent. It wasn't one you heard often anymore, even when he lived in the city. The way the woman dropped the r off of alligators, made house into almost two syllables, the musicality of Judy Holliday.

"Why alligators?"

"I knew someone who had one."

"That's a dangerous pet unless you have a cat. They're afraid of cats. They look at them as if they're crazy people." He knew this because ape actors had talked about this phenomenon when rehearsing accents, the *a* sound in cat and alligator, led to, *hey did you know?* Schusterman immediately regretted using this anecdote and making the comment about crazy people. She might think he was one, a stranger encountered at the rhino enclosure, or that he looked at her as if she were.

"It wasn't a pet. My friend had more of a rescue operation, and the alligator was still very small. You could pick it up and carry it someplace, if you wanted to."

The zoo was closing soon, and she had a long walk. She didn't ask if he wanted to join her, and he didn't offer, only insisting she keep his paper map, and then they went their separate ways.

None of Sauer's propaganda films had been digitalized or could be found online or in any archive Shusterman contacted. They must have existed, still, somewhere. Not only did Shusterman want to see them, but the credits would reveal who had worked for Sauer. In his role as director of a film company, he might have kept production records, and it was possible Alma Mercado had them among the stuff she stole from his apartment. Shusterman wrote to her, and Alma answered promptly. She found no films or even stills in his rooms, just the scripts, but, yes, attached to the last pages were lists of actors and their roles along with illegible penciled-in notes. A typed list was attached to her email. Retaining the original, still hoping someone would offer her a lot of money for it, and knowing that person wasn't Shusterman, Alma wrote that she hoped he would understand, she needed to look out for herself. Shusterman couldn't blame her for it, though he doubted there was any demand for the papers of a sec-ond-rate producer of war propaganda.

All the actors and actresses who worked for Karl were dead or untraceable, but Shusterman tried to find surviving children as best he was able. Mostly he turned up dead ends, or there were names— Gruber, Koch, Stein—that were too common to be found with any accuracy, and these were people who didn't want to be found or re-minded of their parents' or grandparents' performances. Then he lo-cated a Metta Götz, daughter of one of Sauer's stars, Jurgen Götz. Jurgen was a ham in Sauer's B at best movies. His roles were predict-able: a mountaineer cheated by a big city pawnbroker, a Rhineland warrior who vanquished dark-skinned men in turbans.

According to a site about early Austrian cinema, Metta lived in Vienna, and so Shusterman called her up, presenting himself as an American who was producing a documentary about the movie busi-ness in Vienna during and after the war. Much to his surprise, she agreed to see him in her apartment that afternoon. The daughter was seventy, or claimed to be, lived up four flights of stairs, and said that, to be honest, she found her city so full of people she didn't recognize that she had become something of a recluse. She didn't say *foreigners*, but that was the implication, and within the insinuation, she seemed to assume Shusterman would feel the same way. Metta's conversation was sharp and full of references to a vanished youth of outings and parties with children of other actors from that era. Shusterman was sure she could talk about Sauer's postwar years, his visits to their house, gifts of toys, still-rationed chocolate, and friendly pats on the head. She gave him her address, and he was on his way.

The white apartment building, pre-war Bauhaus style, was between a warehouse turned into artist studios and start-up offices and a parking lot. Metta buzzed him up, and he climbed the stairs holding onto the iron banister, its pattern of squares that looked like they were tumbling down the incline, a Modernist design, probably unchanged since it was first installed. Metta's door was ajar, and a voice from within told him to come up, please, and shut the door behind you. A few shallow stairs led to a hall lined with photographs, then at the entrance to a sort of living room, Metta greeted him. A large woman in a blue tracksuit, tall and muscular with iron grey hair held back with rhinestone-encrusted combs, she switched a cigarette to her left hand so they could shake. The apartment smelled as if smoking was her main activity. There were no chairs. Metta apologized in a way that was not really an apology, and explained she had sold them years ago and now used the room to meditate with a teacher who urged her to quit smoking. She made it clear that was never going to happen. The chairs could go, but not this, Metta held up a cigarette. She offered Shusterman coffee, which he accepted, and then sat cross-legged on the floor to wait.

The floor was uncomfortable, so he got up, looked around the room, picking up things and putting them down. He was holding a framed photograph of a castle when she returned with tea in Kurt Waldheim mugs, which she placed on the floor, then she took the picture from him, and positioned it back on a shelf.

"Is that your family estate?" Shusterman asked.

"My family estate was a crap apartment in a building that was demolished to make way for a hotel, but that's the Götz castle. It's a tourist attraction now. Owned by Taiwanese, I think. I like the picture, don't you?" She didn't pause for an answer. "The name Götz is associated with the expression, kiss my ass, going back to the seventeenth century. Götz von Berlichingen was a marauder, a mercenary. Am I related to him? Who knows?" Metta spoke English with an accent that would have worked for the ape scientists. "So, you want to know about Karl Sauer? Why?" She was brusque but stopped talking long enough to fetch a ceramic ashtray from where it was balanced on a windowsill.

"He was an important figure in Vienna's movie business, and your father was one of his star performers. I want to introduce his work to American audiences." This was partly true, but not in the way Metta probably thought.

"Well, really, I can tell you quite a bit." She shifted closer to him, moving the ashtray that was shaped like a man riding a camel.

"Do you mind if I record you?" Shusterman had brought an old Sony cassette tape recorder with him that he thought Metta would appreciate.

"I have not seen such a machine in years. Okay, Mr. Shusterman." She pronounced his last name, Shuster-mahnn, as if it ended in two n's. Putting out her cigarette on the camel, then lighting another one, she continued. "I will tell you what I know, and then I have to return to my meditation. He was a close friend of my father's for a while, and then he wasn't anymore." Metta shut her eyes and took a deep breath, exhaling as if beginning to meditate and communicate telepathically, then she began to speak. Each word was a pinprick of certainty, spoken with authority. Sauer was someone she'd given a lot of thought to.

"Sauer was born in the Austrian town of Kierling in, I don't know exactly, a few years before Archduke Ferdinand met a bullet in Sarajevo. His mother was an unskilled caretaker in the Hoffmann

Sanatorium where Kafka would die. He never knew his father, or much about him, except that he disappeared during World War I, in the Battle of Bir el Abd and was presumed dead. He would say this as if his father was a war hero, but was it true? Who knows. As a child, one of Karl's greatest fears was that his mother would get sick and leave him as well, but as a boy, he also developed an acute fear of contagion. Beset by a storm of anxiety about those he believed were ethnically predisposed to disease, he grew to resent the patients who took up residence in the town and who he saw as wealthy and demanding. Developing theories about the perils of genetic tendencies, he believed those afflicted could also spread their diseases to others. With their bloodied handkerchiefs, slow walks, and chattering families, he saw the sanatorium patients, those who were ambulatory, in town, in the wooded foothills, and hated them. Attached to his mother, despite her constant criticisms about his preoccupations, his choice of friends, his lack of a profession, he reasoned that, accustomed to the rules of her trade, she, too, saw contagion everywhere and couldn't discriminate between healthy and diseased. She behaved toward him as if he was a contagion and kept him at a cold distance. Only later did Karl realize she might have been protecting him from whatever it was she could have contracted at her job."

"How did you come to know his story?"

"Karl often came round to our house to see my father or mother. I was too young to have understood or remembered their conversations, but later my parents had many reasons to speak of him, and so, yes, I know quite a bit about him.

"What Karl loved was going to the movies. There was one theater in Kierling, owned by a Jew, Apfelbaum. Much as he wanted to boycott Jewish businesses, Karl risked contamination to go sit in dark rooms, as far from other people as possible, and watch Buster Keaton, Charlie Chaplin, *Der Golem* and later, both *M* and *Metropolis*. He wanted to make movies, but his mother thought this was utter nonsense; boys like him, from families like his, didn't break into pictures. He had been a good student, but she saw nowhere he could go with being a good student, except that good grades demonstrated Karl was obedient. She apprenticed him to a blacksmith.

"Trapped in the windowless forge, not only was he suffocated by the heat, but smithing bored him to tears. His minimal upper body strength hampered his ability to do the required tasks and failed to improve even with the repetitive motions of the job. When he could, he escaped to the Jew-owned theater on his day off. He saw *The White Ecstasy* in which Leni Riefenstahl played a young village girl skiing and jumping in the Alps, and *The Holy Mountain* also starring Riefenstahl, as a dancer who falls in love with a man living in a remote mountain cottage. In the poster, her eyes were shut like she was in a blissful trance."

As if this were unclear, she shut her eyes to demonstrate. Then she continued.

"After only a few months, Karl could stand the blacksmith no longer, and ran away to Berlin, working as a set painter at Babelsberg Film Studios. At night he wrote Alpine adventure scripts that were never shot. Humans were supposed to win out over nature in these movies, that was the rule, but in Sauer's failed screenplays, sometimes the mountains won, and human skiers or climbers met tragic endings. Karl's thinking was, well, they tried, there was something noble in that, before down a crevasse they tumbled.

"Hanging around Babelsberg one afternoon shortly after his arrival, he saw Leni Riefenstahl drive up in her black Mercedes, and looking up as a door shut behind him, in that moment, he fell in love. Karl followed her from place to place in the film studio, at some distance, so he wouldn't be noticed, and as a small, thin, nondescript fellow, he was easily overlooked. His trailing became constant and turned into stalking. Sauer located Riefenstahl's house, followed her to stadiums and sports arenas, watched Riefenstahl instruct her crew where to set up shots of runners and high jumpers preparing for the

Olympics, marveled at her ingenuity: the underwater camera, the aerial shots of muscled bodies in motion.

"Inspired by Riefenstahl's cleverness and boundless energy, he kept writing, but still no one wanted his Alpine scripts about the challenges of nature. Nature as purity, he thought that was the message of the day, and it was a message he wholeheartedly believed in. Instead they flocked to movies like *The Blue Angel* or *The Testament of Dr. Mabuse*, which Propaganda Minister Goebbels, correctly, in Karl's opinion, banned. He didn't understand how people could pay hard-earned marks for such unmitigated, senseless, degrading crap. Despite stamping Fritz Lang's films as degenerate, Goebbels wanted Lang to be the head of UFA studios. The banks were closed, but Lang fled for Paris that night. This was 1933, and that dog, Karl, wanted his bone. He felt slighted, overlooked.

"Imagine Sauer wanting to say to Goebbels, 'What's up with that? Why'd you ask that guy? Why not me?' Angry and rejected, Karl left Berlin, returning to Vienna, but the Anschluss and the movies changed his life.

"After Kristallnacht, Goebbels wanted to prod any recalcitrant Germans who balked at violent solutions to take up bricks, knives, arms of any kind to eliminate their inferiors post haste. What better motivator than a movie which portrayed a range of stereotypes: the greedy sexually rapacious wily assimilated financier grimy immigrant deviant and duplicitous. Then they were all there in one spectacular script. Goebbels gobbled it up. He wanted ever-increasing spirals of violence, and he got it in *Jud Süß*. The film was a huge success."

"*The Jew Süss?*" Shusterman pretended ignorance.

"The very one. Sauer was one of the twenty million people who saw *Jud Süß* but unlike the other 19,999,999 viewers, Karl thought he could do that shit. He knew a fake beard wholesaler, he had a storehouse of grievances left over from his childhood in Kierling. No, he would insist, his characters weren't cartoon people. They were based on the real deal. Karl began to make propaganda films for the

Reich, small-time in Vienna, not Berlin, but still, he felt, his contribution wasn't nothing. It was his way of getting revenge on the Jew Lang, on Jew-lovers Dietrich and Murnau, on everyone who rejected him, except Riefenstahl. He understood she was out of reach, and he was destined only to dream of mountain fuckfests from afar."

At the word *fuckfests*, Metta exhaled sharply, as if smoking and the word went hand-in-hand, and although she was seventy, she wanted Shusterman to be under no illusions about what she thought she was capable of.

"Through films that exposed foreign infiltration of banking, the film industry, any industry, Karl was convinced that beautiful women would sleep with him, he'd be given villas and chateaux, have boats and trains at his personal disposal. He became an expert at prosthetic noses, hand gestures, dialects, kosher food, and ritual baths. What he got: an apartment requisitioned from a supposedly wealthy Jewish art dealer. It was small, faced an air shaft, and didn't get a lot of light. Box office, such as it was, was not brilliant, but there was a war on and people were busy turning in their neighbors. Though his movies were low-budget, perhaps, in that regard, he did his job too well. Informing on Jews who hid from *aktions* occupied a great deal of time and expense. Back in Kierling, the Apfelbaum theater was now the Reichstheater.

"Then, in 1943, word came from Berlin. Sauer had been noticed. He thought he would be appointed to the SS Panzer, Prinz Eugen Division, but no, the little man was in no shape for that. Sauer was given a title, Assistant Minister of Propaganda, which meant he had to watch and approve movies like those he made and censor or pull the plug on anything that snuck in from Hollywood or Pinewood or, god forbid, Bollywood, though the latter was never a real problem. Lang, Von Sternberg, Billy Wilder, all could be censored, destroyed. We probably have Sauer to thank for the fact that many of Murnau's films were lost. A few of the movies he sent down the gurgle hole: *Sullivan's Travels, Citizen Kane, Suspicion, Wolfman*. He banned Looney Tunes' *The Ducktators* and, of course, *To Be or Not To Be*. He wrote especially to Goebbels that this Benny and Lombard vehicle was a travesty. 'So they call me Concentration Camp Ehrhardt.' He quoted as an example of the movie's depravity. No reply from Goebbels is known to exist."

"I didn't know he was also a censor."

"Being an official censor—that was okay, but not really what Karl wanted to do. He wanted to make films, to be behind the camera, not sitting in front of the projector. Toward the end of the war, who was making movies? Karl and my father would reminisce about the work they'd done together, telling each other that when it was over, they would go back into production. But also, fewer and fewer movies were even in the pipeline to be censored, and he spent the last part of the Third Reich mostly alone in soundproof blacked-out rooms watching pornography sent to him from occupied lands. When Andre Bazin said hooray for dark rooms, this wasn't what he had in mind, I think. Sauer's projectionist had trained with the Fuhrer's personal projectionist. This was an honor, but by the time word reached Vienna that the Red Army was marching through the Brandenburg Gate, the projectionist had disappeared. Sauer was abandoned. He was on his own."

"So how did the war end for Karl?"

"He left Vienna and immigrated to Argentina."

"Do you know anything about what he did there? Did he continue to make even small movies? I've heard that he did. Do you know anything about those films?"

Metta shook her head, reached over to turn off the recorder. She was tired and had nothing more to say. Shusterman turned on a recorder in his pocket.

"Of this, I know nothing. You can go to the address of his former offices on 39 Nachtfalterallee, but the building is being torn down. There would have been little there to see in any case. You know the story of the Wasserturm in Berlin?"

Shusterman did. It had been a water tower built sometime in the 1870s. It included apartments for the machinists who worked there, but then it was used as a torture center, the first concentration camp. It was now luxury apartments.

"The building I'm speaking of had a similar history. Originally owned by a family that manufactured lenses, it was large, had many floors, all requisitioned by the Reich and turned to many uses: offices, Sauer's among them, also an interrogation center, a place to be murdered. Grinding glass machines tossed out, different kinds of grinders brought in. After the war, the building was abandoned. No one would go near it. But finally last year, developers bought the site, intending to tear it down. Conservationists said wait, it should be preserved, even as a ruin. You can go to the address. What would be left of Sauer's activities? Nothing, I would think. Not a sealed-up cave of nightmares, perfectly preserved, just waiting for the door to be opened. It's just a ruin."

"Your father performed in those Sauer films. Can you tell me more about that period?" Shusterman wanted her to keep talking. He couldn't accept Metta would be a dead end.

"My father was a great actor. Perhaps you've heard of him? Jurgen Götz."

"Of course, I mentioned him on the phone. That's how I found you." If he hadn't been on the trail of Karl Sauer he would never have heard of Jurgen Götz. No one had.

"He could have been a *staatsschauspieler* if he hadn't worked with Sauer. Before the war my father performed briefly with Brecht. A small role. Maybe he had Communist leanings for a moment, but then he got a big break. He performed in Mussolini's *Campo di Maggio* at the Vienna Burgtheater. His critics would say of him that he had been around the fence a few times. He was capable of that, but my father was just a working actor. I insist on this point. It was totally unfair what happened to him. He often said, 'This or that is no concern of mine. I'm an actor. I go where there is work.'

He wanted challenging roles. Can you or anyone else blame him for that?"

Shusterman took a swallow of tea that tasted like boiled Hawaiian Punch. Clips of Jurgen Götz performing in non-Saurerian films were available, and from what he had seen, Shusterman doubted Götz could ever have been a *staatsschauspieler*, an actor of national importance.

"Fresh tea? You barely touched your glass."

"No thanks. Why did Jurgen choose to be in Sauer's films?"

"It was the right thing to do at the time." Metta refused to elaborate. "Look at Werner Krauss, star of *Jud Süß*. There was a really big Nazi and what did he get? In 1955 he was awarded the High Decoration of the Republic of Austria."

"Krauss was also Dr. Caligari?" Shusterman posed this as a question, though he knew the answer.

"Caligari, yes, in more ways than one. After the war my father was banned from acting, then had to undergo denazification, and even still he was heckled offstage. People threw rotten vegetables at him, and finally he couldn't work at all. Those same people who had applauded him just a few years earlier now jeered and insulted him."

❖

## ADVERSARIA: ACCORDING TO METTA

*Actor Joachim Gottschalk's wife, Meta Wolf, was Jewish, and Goebbels insisted he must divorce this woman. When he refused, Goebbels said, well fine, then she and your son are off to Theresienstadt, and you get sent to the eastern front. Rather than go to the camps and the army, they killed their son and then themselves using gas poisoning. The truth about their deaths was suppressed and not revealed until after the war. So how was this my father's fault? Yes, he may have harassed Gottschalk who was guilty of rassenschande, and so on. It was, he thought, a wise career move, to criticize his fellow actor publicly, and at the time there was no reason not to believe this would not always be the case. Who kills themselves over such things? My father thought with all the attention, Joachim would do the right thing, demand a divorce, and get back to work. They died in 1941. Jurgen lived until 1984.*

*Look at Paul Wegener. He played the golem in* Der Golem. *He, too, appeared in a lot of propaganda films, but he also hid Jews and donated money to anti-fascist groups. He had a Jewish connection. My father did not.*

*If you want to talk about injustice, let's discuss Jud Süß. Veit Harlan, director of* Jud Süß, *stood trial for crimes against humanity. He was acquitted. During denazification, Harlan and those actors who worked for him claimed they had no choice, but they were paid handsomely for their work. They insisted Goebbels made them do it. No. They did what they did for money. That fat actor, Heinrich George, who played the Heart Machine in* Metropolis, *also played Duke Karl Alexander in* Jud Süß. *He said, hey, wait a minute, I worked with Jews, I'm not all bad. He was arrested as a collaborator and killed by the Russians very quickly in 1946.*

*Just so you know, for your information, the Prinz Eugen Mountain division was one of the most brutal of all the Waffen SS. Prinz Eugen, a dwarf, believed to be queer, was a military commander who routed the Turks from the gates of Vienna in 1716.*

"*Rassenschande*," Shusterman repeated the word.

"Racial pollution," Metta explained. "But then my father became haunted by the suicides, became obsessed with Joachim, and named me after the man's wife. Sauer ridiculed him for his obsession. At my christening Sauer was the evil fairy, making fun of my name."

Metta was clearly offended. She stretched her legs before recrossing them. Toes in yellow socks glanced against one of Shusterman's thighs.

"Back to your father and Karl Sauer."

"Okay, yes, let's talk about the denazification period. Why not?" There was acid in her voice. "When the Allies advanced, Sauer's name was on the lists of those to be arrested, to stand trial for war crimes. 'I didn't do anything. I was under orders,' he pleaded. Yeah, yeah. That's what they all say, isn't it? Karl suspected someone had it out for him. Maybe the family of the man whose apartment he took over, though it was said all had been murdered. Sly Jews, he believed, could turn up anywhere. When the Americans marched into the city, he claimed to have extensive knowledge of Austrian communists, information he would be more than willing to impart in exchange for protection and an ongoing salary. Also, he claimed he had loyal informants from the Channel Islands to the Caspian Sea. Did he? Who knows. The OSS was happy to have him. Names, identities became his stock and trade, people he knew from his film businesses protected or turned in at random as it suited him. He got others on the payroll, black marketeers, actors, even a former Vichy chief of police who had fled east. Sauer had connections. He wasn't a nobody, as he claimed when it suited him. He could get you a new ID card with the red denazification sticker on it if that's what you needed. The Americans protected him because he knew the names of their agents in the just-popping Cold War era, and because of the shifting allegiances, it looked like he would never be arrested.

"Right after the war, Sauer came to my father and said, I can get you a denazification sticker, you'll be okay, you'll be able to work all you want. Of course, my father accepted. He wanted nothing more than to perform again. What did Sauer actually do before he disappeared? He informed. My father was arrested and served time in Sachsenhausen, by then run by the Soviets. He was never the same afterward." Metta pointed to a series of black and white stills she'd framed of her father striking poses in various roles. Some were autographed.

Metta led Shusterman to believe that, in good part because of Sauer, the world outside the city was a terrifying place for her, where, because of her family's affiliations, there were those who wished her grievous bodily harm, so for her entire life, she stuck to the streets she knew. That was why she never left the city, ever, and believed all kinds of strangers were out to get her.

"Karl was always skilled at getting other people to do his dirty work."

Shusterman asked Metta if Sauer himself participated in torture or interrogations that took place in the Kronenberg. She shrugged. She was too young to know personally, and her father never talked about what he did or might have done.

"You know Karl came to see me years ago. He had returned to Vienna. I thought he wanted me to forgive him, but he never admitted that he was the one who informed, thereby buying legitimization for himself in the eyes of the Americans. What he did on the other side of the Atlantic, I neither know nor care."

"So, you didn't forgive him."

"He said he felt terrible about my father's fate, but that there was nothing to forgive, because he would never inform on my father, a great friend and such a formidable talent. Yeah, right. Crocodile tears. Stupid old man. I put blotter acid in his coffee. I have no idea if it had any effect."

39 Nachtfalterallee was near the Prater, close enough so Shusterman could hear the sound of carnival music when he walked down the street. It was an odd place for an interrogation center, whose chambers also accommodated Sauer's offices of censorship and propaganda, but Leopoldtstadt was convenient for overseeing deportations, so many being expelled lived in the vicinity. To get the taste of Metta's tea out of his mouth, he stopped for an espresso, swallowed it in a couple of bitter gulps, then kept going. It was raining lightly, but not enough to turn dirt to mud. When he reached the site, the

destruction, as Metta had indicated, had been halted, but despite the rain and idle machinery, there was an air of productivity to the block. He stood at the edge of the roped-off site. An ornate Deutsche Bank branch loomed to the right, marble Athena glaring over the massive doorway, other figures positioned in aedicules overhead, fenestration heavy with decoration. To the left was a walk-in health clinic, little more than a storefront. You had to know it was there. A few people could be seen in the waiting room: a woman in a hijab, another in a short red vinyl skirt and thigh-high leopard skin boots. In between the bank and the clinic, cold air and the smell of recently overturned earth blasted from #39, the ruin dark due to scaffolding and ply-wood-covered windows. Some walls still stood, other sections had been torn down, dollhouse-style.

A team in bright yellow jackets, hoods up against the rain, was digging in the dirt. Shusterman wanted to go down into the excavation, to see what remains, if any, were lying around from Sauer's days as Assistant Minister of Propaganda. If the building had been in disuse for years, it was possible some film and other kinds of evidence could have survived intact in cabinets or desks whose dented and rusted drawers could be pried open. Shusterman told the security guard that he was a location scout for a television documentary about urban archeology in central European cities.

"When you dig in American cities, you can only go back so far." He spoke loudly in what he hoped was passable German, and the guard seemed genuinely interested. "After lost wallets, tungsten bulbs, laminated driver's licenses, pieces of carriage lanterns, then the human record ends, unless you hit the rare arrowhead, but then it's rock all the way down. Here, in a city like Vienna, underneath the Ottomans are the Romans, and then the Neanderthals." He felt like he was trying to sell the Brooklyn Bridge. All he wanted was to get onto the site.

The security guard nodded, but said no. He could not allow Shusterman to enter the ruins. It was dangerous. No one could go in without authorization.

Shusterman reached for his wallet, wondering how many euro a decent bribe might be. He was unprepared for this and really had no idea. Seeing the wallet come out, the guard reached as if either to take it or push him away. In a moment of split-second confusion, Shusterman held his wallet like a cup of cold coffee he couldn't find a place to throw it out, so just held onto it.

"Let him in, Ivan. No one will ever know. No one cares." A man in a yellow jacket appeared at the top of the ladder. He swung himself over the edge of the basement, removed his hard hat. His skin was coated with a film of dirt, but when he pulled down his goggles, the tan skin around his eyes looked like a half mask. Under his hardhat, he was cue-ball bald, facial hair made up for what was absent from his head. He introduced himself as Petrovic and motioned Shusterman to follow him down a rickety staircase reinforced by wooden beams to what had been the basement of #39. The exterior walls, those left standing, had been smooth, stucco-faced stone, but below street level was a honeycomb of brick walls pitted by what looked like bullet holes and animal burrows. Speaking to Shusterman in English, Petrovic explained he had lived in New York for a few years, working for an uncle who had a company, Rambug, that exterminated roaches and other insects, then when the siege ended, he returned to Sarajevo. Now he was employed temporarily in Vienna as a salvage archeologist.

"This building was known as the Kronenberg from the name of the family who owned the original lens-grinding factory. Watch your step here." He pointed to some large holes as they walked. "It was a prosperous company, but then the owners were relocated, we were told, and the Reich used the Kronenberg for offices. Now we have a heated municipal debate that gives me a job."

Some of the chambers had no ceiling and were open to the sky; others were entirely dark, and Petrovic pointed the way with a flashlight, speaking as if he were giving a formal tour.

"Preservationists say ugly history is a fact you can't knock down and pave over. The burgomeister and his comrades say, enough already with the dead, time to bulldoze this shit and rebuild!" Petrovic knocked a wall with a shovel. It sounded hollow.

"Maybe there's someone there." He told Shusterman a Bosnian folktale about sealing women into the walls of buildings. They die in the walls but their spirits remain, and their skeletons are believed to keep the building upright. "These walls, too, are full of last breaths that may linger, who knows?"

Perhaps the last breaths kept the walls vertical and perpendicular to the earth, or the wreck had become Sauer, the fossilized remains of his work, and the breathing apparatus for dark matter in the present.

"According to the burgomeisterists, there is enough evidence of the country's crimes and complicities extant, still to be found if you travel highways and byways. No secrets. Everybody knows. Why preserve more, you know? They accused their opponents of being hoarders of history, and the builders appeared to have won, until the bodies began to turn up. Some of them dated from the 1940s and showed signs of torture. Some skulls had simply taken a bullet. Then there was another layer of bodies, but truly very old. The site had been the location of a pleasure house during the siege of the city by the Turks in the late 1600s. As soon as those turned up, demolition was brought to a screeching halt."

Shusterman, still pretending to scout locations for an imaginary documentary, told Petrovic this situation reminded him of how evidence of stops on the Underground Railroad were discovered when backhoes began digging in Brooklyn or incidents of Mohawk graveyards that were unearthed when ground was broken for an upstate mall. The urban archeologists would find what there was to be found, make their report and advise on what to do with the site, how best to preserve it and its contents, if that's what the city wanted. Sometimes construction would be stopped, sometimes it wouldn't.

They arrived at a room where a number of the barely identifiable objects were laid out on a tarp: a scattering of typewriter keys, clock gears, electrical cord, a bucket of dark sand that Petrovic said was gunpowder.

"Keep your distance from the explosives." Petrovic pointed with his cigarette, which he then put out on a boot heel with a satisfying sizzle. "The stuff is old, it's probably dead, but we don't know this for certain."

There was also evidence of Karl's work, the tools of his trade: a can of unused film stock, a projector, lens cap rusted in place, but its siding of pebbled black glass was intact.

"This was the first thing we found that revealed an older building lay under the Kronenberg."

Petrovic led Shusterman to another tarp on which lay a single object, a door knocker in the shape of a head with its eyes being pecked at by a raven. He explained it was meant to be the head of a Turk. There were a lot of these heads scattered around in towns all over the country. Heads being attacked by birds appeared as fountain spouts and perched on buildings as gargoyles. It was common in the seventeenth century, when the Ottoman army was reaching north. Petrovic stumbled on the word *infidel* and called them *infidelious Turks*.

Other objects were found from the same era: candlesticks, glass beads from Venice, a copy of *Abelard and Héloïse*, pieces of broken porcelain, all much older than the lenses factory era, so old, in fact, that no one had used these things in hundreds of years. Excavation had to go very slowly and methodically. Petrovic wished for a tea-spoon of neutron stardust, as heavy and dense as Mount Everest—one spoonful would drop all the way to China, and the rest would be easy. The Kronenbergs had built on top of a much earlier building, just as whoever had been the owners of the candlesticks and Turk's head door knocker had built on top of the original thirteenth-century city which was built on top of Roman encampments.

They turned into another room, much larger than any of the others. Skeletons were laid out from end to end, perhaps there were a hundred, Shusterman couldn't tell. Each one had a number. That was the only way to identify them.

"Are all of these from the war?"

"Depends on which war you're talking about. Some were walking around at the time Newton was arguing with the Jesuits about his theory of color."

"What will happen to the bodies?"

"There will be more DNA testing. Maybe there will be some surviving family members who will want to bury the more recent dead, but this is unlikely, just as there are no more Kronenbergs to reclaim their property."

Above Shusterman's head the walls rebuilt themselves, herringbone brick patterns assembled into pointed arches, but no openings were allowed for windows. As Karl Sauer's projector reassembled itself and clicked on, focus adjusted, reels began to spin, and a beam of light hit Sauer's private screen. Screams could be heard, crying, shouting, what did Sauer care? It was all in a day's work. There were many sections in the Kronenberg, even as a ruin, you could tell. It was as if it were a department store of possibilities: interrogation, censorship, imprisonment.

❋

## ADVERSARIA: ACCORDING TO PETROVIC

*When Petrovic studied architecture in Sarajevo, one of his classes was only thirty minutes long and held at different locations which were never easy to find, and it was impossible to predict what would be there when you arrived. The structure could have been reduced to rubble, much more degraded than the Kronenberg.*

*The class studied buildings which were most targeted: hospitals, newspaper offices, mosques, libraries, synagogues, things like that. Because of the constant shelling, at the end of class, the professor would tell the class where they would meet next, so the location was always shifting.*

*For his final project he designed an apartment that could be convert-*

*ed instantly into a survival shelter. Sofa, tables and beds, other pieces of furniture, all had wheels on their sides. Quickly flipped and braked, they could serve as barricades, blocking windows and doors. He also designed containers that could be attached to exterior walls to collect rainwater since all plumbing would be gone.*

*During one of the thirty-minute classes, they were crossing a street when shelling came out of nowhere. This could happen. A sniper from a husk of a high-rise, or someone with a long-range rifle positioned who knows where, put the class in his sights. Petrovic looked around for some idea of shelter. What was a building? Four walls and roof? That could be a rare thing. The shooting could have gone on all day, and maybe it did, only switching to another direction, but when the sound stopped, the teacher and many students lay in the street. Some lived. Some didn't.*

*Petrovic had no expectations that a crane would appear from out of nowhere, hoist him up and out and deposit him in a semi-attached house on the other side of the Atlantic. An uncle helped with his immigration and, almost overnight, he became an exterminator, wearing a green jumpsuit with an apprehensive-looking cartoon roach ironed onto the suit's back. He carried a canister of poison spray from apartment to apartment in an American city, then returned when the war ended and became a salvage man. He gave up on ever making a decision on whether to build or rebuild. Developers love him until he starts finding bodies.*

Petrovic and his team had to get back to work, so he needed to show Shusterman out. Shusterman asked if he could take pictures, and he took quite a few of the chambers, skeletons, bullet-marked walls. At the last minute he bent over the tarp, as if taking pictures for the documentary that would never be made, and put a typewriter key, the letter A, in his pocket.

Walking back through the Prater, he stopped at the ball-shaped structure that was the entire landmass of the Republic of Kugelmugel, a territory established by a man named Edwin Lipburger. The nation, consisting primarily of a spherical house, had seceded from Austria around the time Abril disappeared in another hemisphere. Relocated to the Prater, its self-proclaimed address was #2 Antifaschismusplatz. In the rain, the house's terracotta siding became slick, and the sphere looked like a wet spaceship. If the Republic became unmoored, it could roll wherever gravity and inclines took it. To live in a mobile microstate might not be a bad thing, Shusterman thought: a traveling kingdom, vehicular citizenship. If only he and Abril had known about this place, they could have become citizens and been safe, but if so, would they have found themselves, like Karl Freund, living in the hills above Los Angeles, shooting *I Love Lucy*, glad to be alive, but perhaps dreaming of the lost kingdom of *Metropolis*?

Stopping at an internet café, he sent an email to Alma. Sauer was hallucinating at the time of death, LSD administered by Metta G., but he probably didn't die penniless. Alma had written that she hadn't been able to determine where his resources came from, but where did it all go after he was killed by Leni Riefenstahl in rhino form? Who did he leave his money and personal effects to? Could she go to whatever probate court was in Buenos Aires? Could she find out?

From the café, he made his way back to Leopoldstadt, passing the statue of Karl Lueger, standing on his plinth, hands over his heart, square cut beard stained with bird shit. Four lesser figures representing some aspect of Lueger's tenure as mayor occupied the corners of the base. One of these, a shirtless young worker holding a glass tube, had been painted over with spray paint so he was feminized.

A man and a woman, rival street orators, were screaming at each other from opposite sides of the memorial. The woman was young, in a checkered coat, violet hair stuck out from under her hat. She was drowned out by the man, an older gent, who yelled, despite appearing to be almost in tears, about toxins that crept into their city like a plague of extraterrestrials, they were that foreign, and like aliens, because that's what they were, the contagion they spread in the form of their persons needed to be quarantined, then sent back to where it came from, snail slime trail cleaned up, disinfected. There were people who penetrated their borders who originated in lands of unmentionable horrors, he knew that was true, but those horrors, which must exist for a reason, were their own damn problems. *Dirt is matter out of order*, he yelled. He went on to describe small groups that controlled the flow of information, a form of mind control, you didn't even know it was happening. One of the listeners sobbed that he was telling the truth, finally someone was. A few repeated *Dirt is matter out of order*. Shusterman was mesmerized by the shouting match, trying to identify their accents, native to the city, he guessed. The high emotional register of the tearful but angry man seemed to have an effect on the small crowd of listeners. It was as if they were all hypnotized by his theatrical demonstration of anguish and loss that was not just his alone, but belonged to all of them. Someone started throwing bottles at the young woman, one grazed the side of Shusterman's head. The aim seemed intentional, given where he was standing. He tried to find her bright coat, but she had run away.

Shusterman moved on. He had things to do. He bought a flash-light and a small shovel at a hardware store, then went to a sushi bar that was about the size of a small corridor, and sat as unobtrusively as possible at the counter, shovel balanced on the floor, knocking against his knees. The waitress stared with bafflement and distaste. In New York, he felt, no one would notice if he brought a shovel into a place like this, but here, it registered that he didn't consider the restaurant fine dining, or that he didn't know how to behave, even in a hole in the wall such as this. He apologized and said he planned to work in his garden, but his comment came out of nowhere, she hadn't asked about the implement, why he had it, or requested that he leave. Shusterman followed her gaze and said the shovel had been on sale. He could tell the waitress didn't really understand him, but it was too early in the night to return to Nachtfalterallee, and he needed to spend at least an hour in the sushi bar, more if possible.

He didn't want to go back to #39 too soon, so kept ordering sake. The waitress seemed to have decided it was better to just serve him and leave him alone. There was no one else in the restaurant anyway.

Spiderman climbed up the building's façade, putting one foot on the head of a figure of Neptune and the other balanced on the crook of Apollo's elbow; his gloved hand appeared to grasp a random arrow. Spiderman didn't need statues and friezes to make his ascent, but when film met palace, that was how it appeared. In the plaza below, a dozen people in masks acted out a performance that included enemies of Spidie such as Hobgoblin, Morbius, and Rhino, while other performers played an assortment of prime ministers and presidents. Shusterman didn't completely understand the relationship between the movie in outdoor projection format and the performance, but he was willing to watch for a few minutes. One trio beatboxed in English with undercurrents of their native accents percolating through.

*I'm your Berlin Wall '89*
*You still think everything is fine*
*But you really are behin'*
*'Cause everything you have is mine*

They went on to rhyme about barricades made of gun parts meant to keep foreigners out but which could be scaled by Spiderman, lots of Spidermen, even if the walls were as high as the moon. He wondered if Metta had put anything in his tea, but if she had, he would have felt the effects hours ago, and it would have reacted badly with all the sake he drank, so he went with the assumption everyone in the crowd saw and heard exactly what he did.

Shusterman looked up at the projection again. Spiderman was from Queens, just as he was. In the scene of Peter Parker visiting his aunt and uncle, Shusterman half expected Agent Myers to walk into the frame singing *It's quarter to three, there's no one in the place except you and me,* leaning on a kitchen counter, gesturing to a woman in the audience, one so young she was born after he had died, then he would turn to Shusterman and tell him it was time to hit the road, don't be such a punk, Jesus.

There had been no Spidery wall-climbers in his neighborhood. Parkour and buildering didn't exist back then. Everyone he knew or remembered was earthbound when they were alive, and now they were all dead and buried. None of his friends had been able to shoot strands of spider web from their wrists and swing from tower to tower. If someone had climbed the Unisphere, the giant globe still in place after the 1964 World's Fair closed, Shusterman hadn't known about it. *Spiderman can take many forms*, a trio chanted atonally in German. Shusterman understood that much of what they were saying, so he stayed a little longer. He needed to be sure it was well into the night when he arrived at #39 Nachtfalterallee. The derelict building waited for Kronenbergs who would never return. He had been welcome to visit the site during the day, but the ongoing excavations cramped his style. He wanted access to the forbidden upper floors, dangerous and strictly off limits.

The walk to Leopoldstadt, involved skirting crowds that spilled out of cafés and bars, but the sound of talking and shouting had the effect of an ocean of speech that carried him along in its currents as if he were a plastic bottle tossed overboard with no logical place in the ecosystem he found himself in. Only a few weeks earlier, when he was shutting down his business, giving away his recordings archive, sweeping up the last of the ape fur the cleaner had missed, when he imagined the city he was traveling to, he pictured men with dueling scars across their faces and women smelling of wet felt jackets and chocolate, simultaneously nauseating and compelling. Now he made his way through crowds looking at their phones, adjusting running shoes, or hailing cabs, and to all of them, he was invisible.

On a street corner near the Donaukanal, a woman wrapped in scarves hawked DVDs. She held them out, fan-shaped, in each hand and at arms' length, like a flamenco dancer. She pushed them toward one person, then another. Ignored or shoved away, no one wanted her thin, pirated copies. The packages sealed in plastic could have contained nothing at all—a low-level street scam—but when she pushed a fan of *Hellboy, Dr. Strangelove*, and *Mad Max* at Shusterman, he handed her a fistful of euro. Her German, hard to understand through the scarves, betrayed origins further east. As soon as he was out of sight, he was about to toss the DVDs into the trash, when he stopped, unable to, and instead lined them up, leaning against the windows of a shoe store before he continued on his way.

Shusterman intended to explore unhindered by salvage man, Petrovic, and his crew. They didn't work at night. If no watchman was on duty Shusterman could do whatever he wanted. For what he wanted to do, there should be no one looking over his shoulder. A spade rattled in his bag alongside a hard hat with a light attached. Even during the day, sunlight barely pierced the Kronenberg's abandoned rooms, and he hoped it would be possible to take decent pictures without much illumination. Shusterman had no intention of looting the site, but if he found, for example, a plaque with Sauer's name and title on it, a quick yank with a crowbar, and it would be his. Everything about #39 was a crime scene. Nothing he pocketed was going to change any outcome.

As he was about to turn onto Nachtfalterallee, a man approached him, slowing down when he came within a few feet, and making eye contact, as if to ask him directions. He wore a black and white Liverpool FC away jersey under a black hoodie, but he said nothing as he pointed to a woman in the back of what looked like an Audi that was first driven off the lot twenty years earlier. Shusterman asked in German, then in English, if she were ill and did they need help? English was totally unknown to the man, so Shusterman guessed the shirt came out of a donation bin. Liverpool shirt must have understood some German, because he shook his head. No, she wasn't ill. Taking Shusterman's arm, he tried to steer him toward the back door of the Audi. Nachtfalterallee was a narrow street, two blocks long; it was deserted and likely to stay that way until morning. It dawned on him what the man was selling, and he shook his head, but Liverpool shirt wouldn't leave him alone. Shusterman finally broke away, but when he turned to look back, another man was being detained and did get into the car.

There was no watchman or security guard stationed anywhere on the street, and this was a relief. Although the site had been the subject of public debate and in the news, it wasn't as if a gold mine had been unearthed. Number 39 looked like a dead zone of crap masonry, grids of iron bars sticking out of the dirt, pieces of machinery whose functions were unknown and probably obsolete, or possibly used to administer pain. Though the original entrance to the building was inaccessible from the street, it was easy for Shusterman to duck under the barred entrance and descend the wooden ladder to the pit. With no trouble at all, he was in.

Some corridors and rooms were without ceilings and open to the stars; others supported two or three floors, relatively intact overhead. An interior staircase led from the basement to the ground floor and what had been the lobby of the Kronenberg. It was dangerous to go up into that part of the building already so damaged by the wrecking ball before demolition was called off. The stairs themselves were unstable, but as far as Shusterman knew, they were the only way to access what was left of the offices and rooms where Sauer worked. He began his ascent.

The lobby was full of junk and pieces of plaster that had fallen off the walls in large chunks. Underneath was another layer, an inscrutable palimpsest of markings and rat holes, and above an arch Shusterman made out the letters ℜ r o. An elevator shaft opened onto nothing, its ironwork cage a tangle of bars. A worn leather seat where a uniformed operator would have sat was bent at an angle that would have pinned his ghost to the paneling. Stairs to the second floor were marble, and though the risers were wood and rotten in places, Shusterman continued on.

Missing quite a bit of flooring, the second story looked like Swiss cheese, so he continued on to the third which appeared more solid, though not in great shape either. He tilted his flashlight downward, illuminating the missing patches, but a few yards in, his foot went through the flooring, and he nearly fell through. The sound of splintering wood and crashing tile echoed as the bits and pieces hit whatever lay below, but there was no one to hear it. Shusterman brushed off his pants and kept going. In one wing, in room after room, displayed on trays, racks, and mounted on walls, lenses coated with dust, some shattered, some intact, reflected his beam of light. There were lenses for telescopes, microscopes, cameras, maybe the odd pair of glasses. Scientific charts were still tacked to walls. Mice had long ago chewed through paper and cardboard, and in these rooms only glass remained.

The end of the corridor opened out into a large room, like a loft, bristling with ranks of metal filing cabinets, some upright, some overturned. There were leaking pipes and gaps in the ceiling where rain had been dripping through for years, so many filing cabinets were rusted shut, but when he was able to, he slid open a drawer, dislodging colonies of bugs. Most files were empty or contained moldy lumps of paper reduced to pulp. The fragments were so old and inscrutable, they might as well have originated on Mars.

Then, in one alcove, he found some yellowed envelopes embossed with the Kronenberg logo, an image of an eye behind a lens, and mixed with these were other papers, accounting ledgers and production lists of film equipment. Beyond the forest of file cabinets was a row of metal shelves containing reels of film. Leaking pipes had damaged the labels, but here and there he could make out a few letters of what looked like *Staatliche Filmzensur* on some and *Sauerfilmproduktionfirma* on others. Whether the contents of the cans contained censored films or propaganda, and what those looked like, was impossible to know. Shusterman opened can after can but all were either solid discuses or just flakes of celluloid.

"Perhaps this is what you are looking for?"

The light on a hard hat flicked on. Petrovic stood a few yards away. He appeared out of nowhere, like a twentieth-century holo-gram, but very much aware of his startling appearance, an alien cov-ered in luminous dust, without eye stems, pincers, or advanced and inscrutable technology, yet uncannily able to find and interpret the signs of the dead. Only someone skilled at silence and invisibility, familiar with the building's nooks and crannies, would know how to navigate undetected.

"I heard someone crash through the floor, so I took the lift up."

Shusterman knew only half of this was true. He may have risen through the floorboards, but not via the dead elevator. Even if it wasn't a wreck, there was no electricity. Who was he kidding? The salvage man had a small ax or hatchet stuck in his belt. It was one of the tools of his trade, but Petrovic's pose was reminiscent of one of Sauer's Bavarian woodsman figures, and the idea of being hacked to pieces by someone who, though not Tyrolean, reminded him of them, would have been ideal Sauerian revenge.

"You're living here? Squatting?"

Petrovic didn't answer but told him he was actually glad to see him. He wore black gloves and held up a sheaf of papers. He stepped forward to hold the papers inches from Shusterman's nose, as if they were a prize both explosive and of unimaginable value. The script was old Gothic, illegible to him, and Shusterman's only response was to look puzzled, as the salvage man insisted what he'd found was worth something and he was offering Shusterman a good deal. He used the expression *getting in on the ground floor.*

"It's the deed to this property establishing ownership by the Kro-nenberg family," Petrovic explained. "Looks original, no? I think it is, and there are people who would pay good money for this document."

"I'm sure there are, but you must understand, I'm not one of them." Shusterman slowly began to realize that Petrovic, like himself, had come in the middle of the night to loot.

"The Kronenberg factory is over one hundred years old, maybe more, but what was here before? Nobody cared about #39 until the skeletons started turning up. And then other, much older skeletons raised a finger, gave a nod, so to speak. A forensic architect would have a lot of work here, foundations on top of foundations, the old dead make way for the new dead."

What he described was a cartography of brutality. Abril's disappearance in another city, that would be a map of another kind of brutality, skeletons at the bottom of what? Animated lines of different colors, some dotted, some solid, moving from house to house, taking off from helipads or hidden airports and once airborne, bodies, other animated lines, dropped into the Rio Plata, the Atlantic Ocean. No precise bathymetric maps of that particular underwater terrain, high-pressure aquatic incognito. Human femur nestled against oyster shell or dinosaur bones scattered on the slope of a deep-sea volcano, so gone, so remote: the dream come true of the saurian Sauer.

Petrovic sat in a wooden swivel chair, Shusterman on a pile of film cans. They spoke as if having a business meeting which, in a way, they were. Shusterman could not be persuaded to buy the deed to the site, so Petrovic pulled another object out of his backpack, a series of drawings wrapped in what he explained was acid-free archival paper.

"Maybe this would interest you? They were found in a metal box under one of the really old stiffs. As you can see, they're like cartoon panels but drawn before cartoons existed. For you, a steal. I'll give you the insider discount." Before he let Shusterman take the drawings, he brought out a pair of rubber gloves from the backpack and insisted he put those on first.

Shusterman wasn't an expert, but he would guess the drawing style and the age of the paper were hundreds of years old. The figures of humans looked sort of like medieval manuscript illumination, but wearing clothes of a later era, drawn by someone who was not really trained as an artist, so the figures were flat and expressionless, but looked like porn, or porn of that time. What year exactly? He didn't know. Pornography of the early Enlightenment, whatever that might be.

"Again, thank you, but in this I have no interest, and don't possess those kinds of resources."

"You're an American. You work for a television station. You have resources."

"The deed would mean a lot to someone. Those drawings, too." Shusterman nudged Petrovic's bag away from the water. "You can still make money here."

❋

## ADVERSARIA: ACCORDING TO SHUSTERMAN, 1969

*Shusterman had a summer job in high school, working in a junk store. People found all kinds of trash in their attics, basement, stuff people left behind in their apartments for the next person to find, someone who might think that broken watch was worth something. Maybe that ashtray had belonged to JFK, maybe that rock was an ancient arrowhead. Everyone who walked in had a story. Nothing was simply a broom or a mop, but a treasure that had escaped the jaws of the Russian revolution, or the deck of the Titanic, only to land in a junk shop on Atlantic Avenue. Mostly they were knuckleheads who left with their pockets stuffed with disappointment, but one day a man walked in with a collection of first-edition Superman comics beginning from June 1938. Shusterman thumbed through pictures of U-boats and Japanese Zero fighter planes tossed so far into space, the inker implied, they were landing somewhere outside the frame. The comics were pristine, unread, left by a soldier who went to D-Day and never returned, found years later in the basement of a house in Flatbush. The seller had nothing but disdain for comics and thought they were worth less than the paper they were printed on.*

*Shusterman had looked at the comics with wonder. He still relished talking about the find. The dealer let him touch them because he wanted to convey how valueless they were. In a 1943 issue, Superman dumped Hitler and Stalin on the floor of the League of Nations on charges of unprovoked aggression against defenseless nations. Meanwhile Lois Lane's proto-juvenile delinquent niece, Susie Tompkins, met the S-Man. A few issues later, Lois Lane got a blood transfusion that gave her the same fantastic powers as Superman himself. Shusterman couldn't put them down.*

*His boss sniffed at the cheap paper and offered the man $30, which he grabbed, thinking them fools to pay that much for a stack of comics when new ones only cost a couple of bucks, total. The dealer turned around and sold them for thousands, but he was robbed shortly after that. Someone was watching the shop and knew what time he closed up. As if he'd been touched by, if not an angel, but by Superman, he bludgeoned the robber with a Big Boy. The Big Boy, from the fast-food chain that often featured a revolving figure in red and white pants holding a hamburger aloft, had been about four feet high, made of metal.*

�֎

"Finding the right buyer is trouble. You're here now." It almost sounded like a threat.

"The buyer will come to you."

"I don't want to bargain. I just want to sell." He quickly shed the black marketeer identity when the rich American television producer who seemed to have fallen into his lap turned out to have empty pockets. Petrovic was a shrug-and-whatever kind of looter.

"My point is that you don't always know what you're staring at, even when it seems obvious," Shusterman offered.

"You think I don't know that? Mostly, what I dig up is other people's garbage. I don't want to be the arbiter of what's valuable and what isn't. I need a rich buyer who drives up in his Mercedes and asks no questions. You're not that guy. You sneak around at night and break in. You have no chauffeur. I know this now." Petrovic looked around as if someone might appear who would contradict him, but there was no one.

❀

## ADVERSARIA: ACCORDING TO PETROVIC

*Once his every-meeting-in-a-different-location class was supposed to assemble at a site, ruins like the one on Nachtfalterallee, but maybe he got the day wrong, because no one showed up. As he waited, he wandered around, and you find, when you do this, that maybe someone just like you lived in this place. What he found here: a pinball machine. Petrovic loved pinball. This one was pretty beat up, but still functional, and miracle of miracles, there was electricity in the ruin. You could plug it in and play, so he did until he heard sniper shots, but then a kid arrived with a hand truck. He wanted the pinball machine, and assumed they were going to enter into a slugfest to see who would be the new owner. Petrovic didn't want it and tried to persuade the kid that the mechanical game, any game, wasn't worth it. The shooting was close by. He should quickly go to whatever home was for him and come back when the shooting was over. The kid said, it will never be over. Petrovic couldn't argue on this point, and so helped him load the thing onto the hand truck, and off they went, a moving target.*

❀

Petrovic had a bottle of whiskey and he offered Shusterman a drink, which he accepted. It would be dawn soon. The salvage man turned looter assembled his bits and pieces.

"It's hard to find a black cat in a dark room." Petrovic summed up the attitude of looking for objects that might not want to be found.

"Especially if there is no cat." Shusterman wasn't thinking about things, but people.

"And then, even worse, it turns out there's no room." The salvage man could always do one better.

"Petrovic, look, there is no film about urban archeology in central European cities. I'm not a television producer. My bank account has to stretch for I don't know how long or what will happen when it's empty. I'll limp back to someplace." With another drink, Shusterman divulged the real reason for his breaking and entering.

"Then maybe I have something that will interest you. Let's take these other stairs, here." Petrovic pointed to a narrow stairway behind a bookcase. "The way you came up, those are about to cave in."

"Was this a passage that people could hide in?"

"Who knows." Petrovic's inflection didn't articulate this sentence as a question but a statement of fact, and they descended back down into the basement.

Cold rain made the cellar feel like winter, but despite the darkness and chill, where earth was exposed to even small amounts of sunlight, plants had started to grow. Shusterman hadn't noticed them before, but now they made a brief appearance in the beam from Petrovic's hard hat. The vines, weeds, and saplings were excessively pale, like creatures that lived in caves who evolved without eyes or pigment, these plants were surviving with minimal chlorophyll. They had found cracks in the concrete, in the brick and raw earth, and were reclaiming part of the street for the first time since pre-Roman days. It reminded Shusterman of a tree he'd seen growing out of a chimney of an abandoned church in Queens. The building was at least four stories high, and though it was falling apart, squatters had taken up residence in it. No one was going to remove the tree, its roots heading downwards toward the apse, breaking up a ceiling painting of clouds and angels.

Below a room that had housed a boiler dating from the 1930s, there was another room, very old, Petrovic said, from the seventeenth century, not much of it was left that you would even call a room, it was faced with limestone which acts as a preservative. In this particular pit he found a skeleton without a head. Beside it was a can of film labeled *Sauerfilmproduktionfirma*. Shusterman ran his flashlight around the room. It was empty.

"So days before he was embraced by rhino Leni, Karl was able to break into the boarded-up Kronenberg and take a trip down memory lane, getting reacquainted with the remains of those who were tortured in the same building."

"The skeleton was not from your man's lifetime. He found it and hid this film he didn't want anyone to see. The body, when we unearthed it, was moved to the large chamber you saw, the place where all the remains are kept, dated, and catalogued until it can be determined where they will be housed permanently, in which archive, in which museum, or will they be buried in a cemetery like everyone else? So let me tell you, what was remarkable about this skeleton with whom Sauer left this film was that it was identified as female, originating from Sub-Saharan east Africa."

A slave, Petrovic explained, kept by the pleasure house. Things were found near it, a fragment of a Koran, a map of the Balkans wrapped in vellum that had protected it from the elements, and a knife with an ebony handle. The top of the body had been draped with a shawl, stained with a substance that when tested, and the relevant proteins fluoresced, turned out to be blood. No head was recovered until that afternoon. In pulling up a sapling, Petrovic had found a skull. Tied around it was a piece of fabric that was the same as the fabric found with the skeleton. He had found the head he believed matched the body.

Shusterman wasn't interested in the head.

"Where's the film?"

"It's still here." From the limestone room, Petrovic led him back through the chamber where skeletons were laid out end to end, to a hall of locked rooms where the more valuable artifacts were kept. On a shelf between erotic netsuke was a film can labeled *Versteckt in Einfacher Sicht, Produzent und Regisseur durch Karl Sauer zum Sau-*

*erfilmproduktionfirma. Hidden in Plain Sight, Produced and Directed by Karl Sauer for Sauer Film Production Company.* The can was half covered with olive paint, but it was in much better shape than the ones upstairs. Barely nicked or dented, it was possible it contained not war propaganda at all, but the more recent 1970s footage.

"The outside looks like it's in good shape, but I would need to open it to know the state of the film, and even then, I'd have to find a projector capable of screening the movie, otherwise it's just a plate of plastic you could eat off of." Shusterman wanted the film, but there was no way of knowing if the contents of the can were still a viable movie.

"So this interests you. This you can use. Five thousand dollars."

"I am interested in the film, but I don't have five thousand dollars."

There was no way he could afford to blow that much of what was left of the ape movie money on this relic, but it may have been exactly what he'd traveled to the city to find. They were silent. Water dripped from overhead pipes, and squirrels could be heard pattering on the remains of the ceiling. It would be morning soon.

Petrovic spun the film can on the floor. It looked like a lambent soccer ball before falling flat. "I need the money, that's all."

"The other stuff you have is worth more. You can find buyers if you look in the right channels."

Petrovic repeated the word *channels* as if it were something ridiculous and faintly obscene. Shusterman didn't care. He wanted the film.

"You know, Mr. Shusterman, I'm a preservationist, but also a junk man. I'm supposed to be interested in look-how-rare and care about who owned what, and what is saved, but the truth is everything ends up just ground to bits by the lithosphere."

Shusterman handed him two hundred euro, folded into a wad that the salvage man pocketed without unfolding or counting. They had another drink, then Petrovic told him he should go. It would be daylight soon.

As Shusterman made his way back to the surface, he heard the sound of footsteps somewhere ahead of him that couldn't possibly have belonged to Petrovic, who remained below. He stopped walking, but the tapping of footsteps continued. He called out to Petrovic, but no one answered, so he walked out of #39 with the film under his arm, just as the sun was rising.

*Hidden in Plain Sight* was an invisible nothing if it couldn't be screened, and finding a projector on which to view it would be like looking for another kind of relic. He called the only person he knew in the city: Metta Götz.

Metta's husky voice reflected an undercurrent of irritation. Had he woken her up? No, she was an early riser and was about to meditate with her coach. She wasn't thrilled to hear from him again, and assumed they had no further reason for any kind of conversation. When he said he had a copy of *Hidden in Plain Sight*, her tone became animated and nervous, even high-pitched. She knew the film. In fact, she'd had a part in it as a baby carried by an actress who played an American woman looking across the Atlantic, eager to greet German soldiers who were surely on their way to bring the joys of Reichlife to New England or Florida or wherever mother and baby were supposed to be. Jurgen had also played an American citizen, though he and Metta appeared in separate, unrelated scenes. It was not one of his most important roles, but according to Metta, even his minor parts were emblematic of greatness. Shusterman hoped the label on the can was a decoy, and an altogether different kind of propaganda was spooled within, but he revealed none of this to Metta.

A few hours later, she called with what she stated at the outset was wonderful news; she found someone who had a film projector and a theater, not an actual theater, a tiny storefront of a micro-cinema, what in Berlin were called flea circus cinemas, and, of course, they had them in her city, also. She gave him the address of Das Kollektiv für das Lebendige Kino. There was one other screening that evening, but it was later, so the manager of Das Kollektiv, an American named Frances Baum, would meet them there.

The storefront was on a narrow street in Leopoldstadt, not far from where Shusterman was living. In the window, which was mostly painted over, were posters for Robert Flaherty's *Nanook of the North* and Maya Deren's *Meshes of the Afternoon*. Metta waited for him outside, cigarette in one hand, cane in the other, tapping, impatient. Shusterman wasn't sure if she needed the cane for getting around or was using it for effect. If her expression wasn't so stern, she might break into a song and dance. She wore a fedora and a suit that may have belonged to her mother from the era when *Hidden in Plain Sight* was made. The jacket was tight, and she wore no shirt underneath, so a plunging V of powdered white skin was visible between the wide lapels. A carefully folded handkerchief poked out of one of the slanted pockets. It was a sad hint of formality and solemnity on her part. One passerby stared at her, but another, an oblivious girl listening to music while looking at her phone, knocked into Metta, who stumbled but was able to catch herself.

A woman opened the door for them, introduced herself as Frances Baum, and told her to put out her cigarette, please. Typical American, Metta snapped, oblivious to the fact that Das Kollektiv was doing them a favor. Frances had lived in the city for many years but looked like she still dreamed of *Rancho Notorious*: cuffed jeans, Western-style plaid shirt with snaps and a palm tree stitched over a pocket, black hair cut with bangs that met in a V over her eyebrows. She wore an eye patch over one eye that Metta stared at in a way that was obvious and blunt. The room that served as a theater was narrow, populated by an assortment of chairs from bench seats pulled from cars and buses to dented metal folding chairs that were arranged in four rows. There was no projection booth, just an old projector positioned on a table at the back, and a screen at the front.

Shusterman handed Frances the can and gave her a version of its history. The manager/projectionist pried open the two halves with a jack knife. Shusterman was worried the film stock might suddenly vaporize when it encountered oxygen, and trusted Frances, who was supposed to be a pro at handling the stuff, knew what she was doing, though there was no guarantee this was so.

"That's some old celluloid," Frances said.

"1970s old?"

"No, older, I would guess."

"But you can't know for certain until we screen the film, right?"

They spoke in English, which Metta understood, so she wasn't left out, and she was not amused by the one-eyed projectionist's comments. She sat on one of the seats pulled from a bus, crossed her legs, and looked annoyed.

"Enough commentary. Let's get going already. Miss Pirate, how much time does it take to thread a projector?" Ignored, Metta stared at a poster for an ethnographic film about an Amazonian tribe and snapped her lighter on and off.

Frances held a strip of the fragile film up to the light. It would bear up for one viewing, maybe two, if the sprockets were undamaged. The edges of the stock showed signs of corrosion and a dusting of mold in some places. She could make no promises. As she threaded up the film, Frances explained she worked as a guide for English-speaking tourists, and a couple of years ago started showing old movies to friends. She lived in a small room upstairs accessed by a spiral staircase at the back, but had this storefront, so thought she might as well use it. Eventually a few more people, friends of friends, heard she was doing the odd screening of sixteen- and thirty-five-millimeter films, and so others she didn't know showed up from time to time, but never very many, just enough to be entertaining for a small group. It wasn't a moneymaking venture and was never meant to be.

"You're from Detroit," Shusterman said. "You have the north city vowel shift. Your long e's sound like the i in mirror which you pronounce meer like meerkat."

"I've never been to Detroit," Frances said.

"You have glottal stops at the end of words when you say Detroi. You replace t's with d's as in cidy. Sounds like Chicago but different."

"I've never been to Detroit," Frances repeated, emphasizing the t sound at the end of the word.

"So why are you here?" Metta asked, though she appeared or tried to appear as if mostly ignoring them.

She told them a story about traveling with a boyfriend who had to return stateside for a few weeks. He was supposed to meet her in Vienna, but he never returned. Frances stayed. She didn't have all that much to go back to.

"Accents can be hard to lose. They betray origins, among other things." Shusterman couldn't believe he had been wrong, but now her accent was more deliberately different. He couldn't place it. Some inflection he was sure betrayed childhood origins, as if she'd lived with Russian parents or grandparents. Frances was what was known as an accent chameleon. He wanted her to keep speaking till he got it right.

"Could we please start the film, please?" Metta had unpinned her fedora, stretched her legs. One cracked high heel clattered to the floor.

Frances told her to hold her horses while she finished threading the projector. The process, which he hadn't seen in years, reminded Shusterman of when he was a child and movies would be shown in class from time to time. If he was lucky enough to sit in the back, near the machinery, he would watch the serpentine path of the film through the machinery until it looked like a Brontosaurus in profile. *Hidden in Plain Sight* was in bad shape, it had to be handled slowly and carefully. Frances spoke to herself as she threaded: flat against aperture gate, under the pressure roller, around the sound drum, over the sprung idler, under the snubber roller. Then she turned off the lights, flipped a switch, and the film whirred to life, as Shusterman found a seat. Dust motes floated on rays emanating from the lens.

The first scenes were of a small American town. The voiceover said the town could not be named, but it was just like many others. The burg didn't look particularly American, but there were flags flying everywhere. There were shots of friendly postmen, doctors, teachers, policemen, everyone going about their business with smiles on their faces which transitioned into frowns of concern when discussing the war or listening to the news on the radio. After about ten minutes, the voiceover faded and a scene began with a fireman played by Metta's father, who was supposedly speaking in American English to a woman he encountered on the street. Their own voices were dubbed in German, but if you didn't recognize the actors you might be duped into thinking these were actual Americans having a friendly conversation about how the Reich had some sound ideas, especially regarding the subject of race which was a big issue on their shores. Gradually, it became apparent, this was not an introduction to a dramatic film, but a fiction that was presented as if an actuality, a newsreel, or a kind of bogus documentary film. Minor or unknown German actors who would not be recognized played Americans, dubbing their own speech in German, though the sound track was garbled. The implication was that Americans wholeheartedly supported the Reich and would welcome the troops who would liberate them from the tyranny of Roosevelt and MacArthur. The U-boats would receive a hero's welcome whether they landed in Bar Harbor, Miami, or the Brooklyn Navy Yard. Baby Metta was held up and told to wave toward unseen boats and planes speeding their way across the Atlantic.

Frances howled with laughter.

Scenes of lantern-lit meetings in the bridge between ship captains of opposing navies—one was wearing a Coast Guard's uniform, it looked like. Apprehension turned to smiles and handshakes. Planes landed in fields to welcoming characters, smiling, waving semaphores. Parachutists dropping into backyards got warm receptions, were led into kitchens where they were served hot dogs and pie while blond children gathered round in awe and respect. These interior and exterior scenes could have been shot anywhere. The boat could have been a set, actors swaying to reproduce the motion of waves. What followed were exteriors of cities in which the middle ground contained gothic buildings found nowhere in the United States, despite the American flags draped from every other lamp post. This was all a hoax. Then came a scene in a diner. Two men in fedoras, wearing dark glasses. One passed a piece of paper to the other. A close-up of the unfolded paper. It was a map of the coast.

Frances paused the frame, and they could make out the edge of Maine, arm of Cape Cod, Long Island, and down to New Jersey.

Next: cut to a street scene in New York.

"Wait," Shusterman said. "I recognize that corner."

Frances reversed the film, then played it forward in slow motion.

"That's Thirty-Fourth Street and Seventh Avenue. It looks different now, but I'm pretty sure that's the corner. If you look closely, you can make out the street sign."

"They could have made a city street sign that looked accurate, easy."

"But the rest of the street. That's not a set."

"Whoever shot this part, I don't think his name will be listed in the credits, but he rolled his camera somewhere in New York, sent the footage to Sauer, left no findable trail."

Twenty minutes further into *Hidden in Plain Sight*, Shusterman saw it: Utopia Parkway, followed by his old block in Queens, not exactly his house, his street, but close to it, then cut to Peter Parker's neighborhood. His family hadn't moved there yet. In fact, his parents hadn't even met, but the blocks of brick row houses were the same. Metta was right. Some of the footage was real. Someone shot neighborhoods in New York and possibly other cities, mailed pieces of film to *Sauerfilmproduktionfirma*, where Karl spliced them into shots of temporarily Americanized Berlin and Vienna suburbs, as if to prove, we are everywhere, and we are waiting for you.

The soundtrack gave few clues. The voiceover, where it was intelligible, made absurd statements. Shusterman had thought of speech like an estuary system, linking, connecting, but also creating boundaries. We say speech flows, it's intangible, travels along airwaves, an invisible river, intelligible to many, but not to all. Isolated syllables of accents and continuous accentuation reveal an undercurrent of origins and influences—this he knew, and he strained to hear something that would tell him the truth. Voiceprints, even if he could map them on the spot, would tell him nothing. The dubbing, even if it was theatrical, covered all tracks. For Sauer, information was a weapon. Verbs were machine guns; nouns were tanks. If you were canny, clauses and metaphors were as good as the Luftwaffe.

The final credits rolled, and it was once again affirmed that this was the work of Karl Sauer.

"Welcome to Cape Cod, menschen!" Frances coughed from laughing as she spoke. "We're so pleased to see you! Have some lobster, *etwas hummer*, some saltwater taffy, *etwas salzwasser toffee!* It's like *The Russians Are Coming*, but with Panzers."

"I don't see what is the comedy here?" Metta's eyes were red. "Some people believed. It gave them a morale boost at the end, to believe out beyond the ocean there were Americans waiting for them, who saw us as liberators."

This wasn't the film he was looking for. But if the other film existed, it might look something like this, but cast with doomed people posing as actors instead of actors posing as ordinary people. There was also the subject of who performed as extras, of which there were many. In Riefenstahl's movies, or at least one that Shusterman knew of, Roma were extracted from the death camps to perform in a scene in a bar in which she danced. They were killed immediately afterward. The smiling, unknowing passersby in Sauer's *Hidden in Plain Sight*, the fake American documentary, could have had the same origins and met the same fate. They were expendable lives and they knew something of Sauer's secrets, how he made his newsreels, his theater.

Shusterman wanted to view the film again, to check the expressions—was each and every face truly a happy one? Did any of them look like they knew as soon as the final edit was cut that it was Zyklon B gas for them? Did those in the crowd, the ones who stood on the beach scanning the horizon, did any of them look not quite Aryan?

"Could we watch it again?"

"It will disintegrate. This could only be shown once. I'm not even sure the film can withstand the spinning and slight torquing of rewinding."

"No!" Metta sobbed. She twisted in her chair to look at Frances, as if for the first time. "There were people in your country who would have behaved as you see in this film. It's not untrue. It could be absolutely 100% true. Maybe it happened. You don't know. You weren't there. You can't know for certain. I was only in one scene. The others could have been shot in Atlantic City, in Baltimore, in Rockaway. As you said, the footage exists."

❈

## ADVERSARIA: ACCORDING TO FRANCES BAUM

*Metta isn't entirely wrong. There is footage that recorded a Nazi rally in Madison Square Garden in 1939 attended by 20,000 people, a roaring crowd, many long shots of arms going up like porcupine quills, but I still believe* Hidden in Plain Sight *is ridiculous.*

*One man, one protestor, rushed the stage while the leader of the German American Bund was speaking. The only person to challenge the 20,000 was a twenty-six-year-old plumber's assistant from Brooklyn, Isadore Greenbaum. You can see him being beaten, his clothes pulled off and the fear in his face. A child in uniform dances gleefully on stage while he's punched and kicked. Where is that child now? What kind of life did he go on to lead? Greenbaum was fined $25, a lot of money for Greenbaum and his wife to come up with. The judge said to him, didn't you realize people could be killed because of your actions?*

❈

"Suit yourself." Frances shrugged, then finished rewinding, quickly, no longer keeping an eye on the strip of film as it spun, so as to get rid of them as soon as possible. Returning the movie to its can, she handed it to Shusterman. Tiny pieces of shredded film where the edges of sprockets had come apart from the spinning reels and the motion of projector parts lay on the floor like a dusting of gritty snow. A film restorer might be able to repair *Hidden in Plain Sight,* so it could be seen again, but Frances told them she didn't know anyone who did that kind of work anymore. Maybe in Berlin.

Shusterman thanked the projectionist for her patience and tried to help Metta to her feet, but she pushed him away. She'd been given a brief visit to what was for her a happy, innocent time full of hopeful, scrubbed faces, a *gemeinschaft,* a feeling of joined hands, singing in unison, and she didn't want to let go of it. The truth was she'd been too young to remember any of these imaginary scenes, but since then her life had been one of running home and peering out windows, year after year, so a feeling of *gemeinschaft,* of belonging, that was something. She knew the expression *falsche gemeinschaft,* how the first word was attached to the second, but this feeling was not false. She would insist on it. She asked if she could sit still and meditate for a half hour. Would they leave her alone, please?

Frances said sorry, that she was screening *Jeanne Dielman,* a Chantal Akerman film, they needed to be on their way. She had to clean up, get ready for the next show.

Metta's response was to light a cigarette and blow smoke in her one eye. Shusterman took the cigarette from her and put it out on the concrete floor.

"Who is this Deal Mann who is so important I can't sit for a few minutes in silence?"

"It's the anniversary of the director, Akerman's, suicide. And even if it weren't, I have a show to run."

Metta said Akerman could wait. She wasn't going anywhere. It wasn't clear by *she*, did she mean Akerman, who was dead, or herself, who occupied her seat like a mule? Shusterman forcibly took Metta's bony elbow and told her they really did have to leave.

"Last time I do you bunch a favor," Frances said as she showed them to the door. It was raining lightly, and she handed them an umbrella from a cluster leaning against a corner, accumulated from people who had left them behind, forgotten. The door of Das Kollektiv slammed behind them.

Shusterman liked feeling the rain, so he put the film can under his coat, and didn't open the umbrella. Metta said, do you mind, not as a question, but as a command, and she took it from him. Some of the ribs were bent out of shape, rendering the umbrella marginally functional. She handed it back to him because he was taller, putting her hand on top of his as he grasped the handle. He could feel the warmth of her body, her wet powdery smell, and in trying to be more distant, even if only a matter of inches, walked awkwardly, thinking how she imposed her body, even in small ways. The experiment that was talking to Metta was over. He told her he would put her in a cab, but she shook her head. She wanted to walk.

"You think I'm a sea worm eating at the hull of your ship till we all sink."

"Did I say you were a sea worm? I don't think I did. It's raining. I'll put you in a cab."

"I am not a sea worm, Shusterman. Look, the woman who cleans my apartment is illegal. She's from Izmir, and she tells me she lives in a cardboard box in an alley with her children. I give her a lot of money, really, I do. I donate my castoff clothing to refugee centers, to detention centers, bathing suits, dresses that are too short, sleeveless. Is it my fault they don't wear these things? I tell them to alter the dresses for children, then."

They reached the building on which Spiderman had been projected. It was night, and the plaza in front of the building was empty.

A man in a gorilla suit passed out promotionals for a going-out-of-business sale at an electronics store whose flyers, in German and English, made statements about no more monkey business, the end of monkeying around, and for out of sight deals, shoppers should walk on the wild side. His shift was nearly over, so he bought a bottle of water from a kebab truck, sat on a bench, and removed his head. As he drank he stared at Metta as if she were the one in costume, and in a way, in her 1940s suit, she was. They had paused in front of a shop whose mannequins wore T-shirts with the Thor Steinar logo: an upwards arrow piercing a zigzag or backward N.

"Secondhand clothes, must be. There are no Thor Steinar shops in Vienna."

"You've looked?" Shusterman asked.

She didn't answer.

The smell of cumin, chili peppers, grilled lamb and onions wafted across the square. Shusterman was starving, so he bought some kebabs, offering one to Metta.

"I'm a vegetarian." She wrinkled her nose in disgust.

"Of course."

They sat next to the man in the gorilla suit, who shifted his head from the bench to the ground between his feet to accommodate the two of them. The rain had matted down his fake fur, but it didn't seem to bother him. He shrugged and said what the fuck, meaning, no big deal. Shusterman was reminded of an argument one of the actors had about a line in *Siege of Planet of the Apes*. He was stuck in a cage and was supposed to say, "Hey, what's the big deal?" Meaning, why have you done this to me all of a sudden?

The ape didn't like the expression, complaining that it sounded like a line from a Preston Sturges movie. Shusterman had nothing to do with the script, but he remembered the actor had said, "Maybe *Sullivan's Travels*, you know the one about a wealthy movie director who pretends to be a down-and-out homeless guy. In a moment of frustration, Joel McCrea might say, *Hey chumps, what's the big deal?*

Now, in the twenty-first century, folks say *what the fuck*. Somehow over the decades, *what's the big deal* is now *what the fuck?* I'd say this is a *what the fuck* situation. Stuck in a cage, that's a *what the fuck*."

Metta elbowed him.

"You will give me the film." She pointed to the can tucked under Shusterman's coat. "I'll have it restored, put online. It should be seen again."

"No way. I paid for this. It belongs to me."

"What a Jew. Okay. I'll pay you double whatever it cost you. You're afraid people will believe *Hidden in Plain Sight* is true. This film should belong to the world. Let people judge for themselves."

"*Hidden in Plain Sight* has Sauer's name on it. The credits prove his authority in production, endorsement, and promotion of its story. If the movie were shown to the world, Sauer, even dead Sauer, would be investigated, his assets frozen, restitution paid by his estate, his heirs, even now. As with looted art, heirs, if there were any, couldn't keep the money."

"I told you, I want to preserve the film, to show it widely."

"It would be in your interest to destroy what's probably the only copy."

Metta accused him of being a censor, worse than Sauer. The footage Frances described of the Madison Square Garden Rally, you could watch it in horror and think it could happen again, and in fact, had, but others could view those minutes of film with absolute delight.

"Don't let that dog out." Gorilla man turned to look at them. Up until that moment, he had given the impression that he wasn't listening to them.

"Mind your own business." Metta's voice crackled in German. The man replaced his head back on his shoulders, tossed the empty water bottle in a trash bin, collected his flyers from a plastic bag, and got back to work.

"You'd have to travel to Berlin to get it restored. Are you going to do that?"

"The post has been invented."

"You would trust international mail with the only copy of *Hidden in Plain Sight*?"

"Mr. Shusterman, Sauer is dead. He's unprosecutable. You can't unbury his crimes. Leave him alone. Leave me alone. What does any of it matter anymore?"

BACK IN HIS APARTMENT, Shusterman Skyped Alma. It was early in the morning her time, and when the picture snapped into focus he could tell the laptop was open on her bed. Tangled white sheets looked like a close-up of a mountain range, but he wasn't able to see much of the room itself. Alma smiled at him, got out of bed, carried the screen into the kitchen.

Talking about her late night spent on the roof looking for Magellanic Clouds, dwarf galaxies she'd been told could be seen with the aid of a telescope, but she hadn't found them, she set him on the kitchen table. He had sat in that kitchen every morning for almost two years. Myers had put his feet on the table—not that exact table, but a similar one in the same position, as he sang about clams falling in love.

Her hair was knotted into brown and blond ropes, and she was wearing glasses, squinting at the screen, then taking them off, rubbing her eyes. The rooms of someone who had just woken up were a glimpse into something private, not prepared or staged like the last time they Skyped. The neck of her T-shirt was stretched out around her shoulders, and she asked him to wait a minute while she made coffee. He could hear water running from the tap into the bottom half of an espresso pot, could see her screwing the two halves together and lighting the stove. He wished he were actually sitting opposite her in that apartment. She splashed some water on her face while waiting for the water to boil, rinsed a cup in the sink, and returned to the screen.

"Sorry to wake you."

"I'm hoping you just tapped me on the shoulder to see how I'm doing."

"I am."

"But you also have questions about the old man with a camera."

"Well, yes, but that's not the only reason." It wasn't, but he turned silent, unable to find convincing words.

"Maybe it wasn't quite what we thought, you know?" She poured coffee as she spoke. "There are times when I'm on a bus, for example, and I feel as if I've always been on that bus, and I always will be in some kind of continuous present, and no one knows or gives a shit what I remember."

❈

## ADVERSARIA: ACCORDING TO ALMA MERCADO

*The quest for Sauer's footprints reminds me of one of my clients, International Tango School, their logo: two pairs of dancing feet, one in men's shoes, the other high heels. The family of the International Tango School's director escaped Aleppo in the 1960s, surviving by a trade in relics from their own community, what they could smuggle out, which really wasn't much. Of particular interest was an object called the Aleppo Codex, read by Maimonides, ransomed from Cairo, smuggled out of Aleppo, and now most of it is kept in an archive in Jerusalem. Some pages are missing, believed stolen, and may have turned up in London, in Queens, in Rio, and here, too. Did they profit from this? Answer: unknown, but a few have knocked on the door of Tango International, looking for the missing pages. It annoyed the director of Tango International to no end. She feels culled from suspects because of her Aleppo family, but she was born here. No one believes or cares about her stories of a burning genizah, of searches and people hauled off in the middle of the night in 1957. She just wants to carry on with her business.*

*My client, Tango International, is a business which targets American and European women, a stealthy lonely hearts club, advertising that their happy clients often end up with lasting or semi-lasting relationships with their instructors. You enter the site to the sound of Astor Piazzolla, music selected to have general appeal, nothing too allegro, and animated footsteps mark the screen with tango steps, men's shoes, women's shoes appear and disappear as the music plays. There is actually quite a bit of text to translate besides the school's address and the bios of the instructors, some of which are really impressive, others maybe not as much. Not only does a client pick her instructors, but times of classes have to be coordinated based on travel dates. Later the business expanded into finding hotel accommodations, and Tango Tour Packages was born.*

*What has haunted me about this job, this client, was how I could be one of these women, and maybe I am. If a diaspora stream had taken my parents to New York or London or Amsterdam, provided they all survived, I could be one of these women, time marked by tango steps, a pattern on the floor, making the most of a hand on my back, on my shoulder.*

"Why don't you join me here?" Shusterman asked her.

Alma looked into her coffee. The pictureless telephone used to bevel the edges of awkward invitations; faces were invisible, expressions of joy or embarrassment only to be guessed at. Alma put her glasses back on and looked straight at him, as if to say, listen, you came out of nowhere and could return to nowhere, why should I uproot myself for that?

"Thank you, but I can't."

"I'll pay for your flight."

She talked about her work, what little there was, and how she could lose the lease on her apartment, and Shusterman believed her, sort of.

"If you change your mind." He made a sweeping gesture as if he would give her the entire city.

"You wanted to know about Sauer's will." Alma moved her coffee cup out of the frame. "I can tell you where the money was supposed to go."

Karl Sauer's estate was divided into equal thirds, distributed to: a German language film society headquartered in Berlin, Grenzen Filmgesellschaft, specializing in preserving films from the silent era; Horizontes Dorados hospice outside of Buenos Aires, which catered to the military, closed last year due to financial improprieties, but Sauer may not have known this was going on, or maybe he didn't care; and a Metta Götz, resident of Vienna.

The Republic of Kugelmugel, perched on Antifaschismusplatz, was defended by a chain-link fence and barbed wire, rendering the nation impassable at that hour. With the entire realm off limits, Shusterman walked on to the Wiener Riesenrad Ferris Wheel, stood in line, and boarded a car. The other occupants were French cyclists who refused to lock up their bikes and loaded them into the car, insisting over and over again to the operator that everything was fantastique, and then commenting on the sights, the unreal miniaturization produced as the car began to ascend. While revolving perpendicular to the surface of the city, Shusterman decided he needed to see Frances Baum again, but had no number for her. Das Kollektiv had a website but no contact information; it was entirely fly by night. He'd have to knock on the door in person.

Frances was not pleased to see him. Expecting a delivery, she opened the door, but then shook her head. Shusterman wedged his foot against the jamb and asked if she'd ever heard of Grenzen Filmgesellschaft? He needed to speak to someone who had worked for Grenzen for many years, at least since Sauer's death, if such a person existed.

"Yes," Frances said, "I knew the organization, and if they had such an archive, if they had someone like Sauer's work, they might not admit to it." She opened the door, ushering him into the theater. "Grenzen is run by a pair of eighty-year-olds, a brother and sister. It's only open something like alternate Tuesdays from ten to two."

The flea circus cinema was dimly lit. There was no screening that evening, but Frances had work to do. The show the following night was Lotte Reiniger's *The Adventures of Prince Achmed*, and she was checking the print on a Steenbeck. She could give him Grenzen's address, if it even still existed. Shusterman walked over to a coffee pot sitting on a hot plate and poured himself a cup.

"Make yourself at home," Frances said.

He wanted to see her alone, without the former child actress crying, smoking, demanding to meditate. The cause of anxiety that *Hidden in Plain Sight* hinted at: the cartography of countries yet to come. We're back, the footage said to him. If we were there in your backyard, and you didn't know it, what makes you think we were ever completely gone? He imagined actors turning to face the camera, saying: *Those Thor Steinar-like companies that make our clothing printed with our coded and not-so-coded symbols are very profitable even when bricks are thrown through our display windows. Glass can always be replaced. Orders made online. We're back, yo.*

Shusterman leaned against a wall on which black and white stills were pinned: a man and woman kissing, a sinking ship, a woman aiming a rifle. Frances asked him not to lean against them.

✳

## ADVERSARIA: ACCORDING TO FRANCES BAUM

*Shusterman was looking at stills from the work of an early Danish film company that produced alternative endings for its movies depending on where a film was destined to be shown. Its productions were rescued by re-photographing what was left, but it turned out there were many versions of each story shot. Films heading to the United States—this was just before World War I—got happy endings: true love is found, treasure is discovered, the Pony Express gets through. The same movies, same years, sent to Russia, ended with disaster: avalanche, flood, earthquake. What about the Revolution, some might ask? No, not that. Not yet. But maybe somewhere that film exists, a proto-Potemkin. The question I don't know the answer to is, who decided which ending?* Who decided all's well that ends well *goes to Los Angeles and* clobbered by cataclysm *goes to Odessa.*

❉

He opened the can containing *Hidden in Plain Sight* and shook out the crumbled edges. Maybe it should be preserved as a cautionary tale, like 39 Nachtfalterallee.

"If you took out the soundtrack, *Hidden in Plain Sight* could be almost anything, it might be rendered ambiguous," Frances said.

"You know a lot about old film to be just the manager of a storefront every-once-in-a-while theater."

"I used to work as a film restorer."

Once someone had asked her, would she restore any piece of film? It was in a bar, but she wasn't drunk. Would she do triage on a murderer? She respectfully bowed out. There were faces she wouldn't care if they became obliterated, bodies disintegrated, the silver halide crystals flaked off, emulsion degraded, let the molecules return to their natural state.

"The company I worked for in New York went out of business a long time ago. Almost everything is digitized now." As she spoke, she took a splicer, a bottle of Wet Gate fluid for filling in scratches, and sprocket tape from a shelf, the tools of her old trade.

The last project Frances had worked on was Georges Méliès's film about the Dreyfus trial. It was a series of recreated scenes of the affair, some might argue, just as Sauer created scenes for *Hidden in*

*Plain Sight*, except the Dreyfus movie had been accurate, caused riots when it was shown, and had been banned in France for decades. The *re* before create was really important, she explained. Méliès's audience knew the story. They recognized characters, knew what followed what. The Méliès job had been many years ago, and Frances was long done with the art of preserving old movies. When Alphabet Restoration folded, she packed up and moved across an ocean where no one knew anything about her.

"I have to get back to work on the Reiniger animation."

Frances opened a door to a room off the theater, a sort of storage area, full of junk. They moved some boxes and folding chairs out of the way to clear a passage. There was a popcorn machine and an empty vending machine that had once dispensed cigarettes, it was that old. Its door swung open to reveal it was now used to store cleaning supplies.

"If I have a big crowd, I keep extra chairs back here."

"Do you make popcorn?" There was a lingering smell of burnt butter and salt.

"It's broken. Last time I tried to use it, the reject kernel tray caught on fire. It's a thing that sifts out the duds. Every machine has one."

Frances cleared off the Steenbeck. Shusterman had never seen one of these before. It was a big heavy table; on its blue top were four reels and a series of small rollers like spools of thread. The image would appear on what looked like old double televisions bracketed by speakers. Frances explained the image he would see was produced via a revolving prism that scanned each frame. She made it sound as if the editing table were made of chandelier parts.

Shusterman put his coffee cup on the Steenbeck. Frances moved the cup to the top of the vending machine with distaste, and he felt like one of the images of tourists on Alma's website, blundering in, leaving dirty fingerprints on the glass and expecting someone else to clean up the mess.

Alma hadn't provided that information, and Shusterman didn't want to ask her for another Sauer-related favor. He had a sense that she was on the bus rolling forward, and the bus wasn't headed his way. If she still had the fucking trolls she would eBay them into oblivion and back, ultimate destination: a bank deposit.

"When he visited the city, do you think he tried to retrieve the film from where he'd hidden it in the Kronenberg? He'd want to get it back, to dig it out from under the body."

Imagine Sauer prowling around—it's the end of the war, but he isn't sure whether he really should hide or destroy every piece of evidence. The Americans are at the gate this month, but in a few years' time, someone else's jeeps might roll in, and he might need to prove he had been a minister of propaganda, he had made high-quality, effective films. Give me the money, the artistic license, and I can produce great spectacles. Look at my work. And later—look what I did in the jungles of South America. He needed evidence, and he also needed to hide that evidence. But just in case the right jeeps were blown up, and he was threatened with arrest, in the meantime, the old dead he can put to use, and they become intertwined with the new dead in the basement of the Kronenberg.

There was no way to know, but the film was there when Petrovic found the skeleton. Either the film had been left in the cellar after the war or Karl hid it on his final trip to the city.

"The building was sealed, he would have to have broken in. Perhaps he planned to, but saw Metta first, and had no more time left, though he didn't know this was to be so. He was in a hurry to meet her. She looked a little like Riefenstahl, and perhaps he was in love with her, too."

❊

## ADVERSARIA: ACCORDING TO THE GRENZEN INSTITUTE

*In private they wondered if Karl left part of his estate to Metta as a penance for informing on her father, but Metta believed the reason Karl never asked her to forgive him was because he didn't think he'd done any-*

*thing wrong, ever, and that pissed her off. No amount of largesse would make her feel any less pissed off. She hated him, but he was never aware of it. LSD in his coffee and off to the zoo he went. He needed the youngest person he knew who would believe in his work, and that was Metta, even if only to preserve her father's legacy. Karl's own legacy was important to him, as the bequest to the Grenzen Institute demonstrates. They were happy to take his money, or maybe they weren't so keen to take it, but if they turned down their third, larger shares would go to Metta and the crooked hospice. Grenzen did not want to state the source publicly and stuck to the story of an anonymous gift.*

❋

"Until he met the real love of his life at the Schönbrunn Palace. Turn off the lights." Frances had threaded up the Steenbeck and was ready to begin. Shusterman wanted to see *Prinzen Achmed*, even if it was a cartoon.

On the small screen, the elongated figure of the prince leapt on his mechanical flying horse and flew to the enchanted island of Wak Wak, an orientalist fantasy with minarets, domes, and ogee arches.

❋

## ADVERSARIA: ACCORDING TO FRANCES BAUM

*Lotte Reiniger had also made propaganda in Berlin, but only under duress. She hadn't been an enthusiast, like Sauer. She and her husband had tried to escape, but then returned to Berlin to care for Reiniger's mother and became trapped.*

*Prinzen Achmed, made in 1926, was silhouette animation, before Reiniger became a reluctant propagandist. You can see how she was influenced by Turkish shadow puppets like Karagiozis. The cartoon was meant for children, but it must have seemed subversive at the time.*

*Achmed, feathered turban, shoes with turned-up toes, opened a trap door, danced down a flight of steps to be greeted by lovely women whose limbs bent into scalloped shapes as they danced, offering him fruit and drink. No restrained Disney prince, silhouette Achmed wasted no time.*

⁂

Shusterman's phone pinged with a text. It was Alma. She had persuaded the owner of Tango Tours to send her to Vienna. She would only stay a few days, but Tango got her a flight for the following week.

"I have to make a call," he told Frances. "Sorry to miss the rest of the show."

"If you come back tomorrow, I'll let you into the show free," Frances promised. "I do the door, too, so it's no big deal."

Shusterman said he would look forward to it.

⁂

Petrovic wanted Shusterman to come over to #39 right away. He and his crew were going to quit soon for the night, and he'd found something he wanted to show him. As they dug below the interrogation chambers of the Kronenberg, they had found doorways, sunken threshold slabs, and chandelier prisms, but also a very old Swiss clock which must have been in use in the pleasure house, you could tell just by looking at the structure, the face, numerals and hands that hadn't moved since Halley mapped the changing positions of the stars. Petrovic lowered his voice when he described the clock, and Shusterman hurried to the site.

Near a bus shelter, he saw a poster for the Weltmuseum. The image was of a terra cotta figure holding an arrow, from the collections of Archduke Ferdinand II, Count of Tyrol, originally housed in the Armoury and the Chamber of Curiosities. Objects from Brazil were counted and catalogued after his death in 1595. The poster and others like it were bracketed by graffiti, including a spray-painted ostrich with its head in the ground and a thought balloon coming out of its body which read: *When I pull my head out the*  *will be gone.* Whatever it was that the ostrich was ignoring was blacked out.

"When she was sent to Brazil to marry Pedro I, Leopoldine would have had no images of Brazil, no idea of where she was going," said a woman carrying a book on anatomy and drinking coffee. "She gets off the boat in Rio, no possibility of return, you're not in Europe anymore, sorry, but she collected a lot of stuff and sent it back."

"You've seen the show?"

"I work in a lab nearby."

Shusterman looked up the Weltmuseum, formerly the Museum of Ethnography.

*The foreign policy of the House of Habsburg was characterized by its expansion of power through marriage alliances. In 1817, Austrian Emperor Franz I sent his daughter, Archduchess Leopoldine, to Brazil: still terra incognita for Europeans at that time. A scientific expedition joined Leopoldine across the Atlantic to study the country's people, flora, and fauna.*

*The exhibited objects tell fragmented stories of creation myths, the rise and fall of Amerindian cultures in colonial times, and first contacts with all their catastrophic consequences. They are told from many different perspectives: naturalists of the 19th century, scientists of the 20th and 21st centuries, and by indigenous people themselves. All of these voices speak the language of their time, culture, and individual personality: a language we sometimes may not immediately understand.*

Petrovic met Shusterman at street level and led him down to the corridor of locked rooms where the most valuable objects were kept. There, alone on a table, stood a clock whose snapped-in-half hands hadn't moved in hundreds of years. A pool of gritty black powder leaked from the base. Gunpowder is just sand, dull, nothing, Petrovic explained, the same kind they found in another part of the basement that had turned out to be too old to present a hazard of any kind, but the mechanisms, gears, and so on would still have to be cleaned with caution. He picked up the clock and turned it over. Look, he pointed to a line of engraving: it was made in Zurich, a gift to the women who had lived in the house. When examining the siding and back, the corner of an envelope poked out from between two metal plates that had once been screwed together. He slid it out—there—to demonstrate, as if he hadn't already seen its contents.

The envelope was stamped with the Kronenberg logo, but inside were photographs of Karl Sauer behind a camera, directing a scene, and he looked calm, almost smiling. There were huts thatched with pampas grass and trucks parked alongside them. A man was grilling pieces of meat, another carrying loaves of bread. Some of the people in the background looked serious and studious, holding up pages of scripts, playing musical instruments, wanting to get the scene right. Extras in the background stared into space or looked uneasy. Some wore bell-bottom pants, a woman in a sundress had her hands over her face.

Sauer looked confident, there wasn't a shred of anxiety around the edges, as if he was saying: my self, the self you see before you, is constructed, not discovered, but just the same. The pictures told the story the subject wanted told about himself and his work.

Petrovic told him he was going to take the clock, but the photographs, Shusterman could have.

❋

Initially the bank was identified as the target of the explosion. The news had been full of Panama Papers headlines, stories about money laundering, off-shore accounts, shell companies, tax evasion, and for a few hours, the motives of the bombers were conjectured into life as fabulous conspiracy theories that sparkled like intricate multifaceted diagrams of molecules: here's how noble gas krypton is connected to iridium, tungsten, Copernicium, and carbon.

Then a group in Thor Steinar shirts, faces covered by masks, claimed responsibility, and their target was the clinic next to the Kronenberg, the one whose doctors treated refugees at no charge, they said. So what if the clinic could barely pay its rent each month, or didn't have a name, and operated with a degree of anonymity. You had to know it was there in the storefront, and refugees had invisible networks, crime networks, the group said. The men claimed these so-called patients were freeloaders who should go back to their own countries. They wanted to send a message; sending messages was what they did, and every action they took was about doing just that, making statements.

Investigators were just beginning to sift through the wreckage, and ballistics wasn't yet clear about the exact source of the blast. There was some evidence the walls of the Kronenberg were blown in from an external detonation, but also outwards from a blast within the building. It was anybody's guess how explosives got into the ruin, or who would have an interest in blowing up #39, apart from the developers, who generally projected the outward appearance of being a law-abiding, clean-as-a-whistle concern and may have been willing to just let entropy take its course.

Frances passed Nachtfallerallee on her way to her storefront. When the street came into view, it was blocked off, but she could see heaps of rubble and what remained. The Kronenberg was simultaneously falling down and standing, precarious, dangerous, a few sections still structurally sound, but mostly not.

The police guard at the entrance to the street was watching and listening to something on a small screen. Then she heard the distinctive *two men enter, one man leaves*, and realized it was the Thunderdome scene of *Mad Max*, oblivious to the aftermath of the explosion that was going on behind him while the hoards on his screen screamed for blood and guts. The exciting part was over, and the cleanup and investigation were only of marginal interest. The night shift guard looked at identification papers, let police and a few reporters in, and told everyone else there was nothing to see, so get lost.

Frances stood at the edge of the small group of onlookers, hoping the guard wouldn't notice her. A television reporter positioned herself near the barricade, holding an umbrella and speaking into her microphone, *Not since Carlos the Jackal...* A light rain was continuous, but didn't deter the few late-night spectators. The reporter said the dead had not yet been identified, and it was unknown how many may have died, but yes, there were bodies. She spoke with the serious cadence of television reporters everywhere.

Frances had once seen a drawing titled *All-Purpose Mourning Stadium.*

Level A was for Inconsolable Grief

Tier 1 – A Free Floating Sadness

Tier 2 - Vague Depression

Tier 3 - Bland Indifference

Tier 4- Spectacle Gazers

As she balanced on the curb, she tried several doors to the Mourning Stadium, not sure where she belonged in the architecture of grief, a registry of possible sorrows. Everyone in the city had been present on Nachtfalterallee, in some form, whether physically on the actual street or watching on a screen somewhere: those who were disconsolate, those who breathed the atmosphere of desolation and could go nowhere else, the mere, or mere-ish spectators, tourists whose mission it was to look, to take pictures.

The bodies had been taken away. In the bank and the clinic, it could be said the victims had been alive at the time of the blast.

For the remains found in the Kronenberg, it was less clear. Frances watched the guard watching the fight scene, the scene that was meant to limit the idea of war to just two men fighting, the weight of opposing sides concentrated to Mr. X versus Mr. Y. In the actual street, bodies, glass, steel, and stone were pulverized, but paper survived, floating in the air currents. She caught a paper with an eye printed on it, then let it go.

❧

## ADVERSARIA: ACCORDING TO IRIDIA KEPLER

*When human bodies arrived at the lab, I was surprised. I thought I'd spend the rest of my days turning over extended jawbones of Australopithecines and projecting how a skull would look when glass eyeballs were popped in and synthetic fur was applied.*

*The crates of remains that arrived after the Nachtfalterallee explosion were in very bad shape. What was left of them had to be sorted, matched, and reassembled to be part of an exhibition about the siege of the city. Not only would the skeletons and heads have to be put back together, but models needed to be cast, eventually dressed, posed, given appropriate props.*

*Before the lens factory, there had been a smaller house at that site, and its remains were so buried, the factory owners may have had no knowledge of it. Most of the seventeenth-century skeletons excavated before the explosion had been pretty much crushed, but three of them located in a remote part of the cellar had remained intact. The reports from the deceased salvage crew leader also gave some information in terms of how the bodies were positioned when first found and what objects nestled alongside them.*

*What was known: illness swept through the city in the year of their deaths, large numbers of unsaveables, healthy one minute, corpses the next, cartloads of bodies clogging streets. All that triggered mass hyste-*

*ria. How infection was understood wasn't based on measurements of microbes or testing for contaminated water. What they believed: we were all perfectly fine before foreign armies camped out at the city walls, then infiltrated the city. Foreigners were identified, their residences raided, set on fire, and finally, it was believed that by slitting their throats, contagion ended. Following this reasoning, there was evidence a mob had broken into the house that had been registered at 39 Nachtfalterallee, and as the occupants heard the door splinter and give way at the hinges, they ran to other rooms, but this was futile, because at that time there was no back entrance, no way out. A house full of foreigners during a plague year was seen as criminal, and the women were attacked while they were asleep, eating, working, and if so, then clients were caught with their pants down. They were trapped, dragged into another part of the house and lynched. The thinking being that their elimination was preventative medicine.*

*Skeleton A was the oldest of the three. DNA evidence revealed she was originally from northern Italy, a small percentage of Slavic, also, so maybe from a port city on the Adriatic, a place where people come and go. I gave her a sort of half smile, and the lab called her La Gioconda. Because she was older, we put her in charge of the business of the house. Analysis of her bones told us she had been ill but hadn't yet died of the plague, and never would. La Gioconda met her end violently. She was found with her hands over her head, as if trying to fend off blows. No one buried her. She remained where she fell until found three hundred plus years later. The costume person from another museum dressed her in black with a lace collar that looked like a noose of soap bubbles. That was too buttoned-up, a curator argued; even if she ran the business, she wouldn't look like a severe Dutch burgomeister's wife. But what evidence was there she wore dresses that exposed more than they covered up? There was no evidence either way. So, La Gioconda remained naked for some time because no one could agree on what she would have worn. One of the paleontologists played tango music on his phone and pretended to dance with the naked clay model, while someone else recorded it, then put the dance online. The pattern of elaborate steps around stereo dissecting* microscopes and boom arms did not get as much social network attention as expected. Perhaps it could be said La Gioconda contracted one virus but did not go viral.

Skeleton B, found beside La Gioconda, was Egyptian. Her arms were also trying to shield her face from blows. It looked like they died together. The lab called her Cleopatra, but she was the victim of more violence than was used to kill her boss. One of her legs had been deliberately broken. There was no evidence of disease. Though her death was brutal, I was told to give her a placid life-is-good expression as if she were an indulged princess, taken care of, happy to find herself wherever she was. Cleopatra was to be placed in a diorama inspired by the paintings of Ludwig Deutsch.

Skeleton C was Ethiopian. C had been wearing remnants of European clothing and a knife and map in one of her boots. There is the evidence, then there is the interpretation of that evidence, which I leave to the experts. The Ethiopian, a curator would later write in the museum catalogue, had journeyed just outside the city, then returned, where she met her death. She was an escaped slave who would not have been safe on the road out of the city, but there was no shelter for her within its walls either. Her bones, too, revealed no trace of disease. We had no name for her. I called her Woman with a Knife or Woman with a Map. She was dressed in the period clothes of a servant.

The three skeletons were cast, models made, dressed, posed, sent to the museum. La Gioconda was posed looking out a leaded window, like a figure from a Vermeer painting. Cleopatra lounged on Persian carpets, and the Woman with the Knife held a tray containing a jazvah and tiny glass cups filled with brown resin meant to represent Turkish coffee. Her map was displayed on a stand inches away, as if she could grab it and run at any time. The original bones were sent to storage for further analysis at some point in the future.

Among the remains sent to us, there was one skull that was contemporary. The body was pulverized, and because of my particular skills, that one was given to me to reconstruct. No one knew who he was. When I was finished, he looked like Columbo. I wanted to put a raincoat on *him, but he had no body and no place in the exhibit because he wasn't that old. Though who would know if a costume was put on him and he wre installed in the diorama? Have him say, I can't see you, but I know you're here.*

*The name and identity of the Columbo character was unknown. No one claimed him, and I don't know if by capturing his likeness I will help answer that question. What makes someone who they are? Just when you think you're on solid ground, some celestial homunculus changes the writing on an index card or clicks delete, cuts and pastes, and you're someone else entirely.*

# LEVITATING CITIES

# 1683

A MONKEY RUBBED ITS red eyes, slipped his leash, and ran from tree to tree squawking and flashing his red butt before disappearing into the forest. His owner, naked to the waist, screamed in Turkish that the monkey might think these trees could be a nice welcoming home in July's heat, but sooner or later he would make the acquaintance of something known as snow. For this word he switched to German, as if that were a language the monkey would understand. Frost and ice will coat you down to your tail and make you wish you were back on a rope, he shouted at the empty trees before disappearing into his tent. Clowns, jugglers, poet janissaries trained as boys to sing obscene songs, all this hubbub-producing crowd trailed after the Ottoman army. The number of entertainers whose job it was to provide amusement to the troops was said to total two hundred thousand souls. So big was the Turkish army itself that it required large numbers of panderers, procurers, gypsies, and musicians to provide relaxation and diversion.

Where to put them all was a problem. As the Turks circled the city with hundreds of tents and camels, Vienna became a city within a city. The sultan established his camp in the Rotenhof, a palace whose ogee arches imitated a Turkish style of architecture. Its grounds housed aviaries, orchards, a menagerie, and a walled pleasure garden designed as a labyrinth, originally intended to offer protection only from gossips, snoops, and voyeurs. He set up his personal tent at its center.

The showmen camped in a few nooks and crannies so close to the walls of the city that occasionally the sound of Arabic and Turkish verses floated over the walls of Vienna, only to mix with the fragmented speeches of an itinerant priest or hawker of spiritual remedies. Yelling into the Lindenstrasse or Rosenstrasse at the top of their lungs, these men and women preyed on citizens of our besieged city, people who, at the end of their tethers would believe their terrors would lift if only they could scrape together the pfennigs to buy that one miracle in whatever form whether liquid, powder, or some secret whispered in the ear. Everyone knew that on the other side of the wall lounged monsters capable of unspeakable horrors, creatures who only half watched those invisible jugglers, animal trainers, and dirty songsters meant to amuse. These fiends from the east were only biding their time, sharpening their knives and swords pouring powder into matchlocks while the citizenry inside starved into collections of bones and nervous impulses hardly worth bothering with. It was assumed by the man in the street, dwindling slowly on the other side of the wall, that his enemies weren't asleep, but only waiting so the conquest would require as little expenditure of firepower and effort as possible. The city of stone towers would be pushed aside like a house of cards, a flimsy blockade only temporarily in the way of those Turks who had visions of Berlin and Warsaw.

"Greed, lechery, lust, gluttony, sloth, envy!" The friar, vulpine face animate, described each sin with the accuracy of a former sinner. He knew what he was talking about; he had tasted unnamable embraces, gorged himself on unchecked desire and wished ill to befall those who crossed him. It was the kind of hot July that made the idea of sin most palpable even to those who were sure they themselves had nothing to confess.

"Temptation and I are on intimate terms."

Marco d'Aviano, a Capucine, foreign and hypnotic, had left France for exile in the east, but this only increased his popularity in Vienna. He had a reputation in both courts as a healer, and although much in demand he preferred to stand on street corners, shouting to an audience of rag pickers and hawkers. He spoke a guttural French and German, punching his fist into his hand, looking each tinker or seamstress straight in the eye until he or she dropped coins into the hollowed-out bible he held out to them. D'Aviano had tattoos on his knuckles, and a short-brimmed hat sat on the back of his head. The tattoos were crudely written words in Latin which few if any in his audience could read or even see clearly, although he often punctuated his speech by raising his fists to the sky, or occasionally bending over to hit the hot cobblestones under his feet when he needed to emphasize a point about Hell.

D'Aviano talked with enthusiasm, spraying those who stood too close, letting them know how different he was from his brethren, monks who kept to themselves in monasteries filled with treasure while he walked the streets eating and drinking with everyone else, you and you and you. He rocked back and forth as he spoke, and he was unequivocal on the subject of what the signs meant: complete and total catastrophe, although it was not yet clear exactly who the principal victims of the impending apocalypse would be.

"Calamity and bedlam will reign. The signs themselves are freakish: a two-headed hare that doesn't know which way to run, and at the risk of self-eviscerating, it goes nowhere. A shooting star, divided at its celestial source, also confused, a sign of the ether in a state of chaos. While those at our gates keep fifteen hundred concubines, dressed in lambskin puggarees and heron plumes, we, too, are guilty of our own brand of the most hypocritical and despicable sin."

Sin can scoot up to you in the form of a wink or a smile, and there you are shaking hands, seduced, but maybe, just maybe, there could be a little more change in your pocket when it's over. This is my business. I turn what d'Aviano calls depravity into profit. What would I do if the tattooed priest skilled at projectile spitting turned up at my doorstep? I'd show him in, of course. His money is as good as anyone else's. Then I'd ask how the two-headed hare survives. How can it hop from place to place without tearing itself in two? We are much the same way. I can't be in two places at once, so I make no pretense of who I am.

Every few days d'Aviano got in a shouting match with another street crier, Karl Weisbaden, tall and gaunt, smelling of tar if you got too close, of candle wax if you stood further away, he hated the pope and blamed the church for the siege. Karl was not very popular. D'Aviano shouted at him about the expansioning killing machine Turks who were swallowing piece after piece of the Empire and tossing the bones over their shoulder. Wiesbaden asked d'Aviano how he knew about the wheels and gears of the killing machine? The enemy, he said, is just like you and me. To them, we're the killing mechanismus. It was entertaining to listen to the two hurl insults at one another, but their debate only underscored a sense of precariousness. I have no map and only know the Turks are somewhere over there, and the city sits on the geographical edge of the antagonism both men described, at least I think so.

One night the windows in the palace of the Bishop of Vienna were smashed and parts of the city were looted: proof Wiesbaden must have had his supporters somewhere. It was rumored he was behind the attacks, and I have no doubt this was true. For days crystal shards snapped under foot as I walked down the Rotenturmstrasse, past the ruin, a vacant spectacle. If Wiesbaden knocked on my door, I wasn't sure he wouldn't be any less eager to tally up my moral accounts than his rival, d'Aviano. The sincerity of my repentance, if I were to confess, would certainly be doubted by whoever was doing the balance sheet. Yet under cover of darkness, both men might be loath to turn away when they glimpsed light from doorways opened slightly in an upstairs corridor visible behind my head.

"The Turks laid a big noose around the neck of the city, and while reclining on velvet pillows and smoking tobacco infused with chestnut oil from a gadget called a hookah, designed by the devil. We, friends, are at their mercy." D'Aviano waved his arms. "They are slowly, slowly tightening the rope until we are skeletons, shadows of our former selves. The siege is divine retribution, and we must surrender to God's will and acknowledge our transgressions."

"If that's our fate, then to continue on is hopeless. Why don't we give up, open the gates of the city, and let everyone right in?" Wiesbaden shouted back. His hands made a gesture of strangulation, then he cackled as if he were in on a joke which was opaque to everyone else.

Their voices trailed behind me as I crossed the street. I was wearing a black dress looted from the house of the Spanish ambassador. My mother believed black, unlike any other color, has the ability to erase signs of a working life if one is clean.

She had been brought here from Trieste by her husband, my father, of whom I know very little, except that his name was Primo, and they called me Unna. They fled Trieste, gatekeeper city, between the Republic of Venice and all that lies to the east, but what city isn't a gatekeeper between whatever it lies between? My father was a skilled cardsman, Bone-Ace was his game, but he lost as much as he made at the tables and aboard pleasure ships anchored before they sailed on to Monte Carlo, Nice, Barcelona, Lisbon. One night he left to meet a cardsman colleague and was never seen or heard from again. My mother believed he was abducted, pressed into service aboard one of those ships to pay off a debt to a captain. She had heard of men lured, drugged, waking up in a pitching berth on the Red Sea. Where she would have heard this tale is hard to say, why he would have been followed to Vienna, and why she made him a debtor rather than one who was owed, but in any case this is what she chose to believe.

Alone without a pfennig, my mother began to work in the houses of the Rotenhof district. To many here, she was beautiful. With just the right amount of slightly darker Adriatic skin, round eyes, and a diminutive northern nose, she had a few highly placed clients, a duke of Sachsen, a count from an island between Cyprus and Slovenia. Does such a place exist? Who knows what was true? They paid, that's all we needed to be sure of, and she told me never to lose sight of the fact that her work, what became our work, was commerce, nothing more, nothing less. Her motto was to work so hard you won't have to work anymore, and that's what she did. For each Düsseldorfer or Croatian prince, she saved half or more. By the time clients were eyeing me, she had her own house, and I was whisked away from their gaze. The House of Cygnets had two parts. The part we lived in was not visible from the street, and in this house behind the house I was taught by a priest who had a special relationship with my mother. I learned Latin, read Spinoza, and studied Galileo, those who would turn the universe on its ear. Though when she died I took over the house, and found that men's desires and the need for cash trumps philosophy, science, exploration of the New World. 1783 will be as different from 1683 as it was from 1063. But in the meantime, you have to eat.

Triestino by birth, but Viennese by adoption, my mother had a love of cleanliness, but staying spotless with water shortages required more and more of an effort. Who was I making the effort for during this siege, when it wasn't at all clear anymore who anyone really was, much less how much money their families had? The siege beveled the edges of what had previously been very distinct boundaries between those who ate from rare china plates and those who just ate with their hands. In my mother's time, she had the luxury and the knack of turning down client tinkers and tradesmen who might have given her house a lesser reputation. She was also concerned with the spread of disease, though no one was sure exactly how the contagion jumped from person to person. In its variety of forms, my mother believed it only proliferated in a certain kind of person, and no evidence, even if a king had it, could persuade her otherwise. She would say her precautions were not for herself, but for her investments, the Cygnets themselves.

She herself did succumb to that very disease that affects so many in our profession. It begins with a bumpy, deforming rash, uncontrollable spasms in arms and legs, paralysis, blindness, not knowing a dog from the emperor, and finally death. If I develop this malady, I'll jump off the Salztorbrucke.

So I, on the other hand, take anyone's money, and now everyone is dirty and hungry, part of a mob that has a life of its own.

The city fathers said the threat of attack represented a call for courage, but in the middle of a panicky crowd, where's the courage? Hard to find.

From June to July the bells called Turkenglocken rang every morning. This was a signal for every person in Vienna to stop whatever they were doing in order to pray for deliverance from the Ottoman soldiers. People suddenly came to a halt in the street or in the market, folded their hands, thumbs crossed, heads down, clicking their rosaries. The sound made me a little nostalgic for something I never possessed with any sincerity. The bells meant to inspire courage and put fear into the hearts of the Turks only initiated the day with terror. The ringing seemed to say, yes, they are at the gate. There is nothing you can do about it. I slept late or stayed inside until the middle of the afternoon. Even if I stole a rosary and fumbled with it, I couldn't dispel the visions that accompanied the bells: my house burnt to the ground, masses of turbans like a cataract of blue and white bubbles filling the streets. If I was walking the streets when the bells struck, I would make my way between mumbling, meditating statues. My prayers never stopped anyone before, why should they now?

Refugees began to arrive in the city from the south, and barricades manned by armed children were set up to keep them out. The grown men who remained in the city were needed elsewhere. Warnings were nailed to walls advising citizens to identify and turn in not only Turks, but Hungarians and Serbs, people from Greek islands. It was a long list.

No one can be sure who among you might be a foreign agent, d'Aviano pointed at the crowd. Wiesbaden, on the other hand, had another message, which he demonstrated by pulling his long dirty hair straight up from his head to imitate a Bishop's mitre. Foreign agents, he said, might not be those who speak in unfamiliar accents, but rather come in the guise of those you trust most.

⁂

The biggest asswipe in Vienna actually was Emperor Leopold himself. He and his retinue found a way out of the city, and so while some were trying desperately to get in, he slunk away. A dozen souls with sharp eyes who happened to be up late at night quickly assembled their meager belongings and joined the royal departure, leaving the city along with the crown, scepters, jeweled this and that, thinking in the wake of his royal entourage you could find safe passage out of the siege and across the territory beyond.

The edicts restricting the entrance of refugees into the city proved impossible to enforce with child guards acting as gatekeepers, but for me the flood of outsiders was a boon, and I looked among them for fresh recruits. It was recommended that a story be added to each house to avoid overcrowding, and I had one built with pleasure, there was plenty of need for it.

I saw a woman sitting on a curb, screaming at a boy who had stolen a fistful of Polish copper money from her. The coins were probably worthless, and as the child slipped out of her grasp, I grabbed the young woman's arm just as she was about to chase the thief and asked her the first question I always asked.

"Do you need a place to stay?"

Angry at being held back, the woman told me she couldn't pay me, but I owed her for letting the kid get away.

"You don't need to pay to live in my house, you might only need to work a little. My house is three floors high, and I have several girls like yourself staying with me."

I had picked up girls like this before. Sometimes they stayed for a few nights, sometimes for years. Often, they knew what would be expected of them, before I had to spell it out. I offered a good deal: a place to stay and plenty to eat at no charge. I kept what the men paid, but the girls could pocket whatever gifts were bestowed on them. The new girl had a wide mouth, thick but bowless lips, and a loud voice as if she'd lived with deaf people and was accustomed to yelling to make herself understood. Her hair was matted into clumps that she kept pulling at. As we walked to the House of Cygnets, she told me her story, and I listened because in this way, I learned news of the outside world. There were no other sources.

"I came from a town east of here. The Turks herded everyone into a church, see. I had to think fast. I hid because I figured it was better not to do what I was being told to do. I pretended I didn't exist. I'm not here. I occupy no space. I can't see or hear what people are doing. But from an attic window with the glass knocked out of it, when I looked down, everyone I knew was being marched into the church. Negotiations were conducted about the surrender of property, that much I knew was at stake because land was what the invaders wanted. Everything would have to be turned over because we had nothing to bargain with. Why they would want that little cuckoo clock of a town, I can't tell you. It was a stepping stone to your city to the north, but they came, and they stayed, and are there still."

I nodded as I walked her to my house on Nachtfalterallee, listening, but also not entirely believing her, and told her to lower her voice. There are ears everywhere.

"Finally, when everyone appeared to be satisfied with the arrangements, a small girl in white led the citizens from the church. As they emerged, the Turks murdered every one of them."

"Don't repeat your nightmares," I said sharply, turning a corner onto Lindenstrasse. "Nobody cares." The new girl would need to be bathed. She stank. "Men will look into your face and see an escape hatch, goodbye daily panic. The best part: this they will pay for."

She smiled at me. She thought I was complimenting her pug face and still didn't know what I was talking about.

"When you talk about armies of lunatics, customers will run away from you. They come here," by now I was unlocking my front door, "to forget. If you talk about yourself and burning churches, you will make no money whatsoever."

I've seen paintings of the plague years, and each and every one of them showed people in ecstasy, at banquets, dancing and kissing. These paintings are instructional: adversity, whether war or pandemic, is my most trusted friend and ally. Calamity, sex, money, all went hand in hand.

My house was a narrow, spindly structure with balconies and bay windows sticking out like so many afterthoughts, hammered into place after the house had been built. Because it was sandwiched between two taller buildings, the lower floors were dark. The attic got a little more light, but it was hot, and its single lunette looked out onto a yard piled up with junk. To her it looked like a palace.

Little ivory figures copulated on a shelf. Even in the heat, the windows were shut to the city. She picked one up and played with it. I never learned her real name, so called her Marchegg, the name of her town.

One night when no visitors called, I locked up and went out, leaving the women inside to sleep or play cards. I wandered around the city, just to learn the kinds of things you can learn in the middle of the night, things that are less apparent during the day. The night was so hot, conscripted laborers could not be made to work, and a panic had begun. Ladders remained leaning against brick walls dividing empty spaces, going nowhere; window mullions had been left without new panes of glass. One could reach in and take whatever had been abandoned. Looters ran through the streets carrying candlesticks, pots and pans, half-eaten plates of food. While I walked, I calculated how much had been earned per hour the night before, and the result was barely enough for an entire dinner for all the women I kept. Either the five lowest earners would have to do with less, or everyone would have to endure a few deprivations. Which was the fairer decision? Whichever way I sliced it, there were bound to be serious grievances, if not departures. The possibility that existence was far more precarious outside my door was the only thing that kept the women upstairs in their places, so I did have to thank Marchegg, who talked too about parched earth, burned cities, and bodies lining the roads from here to anywhere else someone might get it into their heads to travel to.

When I returned, she was still awake and seemed to know what was happening in the city, although as far as I knew she hadn't stepped outside since her arrival. In fact, she refused to leave the house at all. Nor had she had the kind of clients who would have information about the state of the siege. The men who requested Marchegg were silent and left quickly, lingering only to listen to her, not to speak themselves. A trafficker in religious incunabula and bogus relics, an engraver so reticent and embarrassed he pushed money at me then pointed to a room, was one of Marchegg's regulars. He had metal filings under his fingernails and silver dust in his hair. An aged gambler, obsessive and focused almost exclusively on card games and the odd bet, used Marchegg as a source for predicting the chances on the bets of those who lingered in the city, haunting betting parlors or houses like mine, men who out of boredom wagered on the likelihood of the attack coming on a Sunday or a Wednesday. Years ago he had lost everything and now lived on the sufferance of an uncle who alternated between indulgence and tightfistedness in matters of the gambler's proclivities. These were Marchegg's customers. Capitalizing on her visions, I began to call her the Futurist.

She opened a window and threw a moldy peach into the street. This irritated me no end. Fruit was expensive, we sucked even the stones, and in my opinion, not only was the peach still edible, but added to the air of luxury and lushness I was trying so hard to maintain, but I had to be careful in my scolding. Her visions had begun to draw attention to my house. This turn of events should have been the cause of satisfaction, but a house of pleasure and forgetting was all I wanted. I began to suspect her stories were rooted, not in the future or the present, but in the past. It didn't seem to make any difference. What happened six months ago would probably happen again next week anyway. She described scenes she saw on her way to Vienna: hundreds of people in chains who would be sold like candles, melting, sticking together in the heat. Some women were acquired by a man who took them to Istanbul for their emperor. They would be kept in a prison within the palace, never to be allowed outside again.

"No, you're wrong," an itinerant clockmaker contradicted her while she ran a finger over the crest of his dried apricot of an ear. "They're taken to ships and set adrift, but even that's not such a monstrous fate. There are many islands in the Adriatic and Aegean Seas, and each one is a paradise, even in their isolation."

The clockmaker also had a reputation for desiring to use some of his delicate but sharp instruments on my employees. I did nothing to stop him; in fact, I always welcomed the man when he was in town. He left no scars on the girls and paid well. His geniality and constant stream of banter and jokes were like blobs of cream disguising a stale, crumbling cake. He fixed house clocks at no charge and compared their inner workings to that of the female anatomy. Only a twist was needed here or there. I admired his careful hands and sharp eyes, the way he could take apart minute gears and silvery chains, then put the machine back together again. Ignoring the girls' complaints, I told them he couldn't have really hurt them. They were being panicky, and the city was full of hysterics already.

In the chaos of hastily locked doors, clogged streets, of packed and lost belongings, I watched as people tore themselves away from those who chose to stay behind. Their anxiety was useless. It really was too late. The rich stuffed massive crates into coaches full of furs, jewels, bottles of wine, destined to become the property of roadside bandits, while those as poor as packrats walked bent almost double from the weight of detritus: the empty bottles, sacks, and worn-through shoes which might be cobbled into some kind of ad hoc usefulness at some point in their travels. Mobs might be omnivorous organisms, but the density of people crowded into a city also provides a version of safety. So I stayed. In the country, travelers were more isolated and vulnerable. Families who departed so late in the day were painful to observe because small children who had to be carried never lasted very long. Children slow you down, my mother used to say, as she dragged me from house to house. Like the clock-maker, I persisted in denying the evidence and refused to believe this summer would be any different from the ones that had preceded it. I looked at the chaotic mass of citizens and strangers, rumors and panic, as if each had no meaning. There would be no siege. They were all extremely mistaken.

At eight o'clock, in a shrouded gilt carriage, the empress, last of the remaining royal family, left the Hofburg Palace, went around the city wall to the canal through Leopoldstadt, and over the Danube to join her family in Linz. The Dowager Empress Eleonora, after moving into the metropolis, was finally leaving for the west. It was well known that she couldn't bear to leave the city, and even after her son snuck out, she stayed until the deprivations of the siege affected even her household. The question of whether to flee the city was finally decided by the empress's lap dogs. The animals ate smoked fish and drank bowls of flat champagne. It was somebody's job, day and night, to pick the bones out of the fish before the dogs were served. When there was no champagne for the dogs, it was time to go, and now, finally, the tinsellated procession, secretive, almost apologetic, disappeared into the hot summer night.

The engraver, in a moment of speech spurred by a sense of abandonment and outrage, chanted, suicidal to escape, suicidal to stay. If the Turks caught up with Eleonora's entourage, he said, they deserved to be cut to pieces.

"They will be taken captive and displayed like prizes from Sarajevo to Salonika. People will pay good money to see a royal family reduced to living on bread and water. The empress will scream and threaten, it's not the kind of life she's used to, being gawked at by the hoi polloi at close quarters. Memories of other imprisoned queens and princes will give her no solace."

During her vocalized visions, Marchegg's eyes glazed over as if not really seeing what was right in front of her, yet still able to scratch her nose, drink, or pick the largest coin out of a pile.

"The empress is not known for her tolerance of personal deprivation, but rather for needing to have her own way at all times. It will not be amusing to see how she behaves as a circus spectacle," I said. "No one will pay to see an old woman scream at them." In other words, I was saying to Marchegg, please be reasonable. Tell your customers something reliable, give them something they can believe in.

"We will be liberated by a French dwarf who shoots a matchlock by day but wears a dress by night. Eleonora will return, but she will always despise this little man to whom she will owe her life and her city."

Customers laughed or looked embarrassed. The engraver obsessively arranged and rearranged the ivory figures. Wrapping her clothes around herself tighter and tighter, Marchegg walked out of the room. That night there would be no income from the Futurist. To believe in a dwarf with an eye like a hawk who carried a gun bigger than himself was to believe Marco d'Aviano got his tattoos from a saint he met on the road.

She wore the blue dress of a Favorita servant, but during the siege, clothing came from any number of sources and could have meant anything. Beggars found abandoned furs and wore them in the heat while fleeing aristocrats had little more than the clothes on their backs. Her rope-colored hair had black roots. I'd seen this before. Serbian women who lived in the mountains surrounding Sarajevo streaked their hair with chamomile. No one else knew how to do this kind of dye job. The woman's name was Nada, and she was happy to follow me to the house on Nachtfalterallee.

❀

The city of Sarajevo was seen as the enemy's northern fringe, his trigger finger, but also something about the antagonist that was secret, wrought with temptation, a way of life that offered the realization of any fantasy, any desire. The house had grown accustomed to the Futurist's canny and precise pronouncements issued in a half stupor, but that I could offer a taste of the myth of Sarajevo doubled my business. Marchegg was right. Baggy silk trousers, a long velvet vest, brimless hat and veil were found for Nada, although none of us really knew if this was what such a woman would actually wear. When word got out that at my house one could savor a taste of the east, Nada was suddenly in great demand. I had a locked box now filled with hard currency. It was a city of insomniacs, and many found their way to my house. Business boomed.

The manners of the men who wanted Nada weren't yet so entirely claimed by fear of loss of simple things: bread, water, a roof over their heads. These were men who seemed to have enough money to pursue an idea of pleasure, men who owned their own houses, had cooks perhaps, and had no hint of food running out. Some had clean clothes. Some were dirty even when powdered over, and in the summer all of them sweat. Nada complained of their stickiness and their unwashed skin. Marchegg considered she had saved Nada's own skin and told her she had nothing to complain about.

No one wanted to hear how the Turks would burn down the city. The clockmaker returned with his pockets full of tiny gold screwdrivers and paper-thin gears, and I sent him to the Futurist, though he owed me. He grumbled. He didn't know what century of horrors Marchegg was in, past or future, and this prevented her from actualizing any pain or pleasure at his hand. I didn't want him to go to Nada. She had become too valuable, and I couldn't risk injury to a valuable investment. In payment, he left me a broken gold watch which he said he would return to mend, but he never showed up again. When I took it to be fixed, there turned out to be nothing inside of it at all. Hardly anyone wanted the Futurist anymore, and it was best to keep her hidden away, talking about the future to herself.

During the summer, refugees broke into empty houses and proceeded to live in them as if they had always maintained residence at those particular addresses. There were rumors that all-night parties took place in these houses, and this wasn't good news to me. Such festivals threatened my business, which relied on payment for pleasure. For the duration of the siege, it was difficult to define what a squatter might be.

The nights didn't cool off, and Nada worried me. The idea of scores of men clinging to the staircases didn't spell riches to her, but a carnival of desperation, and she was beginning to feel the closeness of the siege, I could tell. My description of wartime raucous nights and festivities during plague years fell on deaf ears. Too many of the men climbing the stairs wanted her to speak to them in Turkish, so she invented a nonsense language that amazed me with its music of syllables, declarative and interrogative sounds that appeared to have a grammar and syntax, but no meaning.

Marchegg learned there were women who crept over the broken walls on the north side of the city in order to trade bread for vegetables, and she asked me if she could join them. Ordinarily there would have been no point in asking to slip away even for a night, the answer would have been a flat-out no, but a few days before I had seen a soldier carrying the head of a murdered Turk lying in a basket. Passing him in the street I got a good look at the bloody lump, eyes staring, matted black hair, tongue lolling out. The soldier swung his arms cheerfully and carried the severed head as if the thing were as ordinary as a cabbage he was taking home to cook for dinner. Paving stones had been taken from the streets to be used for fortifications, so our shoes made no sound on the dirt when we passed each other. For days afterward I would not go out, thinking every basket swinging from every hand contained severed body parts.

�֎

One hot afternoon, from the attic window, I saw clouds of smoke beyond the city wall. The clouds spread, seemed to come nearer or were arrested at the wall—I couldn't quite see, and so went into the street to learn what was on fire, taking Nada with me. The destruction of the glacis and suburbs outside the city had been ordered so that whoever laid siege to the city would have no place to hide when they made up their minds to advance. The burning was not thorough; some patches outside the wall remained green with houses standing, while other buildings still smoldered. A spark leapt into the city and started a small fire, but it did not stay small long, soon spreading to the Arsenal where eighteen hundred barrels of powder were stored. A crowd had gathered, but a surge when a bunch of soldiers arrived separated us. I was pushed to the sidewalk while Nada was shoved in the opposite direction. To get a better view, I scrambled on top of a crate before anyone else had the chance.

The sea of people had carried Nada across the street. The fire was spreading, closer to the Arsenal and the gunpowder inside it. An officer frantically searched his pockets for the keys to it. Out came silver coins, bits of paper, half a comb, and a skeleton key. He tried the key, but it didn't fit the lock. Soldiers who had been sent to the general's quarters to look for the proper key came back empty-handed. Fire leapt from spire to balcony, eating through wooden floors and ceilings. Spreading closer, not only to the Arsenal, but to the New-gate, where more powder was stored. None of the lieutenants present had the right keys in their possession. I pressed against panicky people, who shouted about sabotage and keys stolen in a plot.

"Jews stole the keys. Turkish Jews. Maltese Jews. Catalonian Jews."

An explosion ripped through the air, and I fell from my rickety crate, but the blast was the sound of soldiers breaking through the Arsenal door. Scrambling over one another, they moved the powder kegs at the last possible moment. Some fled but others were fascinated by the fire and mesmerized by the possibility of an enormous explosion. Slowly they stopped shoving, spellbound. Waves of people, like myself, froze, rooted to the spot.

"The flag flying from that roof, there, close to the fire," someone shouted, "it's a secret signal to the Turkish army. They'll be coming now."

The crowd grew incensed, taking on a life of its own. One man's laughter was louder than any other voice, and he kept going when everyone around him fell silent. Slobbery, jaundiced, laughing himself silly while leaning against a building for support. Everyone stared. He was wearing the uniform of a Turkish Janissary, but he wasn't a Turkish soldier. None were yet inside the city. He may have stolen the clothes from a body because they were intact and warmer than his own. I'd seen him before, haunting the trash dumps behind cafés, sleeping in the parks, collecting bottles, feathers, anything that didn't move. He spoke in Latin and looked at the sky.

As a soldier rolled a barrel of gunpowder down the street, the laughing man was pulled away and dragged to a tree the fire hadn't touched. A half-dressed woman was already tied to it. Eager to blame someone, anyone, the mob had resolved they were at fault for the fire. They were hanged just at the moment they understood in a terrifying hiccup what was about to happen to them, and in a suffocating screech it was over. I'd done nothing to save them, the homeless or the simple, but no one else had either.

I suffer from that same blindness, that same inability to know how different I might be from those I surround myself with. Am I so different from that slow couple whose nonsensical speech and laughter condemned them to be a source of superstition, to be singled out when a mob decides who lit the match? I think so, but how can I be sure? In my own way, perhaps I, too, can't differentiate between a real potato and one that looks like the saggy-faced Emperor, and so unlike other potatoes, can hold conversations at length.

I shouted Nada's name into the dispersing crowd, but she was nowhere to be found. The fire smoldered in the square, and the two bodies swayed in the wind.

Night, smokey and stinging, arrived with an unusual amount of visitors, proving, once again, that pleasure nips at the heels of catastrophe. Nada didn't return to the house that night, but the Futurist had visions of cafés filled with chocolate and almond cakes dusted with gold, and everyone was happy, or so they appeared.

Three days later, Nada turned up with a tattoo of a crescent moon on her shoulder, nails bitten down to nothing. Where had she been? She made a lot of money for me, and I was relieved she returned in one piece.

As a result of the fire, all cellars in the city were requisitioned for powder storage. Even crypts under churches and convents were taken over.

I didn't want explosives in my house but had no choice. Every house in the city had to store a few barrels. That was the law. One of the soldiers went upstairs with the Futurist, so at least I made some money out of the obligation. To be perceived as unpatriotic, even in the slightest, put one at risk of being tarred with the saboteur brush, ever popular and much in demand. Every time there was a fire, someone was accused of treason and taken off to be hanged. The Futurist had begun to see spies and traitors everywhere. Witch hunts were constant, and I was very careful as to who I let up to see Nada, increasing her desirability even more. Despite the imminence of war, the house had never done better.

One late afternoon near the Hofburg, I came across a partially burned building. I pushed aside a dry branch as if it were a wicket gate to get a closer look. The windows were long, nearly touching the ground, and so I was able to climb over a charred ledge into the chamber as if doors had been left open. The sill blackened the edges of my clothes, but no one was standing guard.

In a large hall with shelves of books from floor to ceiling, mice nibbled corners of bindings and ran over the tops of books at my approach. Toward the western wall the books were entirely black and damaged beyond repair, reduced to bound triangular wedges and shreds, though others were just singed around the edges. Chairs and tables were teetering black skeletons; one push and they would dissolve into cinders. Some gold frames remained eerily intact around seared portraits. Long before his departure from Vienna, the emperor planned a library which was never built. The emperor was believed to have collected more books than any other ruler in Europe and in languages neither he nor anyone in his empire knew. While the library was being designed, books and manuscripts were kept in rooms apart from the palace, and these were the rooms I now wandered through.

The collection included manuscripts handwritten on vellum and parchment, xylographic books, metallographic books, and many different kinds of incunabula, from primitive examples to elaborate imitations of manuscripts, complete with illuminations, rubrics, and borders which overpowered the texts themselves. The emperor especially valued banned and heretical documents, condemned by popes and kings, and they were kept in a separate room, where I found a deck of playing cards stuck in a box between two manuscripts. I took the deck, which looked undamaged, kicking soggy books aside.

A charred drawing fell out of a manuscript: a woman in blue held her arms out toward a haloed, stigmatized figure, an unidentified saint. The marbleized cover and pages were brittle. They crumbled in my hands, blackening them. I was left with a fragment of the head and halo. As the siege forced us to rely on drastic measures in order to survive, and as the evidence of death and dying grew all around me, I had occasionally imagined how I would explain myself to a sexless angel who would come for me. Dante and Boccaccio crumpled in my hands. Since the siege, I, too, had conversations with departed friends and patrons sometimes through the agency of the Futurist, sometimes on my own. I turned over a copy of *l'Epistre au Dieu d'amours*, in which women petitioned Cupid about men who had written badly of them. I would have told them to get over it. Here were the letters of Abelard and Héloïse. Writing about passion, waiting, doing nothing, regretting, repenting, living in an abbey, living in a monastery, doing what someone said were good deeds. These were not creatures of even simple appetites. This is what I think: love = zero, unless money changes hands. The ivory figures in my house were jokes, meant as a form of encouragement, they offered a few suggestions in an instructional mode, but no one fell in love with anyone under my roof. It was never even considered as a possibility. It's not a language I speak or have any interest in.

I would explain my life to the angel so it would understand. There were many reasonable excuses. I needed money, my mother had worked in the trade, so I had the connections, and could expand the House of Cygnets. It was the only trade I knew. There was a logic to my circumstances, all kinds of trades were passed on; mine was as well, and why shouldn't it be? Occasionally I received certain favors as well as cash, but I never did business in barter for essential things: a pair of shoes, bottles of wine, although this primitive possibility was not too far off. In the future if a client had no money but offered a pair of shoes or a bottle of wine, we might need those things badly enough to accept his offer. The angel wouldn't care about my scruples or my history, but it might still be appealed to. I would explain to the angel that I couldn't live under a bridge, scavenging for food and clothing. The angel would understand self-sacrifice isn't for everyone and give me a second chance to alter my means of business in a productive manner instead of closing shop and heading for debtors' prison. After all, I would plead, I do provide a service, not a vice. The angel would fail to be impressed, and would prefer the women on the second floor of my house to be homeless mendicants.

I tore the saint's head in two. It fell into a pile of ashes and burnt leather.

Newton on bending light, Copernicus on the position of the planets, the records of Galileo's trial before the Inquisition, Kepler's *Astronomia Nova*, Tycho Brahe on the life of supernovas; Leopold's scientists were the sum of everything that had happened before them. Pages of Pliny's *Natural History* fell to the floor. Chapters on animals lay at my feet. Antonia, wife of Drusus, fell in love with a lamprey and hung gold earrings from its gills. Aristophanes and an Egyptian elephant were in love with the same woman. Lionesses were often unfaithful to their partners, but the lions could smell the evidence of their infidelity. The lioness, to avoid being mauled, swims in a river or just stays far away until the lingering smell disappears. Here were diagrams of a hydraulic wheel with long-distance transmission built one hundred years ago, an Italian pump with an endless chain, maps of the planets surrounded by astrological signs. Now an abandoned project, the surviving parts of the library were to be packed up and sent north to Passau. Labeled crates lay waiting to be packed, but there was no sign of any workmen.

During the siege it was possible to trespass without consequences. With locks and windows giving way, my curiosity about the contents of the emperor's temporary warehouse could be satisfied, but the blackened doors which connected the library to the rest of the building remained stuck fast. I tried several in turn. One of the library doors did give way to empty blackness, a corridor with no windows. It was growing dark outside, too. I left, taking a copy of Abelard and Héloïse with me.

Soon Vienna was more destroyed than intact, less familiar because landmarks had turned into ruins, bombarded and looted. Like the city, the language grew strangled, and less intelligible. There was no longer one German, but many variations on it. Iron spikes with timber baulks set across were put into the counterscarp. Gallows were erected as a warning to criminals and spies. They stood like bare trees near the city walls. The Turks were said to be digging an elaborate series of trenches and mines, ringing the city. Within Vienna, tunnels were dug to countermine them. I didn't know who would pop out of my cellar, and Nada and the other women were afraid to go down into it. Since the cellar delivery of explosives, the house came to the attention of more soldiers. A census was begun to identify idlers and suspects, and cellars were inspected to be sure there were no traitors tunneling out to meet the Turks. One of Nada's visitors had decided she was more foreign than she admitted. In turning her in, he would save both their souls, before the end of the world, so in order to avoid salvation or martyrdom, she slipped out of the house for a few days until the census passed. She left no note, but then, I wasn't sure Nada knew how to write.

Nada found a place to hide below the stage in a dismantled theater. Others hid in the rafters, but this seemed precarious to her. One could fall off so easily. Under the stage lay the machinery which moved wings and shutter scenery. Flat painted rooms, backdrops of painted forests, coastal scenes with boats, tritons, mermaids, and moveable water all had been carried out by looters. Only the scenery for Hell, with its skeleton characters and airborne demons, had been left behind. The poor who lived in the vicinity of the Hofburg gate could be seen wearing costumes: fake armor, wings, large hats with drooping feathers.

Nada returned, her absence only increasing her popularity, and men eagerly asked after the girl from Sarajevo while I tried to throw a bone to the Futurist or someone else. Sarajevo was Nada's calling card, and when speaking about the city, what she didn't remember, she made up, but she did remember so much, her memory was overcrowded with images of every street corner, balcony, and minaret in painstaking detail, and the callers ate up her every word.

Apart from the Futurist, no one knew what was happening outside the city anymore. It was as if a moat had been dug around us shutting out the rest of the world, leaving an airless island of short-tempered souls.

At the end of July, the bells were silenced. Saint Stephen's bells, it was announced, would ring when the Turks entered the city. On the last day of the month, drums and pipes played very loudly, then Turkish musicians whose instruments seemed to say: we're so close now, and we're coming to get you, growing louder and closer, each side trying to drown out the other.

The Turks cut off the fresh water supply. Nightly forays outside the city walls had stopped. Food was no longer readily shared. I began to hoard every wormy apple and spongy onion. Money was dispensed with. A sack of apples equaled half a night with the Futurist or one hour with Nada if she happened to appear.

On the first day of August, I picked up a loaf of bread which crumbled in my hands into a mass of bugs. Apples and pears in my cupboard were more rotted than fruit. The house was full of rapidly aging food, people, worn bedposts, battered cornices, and dust. Acts meant to slow down the process of decay (sweeping, repairing banisters, leaning over a pot of steaming herbs, or sleeping late) all were useless. Rats and mice took over. Still, I was the only one who should have been allowed to age. I was the invisible mold, the worms inside the bread waiting to turn into bugs. For a few days I found it difficult to eat. I told the women upstairs I was rationing my own food more strictly than theirs, and for a few days this was an honest statement.

Imagine a series of concentric rings: soul, person, city, country, continent, universe, soul, all surrounded, besieged. The dead, the garbage, the sick and wounded increased, accumulated. There were plagues of disillusionment, mad euphoric optimism, violent boredom, and ignorance. Survival seemed a kind of curse dreamed up by the Saint Marinas of Heaven, those who willingly took the blame and got no earthly rewards. In their unrecorded bitterness, they invented the siege to plague survivors.

"Everyone will leave in the middle of the night. When the Turks finally break through, they'll find an empty city, a ghost town," the Futurist foretold.

She also described people found still in their houses, sitting in chairs or lying in beds as if only the clocks had stopped—behind the counterscarps, the whole city will burn to the ground and all that will remain to be conquered will be a huge, black hole. Nada looked like a caricature of misery, such a long face, yet oriental moroseness was a mystery I cashed in on. Even given that the roof was about to cave in around us, life here was surely better than in the peculiar and violent city she came from.

In early September, the Turks closed in. They mined the city walls. The Futurist and Nada were conscripted to carry *chevaux-de-frises*, spiked barricades, used to stop up the holes made by the blasts to the salients. They hadn't wanted to go but had no choice. Everyone was called up. The city became a city of children. No old people were left anywhere. Children became concierges and caretakers. The metropolis seemed to be hollowing out except for garbage, corpses, and their animals, and there was no way to dispose of these outside the walls. As bodies and unsalvageable fragments of possessions piled up, symbolic of fantastic excess, I was forced to practice austerity to the point where I tried to find something useful in piles of ragged discarded things.

Trouser legs became sleeves, a sleeve became a hat, a birdcage became a small table, books were used to line shoes, nutshells were fed to the stove. I served siege veal several times a week. Nobody wanted to know the animal the meat came from, and I never told them.

Houses were searched for any man or boy who could act as a soldier or a watchman, even the very young, ill, and the newly deranged. The rules were considered harsh and unpopular, but there was a penalty of death if a man was hidden.

A Berliner who lisped was afraid of being taken and refused to leave my house. Officers still occasionally visited me, making the house a dangerous place to hide, but he crept into the basement, wedged himself between powder kegs. Sometimes he paced on top of them, but most of his days in the cellar were spent in sleep. There was little else to do in the dark but dream of Nada, and hope a panicky army had forgotten the powder kegs. The cellar was damp, and the Berliner reasoned its wetness muted the volatility of the explosives. He became very white, and his eyes grew accustomed to the dark. I kept buckets of water on the stairs. He drank from these, although the water was precious, and not meant for him. The Futurist knocked against them the single time she descended, and I shouted at her that fire brigades are never nearby when they are needed. She was growing impatient indoors and now always had to be out, to see what was happening, to learn how things were going to end. The Berliner couldn't bear even the idea of going outside, even if the risk of arrest or likelihood of being drafted were suspended. He was forgotten about for days at a time but didn't seem to mind.

"The city has a life of its own," he said grimly, "and it marshals its limbs and emotions to drain everything from everybody. So I hide from it. The image of the burnt desert behind gates and wall is, in part, a welcome one, even if my demise is a piece of the bargain. At least in the fireworks, this awful city that drew me from my home in the north will be destroyed."

An elderly gentleman, Januszki, arrived at my house one night. Januszki had gambled away his fortune, and was therefore reduced to scavenging on the outskirts of the city. He brought me valuable Turkish arrows in place of money. When Turks realized their arrows were being collected, shots were used as lures to draw citizens out, then they killed them or were themselves shot, and in this way, skirmishes began anew, but somehow, Januszki had gotten through. He claimed the Turkish Spahis rode like devils, that the Asiatic hordes had unlimited wealth and arms at their disposal, and if Vienna fell, Europe would be enslaved to the Turkish monster. I imagined a hydra-headed lizard, turbans attached to each head, as it crawled over a map of Macedonia, Bosnia, making its way toward Berlin, leaving a trail of bloody footprints. Januszki was a walking reference book of Turkish customs, and we listened closely. I wanted to know, do Infidels have a human form similar to ourselves?

While he was roaming the outer borders of the Turkish camp Januszki met a French dwarf, the one who was rumored to be a child of the Sun King himself. Eugene de Soissons, now known as Savoy, escaped Paris, and arrived at the Kahlenberg Heights eager to liberate us. I asked if it was true the little man dressed in women's clothing at night, and Januszki said yes, this he'd seen himself.

The end came quickly, but not in the way we imagined it would. On the morning of September 11, the army of Charles of Lorraine attacked Turkish troops guarding a ridge. Ottoman legions occupied a ruined monastery, and in the night, they could be seen throwing books into a huge fire. When Lorraine's army was sighted from Saint Stephen's tower, rockets were fired from inside the city. The battle was brief; by evening the next day, the siege of Vienna was over. The Turks left tents, baggage, camels, orphans. In the grand vizier's tent, the King of Poland found two million pieces of gold. The tent was complicated, divided into many rooms, like a castle of cloth, and it billowed with treasure.

I still posed survival problems to myself. A loaf of real bread which originally cost two kreuzer became sixty. Nada and Marchegg looted houses and scavenged the Turkish camp at the heels of the retreating army. The camp was as big as the city of Warsaw. They found a jeweled copy of the Koran, knives, and a mountain of cooking pots. Also: sacks containing hundreds of pounds of coffee beans and copper jazvahs used for brewing, but no one yet knew what to do with them.

I became interested in coffee. When the original supply of Turkish beans from the grand vizier's tent was depleted, more were imported. Strong Turkish coffee became a source of pleasure and an addiction. Nada began to dye her hair with henna. Sacks of it had also been found in the tents belonging to the grand vizier. Like the coffee beans, its use was not initially clear, and some looters of the ruined tents, thinking it was a powdered spice, ate it until they died. After a year or so, red dye became hard to find, and when she ran out, Nada went for weeks with half yellow, half reddish-brown hair until I was able to procure more.

The empress had not been caught and displayed—that part of the Futurist's vision was uncharacteristically wrong, but she was right about the little man who liked to wear women's clothing. He appeared leading the army of Charles of Lorraine, and it was said that when his soldiers had no food, he too ate acorns. People loved him, or some did. Did I now feel safe? Not entirely. Naturally I began to wonder about the other anomalies cited by d'Aviano and the Futurist: the two-headed hare, the comet with two tails. If they were right about the dwarf, they might be right about the Turks coming again. The powdery sludge leaking from kegs onto the floor of my cellar accumulated in drifts, wet and unusable, until one hot summer my whole house felt like a tinderbox that could ignite any minute. We are capable of exploding ourselves with no help from anyone else, yet from time to time I remember the predictions and start to hoard cash, rice, dried fruit, and coffee beans.

The execution of spies or suspected spies—a practice begun during the siege—became a common occurrence, and always, the little man described by Januszki was present on the scaffold. Savoy's face was long, marked in the center by a tiny nose with enormous nostrils, as if by some whim of nature he'd originally had four eyes. He was hunchbacked, yet had an aloof, arrogant air, and stood to one side counting, giving the order, then the trap door was sprung. In one second the person traveled from, say, age twenty-five to middle to old age to death. How is royal assistant to the hangman a job? How much do you charge for being the officer who gives the signal to the executioner? Is that a well-paid post? Is it part of your morning you look forward to, knowing as you have your coffee, and you look at the clock thinking, two more hours to go, and then two, three, four, or however many convicted agents are present in the tumbrel, each will find themselves shaking hands with Saint Marina or groping in Cerberus' mouth for the hand he's just lost.

Carved gargoyles of round-mouthed angels and demons spouted cataracts of water in the rain, cobblestones were treacherous, and unpaved depressions turned into lakes, runnels into near rapids. Though the city had by now repaired itself from the siege, it was beginning to look like Venice of the north. At this time, during the weeks of endless rain, the Futurist disappeared. This was unlike her. She was making good money again, being showered with gifts, and none of her predictions had revealed any abysses, catastrophes, or just plain bad luck. All that, we thought, had ended with the siege.

A moat had formed behind the theater, and then it turned into a small pond that reflected the windows and mullions of the buildings across the way. It was here where the Futurist's body was found naked, face down. She had injuries consistent with the clockmaker's proclivities. I hired a strongman from Brno to stand at our door at night.

The siege may have been over, but Savoy was not done. The Turks, he said, had large stockpiles of quick-acting giant firearms the size of street lamps capable of spreading havoc and annihilation over vast areas of territory. The sultan had all the metal in the palace melted down to make these super guns, so powerful they could be fired in Istanbul and hit a fly in Berlin.

A man who repaired musical instruments became a frequent guest. Gavrilo traveled from city to city, court to court, restringing and tuning. His nights at the my house were joyous chaos. He held the mysteries of Vienna in one hand, weighed against the promises of Sarajevo in the other. From the city of a thousand delights, Sarajevo, the Turks launched their attack on the lacey edge of Europe: Vienna.

Sarajevo was the city of possibility, and he moved his hands up and down measuring the two cities against one another on a scale that calibrated unknown pleasures. What I can say about this particular guest is that, if possible, he would have ruled over an absurd kingdom. For example, Gavrilo believed interest should be illegal, and in fact, money should be abolished altogether, all monarchs should be deposed, and, in theory, if everyone pretty much followed rational beliefs and their own conscience, peace would roll over Europe like a great, soft comforting blanket. One night he took out paper money printed in patterns of violet, green, and red with the emperor's portrait printed on it and smoothed out the small bills. Nada tried to touch a note, but he snatched it away from her as if she was a thief. He stuck a quill in a bottle of ink, reached for my arm, and holding it tighter than I would have imagined he was capable, began to draw on my skin. The quill pricked and left a tattoo of a word I couldn't quite make out. It looked like kronen. I pushed him away.

# 1697

THE TURKS RETURNED AGAIN, and they were defeated again. This time, they only got as far as Zenta, a small burg somewhere southeast of my door. In the morning after the battle, according to his own telling of the war, Eugene de Savoy claimed to have marched over a bridge made of headless corpses. The battle at Zenta made our French liberator a rich man. His inventory included:

9000 laden wagons
600 prisoners
17,000 oxen
60,000 camels
700 horses
100 heavy cannon
70 field pieces
500 drums
25,000 bullets
553 bombs
505 barrels of gunpowder
74 pairs of silver kettle drums
82 women
Three million livres, the money that was to be paid to the army

Lead casements dug into our arms as we leaned out the windows to inspect the parade of prisoners. What would the dwarf army commander do with them? The women might be considered a treasure or prize transferred from one king to another. They could be given as servants, as factory workers, as a gift to a court musician with tough, pruney hands who never had any wives. We had no idea. I watched the parade disappear until only beggars, dogs, and ordinary citizens filled the street again.

In watching them, I hoped sacks of henna would find their way back into the markets. Nada's hair was turning into gray and rusty streaks. Business wasn't good. At night I envisioned someone else, younger, livelier, with a different set of girls taking over my tenancy, laughter spilling out into the street. My girls would be scattered and, true to their limited talents and abilities, destined for the downward spiral on which the aging of my profession travel. I could find shelter in an abandoned gardener's shed behind the Italienische Nationalkirche for a few months if I was lucky. The landlord gave me a little more time in exchange for a couple of tosses with Nada. I said okay. I was days away from losing my house, and without a house, I was nothing. At my age, homelessness isn't something you recover from. Clients need to trust you, to believe you have a certain amount of stability. You do what you have to do.

The woman wrapped a scarf tightly around her neck and hid her trousers under a dress. Each evening she sat in the park, waiting. Men always knew what she was there for. She never had to say a word; she had only to gesture for money first. This was how I found her, setting up shop in a park, luring away my customers.

"You can't do business here. The gentlemen you stop are on their way to my house." I spoke slowly to her, so she would understand me, and pointed to the windows of my establishment that glowed faintly with candlelight, signs of people and shadows moving in the recesses of rooms. She gave no resistance when I gently pulled her from behind a row of bare lilac bushes, branches like wires, buds just beginning to appear. Walking her across the frozen square to my house was easy; her teeth were chattering.

She was one of the women released into the city by the dwarf, the first of three I would find and introduce into my business.

I brought her paper, pen, and ink, and she drew her story in panels, one after the next. Later that night when Gavrilo knocked on my door, because he had done business in Istanbul, he was able to translate her story for us as she told it.

She used her hands to make shadow puppets on the wall. Gavrilo couldn't stop staring at her fingers and the figures she so dexterously demonstrated. He was spellbound. I had hit gold.

He was thinking that she will see how he, unlike the others, lacks animosity. Gavrilo will be a constant customer, and as he opens her door, he'll imagine he's performing an act of peace and goodwill. She'll make him feel liberal and powerful, bountiful and generous while he speaks to her about Turkish coffee and carpets. Then, when she doesn't understand his constant smiling or half of what he says, he'll ask her to listen closely to his words. He'll speak slowly. She still won't understand all of what he will say, so he'll demonstrate what he wants, then he'll feel humiliated. In the end, he'll be the most brutal of any of the men sent to her because he'll suspect she pities him. I'd seen it all before.

# FROM CAIRO TO ISTANBUL

A MONKEY PERCHED ON her shoulder, grabbed a fragment of bread, and screeched, baring his teeth after gulping it down. One of the servants took the animal away before it could crap on Adila's dress. Because of his gestures she was sure he used the word crap, even though he whispered in his own language. She wanted to hold onto the monkey, but it was carried to another part of the house, happily stuffing its mouth with whatever food could be grabbed from passing trays. His little head turned over his shoulder, yellow teeth grinning, flashing his red butt in a last gesture of defiance before he disappeared. Adila ran her fingers over her dress's gold embroidery until the tips were raw and tasted of metal when she put them in her mouth.

All the women and children lived behind a series of doors and screens in one part of the house, and now in an intermediary room, her father's two other wives and several of her half-sisters waited with her. The wives sat close and held her hand, first one, then the other, but while they lingered, no one except her mother spoke to her directly. Servants also crowded into the narrow high-ceilinged room to catch a glimpse of the Turkish travelers who were expected that day. Hennaed feet and toes drew patterns on new carpets and small children studied how their angular noses turned round and their cheeks became laced with engraved calligraphy reflected on the convex surfaces of brass lamps. As the wait stretched into hours, other half brothers and sisters came and went through the double doors which led to the garden and the rest of the house. While the others could come and go as they pleased, Adila had to stay where she was, watching double doors that led to the street in Cairo where she had spent her entire life. The departure of the monkey must have meant that someone thought the emissaries would arrive soon.

Her father was rich, but by sending his fourteen-year-old daughter away to Istanbul, his tribute money to the sultan was reduced. It was a good deal for him, one he'd been bargaining on for a year with each troop of envoys who were periodically required to stick their noses into his business. Some of her stepsisters had married into families who lived in other parts of Cairo. When they married, each left the house to disappear into the city, but no marriage had taken one of them beyond its borders, or even beyond their quarter.

She couldn't picture the distant city. The house in Istanbul would be identical or closely identical because that was the only kind of house she knew. This is what would happen when she arrived. Someone in a room she couldn't see would be playing the oud. The children would play the same games she had played. Servants would pass through the same arches carrying the same cups of coffee thickened with resin sap and sugar. Her concept of the word journey wasn't a straight line, a dead end marking its conclusion, but implied an elliptical motion: a journey ended either where it began or in a place identical to the one you've left. There were stories about going away. One left poor, learned from adventures, quests, met with adversaries, was transformed into an animal or a djinn, but always returned rich.

Now the women of the household waited all day with her. Tea was brewed early in the morning, then they sat in a white room behind a series of screens. On her last day in Cairo, there was nothing to do but wait.

Her mother told her she would see the ocean, and someone in the group agreed. She had seen maps; there was a sea beyond the Nile, and a sea beyond that, full of islands and tongues of land that led to mountains and inland lakes of no name whatsoever populated by monsters who had virtually no skin and hair as colorless as a glass of water.

If they heard horses one of them would look out at the street through mashrabiya, carved window screens which allowed women to look out without being seen. Across the street tiers of white houses, cypress trees, stray cats, and peddlers presented a picture with few moving parts, but late in the day Adila stared with more concentration, as if by memorizing the view, which barely changed from year to year, she could insure against the loss of forgetting.

Late into the night, when the Turkish agents finally arrived, Adila was asleep on the carpets. The soldiers entered the shaikh's house accompanied by an old woman. Her hair was hennaed and her face was painted; streaks of bright red and green showed under a veil, which she removed when she entered the room. The woman was the only one who spoke, and even then, she would only address Adila's mother, giving her a payment of respect that was entered in the credit side of her imaginary ledger. Her mother kissed her goodbye, and she was carried into the street. Lamps extinguished, carpets swept until no traces remained of the long wait. Oblivious to her departure, Adila's monkey swung from an orange tree in the courtyard. He had already been given to one of her half-sisters.

One of the soldiers spoke some Arabic. Another had light brown hair, and this was the first sign for Adila that the Turks would look different from the men and women in her father's house. She'd never seen light hair and wondered if it would melt in the rain like sugar, then grow back when he was indoors.

❈

Led through a pair of iron doors, followed by pairs of brass doors, Adila found herself in a palace as big as a city. The rooms she was guided through appeared turned in on themselves. Rooms within rooms, folded, nestled, tucked into one another, linked by blue-tiled arcades which gave an illusion of airiness. Adila was told *harem* means *forbidden*. When she felt the walls closing in, she looked up at the high ceilings curved into domes or half-domes. The soldiers handed her over to a group of Ethiopians whispering in Amharic, and three of them, their yellow silk sleeves swishing as they walked, brought her to the inner palace.

There was an inner palace and an outer palace. The residents of each half were invisible to the other. The inner palace, where the women were kept, surrounded a large courtyard and was connected to the throne by the Gate of Felicity. Four hundred women lived there, organized into seven different classes. Many never saw the sultan or the world outside the inner palace. Some were brought up in the inner palace to be educated and married to his pages. There were others who worked as cooks, bath attendants, servers of coffee, and they, too, had no attachment to him. After a sultan's death, some would be removed to the old palace. Considered the possessions of a dead man, the services they might perform for the new ruler were limited. These women remained in the old palace until they died.

They would hear his silver-heeled boots in the hall, and the agha would instruct the women to hide their faces. Because of palace rules, Adila first saw the sultan through a screen. He was older than her father, but larger, and seemed not to see any of the women surrounding him. He would enter the inner palace at night smelling of oiled leather and dead animals. Sometimes he wore a white turban, but more often a gold Venetian helmet that sat on his head like a small house. Engrossed with his advisors, the sounds of fragments of conversations about numbers of dead animals and even the details of imminent invasions drifted past.

❀

Many of the rooms of the inner palace looked out on the garden, and from here Adila could hear the aghas complaining about the sultan, who was obsessed with hunting. Bears, lynx, leopards, otters, fox, rabbits, if it can run, he will shoot it. His mother, they said, encouraged his fanaticism so she could run the empire. Naked to the waist like dervishes, partially hidden by the lattice which surrounded the fountain, the aghas gossiped, unaware of Adila at her window directly above them. They ate pomegranates in lime and rosewater syrup. Blue smoke from their nargile floated over the water.

By listening to the aghas, she learned about how the palace was run. The sultans had miniaturists follow them around so that painters, along with scribes known as the Chroniclers, could record their lives. They were painted hunting and praying, leading parades to commemorate the births of their sons. They were never painted smoking one nargile after another. They were never painted in a semi-conscious stupor. They weren't painted with women. Women weren't painted at all. The sequential history was one of combat, hunting, and prayer. Evidence of excesses disappeared with their witnesses' sudden deaths.

The aghas left the garden and as their voices trailed away, she stared at the ceiling above her head, feeling as if the words lettered in tile on it were not flat but as truly three-dimensional as they were meant to appear.

The older agha whose head was shaved was Ali. The younger agha with the emerald earrings was Gaspar, and he told Adila about the prison full of princes in the middle of the harem, one of the most forbidden places in the palace. Their jail was called the Cage, and they often went mad in it. It was two stories high, with windows covered by iron bars, but contained rooms as ornate and as lavish as the ones they occupied. It was reached along a corridor called the Golden Road, bounded on one side by the Consultation Hall of the

Djinn, but he told her she should never go there or even look for it. Brothers and sons of the sultan were imprisoned in order to prevent any threat to his sovereignty. Although years or decades might pass without incident, death by strangulation could happen to the prisoners any minute. In one second, they could be immensely powerful or find themselves at the bottom of the Bosporus. Their only companions were deaf mutes, clowns, and musicians whose playing is said to cure madness, but it never did.

Adila heard music in the middle of the night and followed the sound to the halls near the Golden Road, where she saw Ali and followed him to the Cage of the mad princes. No one was looking, so she was able to watch him treat the prisoners with a combination of respect and mockery, as if they were children, although any one of them could become his master and could have him exiled to the old palace, reducing a lifetime of the most arch manipulation and politicking to utter futility.

It became a habit, following Ali at night, getting as close to the Cage as she dared while he whispered germs of fears into the prince's cell: *The bars look as if they're gradually moving closer together. It troubles me that if fire were to break out no one, in their panic to escape, would remember to free the princes. I have heard of snakes being introduced into the cages. One should never drink to the bottom of a glass because of poisonous sediment. One never knows what those grains might turn into or what might be revealed about the glass's bottom by consumption of the last swallow.*

❊

His nose was enormous and intrusive. He was a prankster you were supposed to applaud, even when he slipped up and appeared to make things worse. Adila knew he was only made of paper and wood, a shadow puppet, but she felt his eyes follow her, and his arms, she was sure of it, moved even when he dangled from a peg, untethered to any human. She didn't understand the comedy performed by a woman from Ankara and asked Gaspar to find her books, so she could sit in the back, as far from the stage as possible, and read while the Karagiozis plays were performed, but he refused. If no one was watching her, she shut her eyes as if she were asleep.

There was no place more frightening than the corner behind the dark partition where Karagiozis hung on pegs. Adila wanted to see Karagiozis torn to bits, his smile and hooked nose scattered from the window. She was afraid if she touched him, he would spring to life.

Gaspar made things worse. He apprenticed her to the Ankarani mending the fragile paper figures. Only during daylight, small jobs, one at a time, he said. Painting them was like drawing calligraphy. Then she began to enjoy gluing bits and pieces together to form new figures.

One night, Gaspar played a joke on her. The Karagiozis of Istanbul, the one who was performed by men in cafés and smoking houses, had enormous equipment. He was famous for it. In one play, a classic, in order to hide himself from a persistent female admirer, Karagiozis pretends to be an arched bridge, supported by a single pylon: his huge dick. Mobs, armies, marching bands all cross over him with no difficulty. The audience, even those familiar with the story, laughed hysterically every time. Everyone knew about Karagiozis's massive reputation, except for the women of the inner palace, who were given a much tamer version of the colored shadows. Gaspar acquired a real Karagiozis and one night replaced Adila's castrated figure with his café society double. She tore off the outsized body part and handed it back to him in the morning, only saying, did you lose something?

When the Ankarani became ill, lost her voice, and the ability to stand or even sit for long periods of time, Adila took over more and more of the performances, disappearing behind the screen, speaking in deep or high voices, adopting accents not her own. After the older woman's death, Adila became the custodian and manager of the shadow theater.

Karagiozis dressed as a woman to escape the passionate wives of other men. In order to change direction, he would somersault with a twist of a rod. Tiryaki was a hunchbacked opium smoker who carried his pipe and fan. He spoke in a husky voice. Hachivat had a pointed, turned-up beard. He was vain but clownish. In puppet form, women characters might be barely dressed and would find pleasure chasing Karagiozis. Sometimes she saw herself as the Hachivat character, Karagiozis's foil, his straight man; sometimes she was Tiryaki who had an escape.

As women and children entered the inner palace from three continents, Adila would remember their stories after they themselves had forgotten them and put bits and pieces into the performances when she could. Crucifixions and exile weren't funny, but resurrection allowed the characters to die, then come back. A dance from Anatolia performed with lit candles which only girls, happily married women, or women who'd been married only once could take part in became a joke when Karagiozis performed the spectacle of himself because he could find no happily married women. In another episode, featuring a ritual from the south, he was coerced into a rain dance, running naked from house to house while water was poured on him, the perfect way for Karagiozis to perform as seducer, his traditional role. Fire and water had to be engineered as illusions because, in reality, they would mean the end of the shadow figures.

One evening Adila produced the first part of a play which she didn't know how to end. Karagiozis and Hachivat worked as masons for a man whose wife was considered the most beautiful and most vain woman in the world. Every surface in the new house was to be mirrored. Karagiozis and Hachivat were desperate to see her, but didn't know which part of the structure she occupied. They had plans of the estate and pored over them. (Paper was rustled backstage.) The house was vast, and because of the mirrors appeared twice as large as it actually was. To their extreme frustration, her location seemed to change every night. In the morning, when the two came to work, they were taunted by the ribbons, bits of jewelry, and pieces of clothing they found. (Bits of thin red silk and unraveled skeins of gold thread were waved behind the screen.) The owner, they suspected, moved her intentionally because he was a jealous man. Shortly before he was due to leave on a trading trip, he grew especially anxious. Karagiozis and Hachivat reassured him that they would finish their work, and his wife would be safe. After his departure, the two masons spent the night in the house of mirrors, trying to find her. At every turn, at every spangled ogee arch, they banged into each other or their reflections. The day before the owner was to return, they shook and stuttered with anxiety. They'd done no work yet still hadn't found her. Tiryaki, the addict, came to visit them, but he, too, became lost in the house of mirrors. Karagiozis tried to trace him by following the smell of his opium, but the nargile produced so much smoke that he became confused and mistook Tiryaki's reflection, distorted by the haze and gleam, for the most beautiful woman in the world. His desperate embrace met with nothing.

Adila thought Karagiozis ought to find the man's wife at the last minute, just before her husband returned, and consequently be caught by him. This solution would follow the lines of traditional comedy. She described to Gaspar how Karagiozis might then try to escape. Gaspar believed he should never find the woman, never really see her, has no idea who she is and never will know. That was the whole point. But then, Adila felt, there's no proof she ever existed.

The night the play was performed, just as Karagiozis embraced Tiryaki's barely distinct reflected shadow, a thud sounded in the audience. It was one of the henna artists who painted knobby spiral patterns of henna on their hands and feet, framing toenails with ticklish strokes. She was an addict who hid faceted lumps of opium paste mixed with ground pearls or jewel dust where no one could find them.

Rumors began that Tiryaki's disappearance had caused her death, and Adila was a witch, approaching the age of despair, Sin El Ya'as. No one would talk to her. She refused to give up on the shadow plays, though she performed to an ever-dwindling audience. Karagiozis and company were a curse.

Gaspar watched a man coil chains from a heap into a basket, threading them from the confusion of the pile into neat metal spirals, hidden snakes waiting for the charmer's whistle to slither into business. Gaspar had no reason to be in a corner of the palace grounds where the arsenal bordered a treeless courtyard, especially at night, but it was exactly these kinds of spaces he looked for, places where no one would think to search for him, places where men calculated taxes, slapped horses, cleaned matchlocks, fitting sleek barrel into trigger into filigreed rifle butt. This courtyard he stumbled into was completely silent apart from the sound of iron links clinking against one another. Two other men appeared, but none of the three spoke. They looked gray from exhaustion, even torchlight didn't warm the color of their skin, and Gaspar winced as he watched their hands touch iron. He knew how the links stole all the oil from your skin until, with repeated chafing, the metal took skin as well. All three of them were needed to lift the basket onto a wagon already staggering under the weight of identical baskets hiding miles of coils. Every night Gaspar watched as baskets of chains, fetters, and thousands of handcuffs were packed and sent out of the palace. He listened and observed, then he slipped back into the inner palace.

Kara Mustapha planned a hunting expedition to leave Istanbul after the fast of Ramadan and before the feast of Bairam. The destination was set as Adrianople, but the entourage assembled to accompany him was much larger than that which would be required for a hunting expedition. It was no longer a secret that thousands of newly made matchlocks were being oiled, more than even his demented brother ever ordered. The old agha, Ali, clicking amber beads on a string, counting, then swinging the strand back and forth, didn't need Gaspar's nightly wanderings to inform him the entire army was packing up.

One lunatic was as good as or bad as the next. Ali believed you tolerated them or shut up about their obsessions because they held your life in their hands. Discussion was pointless. Gaspar didn't snoop around for his own pleasure, but to learn what lay under the surface of each command and desire, because the knowledge might turn out to be useful at some later date. He wanted Ali to rely on him, to trust him with confidences, to count on his observations, and he was always eager to try again, to offer some useful piece of information. Without question, Ali told Gaspar, what he saw in the courtyard made no sense. Ali insisted even the most deranged of the caged princes wouldn't take hundreds of women to a war in the middle of nowhere.

Everybody wants something, Ali thought, and when they're thwarted they want it even more. Desire, if not fear, eats the soul.

Just as Gaspar had watched lengths of chain assembled by the wagon load, Ali had witnessed the packing of reams of paper. When is a hunt not a hunt? When is wish for a smoke or to hear an oud more than simply a wish for pleasure but a way to delay the inevitable? When is a stack of blank books not a stack of blank books, but a table leg constructed to replace the original when it gives way, or a column of paper might be prepared to hold up the ceiling above their heads when marble shifts or crumbles. Either way the paper stack was a sign of a disaster waiting to happen. This packing, too, was done at night. A massive assembling of writing material could only mean the Men of the Pen, also known as the Chroniclers, were going too. Envied for being so close to the sultan, the Chroniclers taunted the eunuchs because they had pens which the aghas didn't. Whether the Chroniclers wrote an accurate mirror or a corrupting one full of flattery and distortions, few really knew. Ali thought their ink-stained fingers expressed a secret desire to look like him. He had one thing the Chroniclers didn't have, which they would dearly love: access to the inner palace. The writers were the worst transgressors of the boundaries of the inner palace. If discovered in it, the clowns were promptly murdered, but even knowing what they risked, from time to time they would attempt to trespass anyway. It was like a sport to them, and they had all kinds of schemes. One of them stained his skin with walnut dye in order to pass as an agha. When the dye began to dissolve, his own paler skin appeared, and in this way, he was discovered.

Once outside the palace, his job would become impossible. Without the safety of solid walls, Ali needed to be one step ahead. He imagined a building with extra rooms hidden by extra walls with trap doors and escape hatches no one could find unless they knew where to look, but once on the road, no such safety existed.

Adila and the others passed through the Gate of Felicity for the second and last time, walked through an empty palace, crossed the threshold of the Topkapi main gates to find themselves on the street, although every inch above the ground was hidden from them by a long silk tunnel which led to their carriages. The cloth was old and torn, so late afternoon sunlight fell in crescent shapes on the women as they hurried through the billowing passageway. She tried to look through the rips, slowing her pace, but all she could see were blurred shapes: crowds of people, a man's arm, a horse's tail, an edge of stone. Finally she had a glimpse of what would be her last image of Istanbul: a man sitting outside a market, selling piles of olives. The market was shuttered, its stalls closed down. The man sat alone on the ground leaning against a wall, almost asleep.

Gaspar and Ali had an unblinkered view of the parade of spectacles that accompanied their departure: mock water battles between

Christians and Saracens, fireworks which looked like giant luminous asters but sounded like canons. Banners depicting panoramas of battles and victory, versions of Karagiozis and Tiryaki made of clay, wax, and paper, larger than life, carried on poles. The procession went on and on. At the end a trail of köçek, the female impersonators, veiled and skittish, flirted with one another and with the spectators, but at the very end were the beggars who followed the parade. They dove for coins and searched trash heaps for bits of metal, scraps of leather, fragments of glass.

The next day was the occasion of the practical exodus: household cavalry, blacksmiths, cobblers, cooks, and others required for maintaining the army. The last to wander out that day, disorganized and tumbling over one another, were the entertainers. A legion of Janissaries, whose task it was to sing rude songs, was followed by clowns, acrobats, procurers, go-betweens, and pimps.

By twilight, one hundred thousand people had departed, led by the sultan's silver coach and velvet-saddled horses. By now everyone knew they were traveling to Belgrade. Gaspar believed the sultan's desire to take the residents of the inner palace through Kosovo, Montenegro, Serbia, Bosnia, Croatia, and all the way to Vienna had its source in his imprisonment. One of the demons from his years in the Cage had given him the idea that if he could reproduce his palace on the battlefield, he would be invincible. Harem and army, pleasure and defense, both portable, accompanied him. Everyone did as he or she was told.

❊

As they traveled north, they passed through no cities, and the monotony and apparent purposelessness of the trip got on everyone's nerves.

The women were kept next to the sultan's green ceremonial tent, but despite their proximity to guards and soldiers, Ali and Gaspar needed to pace its perimeters from the inside. In a battle, even long before it began, order in the encampment could break down in small ways, and in the approaching chaos, the space between the bottom of the tent and the ground could be cut or widened to let men in. If a man broke through, it would be the agha's body left in a ditch, not anyone else's. They had no illusions. You could go to sleep in favor and wake up a condemned man.

They passed through one dry valley after the next, rocky and nearly treeless. A woman from Venice, who had seen maps, guessed they were far north of Adrianople. Ali told them, if you're captured, give them the gold in your ears, and you might be able to buy your way out. Sometimes they convert you to Christianity, then once your soul is saved, you can go to your death happy, they say. He looked at all the thousands of pairs of handcuffs and fetters had been assembled for the prisoners Kara Mustapha was sure he would take. If they lost, the chains would be used on themselves.

By early September, as they made their way north, some towns greeted them and cheered their passage. Others were like ghost towns, shutters flapping in the wind, birds flying in and out of abandoned buildings.

They reached a small city in northern Croatia, and there they stopped. The town wasn't deserted; clusters of people walked close to the walls and hurried along their way, but no one greeted them. They pitched their tents but were told to be ready to move on in the morning.

The town began to burn; they heard cannon battering a bridge, and the sound of a barricade made of wagons broken through. Ali ran into their tent to tell them detachments from the north were closing in, although there was no reason to hurry. There was nothing for him to do.

Adila didn't see the fighting, but the aghas had been right. They lost. The women were taken to our city, but it was a long march. She watched the landscape turned hilly; granite boulders and acacia trees turned into forests and vineyards. Ominous-looking cloisters, Cistercian monasteries built on low ground near wells, abbeys of the Beggars' Orders with their bell towers and narrow gothic spires, so unlike the domes and minarets Adila remembered from childhood. Crucifixes of all sizes sprung up everywhere. In ruined castles whose towers were full of birds, Adila read signs of calamity. She was certain she wouldn't know how anyone should act in a place where people lived in buildings like these: narrow blocky constructions whose wide-open, shutterless windows and balconies looked straight into the street. The social alphabet would be as incomprehensible as the guttural language barked around her.

People came out of their houses to stare at them, and all kinds of animals crossed the road in front of them. Men and women could be seen bending over rows of plants in fields. They were pulling the plants up, shaking dirt off the roots and stacking them to be carted away. They eat these things, someone said, with pieces of metal held over fire.

The aghas marched far behind with other prisoners. Ali was made to walk in chains with common captives, men it would have been beneath him to speak to in Istanbul, men who had never even seen the palace and could not imagine his power within it.

The women were separated from the prisoners and paraded through the city as part of a mass of looted treasure. At first, they were surrounded by a wall of men on horseback. Then, gradually, the phalanx let townspeople through their ranks. Men and women stared with bare faces like raw potatoes. Their language sounded like braying and honking but must have been made of words, questions, commands. None of them could walk fast enough, but none were allowed to fall behind. They inhaled dust and were given nothing to drink. Adila clutched Karagiozis, silent troublemaker, now outgunned. Half-demonic, half-human, hiding under the bed, behind a column, or peering down from a dome or minaret, he was powerless here. This city was different from anything she'd ever seen: broad streets, very tall gray stone buildings with terrace-less square windows, cathedrals with long, spiky, pointed arches looking prickly and skyward.

At the other end of the procession, Adila saw a very small man who gave orders as if he were in command, yet this seemed so unlikely she couldn't figure out what his position might actually be. He wore metal plates which resembled an assemblage of shallow frying pans, but the metal plates hid a costume of complex frilliness. All the white men surrounding him wore some form of this suit.

Men in metal suits stood in front of buildings that sprouted stone soldiers, monsters, naked women, some winged, some not. The buildings dripped with statues. They were so realistic, Adila expected they could talk, and perhaps did so when no one was looking. Then the crowds dispersed. The procession had arrived at a palace. Adila had never seen a building with so many windows, and as with most of the buildings, the windows had no screens. Its entire surface, vast and carved, was perforated by hundreds of panes of glass, a structure that was meant to be seen from the outside, to be walked past. All the women were assembled outside the palace, and here she saw Gasper and Ali in chains. They were all curiosities and would be displayed together.

Some of the women were taken up a broad staircase whose marble columns were statues of naked men. The men of Herculean proportions were bent over as if the ceiling rested on their shoulders. A naked man holding a club stood at the top of the stairs, a giant seashell behind him, twin angels over his head. There was something disproportionate about the men. Although the weight of at least part of the second floor rested on their hunched shoulders. It was possible, Adila thought, that these people didn't wear clothes indoors at all. Even if they did wear clothes inside, she would not want to live in a house with naked marble giants who woke up at night.

They were led through corridors to a large room whose ceiling hung with bouquets of sharp-edged faceted pieces of glass, and here they were left. A guard shut the door, locking them in. Night came, and they slept on the floor. Early in the morning the doors burst open and a group of metal men barked sentences that melted into waves of speech-like noise.

Then a man she understood to be the emperor walked into the chamber, followed by his court. Adila was shocked by his ugliness. His lank, dark hair framed a long face and the biggest, most pendulous lips she had ever seen. The dwarf who led the army, wig threaded with diamonds, stood beside him, and next to him, a translator shouted out long sentences that were hard to follow. Displayed behind the emperor were three flags taken from the sultan's tent, each marked with horsetails carried into campaigns in imitation of Alexander the Great.

Most of the court were blond and blue-eyed and stood in a glittering ring around them. The women wore dresses which stood out on either side of their bodies like bells waiting to be rung. They had small waists, carried fans which occasionally hid their faces, but for the most part they didn't seem to care who saw them. The men wore short trousers, long coats, lace collars the size of platters, and enormous feathered hats.

Through a translator, the emperor asked them all to be quiet. The heroism of their liberator, and here he pointed to the dwarf, was praised, and his judgment in granting them their freedom commended. At the word *freedom*, a few people clapped. Adila was confused by the sound and translated meaning. The people in this city wanted them dead, everybody knew this, therefore the word pronounced *freedom* must mean *death*, she was certain. The translator had made a mistake. Freedom = Death.

A man and woman in the crowd, bored with the ceremony, leaned their bodies against a wall and kissed openly. Their hands went everywhere, inside and over clothing. Half their necks and faces were wet with sweat.

Finally the translation ended. Three men walked among them and divided the women into two groups. Adila was part of the group that was led from the hall to the gates of the palace. The command was given to open the gates, gestures made that they should leave, and the gates closed behind her. The metropolis seemed to be constructed of corners, hills, arcades, and steps that led nowhere, but she found a doorway, a space under an arch, her back against the door.

The city was organized like a spider web, and days went by when she felt she was walking in circles, but gradually she grew used to it. The others had been swallowed up by paved streets, steep windowed walls, and gardens, never to be seen again. She learned how to find niches in buildings and alleys from the outside. Buildings no one lived in were called churches, but though without occupants, many visitors still frequented them. The visitors would tap their shoulders, forehead, and chest while kneeling, then leave. Buttresses fit into the sides of churches and these corners could be temporary shelter, along with spaces found under outer stairways and under balconies and terraces toward the back of buildings. She learned the difference between various quarters and markets. Some were dark and criminal, others seemed affluent and airy with decorated and crenellated houses which shut her out and gave her nothing. Beyond the clothes she wore, she had little physical evidence the inner palace, as she had known it, had ever existed.

Different inflections of voice suggested certain images, but she stopped just short of really trusting that a particular collection of letters or sounds signified a man, a dog, a carrot. Twisted lines engraved on a plaque could indicate a name on a door or warning. With so little information, with no one to really teach her, the margin for error was infinite. Because she spoke only to herself, she had free range with the new language. Boredom and confusion dictated which names or verbs she assigned to clumps of sounds and gestures. A word might sound like what she thought *Delicious!* ought to sound like but actually meant *Be careful!* It was a question of degree of misreading, of how far off she really was. Her imagined language had a life of its own. *Run for your life!* could mean *I'll give you a drink if you…* Adjectives, adverbs, prepositions, and conjunctions were less troubling. If she mistook *blue* for *green*, *toward* for *by*, the result might be less calamitous, but as time went on, she didn't care if she mistook *poison* for *pillow*.

In late fall, as it grew colder, she lingered longer than usual in a market arcade, hoping that in the evening, when stands shut down, she would be able to pick up the stale bread, discarded fruit and odd scrap of meat left behind. Sometimes she was harassed for scavenging, so she waited until it was dark. As she sorted through a pile of garbage, she heard a man's voice mumbling in Turkish.

"Hey, you, girly, come with me."

The sound of his words was startling. The speaker stood a few feet from her, but reached out his arms as if to grab her. She looked at him closely. His round eyes reminded her of Tiryaki, the addict. Since he had no moustache or beard, his short upper lip exaggerated the overhang of his nose. The speaker appeared comfortable in northern-style trousers, wool jacket, and a broad-brimmed hat, but all were mismatched. He looked like a phantom but spoke a language she understood.

She didn't like the way he held out his arms to her, the kind of assumptions the embrace implied, and she stepped away from him. To the Viennese she was a homeless refugee, human refuse, and she knew it, but to a possible Osmanli in funny clothing, she was due the respect she had been accorded in the inner palace. She tied the sleeves of a velvet jacket around her neck, thinking it ceased being a jacket and looked like the capes she'd seen people wear. The idea of trusting the apparition who appeared as if sprung from a wall was a shaky one. Even though they both had tried to blend in and not be noticed, as they sized one another up, each of them felt confident that he or she had a more accurate eye than the other. He labored under the illusion he could pass if he had to, but so did Adila. She viewed his results as a mixed success. He spotted her from a mile away.

"How did I get here? How did you get here? Need a place to stay? I think you do. I've got a house at the back of the theater. Nobody notices me because even those who work at the theater never go into that back alley."

He spoke in short sentences that came out in nervous bursts. He let her know his adopted name was Henrik, and he was a very busy man. He would not tell her his original name. It was possible he didn't remember it.

"Why? What do you do that keeps you so occupied, so engrossed?" Adila took a few steps toward him, careful to stay out of his reach. What possible occupation could he have found in this city?

"I was one of the agents who was not killed during the siege of years past. At first there were two or three of us. Now there's only myself left. The waters closed over our retreat and any possible route out was impossible. We were marooned in the city as if it were a desert island, still alive only because of the ignorance of those citizens whose doom we had worked so hard to bring about."

He described the characters he tracked, the gunsmiths, forgers, and ambassadors' assistants, and Adila followed him as he made his way through winding streets to a grand part of the city she hadn't seen before. Some of the buildings were mansions, lit up and ornate. Streets were full of people laughing and gossiping, hurrying somewhere. She envied their warmth and collusion, their feeling at home in the world. From time to time the two of them, in their strange clothing, were stared at, but Henrik paid no notice to the attention he received. When he was working, which was virtually all the time, he imagined he was invisible.

Although many years had passed since the great siege, Henrik still wrote his reports to the sultan in a code of his own invention, believing his carefully worded narratives documenting the comings and goings of arms merchants and mercenaries were still urgent. When the war ended, and he found himself stuck within the city gates, he continued to collect information: a design for a rotating cannon that he claimed he found in a pile of garbage outside the arsenal, an overheard conversation about a push toward the Caspian Sea. He did not know how to get his written accounts to Istanbul, and so saved them, convinced his stalled reports were invaluable. No one could be trusted with their transport, but he had no doubt the information they contained would be of great significance, regardless of the year in which the papers might finally find their way to the Topkapi Palace. When the sultan did read them, Henrik had no doubt he would be considered a champion who had risked his life to serve the empire.

"When the day comes, the sultan will personally see that I am smuggled out of Vienna and returned to Istanbul, a hero, a rich man."

"But the man to whom you've addressed your accounts is long dead."

He didn't believe her. Henrik knew nothing about the Topkapi Palace. He had never set foot in Istanbul. He didn't tell her that he was recruited when he was fourteen years old and only as a provincial courier from Cyprus. He looked Adila up and down. Why would a ragged woman know about the Topkapi? She was, he decided, a messenger in disguise, finally come to ferry the volumes of his reports to their destination in Istanbul as soon as he completed writing them.

He took her arm protectively, and she let herself be led along. "In that house," Henrik jerked his head toward a building that looked to Adila like all the rest, "you'll find a moneylender. Everybody owes him. The woman who lives on the corner is an abortionist and an herbalist. She made the poison that killed the mayor's wife."

Adila understood his words, but she had no idea what he was actually talking about. They arrived at the theater, a massive stone building, birds nesting somewhere above them. Henrik had a key to a side door.

"A shortcut," he said. "It's actually safer to go through the theater than around it. My house is at the back, but a tinker has a hut at the entrance to the alley, and he threatens to turn me in every time he sees me." Adila adjusted the jacket that was tied like a cape. "You should only come and go with me. I offer you safety, but also more danger."

Night was approaching, but Adila could see well enough to figure out they were passing through tunnels where costumes, scenery, papers, and musical instruments were stored. She could make out suits of armor and rats running along the walls. It grew darker, and Henrik took her hand as they made their way to the back of the theater. He filled the silence with his history.

"If I did return to Cyprus, I'd be a stranger. I would have to explain why I hadn't come back sooner, if there is anyone left to explain to. At the end of the siege, an informant told me there was nothing left. A vast country from here to Athens lay burnt to the ground. Complicated cities were reduced to simple black rings. It was as if a giant landmass full of volcanoes and deep abysses had risen up between this city and the one I'd left. I had to stay where I was. Even when my knowledge of the language improved, and I realized the story of total destruction couldn't be based on facts, I still had a job to do."

They had reached the theater's back door. In his free hand, Henrik held a metal hand. It was jointed, claw-like, stolen from a suit of armor. The theft had been so skillful Adila hadn't even noticed him detach the hand from any of the metal bodies that lined the corridor.

"What was a theater?" He knocked on a wall before unbolting the theater door. "I'd never seen one before. Why were women allowed to walk down a street alone? What was Eucharist? Meat always tasted like pork, but I've had to eat it. I was forced to scavenge along winding streets, learning the language and manners by imitation. I haven't spoken Turkish to anyone except myself for so long I don't even know if that's the language I'm speaking. Is it?"

A hookah or a metal hand were a source of confusion and clutter, and just added to the pile of junk that composed daily life. He couldn't always sort them out with any accuracy. He stood motionless, still not opening the door.

He had forgotten territories of his original language, without replacing it so much by new words as by intangible, nameless desires. He even dreamed in his adopted language. Gaps appeared when he wanted to explain himself to her, and words in any language failed him. He pushed open the back door.

Behind the door lay an L-shaped alley. At the end of it was a pile of things, an improvised makeshift hut made of sticks, pieces of old doors and shutters. He unlocked the door and ushered her inside, making a sweeping gesture which inadvertently knocked her onto a rolled-up carpet. She sat on it, an unimaginable luxury, and leaned her back against a wall on which another carpet had been nailed into chinks in the mortar. He rummaged through some junk and pulled out a couple of crusty pots which he handed to her, but Adila didn't take them. She had never cooked in her life.

Henrik roasted chunks of meat over a fire, and they ate the crunchy browned pieces with their fingers, dipping chunks of bread into the grease. Adila couldn't identify the salty meat, no food with this flavor had ever been served in the inner palace.

 He ate pork and drank wine if he could get it, and ignoring Adila's repulsion at his eating habits, finished all the food himself. He was just trying to survive, but he was a spy; he had to, sometimes, pretend to be like those he lived among. He stacked pots and plates haphazardly, then got into a bed raised from the ground by short stacks of bricks without offering her a place to sleep, but then he rolled close to the wall so there would be room for her in it. She didn't join him but sat staring at faces of round-eyed devils carved into the door. In the middle of the night, rain leaked through the ceiling and dripped into puddles. Finally she got into bed with him. He smelled of beer, or she imagined that he did. She put her arm around him, because there was nothing else to do, and she wanted the luxury of comfort. It was rare and she would take it where she could find it. Out of the hodgepodge of objects, he had constructed a sanctuary. Even if the carpet had angels on it, the rice was hard white grains, and the coffee was weak, even if everything tasted like sausage, there were echoes of the homes they'd left behind.

During the day when he wasn't spying, Henrik tried to find things to sell. He explained money to her, currency that could be exchanged for food and clothing.

"If you look like them, you can usually be guaranteed a certain level of decency, or what passes as decency in the city, but you will never really look like them." He thought it was too dangerous for her to go out. "People will harass, beat, kill you. The streets are organized like a bowl of noodles. You'll never find your way back here, and no one will help you if you are lost. None of the people here are who they appear to be or who they advertise themselves to be. The herbalist is a poison merchant. The philanthropist is a cutthroat moneylender. A street corner priest exhorts every idler, gambler, and businessman to murder. The streets are full of these chimeras wearing velvet tents. They change their minds as easily as they breathe, and they skewer foreigners as soon as look at them. Let me explain Christianity to you. On certain days in the spring, Christians go mad. The following day, ashes are painted on their foreheads and each person, regardless of age or sex, recovers their sanity. Don't ever leave the house during the day, any day, not only the days I've just described."

She wanted to tell Henrik his reports were useless, he shouldn't bother with them anymore, that no one had heard of him at the palace and no one ever would, but she said nothing.

When it grew very cold, snow arrived, thick and beautiful, unlike anything Adila had seen before, but she hated the chill and slippery ice. When the fire went out, she tried to get into the theater by a back alley entrance, but it was locked. Two men in peaked hats and grey striped beards finally opened the door, but refused to let her enter although she was shivering with cold. Then they saw the hut attached like a barnacle of baroque salvage to the side of the theater. Like birds poking out of a birdhouse only to pop their heads back in, the two men looked at each other, then shut the door with a bang.

At night when Henrik returned, he got them in again, but became angry at her for drawing attention to his house. The men in the theater never bothered him because they never noticed him, and it was important to maintain anonymity in the face of certain hostility. They must never find his papers buried under the hut. It was too cold to answer or even to pay much attention to his mixture of German, Turkish, and Cypriot. She shivered and felt herself falling in and out of sleep all night. When she couldn't sleep, she tried to tell herself the Karagiozis story of the house of mirrors, but couldn't remember if it had been a comedy or a cautionary tale.

The next day after Henrik went out, Adila went up to the roof to feed the pigeons roosting in exposed beams. She imagined they were glad to see her every time, but Henrik insisted the birds felt nothing but hunger. That's what separates us from them. We experience frustration, longing. We have pictures in our heads. They have only jittery eyes, he said. Then why do they keep coming back to us? Do they even know it's my arm they roost on, not a tree branch? No, they know nothing. They're not stupid, that's just who they are, he insisted, but she believed the birds recognized her when she climbed up to the rickety rooftop.

A late morning fog remained, and no sun appeared to burn it off when the men arrived and began to tear apart the house under her feet. She yelled at them, but they laughed at her, pulling down the struts and columns that supported the roof, so she fell as the birds flew off. She was able to get to her feet, started throwing bricks at the men, but one of them picked her up and threw her out of the alley.

She watched from the mouth of the alley as they started a new fire, large and brilliant against the snow. Carved lintels, the beery staves, the door with grisly faces on it were all tossed into the flames. Bricks and plates were scattered.

By the time Adila returned to the alley, it was empty. She poked around in the ashes for the box that might have contained Henrik's reports, meticulously kept for an imaginary sultan. The box was buried, he had said, under a rug, under a trunk, the one with the dented samovar on top. There were so many burnt objects littering the back of the alley, but Adila found a long tin box, a pattern of interlocking spirals embossed in a wide border around the edges of the lid and along the bottom of the box itself. It still felt warm from the fire. When she opened it, the tin was empty. Ashes floated in the air around her. The box's contents? Impossible to know. Perhaps there had never been anything in it to begin with.

In the last hours before night fell, she looked for him in every arcade and blind street, feeling dogged by futility and cold as clocks chimed every quarter hour, but he had vanished, and she became lost. The city was crowded, built of impossibly tall houses. She imagined that if she could climb stairs to those heights she could talk to the stars. It grew colder, and her breath misted in the air. When men and women yelled at her, shouting threats, she grew afraid of drawing attention to herself, so instead of calling out his name, she remained silent, running from street to street. Finding herself in a completely unfamiliar part of the city, she tried to locate a park, one with enclosures, even if only a ring of birch or statues. She slept on the ground under a bench.

The second night she slept in the park she was woken by the sound of rustling a few feet away. A man shambled over to her. She could see nothing in the night, but he smelled of metal shavings, and his fingernails gleamed from filings caught underneath them. At first Adila tried to push him away, then she turned into a limp nothing, to not have to think about anything. When it was over, before he even assembled his clothes, he pressed coins into her hands. She didn't even count the pieces of silver and copper. Like the çengis who danced in the inner palace, she stuck three of them onto her forehead, but in the cold they soon fell to the ground.

Other men came on other nights. She discovered she could earn money in the parks; all that was required were a few simple gestures and being sure kronen or gulden were handed over first. With coins in hand, she could buy hot food. Cafés were crowded with people, and for a moment she felt comforted by so many talking strangers. The pleasure of sitting in a room, even if the chair and table were in the European style, and eating fried fish, roasted birds she couldn't identify, or pastry shaped like small cream-filled castles was extraordinary.

At night, she kept her eyes open, looking upwards at stars, clock towers, darkened windows, bare branches. In the parks and squares, Adila learned how to evade stray dogs and angry citizens. She'd had to run down long stone stairs and under arches spanning portals and alleys. Running hadn't been possible in the inner palace. There hadn't been any place to run to. A corner was something she ran around, not into. She watched her reflection in rows of shop windows and became aware of other people watching her. She learned the language of flirtation for money, ran her tongue over her lips and smiled all the time.

And then I found her, and she no longer had to live on the street.

The girls treated her like a leper, but there were visitors who desired foreigners, and I was more than happy to provide for such cravings. The other girls believed she would do things they would not, but this wasn't true. Nada argued that a foreigner threatened the reputation of the house.

"Use her as a sweep, keep her in the cellar or the attic. If you let her upstairs, no one will ever come here again. They'll fear diseases, plague, fever."

"When you bring in as much business as you used to, I'll retire her." Word had spread about the genuine Turkish girl.

Adila remembered a woman who killed herself in the recesses of the inner palace. You could not be stopped if that's what you wanted to do. She went over the details: the torn twisted sheets, just before dawn, no one was awake. She was curious about what might have been left behind. Not all the evidence of hanging would have been obliterated. Some footprints, some traces of the previous resident would have remained: an earring, a comb, perhaps a book. Those small marginal clues represented the suicide in life, a life which, though unknown to Adila, she could now read any way she pleased. She rejected the idea of dying for love. It didn't make sense. People change their minds, given enough time, and look back on past loves with amazement, sadness, but also, sometimes, embarrassment and revulsion. No, the death had its source in words she knew in my language: siege, engulfed, trapped.

In her room, among her bits and pieces, there was no evidence of her life in other cities. If she smashed a glass and cut her wrists, she would leave no real clues as to who she had been. The next resident might interpret her suicide as death for love, sadness, anything. Survivors are allowed the liberty of interpretation.

The upstairs windows were frosted and lights from the house opposite burned small haloed points into the panes. I knocked on her door to announce another arrival.

# COMMERCE

THE SECOND WOMAN I took into my house was Safiye. She had been given a silver charm in the shape of a sword that she wore around her neck. Carved inside were words too small to be read. The trader who took her from her village removed the rings from her ears, but she was able to hide the charm from him. Reaching Damascus after many nights of travel, the market where they stopped looked like those she knew from her home, but as the caravan moved north, the markets became less familiar to her. Further north still, gold cloth, olive soap, indigo, and other dyes were traded for people. Across Karaman, more women than men were sold, some were bought, and Safiye saw Bursa silk, honey, flax, opium from Beyeshir. The trader did business with a woman from Arabia who was preceded by the sound of heavy jewelry made of many small metal beads. She sifted pearls through a pearl sorter, large ones nestling in the holes, small ones falling through. He held one up to Safiye's throat to demonstrate size. In Istanbul, she was traded for three bolts of cotton and a tax of four gold ducats. The Anatolian merchant would sell the cloth in the Crimea at Caffa, and if he were lucky, he might get some knives from Armenia.

Shortly after her arrival in the palace, she was brought to one of the windows of the Cage, not realizing she shouldn't approach the man she saw there, even if he called to her. The prince gestured for her to reach into his cell, and she put one hand between the bars. The agha, watchful and annoyed, had her punished instantly. Her head was covered. One man held her over his back, holding her arms so harshly they seemed to pull out of their sockets, while another held her feet just off the ground. A third beat her. She could feel the man's back through his robe, bent as he held her arched over him. They could have put her on a table, or forced her to stand, but the man who felt her shrink under each blow and heard her scream seemed to enjoy being part of her torture. His pleasure at her pain was unbearable and humiliating in a way she couldn't articulate to the other women. It was as if she had a kind of power which involved her own degradation. If she refused to flinch or scream, they became bored, so they stopped. After the beating, she kept her distance from everyone in the inner palace.

No one in the crowded room where she slept spoke the same language. Most in the room were assigned to kitchen work or the baths. Some, the agha knew, would make trouble. Some just waited. The sultan's desires were difficult to anticipate or control. The agha was satisfied if the women weren't executed when the sultan grew bored. There were nights when he hid Safiye behind the Karaghiozis screen.

Safiye asked Gaspar what kind of city lay outside their walls. She had traveled up the Nile, had seen boats, crocodiles, and the shore, sometimes barren, sometimes dense with people. By the time the trader made it as far north as Istanbul she'd been secluded and seen little of the city. Gaspar, who seemed to be able to go anywhere unseen, was relied upon to know everything. He described white ambassadors in short coats, barely any pants, and square-toed shoes, all of them speaking in nasally accents.

Safiye wanted to remain exactly where she stood. The rules of the inner palace were bound up with its architecture, its walls and doors, and once these were removed, once all the women began to travel, the rules would be gradually and irrevocably suspended.

Gaspar kicked a box of shadow figures until it was hidden behind a wall. It would only get lost on the journey. There was no point in taking them.

❧

Other men took them from the tent, one group of soldiers replaced another, but with the second group, all the women were treated as prisoners, all the same. It didn't matter who did what in the palace. When they reached Vienna, Safiye tied a piece of cloth over the
lower part of her nose and mouth, the city smelled, but a man leaned
over his horse and yanked it away from her face. He tossed it over
his shoulder, where a child picked it up until her mother snatched it
away from her. The citizens believed the foreigners were the source of
disease. Illness, contagion.

Then the women were separated from the men and taken to a
palace that looked nothing like the one in which she'd spent so many
years. The room where they were kept was enormous, its walls and
ceilings were covered by paintings, imitations of human figures who
she thought might offer clues as to how, in a northern city, inner and
outer palaces might be organized: clouds, spears, halos, nakedness,
eyes looking upward, huge billowing thunderheads, and numerous
sheets that looked like they were caught in a whirlwind. In clouds,
armed or haloed men and women were covered by a few fluttering
bits or nothing at all. Safiye reached to touch an arm or a face that
looked so lifelike, she expected the limb to be warm to the touch.
Among the paintings was a grotesque image of a tortured half-naked
man pinned to pieces of wood. She tried to pull a curtain across it,
but the whole length of fabric came down on her head. At the sound
of metal hitting wood, a guard entered. Everyone ran to one corner
of the room but Safiye, who approached the metal-suited man and
tried to ask him for a piece of paper. She demonstrated the act of
writing or drawing by pretending to mark on her hand, laid out flat.
He took out his sword, shouted words no one understood, then a
translator divided them into groups.

She was taken to a second room whose windows were so huge, it
appeared as if the entire room was made of glass, attached to the pal-

ace. Looking out one she saw two women practicing archery in dresses that seemed to cover acres of lawn. Each pulled back her bow in
turn while the yards of material behind them shuddered like waves.

One by one, or in groups of two or three, they were turned over
to the families of the court. A *bas kadin*, a high-ranking woman who
could read and write Persian and Arabic would now be a servant,
cleaning floors; a *çengi* or a musician would now be polishing silver.
The dwarf in charge was handing them over to this person or that.

A retired army captain who had lost a leg and lived with his sister
approached the pedestal and whispered in the small man's ear. The
military were owed favors, and Ulrich, the retired captain, knew it.
He had already claimed Gaspar and Ali. The two of them stood apart
in chains. The former guardians of the inner palace would be employed working in Ulrich's horse stables. The captain had an interest
in Africa. It interested him more than the Americas or the Orient.
He had a collection of African artifacts: masks, spears, musical instruments, and so on. It was Safiye he wanted more than the others.
He limped out of the room while his sister, leading the way, tapped
a cane against her leg.

Safiye was given castoff dresses but allowed to keep her head
covered. When visitors came, Ulrich called her in to show her off.
He asked her to speak in her language or to do a native dance on the
carpet. Once Ulrich told her to stand perfectly still beside a painting
or a statue and to maintain the pose until his guests left.

He hired a man to teach the new servants the language, and he
also lived in the house, but the lessons were not organized and occurred whenever the schoolmaster felt like giving them. Gaspar and
Ali would be called from the stables and Safiye from the kitchen. In
front of the man, they barely spoke to one another. The schoolmaster
forbade it, since he couldn't understand what they were saying and
believed they were plotting to kill everyone in the house. He taught
enough of the language to follow orders but that was about it, con-
jugating verbs: *to carry, to cut, to dig,* sitting with his feet on the desk

staring into space and asking them to repeat after him. Day after day, the teacher droned on but paid little attention to what they actually said.

He had been to northern Africa and spent evenings with the captain discussing his collection of artifacts. Ulrich didn't know the schoolmaster's time in Africa consisted of only three days spent in the port of Alexandria. He turned those three days into years of exploration and expertise. Ulrich looked forward to their evenings and took notes on the learned man's expositions. The captain acknowledged he was really paying his resident scholar more for these little chats than for teaching his servants, so he assumed everyone was more or less happy.

One morning in March, the schoolmaster was nowhere to be found. Ulrich assumed he would eventually return, but later in the day, when he spent a few hours reviewing the contents of his collections, he found some of his ivories had disappeared too. Ulrich's sister, who had suspected the teacher was an unwashed swindler from the outset, was relieved when he left their service, even if he was a thief. She had been heard to say he always had a poor-me expression, and all the while he was pocketing the spoons. She herself was miserly and so exaggerated the extent of his theft. She didn't care what language the servants spoke as long as they understood her.

More words could be learned under his tutelage than from the thief: *dough, bread, cakes.* Gunter cooked with gusto, throwing handfuls of white powder into bowls, slapping slabs of butter all over the place. She had never seen butter, cream, or cheese before, and found them tasteless. The texture or smell of strong cheese the family loved made her gag. The kitchen was a place of constant activity. Coffee was ground in large metal funnels which ended in small wooden drawers. Meat was hung on rows of partially corroded metal hooks. Vats of soapy water for washing quickly turned into a dirty soup.

Watching the cook, she learned all kinds of tricks. Gunter would occasionally get a deal on meat that was slightly off, but he would put chunks of it in pies to which he added pheasants and chickens, calling it *carne supremo*. If Ulrich and his guests enjoyed the extra spice and maybe got a little sick later without knowing exactly why, Gunter told no one his secret. Safiye, who was in a position to smell the carne supremo cuts, knew he was disguising something bad and inedible. When angry, the cook threw raw meat on the floor, then wiped the cut on the front of his greasy apron before throwing it in the fire.

Gluttony, for Gunter, was an acceptance of pleasure, not a symbol of greed. He loaded his plate, asked Safiye what she was staring at as he ate. Safiye found their food milky and bland. Though she sprinkled her own food with every spice in the kitchen, none of his herbs or extracts ever approximated the tastes she remembered from the inner palace. The jars of ras el hanout, sumac, cumin, and coriander seeds, ropes of red and green chili peppers were nowhere to be found. She couldn't become used to eating with a fork, although Gunter humiliated her for eating with her fingers. He made disgusting gestures as if he were eating and scratching himself at the same time. Gunter's dense chocolate cakes tasted like plugs of butter and sugar, inedible. The thinnest cook in Vienna, the captain's sister said, and asked Gunter to be sure she wasn't stealing food to sell in some unknown market. Gunter defended her, but he did wonder how anyone could resist his concoctions. Safiye actually did steal food when she had the chance, but Gunter never caught her.

Ulrich's house was very large, but Gaspar and Ali lived in the stables, sleeping with the horses and dogs in a small room at the back. Unlike Safiye, they were given the worst food: the truly spoilt, the burnt leftovers from Ulrich's table. Though they lived on what she stole for them and brought out into the stables at night, the two still treated her as if they were sleeping on silk back in a palace they would never see again. The agha insisted that Gunter's domain was insignificant compared to the ten double domes of the Topkapi Sarayi kitchens. Safiye tried to explain how different Ulrich's food was and how it was eaten with forks. Ali couldn't picture any of it and accused her of inventing the dinners she described. When he had first arrived in the palace as a young man, the women had been a terror to him, but as he watched the caged princes, he learned a master who loses control of himself is like a ship already halfway to the bottom of the sea. Ali learned when women were only pretending to be sick, when they lingered too long in the baths or over their hookahs. He had learned how to control by words, chiding, being strict, marshalling all their petty and serious desires. Gunter, waving knives above his head, had no power and was a joke by comparison.

The inner palace had been his empire, yet while he shoveled horse shit his distant domain was a vast cluster of empty rooms. The emptiness was easy to imagine. What was more bitter to picture was a recurring vision: each and every one of them was easily replaced, and soon new aghas and new women would fill the rooms of comfort, pleasure, and boredom they'd left behind.

Ali was too old to become a servant after decades of controlling and ordering others. He lashed out at the horses and beat the dogs until the animals hated him and cowered when he came near. He deliberately brushed the horses with swirling strokes that went against the grain of their pelts and sang out loud while doing so. When the captain found out, he had Ali beaten. Sometimes he had Gaspar beaten too, just for good measure. Gaspar, at first, liked being in the position of scolding the agha, but the old man was tiresome and self-absorbed, even in his insolence. Gaspar wanted to move into the main house and have nice clothes like Safiye. Neither of them could accept the truth, so obvious each time Safiye stepped into the stables; she was much better off than they were and was treated relatively well, sleeping in a small room near the kitchen which was private and always warm. Ali found her presence insulting, although he could no longer control her coming and going, and he often, in spite of himself, enjoyed the curious food she brought. But Safiye ran out of sympathy for him. Even when he grew ill, she threatened to steal food only for Gaspar.

"I used to put women like you into sacks and drop you into the Bosporus." Ali threw a plate. This annoyed Safiye, and she wanted to do more than scold the old man who still thought he could threaten her. She needed to return each plate whole. A broken one would be noticed.

"Where did you keep the sacks? Whose job was it to have more made when the supply ran low?" Safiye shoved him.

"Leave him alone." Gaspar licked a spoon.

Besides the agha, some of the animals, too, became very sick and began to die. Rumors circulated in the house that the new servants carried diseases, but Ulrich's new servants gave him too much pleasure for anyone to dare question their residence in the property.

"It's easier at night. Only the captain, his sister, and Safiye sleep in the house. The servants go home to their families or live in a remote part of the estate. It's three against two. There are knives in the kitchen. We can do it at night. Half a brick in each hand. A torch from the fire. The captain with his one leg and his medals is a fool, overconfident. When he comes downstairs, Gaspar will be ready for him. Safiye can cover his sister's mouth so she won't be able to scream. You'll come from behind. You won't have to see her runny eyes and lips shaped like two worms." Ali stacked horseshoes as if making a tower in an obsessive game. They would fall, and he'd start all over. He couldn't stop making towers.

"Her hair will get in my mouth. I'll suffocate." Safiye gagged at the idea of touching the woman.

"That harmless white hair?"

"It smells." Safiye brushed pieces of straw from the tray she'd carried into the stable.

"We'll take their money and leave the city in the middle of the night."

The sister's friends began to discourage her from letting Safiye handle food. Gunter took her to the market to get her out of the house during the afternoon when visitors called. People in the shops stared at her. Toward evening she saw a woman who looked like Adila, but Gunter turned into another street, and Safiye lost sight of her. Safiye didn't ask Gunter to turn back to look for her. What would Gunter do anyway? All he thought about was cheap meat.

Back in the kitchen she sliced ribs of beef, cut chickens into quarters, chopped onions without crying. The knife was very sharp, and she accidentally cut herself. Angry, she let her finger bleed into the spongy slice of onion when Gunter wasn't looking, making patterns of red on the concentric rings.

An uproar developed in the stables. Ali kicked a horse, and so the captain had him and Gaspar beaten and made to sleep outside in the snow. Safiye wasn't able to bring them food for a week. When she returned Ali lay in the straw, delirious, curled up into a ball, but Gaspar lay on his elbows, eyes bright, uninterested in whatever it was Safiye brought.

"Listen, Safiye, bring us knives tonight. The meal will be cooked, served, and eaten, dishes returned to the kitchen. When Gunter and the others leave, you bring us the choppers."

"Ulrich and his sister will believe anything they are told," Gunter said as he lined up sausages, not speaking directly to Safiye. "They're superstitious and gullible and, in spite of the captain's interest in exploration and charting by the stars, they could easily be persuaded you're some kind of witch."

Safiye took this as a warning, although Gunter was merely talking as he worked.

"They're too old to marry and move away." He looked up as he sliced. "They'll live in this house until they drop dead, so our futures are insured for a little while. I can find work anywhere. High-class chefs are always in demand, but what will you do?" He brushed the back of Safiye's neck with a celery stalk.

Safiye had seen the sister flirt with widower barons and bachelor dukes who knew she was rich. Though elderly, they still looked her up and down, and she coyly teased her potential suitors, who rarely came again unless, Safiye guessed, they really needed money. When they tried to follow Safiye to her room, she was able to lose them in the halls and stairwells with doors that locked behind her, but if she didn't, the house was the kind of place no one would help you or hear you scream.

The captain and his sister were old enough to die in their sleep, and Safiye had no idea what would happen to her if they did. The next house she might find herself in could easily be worse than this one, and she would have no choice as to where she might go. The sister had once spoken of marrying Safiye to a stable boy who belonged to a French count. The Frenchman would pay her for the match by sending her a new kitchen girl. If Safiye helped murder them, stole what could be easily lifted before fleeing south, she would be at the mercy of Ali again, mad and frail. He didn't read foreign customs quickly enough, and in his delusions about who he was, he put them all at risk.

Safiye waited until the house was quiet, then stole maps from a long, flat drawer near the African artifacts. The masks beckoned, pleaded for her to liberate them, but she needed to travel as lightly as possible. Gunter had gone, and the house was dark. She brought knives to the stable while keeping the maps for herself, although she had only glanced at them before stuffing the pages into her clothes. There were two men to deal with the captain; they didn't need her. She planned to leave alone. She was not sure escape was possible, but at least she had the maps and money, two things she'd never had before, and that might make all the difference in the world.

She was in a hurry to leave the city when we found her. Adila said something in their language that I didn't understand, gesturing as if to go with her, but Safiye shook her head. I made the case that she wouldn't get very far. For someone with that face, everyone was a slave trader. I made it clear my door on Nachtfalterallee was open to her. She would be a real moneymaker.

# PAPER MONEY KNOWS NO BORDERS

WITH THE LONG BLONDISH-BROWN roots growing out from artificially blackened hair and surrounding her head like a halo, she had a face like the woman in a Raffaelli painting I saw at the Italienische Nationalkirche Maria Schnee. I followed her until she stopped in front of a shop display full of telescopes, charts, and geographer's equipment. A map of Europe was laid out behind an astrolabe, and she studied it, unaware I was standing beside her. The ink on the map looked fresh, I could see that, though it was of no use to me. A horn blower pointed north, a mermaid pointed south; the cartouche covered Calabria. She tried the shop door, but it was locked, and the man at the counter made signs to indicate his business was closed before disappearing behind a curtain. Only a few stragglers were left on the street now.

"How far am I from Venice?" She spoke a dialect which I still had some knowledge of. It was close to the language my mother spoke to me.

The woman told me her name was Calandra, but this wasn't her real name which was Luna Mezzanotte. When she lived in the inner palace, she kept asking what day it was. Calandra, calandra, she kept saying, so they called her by that name. I took her home and gave her new clothes. In this way, I discovered the third woman from Istanbul. Before she began to work for me on a quiet afternoon, I learned her story, and in doing so, I would know how to sell her services.

Her father said there were no accurate maps of the city. From San Barnaba to the Accademia Bridge, to the merceria, the narrow, tangled streets and canals have never been properly charted. What I've heard: if you were born in the city you learned how to rely on the sound of footsteps ahead, waves lapping beneath you, or to trust in whoever holds your hand, but at night the web of streets and canals presented a different story. You felt your way in the dark by brushing against familiar iron door knockers: a lion's head, a hand, a pineapple.

The Mezzanottes lived in the San Barnaba quarter of Venice, but Luna didn't think of her father as a Barnabotti, an aristocrat who was no longer rich. The word Barnabotti might have been used in other parts of Venice when a rich man suddenly couldn't pay his bills, but the expression was never used in San Barnaba itself. Like the word *fallen*, it suggested gravity and moral shortcomings. Hair, leaves, plates fell or were dropped. Other families lost money, but the word stopped short at the threshold of the Mezzanotte door. Even if they had more money on certain months than others, the differences in fortunes didn't signify an irretrievable fate or fall from grace.

The Argenti family, next door, had fallen. Signor Argenti, a bent old man in a dirty shirt, could be seen talking to himself, as if by describing the gold in the Sudan and rerouting his boats so they wouldn't pass close to Tripoli, he could, with a torrent of words, resurrect both his ships and fortune. When he saw Luna, he would call out to her. *Luna, Luna, I have something for you.* She never ran over to him to find out what that thing might be. Argenti spent his days staring into the canal, wiping his nose on his sleeve, muttering about Tripoli, where his boats had been robbed and sunk by the Turks. One day he hanged himself on a bridge, and from the moment Luna saw him cut down she would never cross that bridge again. On the other side of the canal lived the D'Espiritu family, whose boats lost bales of raw silk and barrels of pepper when Serbian pirates attacked them in the southern Aegean.

Not everyone lost their ships, but everyone was losing money, and even the servants seemed to have empty time on their hands. One hot afternoon their cook told Luna a story she remembered every time something accidentally fell from her hands into one of the canals.

"At Ascensiontide, when floors are swept and carpets shaken out over balconies, the doge stands in front of San Nicolo and throws his gold ring into the sea. The ring, sinking instantly into water, symbolizes Venice's marriage to the sea, the source of the city's fortune."

There was nothing unusual about the practice.

"A ring," she said, one elbow leaning on an iron railing, fanning herself with her free hand, "a ring won't help anyone. It takes something more precious to change your fate. We know because it wasn't always a gold ring that was tossed."

"What do you mean?" Luna asked.

"Before Christ came to Venice, children were tossed from the boat instead. If the sea was hostile, it would have to be appeased. What could you do? Your father would have ten ships today if anyone in this city had any sense and threw a child into the water as it's supposed to be."

When Luna was very young, her father had been nearly ruined by a shipwreck. A storm came on suddenly, and when his boat capsized, its crates full of metals sank instantly. Survivors, picked up by a nearby boat, described winds which came from the east, but her father barely listened to them. He had systems for survival. Following the wreck, even on dry land, he refused to wear heavy clothing which would absorb water, and he ran around in the rain without a coat. He could be seen darting in and out of doorways like a terrier, hair and beard drenched. But his most radical innovation, after he was picked up at sea, was that he would only favor paper money, so nearly weightless it drifted effortlessly from city to city.

"For paper money, the Pyrenees don't exist." He repeated the saying over and over again, as if he believed mountains might literally melt in the face of paper rectangles printed in different languages. Money could be found anywhere, and it went everywhere.

"These are from Genoa," he said, pointing to one pile that lay on the table next to a plate of olives. He bit into one, then pointed the half-eaten olive at another pile. "These are from Antwerp, from Geneva, *Banque de France*." Some had elaborate border designs which took up most of the paper's surface, some were printed with portraits of princes, dukes or kings. A moneychanger told them a rare note with complicated crosses on it came from China. Her father laid them out on the table: kings, popes, and arabesques in all colors.

"Don't handle money where we eat." Her mother was disgusted. "No one knows where those bits of paper have been and who's handled them." She swept it all from the table, saying that as surely as coins and bars of metal sink, printed paper will dissolve into nothing if it falls into the sea. Why hadn't he thought of that?

After the shipwreck, he borrowed money from patrician *piezarie*, underwriters, and had another ship built. He was intrigued by English nautical invention: crosswind bracing on the lower gun deck, replacing the shipstaff by a rope tiller, using a parrell collar (after the Dutch) to distribute the strain on the mast. He made drawings of ships, measured diagrams of holds, spoke of theories of stability and propulsion. Her father loved an audience, and his drawings were complicated, impossible to read without an explanation. Luna listened, elbows on the table, fingers tracing constellations and astrolabes.

Luna's mother left him to his diagrams and monologues about whipstaffs and Dutch masts. The shipping business came from her family but—or perhaps because of this—she had no interest in his drawings. Luna was afraid her mother was a Barnabotti, a woman who paid no attention to the leak in the boat until it was too late. Sometimes she pulled Luna away from the table spread with navigational charts and took her to the markets and shops.

They wandered from stall to stall in the Fondaco dei Tedeschi, hearing unfamiliar dialects of merchants selling chicken and ducks hanging by their legs, baskets of ginger root, jars of white sugar. They pretended not to understand when she asked the way out of the covered market and urged her to buy instead. *Funghi, granchi, galline e caponi, pallia, pignoli*, they yelled. They would be angry at her mother for talking, for wasting their time and not buying. Since their losses at sea they rarely went to the *merceria* between Saint Mark's and the Rialto, where you could examine pearls, real and false, French clothing which resembled nightdresses, cakes shaped like palaces and birds, plates full of small fish arranged as a bouquet of flowers.

Her mother kept a white mask on a stick. There was nothing unusual about it, the mask looked exactly like hundreds of others, but she began taking it with her even when carnival was past. If Luna was with her, the mask was neglected, but wherever it was she went when she was alone, she carried the white mask with her. When winter came, she might forget to have wood put in the stove, but she wouldn't forget the empty, blandly smiling face when she left the house by herself. She began to spend more afternoons out, leaving Luna with her father, saying they no longer had the money to make trips to the *merceria*, although this had been true for a long time. Her father didn't seem to notice when she was gone. He was planning another trip, and everything they owned hinged on its success.

One day she did take Luna someplace. They went to see a painting by Giorgione of two men sitting on a lawn, heads together, engaged in a conversation. Her mother loved this painting, but Luna did not. Alongside the two fully clothed men were two completely naked women, apparently unnoticed, and as far as she could tell uncommented upon; the men's heads weren't turned in their direction at all. A shepherd poked his sheep in the background while the women roamed around without any clothes on: a curiosity without, apparently, any interested spectators. The women might have been invisible. Luna was disturbed by the sight of the exposed women next to clothed men, and the contradictions between who was employed and who sat on bare ground absurdly idle—a spectacle. Either the men were done with the women and had grown indifferent to them, or perhaps the women were supposed to be spirits, or thoughts, and not real at all. The sight of their busy nakedness (one drew water, the other played a pipe) next to the ordinary characters who sat on the grass, languid and obtuse, was troubling to her.

Luna studied the mosaic floor, gray, white, black, and coral tesserae arranged as cubes and angular flowers you could cut your feet on. She preferred Veronese's buffoons, butchers, whippets, and Ethiopian waiters hitting a dwarf with a plate. Veronese recruited models from the street: they argued, bargained, chewed, laughed, and fell over themselves. A dirty dog wandered near Christ. Luna felt she could walk up to the table and take food from a plate. The painter was a realist with his eye on what was just out the window or the other side of the door. People who ate in the street were often eating their last supper without knowing it was to be their last, but Veronese was called up by inquisitors in Rome for painting saints as if they were in some kind of low *banchetti*, and he told them that in Rome Michelangelo painted the saints naked.

Returning to San Barnaba, her mother accused her of looking down into the canals as the city slipped past. Her eyes were on buildings' reflections as well as all kinds of things: a hat, sodden and shapeless, clinging to the pilings of a bridge, a disintegrating section of a painted mask, a white handkerchief embroidered with a pair of initials, playing cards or printed pages spiraling in the current. This was the leftover world of the city: a world of reflection, reversal, and refuse, the decay of which held clues to some past party, dinner, or if a body were found, someone's rush to judgment.

"People live on the street when they have to," the cook explained while she scrubbed oysters in cold water. "Famines come and go in cycles, like the seasons. You've never seen hordes of beggars collapse in the squares, in doorways, everywhere. Families of beggars would try to get into this kitchen. They would rush over the walls and trample you as if you were a melon rind left on the floor."

Their kitchen was accessible from the courtyard. The wall was covered by vines, but it could be easily scaled. The cook held each oyster so that the wider part nestled in the palm of her hand as if it were tucked in a tight groove between rocks. She stuck a thin knife between the valves near its back and ran the knife along its edge until the muscle which held the shell together was cut. Luna picked fragments of shell from a bowl full of blue-gray lumps of oyster and watched the cook's long, narrow hands repeat the same jerking motion when she cut the oyster muscle as if she were angry, and it was the oyster's fault. The cook pointed at window boxes with the end of her knife.

"Beggars go to the Lido now. They're given offal from the cattle slaughtered there. That's why you've never seen armies of beggars. On the island where boats are quarantined, they're kept and sometimes fed."

The cook saved the larger part of the oyster shells and washed them again in cold water. Later she arranged cooked oysters and shrimp on each shell and covered them with citronette sauce.

"This is called *matrimonio di mare*. Because *scampi* is masculine and *ostrica* is feminine, and they are married on this plate. The poor always dress the same," the cook went on, returning to the prior subject. "Year after year, in tatters that belonged to three or four people before them. They can't be kept out of Venice."

Then, dropping crabs into boiling water, she spoke of the battle of Lepanto. Luna spun a green glass bowl full of lemons around the table. The cook yelled at her to stop, or she would certainly break it.

"Lepanto," she said, holding a crab above the pot, "that battle was the end of the Turks."

The cook was dismissed when the last of their ships was lost.

Doctors appeared in masks with long snouts filled with vinegar and dried flowers to overpower the smell of what they were certain was the plague. Their eyes were reduced to tiny irises behind lenses that covered the top half of the face. In their long robes, with covered faces, they looked barely human, like wingless flies or birds with long beaks. Each carried a long stick to feel the patient's pulse so as to avoid actual contact with the afflicted person's skin.

"Signora Mezzanotte is feverish, a sign of imbalance in the body," they said. "The illness comes from the east."

Signor Mezzanotte wanted to say, yes, from water rats that turn crowded boats into ghost ships, but by *east* the doctors were referring to humans, not animal-born contagion. Though her father was fond of saying even the pope couldn't keep Galileo locked up forever. The earth revolves around the sun, her father would say. But even though Mezzanote was a heliocentrist, with death at the door, he was tempted by superstition and, at great expense, he hired a new cook, a hunchback, a traditional Venetian trick to bring luck to the house. She fled when she saw doctors enter the courtyard.

Luna overheard her father make arrangements to leave Venice. Because of the risk of contagion, she wasn't allowed to see her mother. Although she banged on her mother's door, no one on the other side answered. The doctors appeared down the hall and rushed to bar the entrance to the room, pushing her aside with their pulse sticks. They'd read Boccaccio's description of the plague which swept through Florence three hundred years ago. Boccaccio attributed its cause to the planets, to divine punishment.

In another part of the house, her father spread out maps of the Aegean and the Adriatic on floors and tables. After studying them for days, he bundled up the rolls of maps and went around each room closing shutters himself. No servants were left. As her father locked the door, she saw girls she never spoke to looking at them from their balconies. Months from now, would they try to peer through their shutters and whisper about Signora Mezzanotte and her husband's paper money? Calle lunga San Barnaba was dark. She heard footsteps long before she saw the shadows they belonged to. The silhouettes appeared briefly as solid humans, then they became footsteps again and vanished.

At the Grand Canal, her father put her in a boat already packed with their possessions. Early snow fell before his lantern at the prow, melting in the water. The sound of waves lapping against the sides of the canal and boats straining against their moorings were among the last noises of the city she would hear for a long time to come. As they made their way toward the sea, the sounds of the canal at night grew more faint, and then faded altogether.

To the west she saw small clusters of islands, and through her father's spyglass she could make out a few stone forts along the islands' coasts, but they were mostly ruins that made them indistinguishable from rocky cliffs, only part of a dome or column suggesting that something man-made had once clung to the precipice.

"We'll go to Athens, stopping at Montenegro and Preveza, then back," Signor Mezzanotte announced.

If the contagion was traveling west, he thought they would be safe. The wave of malady that caused glass to break, rats to feast, and ships to sink had passed them, was on its way to Rome. He had made the trip many times and was convinced it was a safe passage.

"Saint Mark's lion," her father said, "rules as far as Naxos, Crete, and the Cyclades." He pointed out the islands Venice ruled. It seemed to Luna that, though invisible, Venetian fleets were everywhere patrolling a republic of islands without end.

❈

Near Corfu they sighted a ship with Genoese sails which rapidly overtook them. Just like a Genoese ship, heavy cannon could be seen emerging from portholes. Signor Mezzanotte pointed out the tiers of oars. He waved. No one waved back.

"They can't see you."

"No, not yet."

When the ship drew closer, cannon were fired in their direction. The sharply peaked prow rammed their boat, and men jumped onto their deck. Her father pushed her below. She heard people pleading for their lives followed by yelling in a language she didn't understand and the sounds of bodies falling on the deck above her head, a kind of thunder of body parts. She reached up and flattened her hand against the vibrating wooden ceiling.

The Venetian crew was armed but soon overpowered. Foreign sailors poured below, and she was pulled back above deck. Sailors on any ship came from all over the world, so the Genoese aggressor must have made a mistake. A ship with a Genoese flag could be manned by Irish, Maltese, or Moroccan sailors. Her father employed sailors from Helsinki, Liverpool, Hanover. What were they after? Cargo was taken onto the deck, but the intruders weren't interested in looting. Crates of glass to be sold in Athens were smashed against the mast. Glasses, plates, bowls, red, yellow, green shapes instantly became a rain of shards glittering as they were poured into the sea to slice fish as they fell to the bottom. The other ship was tied to their boat, and she could quickly tell that its flag and sails had been deceptive. The design of the hull was Turkish. Her father was pulled onto their boat and yanked to the other side, but whether he was taken prisoner or pushed over, Luna couldn't see. They mimicked her when she screamed.

Somewhere inside the Turkish boat, she knocked her head against a beam when she tried to stand. There was no porthole or light, and splinters lodged under her fingernails when she tried to figure out where she was by running her hands over the boards. The air smelled vinegary, and she heard people moving on either side of her, men or women trapped in adjoining barrel-like cells.

After what might have been days or hours, she was taken from her cell and delivered to the captain. Although he knew some Italian, he wouldn't tell her where her father was and asked her to speak in her dialect. She soon realized it didn't matter what she said, he just wanted to hear the sound of her language. The captain suffered from headaches and one of his eyes drifted to the right, so she never knew exactly what he was looking at. If he appeared ill, it was a mistake to think he was weak; he ruled the ship by fear. He had commanded Macedonian stowaways tossed overboard as if they were stones.

Luna was offered nothing to drink, commanded only to sit on the floor and start talking. She didn't know what to say to him, so repeated a story her father used to tell her.

"A man sent his only son, Fair Brow, to sea in a large ship so he could learn about buying and selling. He gave his son seven thousand crowns, but at an unknown port, for no reason at all, the boy used the money to pay back the debts of a dead man, a stranger, who lay on the shore. What a waste, you think? Not entirely. When Fair Brow returned home, he told his father he had been robbed by pirates. He lied."

"*Mendacio*," the captain repeated. "In Istanbul liars are branded on the forehead." He traced a shape on her forehead.

"He was sent out again with another seven thousand crowns. This time at sea he encountered a Turkish ship which carried only a beautiful girl, the daughter of a sultan. He captured her, and when he returned to his father, he introduced her, saying:

> *Father, I bring a most precious gem,*
> *You will sing with joy when you see her!*
> *A maiden lovelier than you've ever beheld*
> *The daughter of the sultan of Turkey*
> *I bring as my first commodity!*

"Was his father pleased? No. His father was furious and shut the door in their faces, leaving them paupers.

"She was a painter whose pictures were astonishingly lifelike, almost as good as Veronese. If she painted a man's portrait you would think he was in the room, and if I could do that I would paint a copy of myself and slip away from you." Luna lowered her voice, but the captain had the unfocused look of someone who didn't really understand what was being said to him. She stopped speaking, but he made an impatient gesture for her to continue.

"So they traveled from place to place, selling her paintings. In one town Fair Brow exhibited her pictures in the square when other Turks arrived who immediately recognized the pictures of the sultan's daughter. No one could paint mirrors of nature as she did. They cleverly asked him if they could meet the painter, but when he brought them home, they seized her, and took her back to her city. Fair Brow was disconsolate but could find no ship which would take him to Turkey. After years of wandering, he encountered an old man in a small boat, and he told the fisherman how much he envied him, a fellow who had no troubles. The man, saddened by Fair Brow's story, agreed to take him along under the condition they split everything that came their way. During a storm they were shipwrecked in Turkey, where the two were immediately captured and made into slaves.

"The terms of their enslavement required them to repair musical instruments and to sing as they did so. The sultan's daughter, imprisoned in a tower, recognized the voice of her husband. She had him smuggled up the tower in a large basket of flowers.

The pair plotted their escape by having themselves hidden in a boat full of treasure. The plan went smoothly, but when they were out to sea Fair Brow remembered his friend, the old man left behind, and insisted on returning for him. The boat's direction was reversed, and as land grew visible, the dot on the horizon turned out to be his friend, waiting for them on the shore. Fair Brow gave him half the treasure but the old man, annoyed at being left behind, wanted half his wife as well. Fair Brow said he could have all of the treasure if he would leave him all of his wife."

Even as a child, Luna had known the story wouldn't end with split bodies, but the captain now appeared to be following her story. Bodies cut in half was a circumstance that interested him.

"The old man turned into the soul of the debtor. He praised Fair Brow's generosity, and before disappearing he left them rich and happy.

*Happily from then on did they live*
*But nothing to me did they ever give.*"

They were almost at port, and the captain gestured for sailors to take Luna away. She had no way of knowing how much of the story he understood. As she looked back at the ship, the captain was nowhere in sight, but it was clear he didn't have the soul of a debtor who would reward her with treasure and passage home. She'd told a story to a pirate who sliced people into parts, then had dinner brought to his quarters and charted his next course.

❋

The animal looked like a horse with a hump. Its small eyes were clouded and its body was covered by coarse brown hair. Chewing and spitting violently, the creature knelt, a man showed her what to do, how to ride it, but she kept sliding off.

She was brought to a large house with shuttered windows, left alone in a long, narrow room, and given some flat bread. The men were given candles every night, and after evening prayers, a group of musicians played in a distant courtyard. For five nights, the pattern was unvaried. A woman who brought her food wore a blue glass ball on a silver chain around her neck, pointed to Luna's blue eyes when she entered her room, and called her Frank.

Luna told the woman she wasn't a French coin. She learned that she was in Gallipoli, and all Europeans were called Frank. The blue glass ball was to ward off evil that could emanate from people whose eyes were blue. The charm was meant to deflect the bad luck back to the place it originated.

After five days, she was taken on another ship through the Sea of Marmara to Istanbul. A man who spoke her dialect told her she was fortunate to be sold to the palace. When Christian pirates attack Turkish ships, he said, they kill everyone, even if there were women and children aboard.

She was taken from the ship through the city to the promontory on which the palace stood. Trying to look beneath the skyline of minarets and domes where storks nested, she searched for canals, signs of what were to her a familiar way of traveling in a city. Men sat on the street in front of cafés, smoking hookahs and drinking coffee. A row of letter writers sat before small tables, rolls of paper and brass inkstands before them, writing with frenetic flourishes as men spoke over their heads.

Guards escorted her to the entrance of the palace. From there a man named Gaspar took her through the Gate of Felicity to the inner palace, a series of rooms covered by artificial gardens, pools, fountains, and birdhouses, all made of flat tiles and cool to touch. Plants made of tile, as if espaliered, filled artificial windows. From a distance *trompe l'oeil* plum branches always blossomed. As she walked toward the tree, its bark melted into black and white faience. Flat walls were so patterned they gave the illusion of a series of niches. Her room was covered by mosaics patterned as ogival windows. Green tile plants curled around their edges, but there was no view to the outside. It was all two-dimensional. From the little she had seen of the city, it seemed to her that the outside of buildings mattered much less than the interiors. It was the opposite of Venice. Wearing the dresses they had given her, covered with jagged red tulips and leaves like spiked tongues, she felt she blended in with the walls of her room.

Blond hair was considered plain, and it was a slave's job to dye Luna's hair black. Luna became Calandra. She watched a woman from Crimea hold two inlaid mirrors, one in each hand so she could see the back of her head. Calandra talked to no one. There was no one to talk to, she had no language in common with any of them.

She drew pictures of water steps and canals, gondolas, martyrs and angels barely clothed, and a *banchetti*, a crude imitation of Veronese. Gaspar destroyed her pictures and tried to convey to her that they were obscenities.

Learning there was a library of Greek and Latin books in the palace, she tried to persuade Gaspar to bring her something to read, anything. The room was in the outer palace and forbidden to her. He refused, but then returned a few days later with two atlases and a Spanish book on America written in 1580. It had been translated into Persian, and an accompanying note, which he translated, described the threat posed to Islam by Christianity gobbling more and more. He had also managed to bring out a forbidden book, a work on Copernicus. Calandra looked at the atlas with interest. Here was a representation of the world, the places her father had traveled, the city where she had lived, even though the tongues of land and pools of water were labeled in curved letters she didn't understand. The foreign language claimed those pieces of land, even Venice. Calandra wished for a city without night: sleepless, productive, relentless. If not a city, rooms without night would be enough.

The rest of Calandra's story—years in the inner palace, the long march, and war—all left her with pieces missing. Speaking in a way that could be understood became difficult. She had forgotten certain words and spoke a combination of languages, the dialect of her origin and the languages of her imprisonment. Words kept returning, popping up without warning. We never knew what she would say, and customers who understood parts of her babbling would turn away from her, would want their money back. No pleasure could be gotten from someone who, out of a torrent of incomprehensible words, would describe how she went to Tresaria di San Marco and stood before cases of gold armor, a crown of thorns, bits and pieces of saints' bones, all given by Venetians who recovered their wives kidnapped by Saracens at sea.

Travelers came to my house, people who had returned from the Silk Route, from Lahore, Lucknow, Shanghai, and New Amsterdam. Merchants and missionaries described people who built houses of paper, who danced on fire without burning their feet, who wrote their complicated laws on slats of wood that folded and folded again to fit into tubes you could hold in one hand. Calandra asked for a place on a ship leaving for Alexandria, where she planned to follow one of the spice routes to Goa, and from there look for a route to islands in the South China Sea, where peppers and cloves grow to the size of wagon wheels and music is played on bronze drums. But then she grew homesick and talked about crooked water steps leading into the canal, watching limpets dry as they were brought in from the sea, water rats scuttling close to her feet, and the desire to brush her hand against familiar iron door knockers: a lion's head, a hand, a pineapple. When she disappeared from my house, she wasn't making any money for me, so I made no inquiries.

AT THE TURN OF the century the clockmaker knocked at my door. He had followed the French dwarf to the edge of Sarajevo and worked with the army, so he had learned military time and knew a few things about what was happening to the east.

Savoy had spies who broke into arsenals and laboratories in Istanbul and other pertinent locations, even in Baghdad, but found nothing more dangerous than Chinese fireworks. He wanted his army to believe terrible weapons existed somewhere. Someone else said women from Ankara, who had been captured by Europeans, were paraded around Sarajevo as part of a circus. The clockmaker shrugged, well, maybe, but now let me show you something, and he pushed a row of glasses off a table. Here were the Turks falling over the edge and shattering on the floor. Then he stacked empty plates in the center of a table, bread crusts and crumbs clinging to the parapets of the plate fortress.

"He rode with his army to the foothills outside Sarajevo and looked down at what appeared to be an empty city, but Sarajevo was only playing dead. The citizens had all disappeared."

The city appeared to be a shell, an easy conquest, no people in evidence, just property ready to be commandeered. Spies said the city had been abandoned, but they couldn't say why. The army turned around, and Sarajevo remained a dream city, one he would never enter.

Nada insisted the dwarf had taken the army south into Bosnia, forcing Muslim towns in his path to evacuate to Sarajevo, then burned the city to the ground as revenge for the shooting of his trumpeter and cornet player. I wasn't sure which version was true. There was no way to know for certain.

I stared at the glass broken on the floor and the remains of the china tower. I was annoyed at the damage inflicted so casually, but left the rubble on the floor and on the table. The maid could clean it up. In some other universe I might have been a glass swept off a table at random, falling over the edge, pirates appear on the horizon take me to a palace, a sultan takes me to a battle, he loses the war, a duke is still busy moving boundaries, visiting and revisiting the scene of burned towns and mass graves, and by the time the glass hits the floor I'm back in my city almost as if I've never left. Almost, but not quite.

# SIEGE OF COMEDIANS

THE EXHIBIT, SUCH AS it had been planned, is canceled. The skeletons that had been sent to the archives for storage are exhumed from their acid-free cardboard boxes and returned to the Weissberger Lab. The display figures that had been made of Skeletons A, B, and C are dismantled, disgraced and humiliated, before they even have a chance to be installed in their glass cases. The bells wound around Cleopatra's ankles ring one last time as she is stuck in a corner, and her shoes with turned-up toes, so she looked as if she'd just emerged from a magic lamp, disappear into someone's closet.

Okay, I confess I took them. They were iridescent, and no one else was going to claim them. They fit perfectly. La Gioconda's wig, threaded with fake pearls, is repurposed and donated, her flying saucer lace collar turned up on top of the lab's microwave. It is partly synthetic and can be used to handle hot objects.

The museum says, we've changed our minds here. No frozen-in-time tableau that implies all is well, we're tolerant citizens who embrace the foreigners who have been forced on us, and let us show them to you living a tranquil existence. We'd prefer, says the curator who accompanied the returned figures and boxes of remains, at this moment, to reenact the scene of their murders. The curators, the director and technicians of the Weissberger Lab, didn't know I had that job once, reconstructing the faces of murder victims.

It isn't enough to put them back together. They want to know what happened to the bodies. What actions might have been recorded by how they fell and by what's no longer connected, a piece of cervical spine here, a jaw bone there. Go back, I was told, what are the anatomical landmarks, places on the skull, cheekbone, chin, jaw, where you can say, here the average depth of tissue will reveal this particular face. Are you sure you want to see Cleopatra, the most intact of the three, open-mouthed, still screaming?

An adversarial curator takes a moment to say, we're not a wax museum of horrors. He goes on to ask who needs a diorama of blood and body parts scattered among candles, lanterns, maps of the New World that make the Horn of Africa the size of Calabria? If a head is far from a body, we know it didn't walk there all by its lonesome.

He is overruled.

Forensic archeologists from another city arrive with laser scans and ground-penetrating radar to give a worm's eye view. Cracked lintel above a bricked-up door, Romanesque arches, barrel vaults, stratas of memory. One layer elbows aside an earlier tier and says, get lost, we're the enhanced design, improved material, more resistant, make way, our imposition is a way of sending you to the path of forgetting.

The forensic architects create an animated digital model of #39, complete with figures who walked through the earliest rooms. Here are the bedrooms, the kitchen, a narrow, spindly building of wood and stone, a fireplace where clients warmed themselves before going upstairs. What they showed us, augmented reality, was very cool.

They scanned the onsite photos taken of the bodies before the explosion, before they were moved. With their photogrammetry, ghosts begin to take shape and tell us what to do. But then, a mob broke down the doors, and you could see what happened to the faces and bodies I worked on. Photos taken from the site before the explosion spin around on a screen, then fall into place on the scans, slipping into place like wallpaper. The women tried to hide, but it was hopeless—every hall, every room was a dead end. Sound of doors break-ing down, thumping of footsteps on the stairs, knives, ropes, yelling.

Skeletons A, B, and C died horrible deaths when the crowds came for them.

The red-rimmed eyes of the crowd receded. Decades, centuries fly by, pages flip off a calendar.

Fade in. Fade Out. Fade In.

Then a stone edifice of many stories, a sign of prosperity and industry—and inside, lenses ground, held up to the light, put into telescopes, microscopes, ordinary eye glasses. Some are as big as din-ner plates, some as small as a coin. The sun is shining on #39, pretty much, but this period was not destined to last either.

Doors splinter. Tables and chairs pushed against the door, run down steps to the cellar. Tapping of footsteps. At first just a few, then many. The Foley artist (who recorded the stomping we hear) wore rub-ber boots on tile, it sounds like. Herr Kronenberg tries to protest, we've lived and worked at #39 for years, never disturbed anyone, but he's shot, body dumped. Other members of his family and the employees are pushed into the street, and from there to the Nordbahnhof train station and certain deportation to points north by northeast. The fac-tory becomes a series of offices, a screening room, underground prison.

A man the voiceover identifies as Konrad, no Karl Sauer, arrives and surveys what is now his small principality, Ministry of Propaganda. Books and films are debated, put on trial. Producers of banned ma-terial are rounded up and questioned, right this way please, to this office, to that cellar chamber. If it were possible to open their skulls, clean their brains, and then gently put them back, Sauer says through crocodile tears, he would do just that, and all would be well with the world, but once the brain is removed, there's no returning it in work-ing order. This is his actual voice, an old recording unearthed from a toppled file cabinet.

Men in uniform scurry to bring Sauer paintings and books. He checks for names he recognizes, because when he does, that's it, pull the eject lever, down the chute, and into the furnace they go: Georges Grosz, Hans Richter, Otto Dix, Elfriede Lohse-Wächtler who wasn't even safe in an asylum, or in an asylum least of all. The movies he watches alone in dark rooms, and here he simmers with outrage, but also sometimes with jealousy. Sauer wants to make his own films and once in a while he does. A few minutes of a stop-motion animation featuring wooden Tyrolean dwarves plays on the screen.

In the basement under his feet people are turned into bodies. Sometimes he oversees this process, sometimes not. Here, at first, there is not a lot of identifying detail in the simulated 3-D model. The representation of torturer and tortured are gray figures like those anatomical dolls made of jointed wood. Bodies dissolve into bone and fall on top of others. Sometimes the generic are given names and faces which adhere onto the blank heads like masks, but they are real photographs of actual victims, and this is very unsettling. These were not sculpted by me. The new dead have been given precise and accurate identities thanks to FaceIt software. The voiceover goes further. This one was a doctor who treated panic disorders; that one photographed bakers, railway workers; another made collage cartoons. A children's book illustrator drew a duck dictator.

Then round silver and rust-colored objects come into focus. Cans of film are found in the cellar that had fallen through holes in upper floors, coming to a rest near bodies. Most of the reels are so corroded as to be unwatchable on any known machine, but held up to the light, a few frames are visible: scenes of people doing experiments, walking on re-named streets, smiling when no smiles were called for.

But next, and without much explanation, the tenure of the Ministry of Propaganda ends—the figures run out of the building, get arrested, or, in the case of Sauer, hide in the cellar and then escape into unguarded night.

More years fly off the calendar. #39 remains dark, empty, and unclaimed. No one is alive to say, that's my name on the deed.

A salvage crew arrives and clears away collapsed brickwork, props up walls and staircases until an explosion nearly levels what's left. The Foley artist drops a metal can filled with nails, screws, wing nuts to simulate the sound of an explosion, snaps celery to indicate shattered bones. The crew, the voiceover says, came from the same geographic locations as Skeletons A, B, and C. The remains I was calling Columbo share similar DNA as the Kronenbergs, though he was a member of the new dead, not from their era, and too old at the time of death to be working salvage. Who he had been and what he was doing at #39 has never been established. In the new diorama, he stands in front of a food truck, coffee in hand, talking to the salvage crew. We don't know what to do with him.

Clothing and props are gathered for the new diorama, texts written about how each of the figures got into the city, attached to armies, smuggled across borders, how they were sold while fortifications are built stone by stone, streets are paved, van Leeuwenhoek looks at his own sperm under a microscope (yuck, frankly), synthetic radium is hatched, radios operated by turning knobs, the concept of the Turing Machine is introduced, and all the while the animated figures that are Sauer's ancestors are meeting and creating more of themselves, and eventually, this way for the gas, ladies and gentlemen. The diorama ends with migrants in life vests and photographs and Euros sealed in plastic bags. But then the waves wash over and #39 becomes a luxury apartment building with a doorman and rooftop swimming pool. That's the future as we know it.

In the very last few feet of the diorama, I could step in, like those golden statues that are really an actual person covered in metal paint who don't move until someone puts a coin in their hat, but nah, I don't think so, not today, not anytime soon.

In an office building with no signage to inform you this is where Missing Persons resides, in a basement storage area known as the

Evidence Room, sit three heads of people who don't exist and never will. To get to this unmarked building, I take the A train to Howard Beach, then a bus. It's late at night, so it's quite a wait for the Q11, but I haven't been here in a while, so I'm enjoying the dark and the quiet, how the air smells like the ocean when you're at a far edge of the city, almost no longer the city, like you could launch yourself into the sea and thereby leave anytime, though this isn't actually possible. Obviously, there would be technical problems.

I arrive at the boxy white building, slide my old ID at the door, and what do you know? It works. Someone never hit delete, erase, sayonara, Iridia Kepler, you're obsolete, and you haven't shown up since God knows when. Hoodie over head, dark glasses, back to security cameras, not sure if this will work. The Evidence Room will be locked, but I know who has a key, and I know he's been high on whatever because Suicide Bunny isn't totally working for him anymore, so yes, he graciously forgot to lock his office door, or maybe caring, as far as he's concerned, is obsolete, too. So many people are missing, piled up at borders, laws are laws and then they aren't, and he doesn't know what to do, he says.

Key in desk drawer, patter downstairs because the elevator spooks me at night. The Evidence Room, behind a pebbled glass window, is a treasure box of mostly dead ends. There are two things I need to find: the original bones and the heads I cast for the Pianist. The bones should be in this room since they didn't portray any actual once-walking-around humans and couldn't be returned anywhere.

I have to work quickly. Someone unexpected could saunter in, even in the middle of the night, some insomniac mulling over a cold case, just like I am. *Hey, I was looking for the knife that was used in that 1986 unsolved triple nothing. What's all that clay on the floor? Who the hell are you?* Honeybunch, I'll say, I wish I knew.

So I have to work fast. The shelves are organized by year, but I don't know the date of the case. I walk down rows of gray metal shelving spilling over with files, boxes of evidence of all kinds including heads I once made, so many of them that parts of the room looked like the Capitoline Museum for the unfindable, the disappeared, trafficked, eliminated. Then I see them, the three women who don't exist, sitting at the end of a shelf conveniently located near an electrical outlet, which I'll need. Beside them, in what look like hat boxes, are three skulls. I put down my backpack and bags. A lot of equipment is required, and I set blocks of wet clay, jars of resin, small stands, and my tools on the floor. Standing, bending over, sitting cross-legged—whatever works because there is no table—I make molds, pour resin, sculpt clay, wait for features to dry. It's a Friday night, I have the weekend and will need most of it. No one's around to hear plastic bags being torn apart, or the snap of potato chips so I crunch away when I'm hungry, keeping crumbs away from my work. I think about going upstairs to the coffee machine but don't want to risk more cameras.

The heads finally look like who they're supposed to. I wave the blow dryer around. I want to get out of here already but don't want to risk faces getting squished from being moved too soon. By now it's the middle of Sunday night. When they're reasonably dry, I repack my bags, putting the old heads in one and the new heads in another. Leaving the revisions in front of the door of the only highly placed employee I still know at Missing Persons, I also put the hat boxes of bones close by, so he'll know what case they reference. I won't be here, but they'll be discovered in the morning when everyone who works at Missing Persons clocks in.

It's a short stroll to the boardwalk. To the west is Coney Island, and if I walk a little farther I'll see the top of the Cyclone and the Wonder Wheel, and I imagine what it would be like if an army were to lay siege to it, sandwiching visitors and employees between Surf Avenue and the beach. Forced to survive on hot dogs and candy apples, they would sleep in the Sideshow house and burn roller coaster railing to keep warm. There's always someone who believes it's not really happening, it's a movie, the amusement park is a set. It's one way to keep going, to put one foot in front of the next, and the amusement park looks like a set anyway. Gulls looking for Saturday night party garbage, though Sunday at the beach garbage will do, squawk overhead. There are no boats in the distance but small barren islands, possible Republics of Kugelmugel, I know they're out there somewhere if anyone were interested in founding a new nation-state big enough for one, maybe two. I have no way of getting to those islands and setting up shop there. I'm not sure anyone does, so I settle for staying where I am for the moment, but before I walk back to the bus stop, I take out the old heads, the fake kissers, and throw them into the waves that carry them out to sea.

# ACKNOWLEDGMENTS

THANK YOUS, THANK YOUS, and more thank yous to Michelle Dotter, editor par excellence, Anna Di Lellio, Sam Crawford, Anna Brodsky-Krotkina , Kevin Crotty, Leslie Camhi, Lisa Cartwright, Rachel Cohen, Alex Aleinikoff, Mark Cohen, Ivone Margulies, Margo Cooper, Rachel Danzing, Marion Falk, Bill Kanemoto, John Foster, Alice Kaltman, Mary Kanemoto, Richard Kaye, Lata Mani, Regina McBride, Bill Nericcio, David Shields, Brooke Stevens, Karen Weltman, and of course, Nissim.